MW01029279

*Praise for
Constance Bennett's
previous romantic novels:*

MORNING SKY

"WONDERFUL!"
— Linda Ladd, author of *Frostfire*

"A BEAUTIFULLY WRITTEN LOVE STORY
. . . COMPELLING!"
— bestselling author Lori Copeland

BLOSSOM

"DEFTLY PLOTTED AND EMOTIONALLY
RICH, *BLOSSOM* IS A MARVELOUS BOOK . . .
BREATHTAKING!"
— Suzanne Ellison, author of *Eagle Knight*

"A BEAUTIFUL LOVE STORY, FULL OF IN-
TENSE EMOTIONS, TENDER LOVE SCENES,
AND UPLIFTING FAITH . . . FASCINATING!"
— *Romantic Times*

Diamond Books by Constance Bennett

MORNING SKY
BLOSSOM
MOONSONG

MOONSONG

CONSTANCE BENNETT

DIAMOND BOOKS, NEW YORK

This book is a Diamond original edition, and has never
been previously published.

MOONSONG

A Diamond Book / published by arrangement with
the author

PRINTING HISTORY
Diamond edition / November 1992

All rights reserved.
Copyright © 1992 by Constance Bennett.
This book may not be reproduced in whole or
in part, by mimeograph or any other means, without
permission. For information address:
The Berkley Publishing Group,
200 Madison Avenue, New York, New York 10016.

ISBN: 1-55773-809-2

Diamond Books are published by The Berkley Publishing Group,
200 Madison Avenue, New York, New York 10016.
The name "DIAMOND" and its logo are trademarks
belonging to Charter Communications, Inc.

PRINTED IN THE UNITED STATES OF AMERICA

10   9   8   7   6   5   4   3   2   1

Prologue

New Mexico Territory, 1863

THE DEEP MASCULINE voice woke her. It wasn't loud, but it was enough to infiltrate the restless slumber of five-year-old Rayna Templeton and bring her upright in her bed. She paused a moment, listening carefully, hardly daring to breathe until she heard the voice again. There was no mistaking it. Papa had finally come home!

Her face wreathed in a joyous smile, Rayna threw back the coverlet and scrambled out of bed. Her bare feet were virtually silent as she flew across the room and onto the balcony that overlooked the interior courtyard of the hacienda. Overhead, the sky was awash with stars, and lanterns at the foot of the staircases cast patterns of light and dancing shadows, but otherwise the courtyard was empty. The voice was more distinct, though, and Rayna knew she hadn't been mistaken.

Her father had left for Sonora to buy cattle five weeks ago, and every day he'd been gone had been an eternity for Rayna and her mother. There were so many dangers between Rancho Verde and Mexico—deserts and mountains, scorpions and snakes, bears and mountain lions—but those were simple hazards that Raymond Templeton was more than equipped to handle. The Apache were far more dangerous than all the others combined, and every moment he'd stayed away had meant one more day of waiting and praying.

But now he was home.

Imagining how he would sweep her into his arms and toss her into the air with a big barrel-chested laugh, Rayna hurried down the stairs and into the courtyard, straining to hear his voice. The way the sound carried up told her he was in his study, and the second voice that joined his indicated that her mother was with him. Colleen would be irritated when she learned that her daughter was out of bed at this late hour, but Rayna didn't care. She was accustomed to being in trouble, and besides, she knew from experience that the worst punishment she was likely to get from her softhearted mother was a mild scolding. Seeing Papa again would be worth that and much more.

Her feet barely touched the cool flagstone as she dashed across the courtyard and down a darkened corridor toward the study. Her parents' voices grew louder, bringing Rayna to a halt a few feet short of the pool of light that beamed out the half-open door of the study. She crept closer and listened.

"But, Collie, what else could I do?" Raymond Templeton was saying. "Look at the poor thing. She's not even as old as our Rayna, and already she's been through a hell you and I couldn't begin to imagine."

"You can't know that," Colleen argued.

"Of course I know it—and so do you. Those damnable Mexican slave traders didn't just find the poor thing wandering alone in the mountains. She wasn't rescued—she was stolen, probably after watching her parents be murdered and scalped. I couldn't just leave her in Sonora, could I? God only knows what would have become of her!"

"But, Raymond, she's—"

"She's a frightened little girl," he said, overriding whatever objection Colleen had been about to make. "What else matters? Rayna has been begging for a sister—"

"That's not fair," Collie said quietly, her voice filled with pain. "I've tried to give you another child."

Heavy footsteps crossed the room, and when Raymond spoke again, his tone conveyed nothing but love. "I know, Collie. And I also know how many nights I've held you while you cried because you have so much love to give and only Rayna to lavish it on. But look at this little one, Collie—really look at her, and you'll see how much she needs you."

"I don't want to look at her."

"That's because you know you'll fall in love with her the same way I did. Just look, Collie."

There was a long pause and then the sound of footsteps softly padding across the study floor.

Tossing her long fall of golden hair over her narrow shoulders, Rayna held her breath and peeked around the door. She spied her father first, but as much as she longed to greet him, she was even more curious about the present he had brought her. A sister! What could be more wonderful than that?

Rayna was the only child at Rancho Verde, and she was lonely. Now she'd never be alone again. She would have a playmate and a friend, someone to run wild with and to ease the boredom of the hours she spent doing her lessons in reading and etiquette, someone to share her chores with and dream with and talk to.

Her heart filled with hope and expectation, Rayna looked deeper into the room, past her mother, who was moving toward the hearth, until her rapt gaze finally fell on a small, dirty bundle of black hair and buckskin cowering by the fireplace. A pair of enormous dark eyes stared up at Collie Templeton out of a gaunt face covered with dirt. Despite the smudges, there was no mistaking the origin of that face. The hair, the high cheekbones, the square jaw, the copper-colored skin, all told Rayna that her new sister was an Apache!

With a pitying moan, Collie knelt by the hearth, but when she extended her hand, the child scurried away like a cornered animal fleeing its would-be captor. The wild-eyed little Apache threw herself at Raymond Templeton's feet and clung to his leg, shielding herself from the strange white woman. Collie followed, stopping a few feet away to look at her husband.

"Oh, Raymond, she's so frightened. How did you get her to come with you?"

He looked sad and tired. "I wish I could say it was hard, but it wasn't. The poor little thing had been whipped into submission long before I found her. Some hot food and a few gentle words were enough to convince her she was better off with me than with those slave traders."

Collie looked down at the pitiful waif, her eyes swimming with unshed tears. "You'll be all right, little one," she said softly.

Raymond smiled. "Thank you, Collie."

She shook her head. "Raising an Apache won't be easy, Raymond. How much do you know about where she came from?"

"Not much," he admitted. "The traders I bought her from claimed they purchased her and several other children from a band of renegade Chiricahua. From the looks of her clothes, they guessed that she was from the White Mountain tribe."

Collie nodded thoughtfully. "Do you think she might be able to communicate with the Mescalero Apaches here on the ranch?"

"That's what I was hoping. Surely Gatana can help us."

"We'll need all we can get." She knelt, and the little Apache skittered away again, this time moving unerringly toward the door. Raymond uttered a soft, firm no, and she froze, squatting on the floor with her hands wrapped tightly around her knees, her head bent in submission.

Rayna, who had never been afraid of anything, could hardly believe what she was seeing. Witnessing a display of hopelessness and fear like this was more than she could bear. Acting with the same instinct she had used to tame the menagerie of wild animals that were her only friends at Rancho Verde, Rayna slid to her knees, gathered the tail of her nightgown in one hand, and crawled into the room, heedless of her startled parents.

"Rayna! No, don't!" Collie called out in alarm, but Raymond placed one hand on her arm.

"Let her," he counseled.

Rayna ignored them both. The frail Apache raised her head, and her eyes widened. Her fear seemed to ebb away, replaced by cautious curiosity. She lowered her knees to the floor and sat upright, motionless but poised for flight as Rayna came closer and finally mirrored her position on the floor only a few inches away.

They studied each other for a long moment. The Apache looked terrible and smelled even worse, but Rayna ignored the odor; she knew from experience it was nothing a good hot bath couldn't cure. The hard part would be earning her trust enough to get her into a tub. It was the supreme challenge to the adventurous five-year-old, and there was nothing she liked more than a challenge.

"My name is Rayna." The healthy blue-eyed blond child placed a hand on her own chest. "Rayna."

The solemn little Apache mirrored the movement, but made no sound.

Rayna smiled. "I am your sister."

The little girl's matted black hair spilled over her shoulder as she cocked her head to one side. Timidly, as though she feared she might be punished, she reached out and touched one of Rayna's golden curls. A fearful glance darted up to the adults nearby, but they only watched, and she grew bolder, her curiosity getting the better of her fear. Wrapping the lock of hair around her hand, she tugged gently and seemed mystified when nothing happened. Puzzled, she raised the curl to her face and sniffed.

Rayna had to lean forward to keep the lock from being pulled out of her head, but she patiently submitted to the examination. "She's never seen blond hair before, Mama," she said quietly without looking at her parents.

"Rayna, be careful," her mother cautioned.

"Oh, she won't hurt me," she replied confidently. "You won't hurt me, will you?"

The little Apache studied the lock of hair and the child it was attached to. Finally she released it and gathered a handful of her own hair into a tiny fist. Tears appeared in her dark eyes, and her chin quivered. "Pr'ncess pretty?"

Collie gasped and glanced at her equally amazed husband, but Rayna never took her eyes off her sister. "Princess very pretty." She held out her hand. "Come."

Dark eyes darted again to Raymond, and when he nodded his head the little Apache took Rayna's hand.

Collie breathed a sigh of relief. "Raymond, you send for Gatana while I heat some bathwater. It's going to be a very long night."

Her prediction proved to be something of an understatement.

Chapter One

New Mexico Territory, April 1882

"THEY'RE LAUGHING AT us, Samson, and it's all your fault," Rayna Templeton muttered as she trudged through the gates at Rancho Verde leading her Appaloosa stallion. Samson whinnied what could have been an apology, but his mistress suspected that he wasn't at all sorry he'd thrown a shoe for the second time this week. For the last four miles Samson had been quite content to poke along unencumbered by his rider, but Rayna was disgusted and bone-deep weary. She was also covered with dust from her wide-brimmed felt hat to the toes of her leather boots. Since dawn she had been scouring the countryside for calves that had escaped the spring roundup, and now she wanted nothing more than a hearty meal and a hot bath.

But first she had to get past the cowhands who had gathered at the corral to poke fun at her.

"Out fer another stroll, Miss Rayna?" Charlie McGinty hollered, making no attempt to hide the smirk on his weathered face.

"Yes, indeed, Charlie," she replied facetiously. "The air is so invigorating at this time of year I just don't seem to be able to resist."

While Charlie scratched his head, apparently trying to figure out what "invigorating" meant, Flint Piper took his turn. "Didja pick any pretty wildflowers, miss?"

Everyone guffawed at that, and even Rayna had to bite

back a smile. Dainty pursuits like picking posies were as foreign to her as words like "invigorating" were to Charlie. "No, Flint, I'm afraid the verbena and Indian paintbrush are past their prime. There'll be no flowers on Mother's dinner table tonight."

"That's too bad," Flint replied. "Miz Collie's gonna be mighty disappointed."

Rayna stopped and affected an air of sadness. "No more so than I, Flint. You all know how much I adore a pretty bouquet."

The men were still laughing at that when someone else called out an admonition against strolling in the sun without a parasol. He earned a back-slapping guffaw because he'd done such a good impersonation of Rayna's mother. The object of their mirth put an end to the laughter by dusting her hat on her trousers, sending up a cloud of dirt that set everyone to coughing.

Chuckling, Guillermo Rodriguez jumped off the top rung of the corral fence. "All right, vaqueros, the fun is over. The sun is high and there is still work to be done."

"Not the least of which is shoeing this horse," Rayna muttered to the range boss as the other men scattered. "Something has to be done about that new blacksmith, Gil. I knew he was too good to be true when he showed up last week looking for a job. I can do a better job of shoeing horses than he can, and that's not saying much."

Rodriguez grinned. "Do you want the job, señorita? I am sure Señora Templeton would be happy to know that you are working closer to home instead of being out on the range every day."

Rayna slanted an exasperated glance in his direction. "Don't you start on me, too, Gil."

"Oh, but the men, they love to tease you, señorita."

She patted Samson's neck. "That's because a walking target is easy to hit."

He laughed and held out his hand for the reins. "Here, I will take care of Samson—and the blacksmith."

Though normally Rayna stabled her own mount, she handed the reins over gratefully. "Thank you, Gil. And by the way, I struck gold this morning. I rounded up ten head and drove them into the corral above Diablo Canyon. There are two maverick calves and a sleepered yearling in the bunch."

"Bueno!" he said, his eyes shining with respect. A sleepered yearling was a calf with an earmark but no brand—indicating that the animal had escaped spring roundup for two years in a row. That usually meant the herd he traveled in was quite wild, and single-handedly corralling a wild herd was no small feat. "I will send Flint and Charlie out now to bring them in for the brand."

"Thank you, Gil."

"Will you be riding out again today?" he asked.

"No, I don't think so," she replied, removing her rifle from its scabbard. "I've eaten enough dust for one day."

"Bueno."

Slinging her saddlebags over one shoulder, she patted Samson's hindquarters as the range boss led him away to the stable. The house lay in the opposite direction, and Rayna headed for the nearest entrance, through the walled garden that sheltered the hacienda's western exposure. The iron gate creaked a scratchy welcome as she slipped inside and moved across the flagstone patio toward the house.

The magnificent old two-story home had been constructed in the Spanish style over sixty years ago. Shady *galerías* encircled it on both floors inside and out, and each room had doors that led to the exterior galleries and interior courtyard.

The stucco hacienda had a long and colorful history, having survived Mexico's revolt against Spain and the American incursion that subsequently wrested the territory from Mexico. What mattered to Rayna, though, was that Rancho Verde was the only home she had ever known. She loved the house and the lush green Rio Grande valley that sheltered it. She loved the mountains and deserts beyond the valley, too.

It was a harsh land that could be cruel and unrelenting, but it was her home.

Her mother had insisted that she and her sister, Skylar, received a proper education back east, so Rayna had seen other parts of the country—places where water was never scarce, neighbors were plentiful, and the greatest danger to life and limb was being run over by a runaway carriage on a cobblestone street. Her brush with civilization had done nothing to change her opinion of Rancho Verde. It was the most beautiful place on earth.

The house was quiet when Rayna slipped through the arcade that connected the patio with the courtyard. Through the open doors of the dining room on the other side of the enclosure she spotted one of the servants laying the table for supper, and she heard muted voices drifted down from the upper floor. Anxious to tell her father about the bonanza she'd corralled, she headed across the courtyard to the study. The desk was littered with open ledgers, but Raymond Templeton was nowhere to be seen.

Disappointed, Rayna ejected the shells from her Winchester, placed it in the polished gun case by the door, and returned her cache of ammunition to the drawer below the rack. She performed the ritual with the ease of someone who had been well trained in the proper care of weapons, as indeed she had been. Rayna had been working the ranch alongside her father for as long as she could remember, and only a fool roamed the countryside unarmed.

That chore completed, she returned to the courtyard and dashed up the nearest staircase with her usual abandon.

"Unless you're trying to escape a stampede, I suggest you slow down, dear."

Her mother's quietly spoken admonition brought Rayna up short, and she turned. Collie Templeton was approaching the stairs with an armload of fresh linens. "No stampede, Mother. I was just trying to see how quickly I could get into my room and out of these dusty clothes."

Collie gave her daughter a once-over as she started up the

stairs. "In this instance I could almost approve of your haste. Did you have trouble with Samson again?"

"How did you know?"

Collie's blue eyes, so much like her daughter's, glittered with amusement. "Marie spotted you walking in."

Rayna groaned. "Marie and everyone else on the ranch. I told Gil to get rid of that new blacksmith. He's absolutely worthless." She extended her arms. "Here, let me help you with those."

"Not until you've had a bath, young lady," she replied sternly, shifting her bundle out of Rayna's reach. "Consuelo would skin you alive if she had to wash these over again."

"No, she wouldn't," Rayna argued good-naturedly as she turned and strolled with her mother down the gallery. "She's been threatening that for years and hasn't caught me yet."

"Lord knows you've given us both enough excuses— muddy boots, soiled gowns, disgraceful tattered Levi's that no woman should ever be caught dead—"

"Yes, yes, Mother, I know," she said, silencing her with a kiss on the cheek. "I'm a wretched hoyden, the bane of your existence, and the most unrefined lady in the entire territory of New Mexico."

Collie sighed with exasperation. "You don't have to sound so proud of it."

Rayna chuckled as she stripped off her gloves. "Mother, you've been trying to domesticate me for twenty-four years and haven't succeeded yet. When are you going to face the fact that I'll never be anything but the son you and father always wanted? Skylar is the domestic one."

Collie wished she could debate the issue. She loved both her children dearly, but they were as different as night and day. Skylar was quiet and shy. She had mastered the fine art of running a household and was in all ways a dutiful daughter. Rayna, on the other hand, was stubborn, headstrong, and willful. She had inherited her father's business sense, and her only desire was to someday assume the responsibility of running Rancho Verde. If Raymond Templeton had ever once discouraged his daughter from such an unladylike pursuit, Collie hadn't been within earshot when he'd done it.

"Marie is preparing your bathwater, dear," she said, resigned to the knowledge that nothing she could say would change her daughter's deportment. "I may not be able to domesticate you, but I can at least make certain you don't appear at the dinner table smelling like a horse stall."

"Thank you, Mother." Tugging at the strip of rawhide that held her blond hair into a tight queue, Rayna glanced into her sister's room and found it devoid of life. "Where's Skylar?"

A small frown furrowed Collie's brow, but she kept her voice carefully neutral. "I believe she went out to the Mescalero encampment."

Rayna wasn't fooled by her mother's even tone. "Why does that upset you? She's always felt a special connection with the Apaches at Rancho Verde."

"I know that, dear. But she's spending more and more time with them lately. She goes out to the encampment every day now."

"Really?" Rayna stopped in front of her bedroom door.

"You didn't know?" Collie asked. Usually Rayna knew far more about what her sister thought and did then either of her parents. Since the day Raymond had brought Skylar home, the two girls had been virtually inseparable.

"No, I didn't," she replied, her own brow furrowed with worry now. It wasn't like Skylar to keep things from her.

"I believe Gatana is teaching her some sort of ceremony."

Her voice was laced with sadness, and Rayna finally realized what was upsetting her. Collie felt betrayed because she feared that all the advantages she'd given Skylar hadn't been enough for her adopted daughter. She had loved her and protected her as best she could from the inevitable prejudice the girl had faced. She had seen to it that she received an excellent education back east that had broadened Skylar's horizons far beyond the scope of most other young women in New Mexico, white or Apache.

Unfortunately a connection to her heritage was the one thing Collie couldn't give her daughter, but it was the one thing Skylar seemed to want most.

Rayna searched for something to say that would lift her mother's spirits, but she couldn't think of anything. She knew that Skylar loved her adopted family, but there was a certain sadness in her that seemed to be growing stronger every day. Rayna thought she understood it, but she knew she could never explain it to the woman who had raised Skylar with the same love and devotion she'd bestowed on her flesh-and-blood daughter.

"I wouldn't worry about it, Mother," she said, trying to sound reassuring. "She's probably just looking for a little diversion to ease her boredom. I know that if I had nothing to do but change bed linens and embroider sofa cushions every day, I'd go stark raving mad."

"Yes, but you're not your sister," Collie retorted, then fanned the air to shoo away the words. "I'm sorry, dear. I'm just being silly."

"Yes, you are," Rayna agreed. "Learning a Mescalero ceremony isn't going to change the way she feels about you. You're her mother. She loves you."

"I know she does, dear." She started to pat Rayna's arm, then remembered the layers of dirt and the clean sheets she was carrying. She withdrew her hand so quickly that both of them laughed.

"Oh, go ahead, Mother," Rayna teased. "I'd love to see Consuelo threatening to skin *you* alive."

"Collie!" Raymond's deep voice reverberated through the courtyard, startling his wife and daughter.

"What is it, dear?" Collie stepped closer to the gallery railing and found herself looking down on the top of her husband's balding head.

Raymond twisted around and looked up. "Riders coming in."

Rayna joined her mother at the rail, her unbound hair spilling over her shoulders. "Who is it?" Visitors were rare and always a source of excitement because they varied the routine of ranch life.

"Looks like Ben Martinez and that Hadley fellow from the newspaper in Malaventura." Raymond grinned up at his daughter. "Hullo, missy. Hear you had a little trouble with Samson again."

"You don't have to look so smug about it, Papa. You're the one who hired that no-account drifter who *claimed* to be a blacksmith."

"Live and learn, missy. Live and learn. Gil's already given him his walking papers."

"Well, if he leaves on a horse he shod himself, we can expect him back by nightfall."

Raymond's hearty laugh bounced off the walls of the courtyard as he made his way toward the parlor at the front of the hacienda. "Are you two ladies going to come down to greet our guests, or not?"

"I'm on my way, Papa," Rayna said, tossing her saddlebags and hat on the chair just inside her door before heading for the stairs.

But Collie had other ideas. "Not until you've had a bath and changed into proper clothing, young lady," she said sternly. "You cannot receive visitors looking like a common cowhand."

"Don't be silly, Mother," she replied without stopping. "I've worked the herd right alongside Ben Martinez during roundup for the last six years. If he saw me in anything other than Levi's and boots, he'd have a fit of apoplexy."

She was right about that. Ben was Rancho Verde's nearest neighbor, and he was well acquainted with Rayna's unusual habits. The man with Ben was another matter entirely, though. "That may be, but Mr. Hadley is a fine gentleman from Boston. You should greet him properly."

When Rayna realized what her mother was getting at, she stopped at the head of the stairs and gave her the most wicked grin in her repertoire. "You mean he's a fine *unat-*

tached gentleman from Boston, and I should pretend to be the delicate flower we both know I'm not."

Collie sighed with exasperation. "You do have manners and breeding, Rayna. It's just a matter of recognizing the appropriate time to display them. *This* is one of those times."

"Sorry, Mother, but I'm not about to trot out my best behavior for that Boston dandy," she said, continuing down the stairs. "He can't even sit a horse properly."

"There's more to life than sitting a horse!"

"Not my life," Rayna replied.

"I give up," Collie muttered, hurrying down the gallery. She had raised two of the most beautiful young women in the territory of New Mexico, and both, it seemed, were destined to remain spinsters—Skylar by circumstance of birth and Rayna by choice, or just plain stubbornness, Collie wasn't sure which.

For safety's sake, Rancho Verde had been situated in the center of the valley so that riders approaching from any direction would be visible long before they reached the hacienda. That gave Collie ample opportunity to dispose of the bed linens and instruct Consuelo Rodriguez, the Templetons' housekeeper, to prepare refreshments for the guests. Then she went in search of her husband and daughter. She found them on the front veranda watching the riders approach. Rayna was telling her father about the unbranded cattle she'd discovered and the merry chase they had led her on.

"It's fortunate Samson didn't lose that shoe until after I'd corralled the herd."

"Fortunate for the blacksmith," Raymond commented with a chuckle. "I'd hate to see what you'd have done to him if you'd lost that yearling."

Rayna didn't share her father's mirth. "Rest assured, Papa, if that had happened there wouldn't have been enough left of that charlatan's hide to—"

"That's enough, Rayna," Collie said, then turned a stern

eye on her husband. "And that's enough out of you, too. If you didn't encourage her—"

"Oh, now, Collie . . ." Raymond threw one arm over her shoulder. "You oughta know by now that nothing either one of us says is going to discourage Rayna from speakin' her mind or doing what she wants to do around the ranch." He winked at his daughter. "And she does it so well that I can't hardly complain, now, can I?"

Though Rayna smiled at her father and the affectionate way he gathered Collie to him, the mild disagreement between them made her uncomfortable. The only real quarrels she'd ever heard them engage in had been over her. Her earliest memories were of her father teaching her to ride and her mother protesting because she was too young. The same had been true when he taught her to use a rifle and a revolver.

Raymond had allowed her to ride herd as soon as he was confident of her ability to manage a cow pony from a side-saddle, and Collie had objected to that, too. They had fought over Rayna's determination not to be sent away to school, and an even bigger argument had ensued when Raymond had supported Rayna's decision to abandon her inconvenient sidesaddle in favor of a more practical stock saddle. Collie had given in on the issue of riding astride only after her husband convinced her that cutting range stock from a sidesaddle was not only impractical but exceedingly dangerous. Collie had argued that Rayna shouldn't be working alongside the men like a common cowhand, but she'd lost that argument along with the original one.

In fact, with the exception of the issue of education, Raymond and his namesake had won nearly every battle. Rayna knew that would never keep her mother from trying to reform her, and she didn't mind. Collie might protest her behavior, but she would never stop loving her. That was all that mattered to Rayna. Being a bone of contention between her parents did disturb her, though.

But Rayna knew this argument wasn't going to get out of hand because their visitors were riding through the gates, and Collie would never have aired the family's quarrels in front of guests.

"Howdy, Ben. Mr. Hadley," Raymond greeted the two men as they neared. "What brings you all the way out here?"

Though Raymond's greeting was friendly, the two riders showed no sign of returning the affable welcome. They doffed their hats to the ladies, but their faces were grim as they dismounted.

"We got trouble, Raymond," Ben Martinez said.

"Oh?" He looked from one man to the other.

Samuel Aloysius Hadley nodded a confirmation. "Big trouble, Mr. Templeton."

"Well, spit it out," Raymond demanded.

Hadley looked at the two ladies uncomfortably, then made his decision. "Geronimo's on the warpath again."

"And he's headed this way," Ben added.

Raymond sighed heavily. "Hellfire and damnation. Come on in, boys. We got some plannin' to do."

The men adjourned to Raymond's study, and though Collie tried to discourage Rayna from participating in the conversation, a team of wild horses couldn't have kept her away. Their guests settled into the twin armchairs opposite Raymond's desk, and Rayna took a seat on the small sofa behind them.

With a minimum of embellishment, Hadley related what he'd learned of the Chiricahua renegade's bloody escape from the reservation at San Carlos in Arizona. Telegraphed reports gave several different versions of the outbreak, some stating that as many as thirty and as few as ten civilians and soldiers had been slaughtered.

Though Rayna had no direct knowledge of the attack, she would have been willing to guess that all the reports were exaggerated. As a general rule, anything that had to do with Apache depredations was blown out of all proportion by the press. Still, having Geronimo on the warpath was a dead serious matter. There wasn't a man, woman, or child in New

Mexico who had forgotten the massacres of the previous spring when Chief Nana, one of Geronimo's most trusted allies, had terrorized the Rio Grande valley. His raids had lasted only six weeks, but before he disappeared into Mexico he had killed nearly fifty New Mexicans, taken several women captive, and stolen more than two hundred horses and mules. All that . . . accomplished by a seventy-year-old chieftain and forty Apaches who had a thousand soldiers hot on their trail.

If Geronimo was headed for New Mexico, Nana would undoubtedly come out of hiding to join him, and blood was going to flow like water.

Rayna was impressed by the way Hadley told the story of the recent outbreak. Obviously he had received several telegraph dispatches, sorted through them, and come up with the best conclusions he could draw, considering the limitations under which he worked. And unlike Ben, who was punctuating Hadley's tale by interjecting an occasional wild speculation, Samuel was remarkably calm. But then, he'd been in the territory for only a few months. He hadn't experienced the terror caused by Nana's raids or those of the Mescalero chief, Victorio, before that. Rayna had seen firsthand what destruction the Apaches could wreak.

"Tell 'im about the head," Ben encouraged, getting carried away with the story.

Hadley looked uncomfortable. "Well, it seems that . . . This is just an unconfirmed rumor, you understand. . . . But it seems that one of the men at San Carlos was decapitated, and the savages . . . played football with the dismembered head."

"Dear God," Rayna murmured, then instantly regretted having spoken. She was behind them, and the men had forgotten there was a lady present or they never would have spoken so freely.

Hadley was instantly apologetic. "I'm sorry, Miss Templeton. I shouldn't have mentioned that."

"It's all right, Mr. Hadley," she reassured him. "I've heard worse."

"That may be, ma'am, but such matters aren't—"

All her life men had been giving her the condescending speech about matters that were unfit for ladylike sensibilities, and she didn't want to hear it again. "How reliable are the reports that he's headed this way?" she asked, cutting him off.

Hadley cleared his throat. He was never quite sure what to make of Rayna Templeton because she was so different from any woman he'd ever met. She hadn't fainted dead away at the mention of the head, and since her father showed no sign of being uncomfortable at having her in the room, he decided to continue.

"As reliable as they can be at this point. Apparently word was slow coming out of San Carlos because the telegraph lines had been cut, but the renegades also killed five teamsters near Clifton. That means they headed due east from the reservation." He wiped a hand over his pasty white face, and Rayna wondered if he'd gotten more than he bargained for when he decided to pursue his journalistic trade in this rugged, dangerous part of the country.

"This is a big territory, Raymond," Ben commented, "but we can't afford to take the chance that those savages won't come up this way. We'd better start preparing now. I've got some of my men out already, warnin' the ranches to the south. We were hopin' you'd be able to spare a few to ride north and west."

"I'll have Gil get some men out first thing tomorrow," he replied. Ben started to protest the delay, but his host overrode his objections. "Ben, you know as well as I do that it would take nearly a week for Geronimo to get this far."

"That may be, but what about the Mescalero?" he asked defiantly. "If they hear that Geronimo is on the warpath, they might decide to join him the way some of them did with Nana last year."

"The Mescalero reservation is well south of here, Ben. I don't think we're in any immediate danger."

"Yeah, but those ain't the only Mescaleros in the territory, Raymond," he said significantly.

"Now, just a minute—" Rayna was on her feet instantly, but her father silenced her with a wave of his hand.

"I'll handle this, honey. I think Ben knows he's gone too far."

"No, Raymond. You're the one who's gone too far," Martinez countered. "You got nearly twenty Apaches workin' for you, and it ain't right."

Raymond exchanged an exasperated glance with his daughter. He had lost count of the number of times he'd had this argument with his neighbors. When he purchased Rancho Verde he had inherited a small group of Mescaleros and had quickly seen the advantages of befriending them just as his predecessor had. Their leader was Consayka, who as a boy had broken away from his own people after being converted to Christianity by Spanish monks. When the land that was now Rancho Verde had been given to Don Diego Sebastian in a vast Spanish land grant, the don had allowed Consayka and his people to stay and had put them to work on the ranch.

Consayka was old now, and he had strong feelings about continuing the traditions of his Mescalero ancestors, but Raymond had no doubts about his commitment to peace. There was no way the ancient Apache would give a second thought to joining Geronimo on the warpath.

Unfortunately, getting his Johnny-come-lately neighbors to understand that was another matter entirely. "Ben, Consayka's people haven't made any trouble for sixty years. Most of them were born on Rancho Verde and have never even lived among their own people."

"Can you deny that they still hold their heathen ceremonies?"

"No," Raymond answered reluctantly. "But that doesn't

mean they have any interest in joining their brethren on the warpath even if the reservation Mescalero do revolt."

Rayna could be silent no longer. "Ben, our Apaches are farmers, cowhands, and house servants. I seriously doubt whether they could even survive among their own people now."

"All the same, you're taking a terrible chance," Martinez warned them.

"I'm afraid I have to agree," Hadley said somewhat apologetically as he glanced between Rayna and her father. Rayna gave him a disgusted not-you-too look, and the young journalist hurried to explain, "It's not that I doubt the peaceful intent of your Apaches, Miss Templeton. You may be entirely correct in your assessment, but not everyone in Malaventura agrees. I've noticed a rising tide of sentiment against them."

"What have you heard?" Raymond asked, scowling.

"There have been no specific threats, but the community is growing increasingly uncomfortable with having a band of non-reservation Apaches in the area. Once word of Geronimo's depredations spreads, I'm afraid the citizens of New Mexico will begin to retaliate. The history of this territory suggests that they may not care whether the Apaches they retaliate against are peaceful or not."

A cold chill ran down Rayna's spine. Hadley may have been scrawny, pasty-faced, and a poor horseman, but he had an excellent point. If a panic started, no Apache would be safe from attack. During Victorio's raids several years earlier, rumors had abounded that the Rancho Verde Mescaleros were secretly aiding the renegade. Nana's raids last year had wrought similar rumors.

For that reason, neighbors—even good ones like Ben Martinez—had been seeking the removal of the Rancho Verde Mescaleros for years, and this recent outbreak would undoubtedly fuel even more unfounded rumors. According to Samuel Hadley, the kindling for a conflagration was already being laid.

Raymond launched into a vigorous speech about his commitment to protecting the Apaches on the ranch, then moved on to the topic of stationing lookouts at strategic passes throughout the area. Hadley and Martinez apparently felt it was wise to let the argument drop, and once they had a firm plan in mind, they took their leave. Rayna and Raymond escorted them to their horses and watched as they rode away.

"This is going to upset Skylar," Rayna said quietly as they turned back to the hacienda.

"I know." He shook his head. "When is this all gonna end, honey? I feel like I been fighting Apaches all my life, and for the life of me I can't figure out why. This country should be big enough for all of us."

"But it's not. Mankind is basically greedy, Papa. We always want what our neighbor has, and only laws and the constraints of civilization keep us from preying on one another. Unfortunately those same laws don't apply where the Apache are concerned, and they don't seem inclined to accept our views on the value of civilization."

"Very nicely put, honey," Raymond said, his eyes twinkling with mirth as he threw one arm over her shoulders. "And here I thought your sister was the philosopher in this family."

"Don't poke fun at me, Papa," she said, slipping one arm around his ample waist as they strolled inside. "I've had enough of that for one day."

"All right. What other views of the Apache would you care to share with me?"

"None, because you'll only tease me about it later. I think, instead, I'll stroll out to Consayka's camp and fetch Skylar. Word of Geronimo's outbreak is probably spreading all over the ranch already, and I'd rather she heard it from me."

"That's a good idea."

"Tell Mother I'll be back shortly."

It was a brisk ten-minute walk to the tiny encampment behind the hacienda. Unlike most other Apache tribes, the Mescalero lived in tall, stately lodges similar to those of the

Plains Indians. The eleven homes were grouped together in a seemingly haphazard fashion, no two exactly alike except that each entrance faced the sunrise.

As Rayna approached, she saw her sister and two elderly women sitting under the brush-covered ramada the ranch hands called a squaw cooler. Skylar's head was bowed, and her hands were working busily on an object that rested in her lap. Rayna had always envied those delicate hands and the genteel way her sister carried herself. In fact, there were many things about her sister that she envied, not the least of which was Skylar's gentle disposition. But it had never occurred to Rayna to try to be more like her demure, ladylike sister. It would have pleased their parents no end, but Rayna didn't know how to be anything but what she was.

Under the ramada, Consayka's wife, Gatana, was facing Skylar, deep in concentration as she studied the young woman's every move. The third woman, Tsa'kata, sat apart from them and seemed to be paying no attention to the others. Rayna knew that was not the case. Tsa'kata's eyesight was poor and her hearing even worse, but little happened on Rancho Verde within her sight—or out of it—that she was unaware of.

Of all the Apaches on the ranch, Tsa'kata was the one Rayna knew and understood least, for she had never worked as a house servant, as her daughter Gatana had. Her face was a leathery mask of deeply cut wrinkles and sagging flesh, yet no one would have guessed her to be nearly a hundred years old. She spoke enough Spanish to make herself understood when necessary, but she had refused to learn English—or at least she refused to *speak* it; Rayna had always suspected she knew far more of the white man's language than she let on.

As a child, Rayna had been secretly terrified of the old woman, and even now Tsa'kata was one of the few people in the world who had the power to intimidate her.

Though the women had undoubtedly seen her coming, no one acknowledged her presence, so she slowed her pace as she neared the ramada. If Gatana was teaching Skylar a rit-

ual ceremony, it would be disrespectful for Rayna to interrupt, and she had no desire to incur Tsa'kata's wrath. Instead, she moved to a nearby outcropping of boulders and
sat, giving every appearance of someone who'd been out for
a casual stroll and had decided to stop and rest.

Watching covertly, Rayna finally identified the object in
Skylar's lap as a necklace of some sort. Her small, graceful
hands were carefully weaving beads and strands of grama
grass into an intricate bib that was suspended from a beaded
choker. Rayna could vaguely hear Gatana and Skylar speaking, but their voices were too soft to allow her to catch any of
the words. It was just as well, she reasoned, for they were
undoubtedly speaking Apache, and Rayna's knowledge of
the language was limited.

When Skylar had first come to Rancho Verde, Rayna had
taken on the job of teaching her new sister English, and
Skylar had tried to reciprocate. Skylar had proved to be the
better pupil. Over the years, Rayna had kept trying, but
whenever she used her limited vocabulary with the Mescaleros she invariably received snickers or outright laughs because she was so bad at it. She had finally given up
completely after she mispronounced a phrase that had conveyed some terrible insult and had received an incomprehensible tongue-lashing from Tsa'kata. Now she left the
difficult language to Skylar.

Out of the corner of her eye, Rayna studied her sister. Her
simple white shirtwaist and beige skirt were a striking con-
trast to the loose overblouses and colorful calico skirts of her
companions. Only those clothes and her age set her apart
from the other women, though. Her hair, which she normally
wore in a loose chignon or a braided roll at the nape of her
neck, was unbound today. Jet black, it fell in gentle swirls
around her shoulders and framed a face of such delicate
beauty that all who saw her felt compelled to comment on it.
Hers was an exotic, intriguing face—or so it had seemed to
the easterners Skylar and Rayna had encountered while they
were at school in Boston. While no one had feared the Indian

named Templeton, her appearance had set her apart from the other girls, making her an outsider.

In this territory, however, Skylar's square jaw, high cheekbones, deep-set black eyes, and light bronze skin labeled her an Apache. No amount of culture, grace, education—not even the considerable influence of Raymond Templeton—could overcome the prejudice that kept Skylar from being totally accepted. She was still an outsider.

Was it any wonder that Skylar felt such a bond with the Rancho Verde Apaches? Rayna wondered, remembering the pain she'd seen in her mother's eyes earlier. As much as Collie loved Skylar, she couldn't understand her daughter's need for a connection with her past. But Rayna understood. Skylar was a beautiful, demure young lady trapped squarely between her vague memories of life as an Apache and the Anglo world she had been raised in. The tragedy was that she could never truly belong to either.

Even the Rancho Verde Mescaleros, who had accepted Skylar and indoctrinated her in their ways, were not really her people. She had been stolen from a band of White Mountain Apaches, whose culture was in many ways different from that of the Mescalero. Over time, Skylar's memories of her first family had fused with the beliefs of the Mescalero and the legends Consayka told around the fire on winter evenings.

Rayna ached at the sadness she often saw in her sister, but she didn't pity her. Skylar would never have stood for that, and Rayna loved her far too much to demean their relationship with pity.

Never one to enjoy being inactive, Rayna soon grew tired of pretending to admire the scenery. She kept still, trying not to fidget, but by the time the ceremony was complete, Rayna had exhausted her meager supply of patience. She sighed with relief when Skylar wrapped the necklace in a cloth and placed it along with several other bundles in a beaded buckskin pouch. As she rose, she spoke quietly with Gatana and Tsa'kata, then slipped out from beneath the ramada.

"Hello, sister. What brings you back to the ranch so early today? Did Samson throw another shoe?" Her dark eyes were twinkling merrily, and though Rayna didn't know how it was possible, she suspected that Skylar already knew the answer to her question.

She stood and stretched her legs. "Yes, he did, and if you're going to tease me about it, too, you can walk back to the house by yourself."

Skylar stopped in front of her. "You've had a difficult day," she said sympathetically.

"That is something of an understatement," she replied, all hints of teasing gone. For the sake of courtesy, she moved to the ramada and greeted Gatana and her mother. Tsa'kata did not deign to acknowledge her, but Rayna spent a moment conversing with the old woman's daughter, who had long since stopped working at the hacienda because of her advanced age.

"What brought you out here?" Skylar asked when she and Rayna finally started for home.

Dreading having to tell her about Geronimo's outbreak, Rayna stalled for time. "Mother said that you were learning a ceremony, and I thought I'd better see what you were up to. What is Gatana teaching you?"

Skylar's eyes danced with excitement. "You won't believe it, Rayna. I've been asked to participate in Mary Long Horn's maiden ceremony. Gatana is teaching me the ritual prayers for making the necklace of the *sons-ee-a-ray*."

Rayna gave her a sidelong glance. "Would you care to translate that for me? You know how good my Apache is."

"It's the symbol of the morning star, one of many that will decorate Mary's dress. Once I have learned the prayers, I'll make the actual necklace that she'll wear in the ceremony. The one I was working on today is only an imitation. We use several different necklaces for practice so that none will be invested with the power of White Painted Woman."

Rayna needed no explanation of that. White Painted Woman was the deity revered by the Apaches as the mother of their race. Apparently the symbol of the morning star belonged to her. "When is the ceremony?"

"In July, four days before the full moon. I suppose that would make it somewhere around the eighteenth."

"Hmmm . . . That doesn't give you much time to learn the ritual and complete the necklace."

"I know," Skylar answered, growing pensive. "And there's more, Rayna. I have been asked to attend Mary on each of the four days of the ceremony." She paused a moment. "Will Mother be upset, do you think?"

Rayna couldn't lie to her. "It's possible, but she won't try to stop you from participating."

"I know that. I hate to cause her pain, though."

Rayna slipped her arm around her sister. It made walking difficult, since Rayna was several inches taller, but Skylar needed the comfort. "You're a grown woman, Skylar. You have to do what you think is best."

"Even if it hurts someone I love?"

"Mother understands."

Skylar shook her head sadly. "No, she doesn't."

"Then we'll find a way to make her understand how important this is to you."

Skylar glanced up at her, grateful for her support. For nearly as long as she could remember, this sister had been her buffer against disappointment, frustration, and anyone or anything that tried to harm her. Skylar had vague memories of another sister, older than Rayna, who had also watched over her—who had, in fact, died while trying to protect her from the Indians who had kidnapped her. The memory saddened her, but she couldn't imagine loving that sister in the shadows any more than she loved this one.

"It is important to me, Rayna, but I don't think I could make anyone understand why—not even you."

"But I do understand," Rayna insisted.

"No, you don't." Skylar stopped suddenly and glanced at the high blue sky near the horizon to the east. She seemed lost in thought, as though looking for something that wasn't there.

Rayna stopped, too, facing her. "Then explain it to me."

Skylar did not look away from the horizon as she spoke. "It's the necklace," she said softly.

Now Rayna really did understand. Or thought she did. Years ago Consayka had told Skylar the romantic tale of a young Apache brave who had married a maiden from an enemy clan and united both their peoples. The brave had defied custom and given his bride a magnificent necklace of turquoise and silver with a medallion carved in the image of the Thunder Eagle.

Consayka told the story often, and not always in the same fashion. In one version the brave had been from the Jicarilla Apache tribe; in another, he was White Mountain. Depending on Consayka's mood, the handsome brave and his wife had many children and lived to a ripe old age, or died tragically at the hands of a Chiricahua renegade. Rayna had heard so many versions of the story that she found it virtually meaningless.

Skylar, on the other hand, believed the story was true. What was more, she believed that somehow she had been a part of it. When she was fifteen, she had even made a replica of the necklace Consayka had described. She kept it hidden, and no one but Rayna and a few of the Mescaleros even knew of its existence.

"Making this necklace has reminded you of the Thunder Eagle legend, hasn't it?" Rayna asked.

"Yes, but that's not all." She looked at her sister. "It's *sons-ee-a-ray.*"

"Morning star? What has that got to do with the legend of . . ." She searched her memory for the names of the couple in Consayka's story, but drew a blank. "Oh, what were they called?" she muttered impatiently.

"He Stalks the Gray Wolf and She Sings by the Willow," Skylar supplied, her voice almost reverent as she spoke the names.

"Right. What has the morning star got to do with them?"

Skylar shook her head helplessly as tears shimmered in her eyes. "I don't know. I can't remember. There's a memory in my head that tantalizes me like a mirage in the desert, but when I reach out to touch it, it vanishes. All I know is that *sons-ee-a-ray* should mean something to me."

Rayna had no idea how to ease her sister's distress, and there was nothing she hated worse than feeling powerless. "Perhaps the memory will come to you in time," she suggested lamely, and earned a small smile for her effort.

"I was taken from my people nineteen years ago, Rayna. It's not likely that I'll suddenly wake up one morning with all those memories intact. My old life will never come out of the shadows. I have learned to live with that."

"Until something like this reminds you."

Skylar nodded. "The feelings will pass. Come. Mother will be wondering what's keeping us." She started again toward the hacienda, and Rayna fell into step beside her. "All right, now, sister. You may tell me the real reason you came to fetch me."

Rayna laughed. "I never could fool you, could I?"

"Not for very long," Skylar replied, sharing her sister's amusement. "Your eyes betray your emotions. Others can't always see it, but I can. Something has troubled you deeply, and you don't want to tell me about it."

Rayna took a deep breath. "Geronimo has fled the San Carlos reservation and is rumored to be heading this way."

"I see." Though Skylar continued to walk, her body became very still, as though she had somehow drawn into herself, and a curtain fell over her features, making them unreadable. Rayna had seen it happen before. Her sister had inherited the stoicism of her ancestors, and when she chose to shut out the world, no one—not even Rayna—could penetrate the barriers she erected.

In an evenly modulated voice, Skylar asked questions, eliciting all the information her sister knew. Most of it was speculation, but even that was enough to cause concern.

Where the Apache were concerned, everyone always assumed the worst.

"Did Mr. Martinez try to persuade Father to send the Mescalero away again?" she asked quietly.

Rayna knew Skylar wouldn't believe a lie. "He did mention it, yes. But Father stood his ground. Nothing is going to happen to Consayka's people."

It was a long moment before Skylar replied. "I pray you are right, sister."

They completed the long walk to the hacienda in silence.

Chapter
Two

Arizona Territory, April 1882

EVERY WINDOW ON the first floor of the modest two-story ranch house blazed with light, and the strains of a vigorous fiddle tune wafted out over the valley floor. There was no other sound for miles in any direction save for the occasional lowing of cattle in the distance and the haunting bay of a coyote somewhere up on Windwalk Mesa.

Keenly aware of the isolation of the Longstreet ranch, Major Meade Ashford relaxed against a post that supported the porch roof and extracted a slender cheroot from his pocket. His match flared briefly in the darkness, then arched through the air as he flicked it into the front yard. It landed in one of his sister's flower beds, and Meade winced. If Libby found it tomorrow, there would be hell to pay. She'd been trying her hand at horticulture since the day he'd brought her to Arizona eight years ago, and she protected her garden almost as fiercely as she protected her two young children.

As far as the flowers were concerned, Meade had to admit that her results had improved tremendously over that first dismal year at Fort Apache when her garden had consisted of a heavy wooden container that looked more like a watering trough than a window box. She had placed it on the porch that connected their quarters with the post hospital, and though people had told her that flowers wouldn't grow in the baking Arizona sun, she had been determined to prove them wrong.

Undaunted by her failure in '74, she had tried again the next year here at the ranch . . . and the year after that. After years of diligence, irrigation, and far more trouble than they were worth in Meade's opinion, she had finally coaxed her roses into blooming.

Meade smiled down at the pitiful little bed of roses and realized that he was going to miss watching them bloom this year, despite all the teasing he had subjected his sister to over the years. He was going to miss the quiet solitude of this ranch, too . . . and his niece and nephew. He would miss them very much. Of course, it went without saying that he would miss Libby, and if pressed to admit it, he might even have confessed that he was going to miss his brother-in-law, Case Longstreet.

The one thing he felt certain he wouldn't miss, though, was Fort Apache. Eight years as post surgeon at that misbegotten hellhole had taken their toll on Meade. He had come to the position one year out of medical school at Harvard eager for adventure and challenge. Instead, he had been forced to witness more kinds of suffering than he had ever dreamed possible. Had it not been for Libby, he would have transferred long ago to some more hospitable climate and to a place where constant battles with the Apache wouldn't have left so much blood on his hands.

But all that would be over soon. In four days he was being involuntarily transferred to Fort Marcy in New Mexico, and six months after that, he was leaving the army forever. Though he wasn't looking forward to the transfer, he readily acknowledged that it would be nice to enjoy the relative quiet of Santa Fe for a while. It was a beautiful old city, situated far enough north to be somewhat removed—geographically, at least—from the army's perpetual conflict with the Apache.

After that, he would return here, to the ranch he had helped his brother-in-law purchase shortly before Case and Libby's wedding. Though he was only thirty-six, Meade felt like an old man who had earned a quiet retirement, and he

Moonsong
33

was looking forward to becoming a gentleman rancher. In the back of his mind was the idea that he might someday set up a small medical practice somewhere, but that wouldn't be for a while yet. At the moment, his chosen profession was anathema.

"Meade? What are you doing out here?"

Libby's quietly spoken question startled Meade. "Good Lord, Lib, don't sneak up on a man like that."

"Sorry. I suppose some of my husband's skills at stalking have rubbed off on me."

"Among other things," he grumbled.

"Don't be contrary, Meade," she said gently. "I know you'll never admit it to me, but you and Case have become good friends. You can stop glowering every time something reminds you that he's an Apache."

Meade squared his shoulders with a hint of indignation and straightened his dress-blue uniform coat. "My dear Liberty, I do not *glower*. I do, on occasion, bristle, and I have been known to fume from time to time, but I most emphatically do not glower." He turned his profile to her. "It wouldn't be seemly."

Her gentle laugh drifted out over the rose garden, and she tucked her arm through his. "Oh, Meade, I'm going to miss you. No one has ever been able to make me laugh the way you do."

Meade dropped a kiss on her forehead, a gesture that was an old and comforting habit for both of them. "I'm going to miss you, too, Libby."

"Then why did you sneak away from my party? I invited all our neighbors just to give you a magnificent send-off, and you pulled a vanishing act. It was everything I could do to keep Drucilla Metcalf from coming to look for you herself. She was positively frothing at the mouth when she realized you'd escaped her clutches."

"Why do you think I disappeared?" he asked as he sat on the porch railing. "That hellcat has spent the better part of the last two years trying to rope me into matrimony, and she seems to think that this is the last opportunity she'll ever have." Meade shook his head in bewilderment. "Why in the name of God is she so intent on me? I just don't understand it. I'm nearly twice her age!"

"Yes, but you look incredibly handsome in your uniform."

Meade groaned. "One more excellent reason to leave the military posthaste."

"I agree with your goal, but not your reasoning," Libby said, smoothing his lapel. "You see, you may eventually leave the uniform behind, but that will not keep you from being incredibly handsome. What's more, you're a respected physician and a landholder of some repute. That makes you the finest catch in this part of the territory."

"To be a fine catch in this godforsaken territory, you need only be breathing, Libby."

"Meade, you're being contrary again," she scolded lightly, though in truth she could hardly blame her brother for his attitude. There was a marked scarcity of unmarried women in the territory, and it seemed that the ones near Fort Apache always gravitated toward Meade. Over the years that number had included several officers' wives as well. To the best of Libby's knowledge, which might or might not have been accurate, he had successfully evaded those amorous women, and had also eluded the clutches of the unmarried ones.

Yet she could scarcely blame the women for being attracted to Meade. Not only was he a mannerly, educated gentleman, he was incredibly handsome as well. Even the rigors of his career had not changed that. He was tall, with a lithe, athletic physique, and the youthful softness that had marked his features when he arrived at Fort Apache was no longer evident. His face was harder now, and deep lines framed his mouth when he smiled or frowned. His eyes, an odd color of hazel, were much more piercing than before. They no longer twinkled with gentleness and mirth except when he looked at Libby. The sun had lightened his dark brown hair, giving it highlights of gold; the things he had seen and done had added flecks of silver.

In many ways those changes had only made him more attractive. No longer was he a boyishly handsome young man. Fort Apache had transformed him into a ruggedly handsome man of depth and maturity. Unfortunately it had also twisted his idealism into cynicism, and Libby grieved for the parts of her brother that had been lost bit by bit with every limb he'd been forced to amputate and every patient who'd died a hideous, agonizing death before his very eyes.

Though Libby dreaded seeing Meade leave for Santa Fe, she was more than anxious for him to retire from the army. He was weary of death, and only time would heal the ravages of his soul. Time . . . and perhaps a loving woman—though Libby knew she would never be able to convince Meade of that.

"I have a right to be contrary where Drucilla is concerned, Libby," he was saying. "She is a most determined young lady."

"Then perhaps you should succumb to her charms."

Meade looked down at her, frowning. "What charms? She has buckteeth, and her eyes cross when she laughs. And that laugh! She sounds like a braying army mule."

"Meade! That's unkind and untrue," Libby said, slapping his arm lightly. "Drucilla is quite attractive, and you know it. Granted, her laugh is a little . . . exuberant, but that only proves that she enjoys life to the fullest."

He made a disgruntled harrumphing sound and flicked his cheroot into the yard, making sure it fell far beyond Libby's rose bed.

"Tell me the truth, Meade. Why don't you like Drucilla?"

He sighed wearily. "I told you before, I'm practically old enough to be the girl's father, and if I were, I'd apply my hand liberally to her backside. She's boisterous, loud, opinionated . . . Most of the time she dresses like a man—and behaves like one. Frankly, I prefer more demure women, and Drucilla Metcalf doesn't have a ladylike bone in her body."

He raised one eyebrow sharply. "Are those sufficient reasons for you? They certainly are for me."

"Meade—"

"Enough, Libby," he said placing his hands on her shoulders. "We've covered this territory before, and you're never going to wear me down. I'm too old and set in my ways to ever marry."

"Thirty-six is not old!" she said adamantly.

"It's not a matter of chronological age, Libby," Meade replied, his voice tinged with sadness as he stood and looked out over the still valley. "I *feel* positively ancient. All I want from my life now is a little peace and quiet."

For a moment, with his face couched in shadow, he looked as old and tired as he claimed he felt. Libby's heart wrenched at the sight, but she knew there was no way to ease his pain. Slipping one arm around his waist, she leaned her head against his shoulder. "I wish you didn't have to go to Fort Marcy."

"So do I, little sister, but I don't have much choice in the matter. I've been reassigned to the One Hundred-fortieth, and whither they goest, I go, too."

He said it blithely, but to Libby it wasn't a matter for levity. As post surgeon, unattached to any specific army unit, Meade had rarely been required to venture out with the troops and engage in battle. Those occasions when he had done so had always been devastating for him. This new assignment with 140th Regiment might place him almost constantly in the field . . . constantly in danger. Libby didn't want to think about what could happen to him.

"Damn him," she muttered vehemently. "This is all Geronimo's fault. If that accursed Chiricahua hadn't gone on the rampage, none of this would be happening. I don't know why the army didn't hang him back in '77 when John Clum brought him in. We'd be at peace now, and you wouldn't be going away."

Meade looked down at his sister in surprise. When it came to the Apache, Libby was the most moderate and sympathetic supporter the Indians had. Considering that she had married into the White Mountain tribe, that was only to be expected. Generally when there was trouble, she blamed corrupt Indian agents, unenlightened army officers, or inconsistent government policies. He'd never heard her speak out so passionately against any Apache before.

"I certainly wouldn't argue with you on that point, Libby, but there's no sense in looking back. We have to deal with the situation as it exists now, and that means preparing for a long and bloody war with Geronimo. When his braves killed those two San Carlos policemen, his fate was sealed. He'll never surrender, because he knows that if he does, he'll be hanged."

"But so many good men are going to die because of him." Libby felt tears stinging her eyes. "I don't want you to be one of them."

"Libby, I'll be fine," he insisted. "I swear it. In six months I'll have completed my obligation to the army and will retire for good. In the meantime, I plan to be very careful."

She wasn't reassured. "Well, I hope that course you took at Johns Hopkins was worth it, Meade," she said testily. "If it hadn't been for that, you could retire any time you liked."

"It was worth it, Libby. It gave me some much-needed time away from Fort Apache, and I learned a great deal about the new surgical procedures that are being introduced. At the time, trading attendance of that course for an additional two years of service to the army seemed like a good deal."

"Well, it wasn't."

"In your opinion."

She glanced up at him. "Hasn't Case told you? In this house, my opinion is the only one that counts."

Meade laughed because he knew that was far from the truth. The love and respect Case and Libby felt for each other had made their marriage one of harmony and equality. In the beginning Meade had violently opposed his sister's relationship with the Apache army scout who had been raised and educated by frontiersman Jedidiah Longstreet after Case's parents were murdered. Even after their love was put to the ultimate test and survived, Meade had still had reservations.

He couldn't deny, though, that despite the prejudice they often encountered, they had made a good life together. Case was respected and accepted by most of their neighbors because they knew that his close ties with the nearby reservation Apaches was responsible for much of the serenity they enjoyed at a time when most ranchers in Arizona lived in constant fear for their lives and property.

"Laugh at me if you like, Meade, but I won't rest easy until you're back here in October."

Meade sobered as he studied his sister's worried countenance. Thoughtfully he reached out and touched the medallion hanging from the turquoise and silver choker that encircled her throat. Four eagle feathers representing Case, Libby, and their two children were suspended from the medallion, which was carved with the symbol of the Thunder Eagle, Case's guiding spirit. The necklace had been a gift from her husband, a legacy left to him by his parents, and Libby wore it only on special occasions.

"Libby, does your concern for me have anything to do with this?" he asked as he fingered the medallion. "Has Case had a vision about me?"

The question surprised Libby so much that she couldn't keep from smiling. "Why, Meade! I didn't think you believed in Case's visions."

"I don't," he said quickly, then hesitated. "But I do have to admit that he sometimes has an uncanny ability to foretell coming events."

"Like Geronimo's outbreak?" she asked slyly, remembering the somewhat heated discussion Case and Meade had engaged in when her husband tried to warn her brother that the Chiricahua was stirring up trouble.

"Oh, well, that . . . that could probably be attributed to rumors he'd heard around the reservation."

"Or a vision from the Thunder Eagle."

Meade raised one eyebrow again. "Of the two explanations, I prefer the former."

Libby laughed. "You are the most stubborn man I have ever known, but I do love you."

She looked at him expectantly, as though innocently waiting for a new topic of conversation to crop up, and the small silence extended into a long one as Meade wrestled with his pride. Damn her, she was going to make him ask for it.

"Well? *Has* Case had a vision about me?" he finally demanded with a burst of disgust at his own curiosity and superstition.

"No," she assured him with a smug chuckle.

"Would you tell me if he had?"

Libby thought it over. "Probably, though I doubt that Case would tell me if he foresaw some tragedy ahead for you. He would be far more likely to warn you directly."

"I wonder about that," he mumbled.

"What?"

"Nothing," he said smoothly. "Nothing at all."

The front door opened wide, spilling another patch of light onto the shadowy porch, and Case stepped into doorway. *"Cida'ké?* I'm sorry to interrupt, but our guests are beginning to ask about you." The tall, broad-shouldered Apache smiled at his brother-in-law. "And Miss Metcalf is organizing a scouting party to track you down."

"Typical," Meade muttered as Libby went to her husband and slipped her arms around his waist.

"I'm sorry I abandoned you, beloved. I'll see to our guests while you talk to Meade." She turned a pair of sparkling brown eyes on her brother. "I believe he has a question to ask you." She stretched up, brushing her lips lightly against her husband's, and Meade felt a swift stab of envy. He didn't really believe in the kind of romantic love Case and Libby felt for each other, yet lately he found himself becoming more and more envious of their relationship.

Of course he rationalized the emotion by convincing himself that it had only to do with the kind of woman Libby was.

She was truly a lady—a gentle, loving, nurturing spirit who seemed too fragile for this world, or any other. Yet beneath that gentility lurked a core of iron, capable of withstanding the worst the world could throw at her. Case Longstreet was a very lucky man.

Meade had often reflected that if he had found a woman like his sister, he might have considered marriage despite his dislike of the institution. That hadn't happened yet, though, and it seemed unlikely that it ever would, since Libby was one of a kind.

She disappeared into the house, closing the door behind her, and Case joined his brother-in-law at the porch rail. "What did you want to ask me?"

Wild horses couldn't have dragged his question about Case's visions out of him this time. "Nothing. Libby was just teasing me."

"She's very concerned about you," Case noted.

"I know. Frankly I'm concerned about her, too. Are you sure Libby and the children are going to be safe here, Case?" he asked bluntly. "Perhaps you should send her to Fort Apache until Geronimo is captured."

"That's not necessary," Case replied with the certainty that never failed to irritate Meade. He was always so damned sure of himself. And most of the time he was right, which irritated Meade even more.

"How can you guarantee that?"

"Because Geronimo will not come back here for a very long time."

"But what about the rumors that the Chiricahua who stayed behind will take to the warpath, too? If that happens, there could be trouble here."

Case's dark eyes met Meade's. "I give you my word that no harm will ever come to Libby or our children."

Meade didn't see any way to argue with that. If anyone could live up to that promise, it was Case Longstreet. He glanced up at the shining silver-slipper moon on the horizon.

"Do you have any predictions about what the future holds, Case?"

Case smiled into the darkness. "I'm not a soothsayer, Meade."

He sighed irritably. "Is that a yes or a no?"

The Apache was silent for a long moment as he tried to decide how much, or how little, to tell his skeptical brother-in-law. The fact that he had asked the question was remarkable in itself, but Case knew that Meade didn't really believe that a phantom Apache spirit sometimes visited him, showing him shadowy visions of the future. Case was hesitant to relate the visions he had experienced recently, but not because he feared Meade's ridicule. Case simply didn't understand them all himself, and until he did, he would never speak of them to anyone. Not even Libby.

There was one thing he could relate, though. "The Gray Fox is coming back," he said finally.

Shocked, Meade turned toward him. "General Crook is being reassigned? When?"

"That I do not know," Case replied. "But I believe it will be soon."

Though he wanted very much to believe it was true, Meade found it difficult—not because it was one of Case's visions, but because he didn't credit the army with enough good sense to bring the general back. George Crook was the only military man who had ever engineered any kind of meaningful peace with the Apaches. The Indians trusted him because he had proven himself a man of his word during his campaigns against them in the mid-1870's. Had he been left in charge, Meade had no doubt that the Apache menace would have ceased to exist long ago.

Unfortunately the army had transferred him to the Department of the Platte to fight the Sioux in 1875, and the corrupt "Indian Ring" of bamboozlers and outright thieves had systematically destroyed what little confidence the Apache had in the word of the white man.

"I sincerely hope you're right about that, Case. With Geronimo on the warpath, bringing Crook back would be the smartest thing the army ever did." He grinned at his brother-in-law. "You think they've got that much good sense?"

Meade was treated to one of Case's rare laughs. The deep, melodious sound started deep inside him and overflowed into the night. "Frankly, my brother, I don't," he said with a smile once his laughter had subsided. "But I believe in my vision. Crook will return."

"If he does, you know he'll come to you," Meade commented, his tone serious.

Case's smile faded. "I no longer wish to scout for the army."

"But will you be able to refuse the Gray Fox? He's a very persuasive man, and he trusts you implicitly. You know as well as I that the first thing he'll do is recruit Apache scouts for the campaign against Geronimo, and he'll want you to lead them."

"I'm a rancher now, not a soldier." Case's voice was very quiet as he added, "And sometimes I am not even sure I am an Apache any longer."

Meade allowed the comment to hang in the air. One of the things he respected most about his brother-in-law was his ability to walk the fine line between his Apache heritage and the white world he had chosen to live in. For Libby's sake, Meade didn't even want to consider the possibility that Case would ever doubt the choices he'd made.

The fiddle music in the house seemed very far away as a companionable silence stretched out between the two men. Meade lit another cheroot, then offered one to Case, who refused it with a simple shake of his head. On Windwalk Mesa the mournful coyote bayed again.

"We should return to your party now," Case said when the cheroot went sailing into the yard.

Meade nodded. "Yes. Libby probably has Drucilla hog-tied to a chair."

"That's unlikely," Case replied as they turned toward the door. "Libby is terrible with a lasso."

It was Meade's turn to laugh. Case's quiet humor always caught him off guard. But he was in for another surprise, too. Just as he opened the door, Case stopped him by placing one hand on his arm.

"In case you are wondering, brother, you *will* be returning to us unharmed in October."

Meade didn't bother denying that he'd been curious. "Thank you . . . brother."

Case's normally stoic face was suddenly softened by a devilish grin. "But you will not be alone."

With that, he disappeared into the house, leaving Meade to wonder just what the devil he meant. Case's knowing smile troubled him a lot more than the prediction itself.

The campfire crackled and shifted, sending a shower of tiny golden sparks into the air. None of the braves at the Mescalero war council noticed. Calm voices and reasonable words had deserted them hours ago; now they shouted at one another and hurled insults. They made threats. One stalked off in anger, then returned minutes later, ready to take up the fight again.

The old ones, who had seen too many of their people destroyed, counseled for peace. The young ones, who were outraged by confinement to the reservation, wanted to join Geronimo on the warpath. Fed by the fuel of their rage, the young voices were much louder than the old ones—with one exception. Sun Hawk sat in the midst of the fray watching the others expend their wrath. His face was an impassive mask, but his dark eyes were alert to every move and gesture his Apache brothers made. He had spoken once, earlier, before the talk had decayed into a contest to see who could shout the loudest. Now he was waiting until the time was right to speak again.

"How long must our children go hungry because there is not enough food?" Dull Knife asked, his voice raised with the passion of his oratory. The guttural traits of the Apache language made him sound all the more fierce. "When the

White Eyes told us we must live in this valley and nowhere else, we believed their promises to give us blankets, horses, and beef! They robbed us of our right to feed and clothe ourselves, but do they keep their promises? No! They give us one steer to feed a family of twenty for a month!"

"And how many beeves will Geronimo give us?" one of the elders asked.

"Enough to feed our families, Grandfather!" Dull Knife said, though the old man was not related to him. He used the term only as a token, since it was considered an insult to use an Apache's name when addressing him.

Klo'sen shook his head. "I do not think so. Even now the horse soldiers are hunting him like an animal. They will chase him and his people into mountains—"

"But they will never find him!" Dull Knife insisted.

"Perhaps, but Geronimo will not find cattle in the mountains, either. The deer he kills will be barely enough to feed those who follow him now. His women will not be able to gather juniper berries or harvest the mescal. His children will go hungry, too, and for what?"

"For freedom!" Dull Knife shouted.

"At what price?"

The hot-headed brave leapt to his feet and glared down at the old man. "At least he is a warrior, not an old woman."

Sun Hawk could be silent no longer. "Enough, cousin," he said quietly as he rose and faced the would-be renegade. His height and the breadth of his shoulders gave him an advantage over the other brave, but Dull Knife did not back away. "You will not speak to our grandfather with disrespect. The battles he has led have brought glory to our people. He deserves better from you."

"That was long ago," Dull Knife replied, unintimidated by the reminder that the others regarded his distant cousin with great respect. "He has forgotten—"

"He has forgotten nothing," Sun Hawk said forcefully, but still he did not raise his voice. When he turned and surveyed the faces around the fire, everyone including Dull Knife fell silent. "Listen to me, and mark the words well, my friends. To follow Geronimo would be madness. Once our people numbered in the thousands. We hunted buffalo and traded blankets for horses with our sometime friends, the Sioux. Our hunting grounds stretched farther than an old man could walk in a year.

"But now"—his voice took on a haunting sadness—"now we are only a few hundred, and I could run the length of our land between the rising and setting of the sun."

Dull Knife smiled triumphantly. "What better reason do we need to join Geronimo?"

"It will change nothing for the good," Sun Hawk replied calmly. "If we follow the way of the Chiricahua, we will no longer be Mescalero. Too many of our people will die, and what little land we have now will be taken from us. For the sake of our children, we *must not* fight."

Dull Knife spit on the ground at Sun Hawk's feet. "What do you know of our children, Iya'itsa? You have none to awaken you in the night with their tears of hunger, and you allowed your own to die unavenged."

A gasp of shock went around the fire, and a shadow of sadness passed over Sun Hawk's face before it hardened into stone. "You go too far, cousin," he said, his quiet tone edged with steel.

"He is right, Dull Knife," Klo'sen said, deliberately insulting the young brave by using his name. "We do not speak of the dead, nor do we remind the living of the pain they have suffered. Leave the council. We no longer wish to hear your words."

"I will not leave!" Dull Knife shouted in outrage, but when he looked to the other men in the council for support, he found no one willing to meet his eyes. Even his friends who believed as he did would not look at him.

Only Naka'yen, the oldest and most revered of the Mescalero chiefs, met his intense gaze, but support was not on the old chief's mind. "Go, Dull Knife. Return when your blood

is not so hot that it clouds your mind, and hope that your
cousin will forgive you."

Shame and anger warred within the young brave, and after
a moment he whirled away from the fire and disappeared
into the night. With the most outspoken dissenter gone, the
war council ended soon after. Though many still believed
they should join Geronimo, all agreed to abide by the decision of the elders.

As the others dispersed into the night, Naka'yen stood and
looked with pride at Sun Hawk, his youngest child, who was
a child no more. He was a great medicine chief who would in
all likelihood lead their band when Naka'yen no longer
walked the earth. "You spoke well tonight, my son. I am
proud of you."

"I spoke what was in my heart, Father," Sun Hawk replied. "I have no more reason than Dull Knife to trust the
white man's promises, but following Geronimo will not help
our people." The shadow of sadness passed over his face
again. "Or feed our hungry children," he added quietly.

Naka'yen ached for him—and for himself. The wife and
two sons Sun Hawk had lost had been a part of Naka'yen,
too. "You have the right to challenge Dull Knife for the thing
he said to you," the old man said softly. "Some might even
say it is your duty."

Sun Hawk's eyes were as black as the night as he looked
at the old chieftain. "Father, when it becomes my duty to kill
one of my Apache brothers, I will no longer be an Apache."

He turned away from the fire and became one with the
darkness.

Chapter
Three

MEADE HAD ALMOST forgotten what civilization looked like—and felt like. Santa Fe wasn't as cosmopolitan as Washington or the other eastern cities where he'd lived in his younger years, but compared to Fort Apache, it was sheer heaven. It was a charming old city with the Military Department of New Mexico sitting squarely in the middle. Fort Marcy itself stood on a hill overlooking the town, but Meade's assignment placed him in the Military Headquarters. His quarters were on Grant Street less than a block away from the finest hospital in the southwestern territories, and there were excellent restaurants, gaming halls, and a new opera house within walking distance of the post.

In the three months he'd been in Santa Fe he had put each of those amenities to the best possible use. He'd been out on brief details with two cavalry companies, but both assignments had consisted of nothing more than escorting visiting dignitaries to the elegant Montezuma Hot Springs Hotel near Las Vegas. Since there had been no Indian trouble in that area since the Pueblo uprising several decades ago, the details had been less than hazardous.

Meade was far from bored by the lack of official duties. He had made good use of his time by persuading General Whitlock, commander of the Department of New Mexico, to allow him to teach a class on new surgical techniques to the hospital staff.

Having just completed one such lecture, he left the hospital and paused a moment to consider his options. He had been considering walking down to the Palace Hotel for supper, but the late afternoon heat made the very thought intolerable. Captain Manlove and his wife were hosting a card party later in the evening. . . . That was a possibility. The Manloves were pleasant enough, and there was always a last-minute need for a fourth at whist.

Then again, he could always—

"Major Ashford! There you are, sir." Colonel Collingswood's young aide-de-camp hurried out the hospital door and offered him a brisk salute. "I've been looking for you everywhere, sir," he said pleasantly as soon as Meade had returned the salute. He seemed slightly out of breath. "It's a big hospital."

"That it is, Lieutenant . . . Bascomb, isn't it?"

"That's correct, sir."

"Well, now that I've led you on a merry chase, what can I do for you, Bascomb?"

The fresh-faced officer pulled a folded sheet of parchment from his coat and handed it to Meade. "The colonel requested that I deliver this to you. New orders, I believe, sir."

So much for my daily lectures, Meade thought as he opened the directive, which was nothing more than a request for him to attend the colonel immediately. "Thank you, Lieutenant. Any idea what those new orders might be?" he asked, though he thought it unlikely that the officer would tell him, even if he knew.

"None, sir. If you'll excuse me, I have other duties to attend to."

"Of course, Lieutenant. You are dismissed."

Bascomb hurried off, most likely to deliver another message like the one he'd given to Meade.

Knowing it was pointless to speculate on the new detail to which he was about to be assigned, Meade turned down Grant Street past his own quarters and then moved along the edge of the parade grounds to post headquarters. Several minutes later he was ushered into Colonel Collingswood's office.

The colonel was a brisk, no-nonsense fellow with graying muttonchops that added to the already considerable width of his face. Privately Meade considered him a pompous ass, and though he kept the opinion to himself, he knew others who were less discreet in voicing similar opinions.

They went through the ritual amenities; then the colonel got right down to business. "Major, I want you to make ready to depart tomorrow at dawn. We have finally received authorization to move against the Mescalero. You'll be attached to Company B and will take your orders from Captain Greenleigh."

It was everything Meade could do to keep from groaning. If Collingswood was an old pompous ass, Greenleigh was a young one. In Meade's mind, that was much worse. At least Collingswood was a seasoned soldier whose experience could sometimes be counted upon to keep him from making foolish decisions. But only sometimes. Greenleigh was just plain arrogant.

"Yes, sir," Meade said, trying not to grit his teeth. "May I ask a question, though?"

"Of course."

"I was under the impression that the Mescalero were living peacefully on their reservation. Has there been an outbreak of violence?"

"No, no, no," the colonel said irritably, plucking at his muttonchops. "There are a few agitators on the reservation, but so far old Naka'yen and his son have kept their people in line."

"Then why are we moving against them? Sir," he added quickly.

"It's not the reservation Mescalero we're concerned with, Major. For a number of years now we've been receiving citizen complaints about a large group of Apaches who have been working on a ranch south of Albuquerque. General Whitlock has *finally* decided that it would be prudent to incarcerate them with their fellow Mescaleros on the reservation."

His smug expression and the way he emphasized "finally" led Meade to conclude that Collingswood had been lobbying for this action for some time. It didn't make much sense to Meade. "Have they made any trouble, sir?"

"They're Apaches, Major. That alone makes them trouble," the colonel replied, giving him a withering look that might have sent a lesser man scurrying for the door. "Of course, your perspective may be a little different, Ashford. Your sister is married to one of them, isn't she?"

"That's right, sir," Meade said pleasantly, though inside he was seething. "And I'm happy to say that my brother-in-law is one of the finest men I've ever known."

Collingswood clearly wasn't impressed. "How fortunate for you. Have you any other questions?"

"No, sir."

"Good. You will accompany Captain Greenleigh and subdue the Mescaleros. Offer any medical assistance to the hostiles that may be necessary, but in the event that they resist, I trust you will remember that tending to our own wounded men comes first?"

The sarcastic question went through Meade like a hot poker. "Having served for eight years in the Apache war theater, Colonel, I can assure you that I know my duty."

"Good. Dismissed."

Meade offered a brisk salute and departed quickly, reminding himself that in three months he'd never have to smile at another pompous ass for as long as he lived.

After hours of standing in the miserable July sun, the shade offered by the cottonwood looked like heaven to the Templetons. Rayna had been eyeing it covetously through most of the last maiden ceremony ritual, and as soon as Mary Long Horn disappeared into her lodge to rest, Rayna tried to usher her mother and father toward the tree. Raymond hung back, engaging in conversation with Consayka and several other Mescalero ranch hands, but Collie and Rayna headed directly for the shade.

They were only midway through the third day of the ceremony, and though Rayna had done very little but watch, she was exhausted. For Skylar's sake she had been on hand for every ritual from sunup to sundown, and tomorrow she would do her best to stay awake during the final event, a dance that would last all night long. She had attended other maiden ceremonies, but only in bits and pieces because Skylar had not been a major participant in those events. Since this was such a special occasion for her sister, Rayna felt it was important to support her.

At least once a day Collie also came out to watch the ceremony. For the past two nights she and Rayna had given Raymond an account of the rituals his daughter was participating in, and he had decided this morning that he would attend, too. Had it not been for the intense heat, they all would have been enjoying themselves tremendously, but Rayna could tell that her parents were getting tired. She couldn't imagine how Skylar was going to survive the ordeal; yet from all outward appearances, she was thoroughly enjoying herself.

"How much longer today, dear?" Collie asked as they settled onto a blanket under the cottonwood.

Rayna spread her skirt out around her, leaving her ankles exposed, then unpinned her wide-brimmed straw bonnet and used it to fan herself. Neither effort cooled her off even a little. "If I remember Sky's description correctly, there's only one more song this afternoon. Then there will be feasting until sunset."

Collie's smile was strained as she closed her parasol and laid it aside. "Do you think Skylar would be very upset if Raymond and I skipped the feast?" She glanced at her husband, and her smile faded altogether. "I don't like your father's coloring, Rayna. He would never admit it, but he hasn't been feeling well lately. I think I should get him out of this sun."

Though Rayna had always viewed her robust father as invulnerable, she had to agree with Collie. He hadn't been looking well for quite some time, and she was beginning to worry. "Mother, if you and Papa want to leave now, I'm sure Skylar would understand. Having you here has meant a lot to her, but she wouldn't want either of you to suffer."

"Then I think we'll ride on back to the house. I'll have one of the hands bring the buggy back for you."

"Oh, don't bother with that. I can walk."

Collie patted Rayna's arm in her most motherly fashion. "Not in this heat, dear."

Rayna was too hot to argue. She glanced around, looking for her father, and was surprised to see Skylar coming toward them. Though this was the third day Rayna had seen her sister in her ceremonial dress, she was struck again by how beautiful Skylar looked in her costume. As Mary Long Horn's attendant, she wore a buckskin dress very similar to the celebrant's. The waist-length cape and calf-length skirt had been tanned and bleached in the sun until they were nearly snow white. Layers of fringe adorned with tin cones and beads hung from the waist of the cape and down the sleeves, and the fringe of the skirt dangled to the tops of her beaded moccasins.

As she walked, the fringe swayed gently, creating swirls of motion around her. Her unbound hair hung to her waist, adorned only by a single feather that had been braided into her hair so that it fell onto her right shoulder. What had surprised Rayna most about her appearance was that she had also donned the necklace she had made years ago. The bone, silver beads, and turquoise choker fit her throat snugly, and the crudely carved Thunder Eagle medallion that hung down between her breasts swayed lightly as she walked.

Whatever its significance to her, whether real or imagined, it was a lovely adornment. In this native costume, Skylar was stunningly beautiful. She was also thoroughly Apache.

The strained smile on Collie's face told Rayna that her mother was thinking the same thoughts. "Is something

wrong?" Rayna asked as Skylar knelt on the blanket in front
of them. "I didn't think you were supposed to leave Mary's
side."

"White Painted Woman is resting," Skylar said, careful to
follow the proscription that during the ceremony Mary be referred to only as the Apache deity she represented for these
four days. Skylar looked at her mother. "I am concerned
about you and Father. I know that you came to show your
support of me, and that means more than you can ever know.
You mustn't feel obligated to stay, though. It's much too hot
to stand in the sun all afternoon."

Collie reached out and brushed a lock of hair over her
daughter's shoulder. "It's hot for you, too, dear."

A radiant smile lit Skylar's face. "I've hardly noticed the
heat, Mother. Attending White Painted Woman has kept me
too busy. And besides"—she gestured toward a tall ceremonial lodge that was open at the bottom but covered with
brush and yucca leaves at the top—"I spend most of my time
in the shade. You and Father are suffering far more than I."

"What about me?" Rayna asked, affecting a teasing pout.
"Don't I get any credit for suffering, too?"

Skylar laughed and took her sister's hand. "Not a bit. If
you weren't here, you'd be out scouting the herd, and you
wouldn't feel the heat, either." Her look of gratitude was
enough to tell Rayna that Skylar understood why she was
here and that she appreciated the sacrifice.

"Actually, dear, I was thinking of taking your father home
after the next ritual," Collie said.

"Good. He doesn't look well." Skylar glanced around. "If
you can drag him away from Consayka, you should take him
home immediately."

"Thank you, dear. I believe I will."

"I should be getting back now," Skylar said. As she rose,
she glanced in the direction of the house, barely visible in the
distance, and she frowned. "What is that, I wonder?"

Collie twisted around and Rayna stood. A cloud of dust
was rising out of one of the shallow flats between the Mesca-

lero encampment and the hacienda. A murmur of voices nearer to the ceremonial grounds suggested that the Templetons were not the only ones to notice the phenomenon.

"Looks like company's coming," Raymond said as he joined his family under the cottonwood. A moment later that prediction was borne out as two flags appeared on the rise, announcing the arrival of a long column of cavalry troops.

"What the devil are they doing here?" Rayna muttered.

Collie chided Rayna for her language, and Skylar glanced nervously behind her at the cluster of Mescaleros who were gathering near the ceremonial lodge. "I must get back to White Painted Woman." She placed one hand on her father's arm, drawing his attention down to her. "You won't let them disrupt the ceremony, will you, Papa?"

Raymond wrapped one arm around his daughter and gave her an encouraging hug. "Of course not, princess. Don't you worry about a thing. They probably just want to ask permission to make camp nearby."

Wanting to believe it was that simple, Skylar hurried off, the cones on her dress tinkling lightly as she walked.

As the cavalry drew closer, Rayna spotted Gil Rodriguez riding alongside the officers at the head of the queue. That made sense, since Gil would have been on hand to greet them when they arrived at the hacienda. He had undoubtedly offered to take them to Raymond, but if they only wanted permission to camp on Rancho Verde land, why hadn't the officer in charge come out here alone? Why bring his hot, dusty troops along?

Whether their slow pace was a concession to the heat or a sign of the lack of urgency, Rayna couldn't have guessed, but it seemed to take them forever to arrive. As they drew close, Raymond finally stepped out of the shade to greet them, and though Collie hung back a few paces, Rayna was right at her father's side.

At the head of the column, Meade Ashford studied the scene before him with dread. He had disliked this detail from the moment he had been assigned to it three days ago, and what he saw now made him detest it all the more. A man was coming toward them with an attractive young woman at his side and another lady slightly behind. All three were tall and fair-haired with complexions more suited to Nordic winters than to desert summers. They looked like a pleasant family out for an afternoon picnic.

The fact that they had permitted a group of Apaches to live and work on their land indicated that they had some attachment to the Mescalero the cavalry was about to incarcerate. This wasn't going to be a pleasant confrontation for anyone, with the possible exception of Robert Greenleigh. In Meade's opinion, the captain was displaying far too much relish for the task at hand. His intolerance of all Apaches, friend or foe, was well known, and Meade was certain he couldn't be counted on to bend an inch.

The ranch foreman, Rodriguez, had said the Mescalero were engaged in some sort of ritual, and from the looks of things, Meade guessed that it was a maiden ceremony. Over the years, Libby had coerced him into attending a number of Apache rites, and the maiden ceremony had been his first. It wasn't one of his fondest memories, but neither was it something he was likely to forget.

Looking beyond the man and two women near the cottonwood, Meade studied the cluster of Mescaleros near the ceremonial grounds. A maiden ceremony indicated the presence of a teenaged girl, but Meade was struck immediately by the noticeable absence of young children. Usually they were everywhere at events like this. The Indians he saw were mostly old men and women, and a few middle-aged couples.

These were the Apache he'd been sent to subdue? It was absurd. These people weren't about to make trouble for anyone.

Captain Greenleigh, whose pomaded muttonchops and bushy mustache had long since wilted in the heat, gave a signal to the sergeant behind him, and the troops came to a halt a short distance from their welcoming party. "Mr. Raymond Templeton?"

"That's right, Captain," Raymond said cautiously.

"Mr. Templeton, I am Captain Robert Greenleigh, and this is Major Meade Ashford of the One Hundred-fortieth Regiment of the United States Cavalry."

"Gentlemen," Raymond said with a nod. "My wife, Colleen, and my daughter, Rayna."

Both officers touched their hats in acknowledgment of the ladies, then dismounted. As they came off their horses, Rayna noticed the gold oak leaves on the shoulder of the second officer and wondered why a major would allow a subordinate to do the talking. They handed their reins to a waiting sergeant and stepped forward.

Meade removed his hat. "It's a pleasure to meet you, sir, ladies. We apologize for the interruption." He gestured toward the brush-covered lodge. "This is a maiden ceremony in progress, isn't it?"

"Yes, it is," Rayna replied, surprised by his knowledge. "How did you know?"

"I recognized the maiden lodge and some of the other accoutrements," Meade replied, looking at her closely for the first time. She wasn't quite as young as he'd first thought, but she was even more attractive. She was, in fact, quite beautiful. Her simple skirt and shirtwaist highlighted a trim but well-curved figure, and delectable wisps of her upswept blond hair clung damply to her face, framing her lightly tanned skin and arresting blue eyes.

"You've seen this Mescalero ceremony before?" she asked.

"No," Meade replied. "My knowledge of Apache rituals comes chiefly from the White Mountain tribes. The similarity is inescapable, though."

Since the moment she had seen them approaching, Rayna had been gripped by a feeling of impending disaster, but this courteous, knowledgeable officer gave her hope that nothing was amiss. He was considerably older than the captain, but he appeared far more approachable than the arrogant, wooden-faced officer at his side, who seemed irritated and impatient with the exchange of pleasantries.

Major Ashford was also much more handsome than the captain, Rayna noted in a purely analytical manner. His face, lacking a fashionable mustache or beard, had a rugged quality to it that appealed to her—as did his eyes. There was an innate kindness in them.

The tiny caduceus on the choke collar of his tunic indicated that he was a physician and, as such, was only an addendum to the military detail rather than an important part of the command structure. That explained why the captain appeared to be in charge.

"Our friends are preparing for the next ritual," she informed the major. "It is Cane Set Out, I believe. You're more than welcome to watch, gentlemen."

"Thank you for the invitation, Miss Templeton, but that won't be possible," Greenleigh said tersely, darting an irritated glance at Meade.

"Then what can we do for you, Major Ashford?" Raymond asked.

"We're here about these Mescaleros," Greenleigh said, drawing the attention back to himself. Clearly he didn't want anyone attaching importance to the presence of a superior officer.

"What about them?" Raymond asked.

Greenleigh dug into his tunic and produced a packet of papers. "By the order of General Samuel Whitlock, commander of the Department of New Mexico, I have been instructed to round up these Apaches and transport them directly to the Mescalero reservation."

Rayna's feeling of dread blossomed into fear. Skylar would be devastated if they took her friends away. "You can't be serious," she said as her father reached for the official documents. "These Indians have been living peacefully on Rancho Verde for three-quarters of a century."

"That oversight is about to be corrected, Miss Tem-

pleton," Greenleigh said haughtily, as though he didn't wish
to be bothered speaking with a woman.

"Over my dead body," Rayna replied hotly, incensed by
his condescending attitude.

"Rayna, please. I'll handle this," Raymond said softly. He
glanced through the papers, then handed them back to the
captain. "These seem to be in order, but frankly I don't understand why such a drastic action is being undertaken, Captain Greenleigh. The Mescaleros you see here are no threat
to anyone. They never have been."

"That is a matter of opinion, sir. Your neighbors see things
quite differently. Having these Apaches free to roam the
country is a source of concern to all of the settlers in these
parts, and they have a right to expect the army to deal with
the problem."

"But there is no problem!"

"General Whitlock feels differently. What with Geronimo
on the warpath—"

Rayna could be silent no longer. "Geronimo is in Mexico,
and even if he were camped on the outskirts of Albuquerque,
it wouldn't have anything to do with these Indians."

"There is concern that they may be abetting the renegade."

"Or, for God's sake, Captain, how could they possibly be
giving aid to a man who is several hundred miles away?"

Greenleigh sighed heavily. "Miss Templeton, I have no
desire to debate this issue with you. We are here to subdue
the Mescalero and take them to the reservation."

"Subdue!"

"Rayna, that's enough," Raymond said sternly.

If the situation hadn't been so dismally serious, Meade
might have laughed. Miss Templeton was not at all the demure young lady she had appeared to be at first glance, and
she seemed more than adequate to the task of bringing
Greenleigh down a peg or two. Despite her father's warning,
she showed no sign of calming herself.

"No, Papa, it is not enough," she argued, though her angry

glare never left Greenleigh. "Captain, these people do not need to be *subdued*. They are house servants and ranch hands! Most of them have never even lived among their own people. You can't uproot them from the only home they've ever known!"

"I can, and I intend to, Miss Templeton." He looked at Raymond. "I see no reason for further discussion of this, sir. We will give the Mescaleros one hour to collect whatever belongings they might need, and then we will move out."

"Now, just a—"

Greenleigh overrode Raymond's protest. "Do you have someone who can act as an interpreter to explain to them, or would you prefer our interpreter break the news to them?"

"They speak English," Rayna said viciously, spitting out every word. "And most of them probably *read* the language better than you do, you ignorant clod!"

This time the captain didn't look at her. "Mr. Templeton, will you control your daughter, please?"

Meade had finally had about all he could stand. "That's enough, Captain. We're not here to bully these civilians—or the Mescalero, for that matter."

"Then do something to stop this," Rayna snapped.

Greenleigh clenched his hands into fists. "Major Ashford is—"

"Major Ashford is perfectly capable of speaking for himself, Captain," Meade said briskly. He took a step toward the Templetons, but his gaze was on Rayna. "I am sorry to say, miss, that while I disagree with this action, there is nothing I can do to stop it. General Whitlock's orders are very specific, and irrevocable. I'm sorry."

Raymond knew a reasonable man when he saw one, and he was grateful. "Major, is there anything in those orders that would make it possible for you to delay this action long enough for me to get to Santa Fe and talk to Whitlock? I've met the general a number of times, and I feel certain that if I could speak with him personally we could clear this matter up."

Meade hesitated. If it had been up to him, he would gladly have given Templeton the time he needed, but it wasn't. Greenleigh jumped in at once to make that clear. "Major Ashford is not in charge of this detail, Mr. Templeton. He is a surgeon, here only to render whatever medical assistance might be necessary."

"Expecting a lot of casualties, are you?" Rayna asked Meade sarcastically, cutting him dead with a killing glance.

"Rayna, be still," Raymond ordered. "In case you hadn't noticed, Major Ashford is on our side."

"Yes, but he isn't doing anything constructive, is he?" she asked, too angered by the injustice of it all to distinguish between friend and foe. "You can spout all the pleasantries you want to, Major, but unless you can take action to stop this, you're just as bad as he is," she said with a jerk of her head toward Greenleigh.

Meade stiffened. Being lumped into the same category with officers like Greenleigh didn't sit too well. Still, he couldn't blame the lady for her opinion. "I'm sure that's how it must appear to you, Miss Templeton." He looked at his companion. "I'd like a word with you, Captain. Will you excuse us?" he asked the Templetons, then turned on his heel and walked toward the horses.

Though it obviously galled Greenleigh, he didn't have any choice but to obey this particular request of his superior officer. "Yes, Major?"

"I want you to consider granting Mr. Templeton's request," Meade said. "Give him time to speak with Whitlock."

"My orders are specific, Major, and I have no intention of disobeying them."

"Damn it, Robert, I'm asking for latitude, not disobedience. For the love of God, look at those people," he said, pointing toward the Mescalero. "Those old men and women are no more of a threat to this territory than I am."

"They're Apaches," Greenleigh argued. "Are you forgetting that Chief Nana was nearly ninety years old when he went on the warpath last year? He and his braves butchered dozens of innocent citizens, and I don't blame General Whitlock one bit for incarcerating these Mescalero, regardless of their age. I wouldn't want their depredations on my head, either."

"Be sensible, Robert."

"I am, *sir*," he said, using the most sarcastic tone he dared. "It is you who are out of line here. If I may *respectfully* remind you, this is my detail, and you have no right to interfere. I will not hold my men over while Templeton puts his suit to the general. I consider that the end of this discussion."

With a brisk salute, he turned away and rejoined the Templetons. Feeling as thoroughly ineffectual as Miss Templeton had accused him of being, Meade followed.

"I'm sorry, sir," Greenleigh said to Raymond, "but my orders do not allow for the type of latitude you requested. These Indians have one hour to collect their belongings and be ready to move out, or we will take them forcibly. Now, sir, do you want to tell them, or shall I?"

"I will," Raymond said after a moment.

"Papa!" Rayna whirled toward him and discovered that her father had aged a dozen years in a single, telling second. The sight of him nearly broke her heart.

"I'm sorry, honey," he said quietly, placing his hands on her shoulders. "Short of fighting the U.S. Cavalry, there's not a damned thing we can do for now. I'll be on the next train to Santa Fe, and we'll get the Mescalero back, but in the meantime, Consayka's people are going to have to go."

"You know what this is going to do to Skylar, don't you?" she asked, gentling her voice. "Consayka's people are like family to her. Almost as much as we are."

"I know that, honey. I just don't see any other way." His face paled as he glanced over her shoulder. "I'd better tell Consayka, although I suspect he's already figured it out by now."

"I'll go with you, dear," Collie said, stepping closer to his side, her face deeply etched with concern.

"Your father has made a wise decision," Greenleigh told Rayna arrogantly.

"Oh, shut up," she snapped. "You don't know anything about my father or me or these people you're treating like a herd of cattle."

"That is quite true, and quite regrettable," Meade said. "For whatever it's worth, Miss Templeton, I can assure you that your friends will be well cared for on the journey. I'll see to that personally."

Rayna wasn't comforted. "Oh, really? Did you bring army ambulances to transport them in?" she asked, looking down the rank and file to the two wagons that brought up the rear. One was a chuck wagon, and the other appeared to be loaded to the brim with supplies.

"Of course not," Greenleigh replied. "They will walk."

"You would make those old men and women walk a hundred miles in this heat?" she asked, aghast. "That's inhuman."

"They're Apaches," the captain said negligently, as though that explained everything.

Rayna stepped closer to him, and Meade realized that she was really quite tall for a woman. She was nearly able to meet Greenleigh eye to eye. "You, sir, are a bastard," she said, shocking both officers. She turned on her heel and called to the foreman. "Gil, get back to the house. Hitch up both of our supply wagons and see if you can rig some sort of canvas covering for one of them. And have Consuelo throw together some food supplies—as much as she can manage in what little time we have."

Meade wasn't surprised that the foreman didn't question the order or the young lady's authority to issue it. She was obviously a strong-willed hellion who was accustomed to getting her own way. Though Meade sympathized with her predicament, his initial attitude toward her had changed somewhat during her heated exchange with Greenleigh. At first she had reminded him of his sister, whose outspokenness was something Meade had learned to live with—and occasionally enjoy. But unlike Libby, who was a lady through and through, Miss Templeton was a little *too* outspoken for Meade's taste.

Still, he felt obligated to give her what little reassurance he could. When she stalked away, heading toward the ceremonial grounds, he hurried to catch up with her. "Miss Templeton?"

She stopped and turned, her expression impatient. "What?"

"Your loan of transportation is very generous."

"Well, it's kind of you to say so, Major, but I'm not lending *you* the wagons," she responded scornfully. "They're for Consayka and his people."

Meade was getting a little fed up with her hostility. "I understand that, miss. I just wanted to assure you that I will take personal responsibility for seeing that the wagons and teams are returned."

"That's very reassuring, Major . . . Ashford, isn't it? Forgive me if I don't go down on my knees in thanks."

He stiffened. "No thanks are necessary," he said tightly. "I'm just doing my duty."

Rayna gave him a thoroughly insincere smile. "And you're doing it admirably, too." The smile disappeared. "Now, if you'll excuse me, I have to speak with my sister. This is going to devastate her."

"I'm sorry."

"I'll be sure to tell her that."

She whirled away, and Meade cleared his throat, fighting down a surge of anger. In the space of thirty minutes, Miss Rayna Templeton had gone from attractive to outspoken to offensive to downright infuriating.

He turned and came face to face with Greenleigh, whose smug expression suggested that he'd heard the exchange. "So much for trying to do a good deed, eh, Major? These

Indian-lovers are all alike. If they think so highly of the
Apache, they ought to go live on the reserve, too."

Meade took a step closer to the captain, but unlike Rayna,
he was able to look down at the obnoxious ass. "The lady is
right, Robert. You really are a bastard."

Chapter Four

BY THE TIME Rayna arrived at the maiden lodge that had been constructed for White Painted Woman, Skylar was standing just outside, waiting for her. The other Mescalero were still deep in discussion with Raymond.

"Rayna, what's happening?" Skylar asked, her voice tinged with desperation. "I saw you and Papa arguing with the officers."

"I'm so sorry, Sky." Rayna took her sister's hands. "We couldn't stop them."

Skylar's jaw stiffened with the twin emotions of grief and fear. "The soldiers have come to take Consayka's people, haven't they?"

Rayna nodded. "Yes. Apparently Ben Martinez and our other good neighbors succeeded in convincing the military that the Rancho Verde Mescaleros are a threat to everyone's safety," she said with disgust. "Papa is going up to Santa Fe to see what he can do about getting them back, but for now we have no choice but to let them be taken to the reservation." She went on to explain her orders that would supply the Rancho Verde Mescaleros with wagons and food.

"This is so unfair," Skylar said. "These people have done nothing wrong. They're decent and hardworking."

"And they're your friends," Rayna added softly.

Skylar nodded mutely, trying to fight back the tears burning her eyes. "There's nothing I can do to stop this, is there?" she asked after a moment.

"No."

"Perhaps if I went with Papa to Santa Fe?" she suggested hopefully.

Rayna smiled. Skylar was gentle and tenderhearted, but there was nothing weak about her. In her own quiet way she was every bit as much of a fighter as Rayna. "That's an excellent idea. In fact, I'll go, too. Faced with all three of us, General Whitlock won't stand a chance."

Skylar actually managed a smile, but it faded quickly. "I'd better tell Mary what's happening, and help her and the others prepare for the trip."

"You'd better hurry," Rayna advised. "We don't have much time."

"Why don't you go to Gatana and see what you can do to help her. I'll take care of Mary."

The girls separated, and as Rayna skirted the ceremonial grounds she noticed that Consayka was now talking to Greenleigh, but even from a distance she could tell he was having no luck changing the officer's narrow mind. The women were hurrying toward their lodges, but some of the ranch hands were still clustered together, deep in conversation.

Were they thinking of trying to escape? she wondered. The younger ones could disperse and disappear before the cavalry knew what was happening, but would they leave the old ones? Rayna doubted it. They had too much honor to desert their elders, leaving them to the privation of the difficult journey and life on the reservation. It would be up to them to provide for and protect the old ones, and Rayna couldn't believe they would shirk their duty.

And besides, Raymond had undoubtedly promised them that he would do everything he could to effect their release. They had good reason to trust him, but the grim looks on their faces told Rayna they had little hope that he would succeed.

An eerie silence had settled over the encampment, and as Rayna tried to help the Mescalero women prepare for the journey, she saw a kind of sad bewilderment and resignation in the old faces and deeply burning anger in the younger ones. Only Tsa'kata seemed unsurprised by the tragic turn of events. Her ancient eyes held a spark of fire that betrayed her dislike of all whites, even the ones she had lived among most of her life.

As the shock began to wear off and the deadline grew nearer, the unearthly quiet of the camp turned into utter confusion. The Mescalero began bringing their belongings to an area Captain Greenleigh had designated. Gil returned with the wagons, one shaded by a canvas canopy, the other heavily laden with supplies.

The captain had deployed his men so that they formed a semicircular perimeter around part of the camp, and several soldiers had gathered near the wagons to "assist" the Apaches. All of the ranch hands had their own horses, and there had been a brief disagreement over whether they would be allowed to take the animals with them. At Meade's insistence, Greenleigh had finally relented on this one point, and the men had gone off under heavy cavalry escort to collect their animals from the corral behind the encampment.

The tepees were stripped of their outer coverings, and by the time the deadline expired, the Mescalero camp looked like a barren valley littered with the bleached bones of some prehistoric animal. The soldiers grew impatient with their slow-moving captives and began throwing their bundles unceremoniously into the supply wagon. When the braves finally returned, mounted on their horses, the soldiers herded the women toward the canopied wagon.

Rayna was too angry to even consider crying as she helped Gatana climb into the wagon, but next to her, Skylar was valiantly fighting the crippling weight of her emotions. Mary Long Horn was weeping openly as the two Apache women embraced, and the tears were nearly Skylar's undoing.

"Everything will be fine, Mary," Skylar promised, stroking the young girl's hair. "You'll be back here soon."

"I do not think so," Mary replied, raising her head from Skylar's shoulder. "I will never see you or my home again."

"You mustn't say that," Skylar told her sternly. "You must be strong." Lapsing easily into Apache, Skylar told the girl it was her responsibility to help care for the old ones.

Though Rayna understood little of what her sister said, she was amazed at the transformation in Mary as pride overcame her fear.

"Come on, squaws, get in," one of the troopers said gruffly, giving Mary a shove that nearly sent both her and Skylar stumbling into the wagon gate.

Outraged, Rayna shouldered her way between her sister and the soldier, forcing him back a step. "Stop that! There's no reason for brutality. She's just a frightened young girl!"

"Sorry, miss, but I got orders to get these squaws loaded so's we can pull out, and that's just what I'm gonna do."

"Then do it without pushing anyone around," Rayna snapped.

"It's all right, Miss Rayna," Mary said quickly. "I'm ready to go."

With Skylar's help she scrambled into the wagon and Rayna stepped back, looking around. Mary was the last. The braves were mounted, and all the women were in the wagon. Raymond and Collie were some distance away conversing with Captain Greenleigh and Major Ashford, and from their gestures, Rayna guessed that her father was making one final attempt to change Greenleigh's mind. He didn't appear to be having any success. Nothing was going to stop this travesty.

"Rayna, I have to speak with Consayka," Skylar said, moving toward her sister.

But the trooper's patience was gone. "Oh, no, you don't, squaw," he said, grabbing her arm as she moved past him. "There's been enough lollygagging. Into the wagon, now!"

"What?" Skylar gasped, straining against his rough grasp as Rayna whirled toward them.

"You heard me, squaw. Get in the wagon."

Incensed, Rayna flew toward the trooper and gave him a

stout shove that sent him stumbling back a pace just as Skylar wrenched her arm away. Her ceremonial dress tore at the shoulder, and the trooper was left with a handful of beaded fringe.

"You keep your filthy hands off her, soldier!" Rayna said hotly, stepping between them.

Disgusted, the trooper hurled the buckskin fringe away and made another grab for Skylar. "I got my orders, miss."

"Your orders don't include my sister!" She brought her fist down hard on his hand and rammed her elbow into his ample midsection. He buckled over with a soft "whoof," and Rayna whirled toward her sister. "Get out of here, Sky. Go to Papa quickly!"

"But—"

"Go!" Rayna gave her a push, but by that time other troopers had seen the tussle and stepped in, blocking her path. One of them grabbed Skylar and propelled her back toward the wagon.

"What the devil's going on here, Gless?" Corporal Lawton demanded of the trooper who was rubbing his stomach and glowering at Rayna.

"That squaw won't go into the wagon, and that one punched me," Gless replied.

"He was manhandling my sister," Rayna said, moving toward the corporal who was holding Skylar. "Now, let her go!"

"Sister?" Lawton looked around in confusion. "What sister?"

"This one, you oaf!"

Though her eyes were wide with fear, Skylar tried to keep her voice even. "Rayna, please, calm down. Considering the way I'm dressed, I'm sure this must be very confusing to these gentlemen, but if we explain—"

"You ain't explainin' nothin', squaw," Gless said. "You're goin' in that wagon with them other heathens." After shoving Rayna out of the way, the trooper snatched

Skylar away from the corporal and propelled her roughly toward the wagon.

Acting on outrage and instinct, Rayna lunged toward Gless, her hand moving unerringly toward the revolver holstered at his waist. Before anyone could react, she had the Colt pressed firmly into the nape of his neck. "You let her go, you bastard, or you're dead," she said softly.

The dangerous quality of her voice might not have been enough to stop Gless, but the sound of the hammer being cocked and the feel of the warm steel on his neck was more than sufficient to freeze him where he stood.

Around her, Rayna heard the sound of other guns being drawn and cocked, and these, she knew, were leveled at her. She didn't move an inch. Someone shouted for Captain Greenleigh, but that made no difference to Rayna. Her only objective was freeing her sister. "Let her go, trooper."

"Rayna, stop this!" Skylar cried, wincing against the pain of Gless's brutal grip. "They'll kill you!"

Lawton stepped forward. "Miss Templeton, please put that revolver away before someone gets hurt."

"Corporal, the only one who's going to get hurt is this trooper if he doesn't let my sister go this instant," Rayna replied without taking her eyes off Gless. "Skylar is not a Mescalero, and no one is going to take her off Rancho Verde. Now, you order this man to release her, I'll uncock this Colt, and we'll consider the matter settled. Otherwise, you'll be taking Private Gless back to Fort Marcy over the saddle of his horse!"

"What the devil is going on here?" Greenleigh shouted, muscling his way through the knot of soldiers at the back of the wagon. The crowd parted, and the captain, Meade, and the Templetons moved into the circle. "Miss Templeton! Put that revolver down at once!"

"For God's sake, Rayna, have you gone mad?" Raymond asked, moving to her side. "Give me that Colt."

Rayna felt a surge of relief now that her father had arrived, but she wasn't about to back down until she had a few assurances. "Papa, this idiot is trying to take Skylar away with the others."

"What?" Raymond said with a gasp, and Rayna heard her mother mutter a fearful "Oh, dear God."

"Corporal Lawton, explain this situation at once," Greenleigh ordered.

"Yes, sir. Private Gless was attempting to place this squaw into the wagon when Miss Templeton attacked him. She claims the squaw is her sister, sir."

Raymond rounded on Greenleigh. "She's my daughter, Captain, and I want her released at once. Those papers in your pocket give you no right to kidnap an innocent American citizen."

"Citizen?" Greenleigh's arrogant brows went up in surprise as he looked Skylar over, taking in everything from her raven-black hair to her beaded moccasins. "I don't know what you're trying to pull, Templeton, but this squaw is obviously an Apache, and as such, these papers give me the right to take her into custody. Now, take that gun away from your daughter, and let us be on our way."

"No!" Rayna shouted. "Papa, do something!"

"Private Gless! Release Miss Templeton at once," Meade demanded, moving around Rayna and Raymond.

Beads of sweat that had nothing to do with the heat were streaming down Gless's face. "Beggin' your pardon, Major, but I ain't got Miss Templeton. The little she-witch has got *me*."

"I meant *this* Miss Templeton." Though his voice was angry, Meade's hand was gentle as he touched Skylar's arm. When Gless released her, Meade ushered her away a few paces and looked down into one of the most beautiful faces he had ever seen. Wide dark eyes like those of a startled doe looked up at him with gratitude.

"Thank you, Major."

"Are you all right, Miss Templeton?"

"I will be once this matter is settled."

Meade nodded and turned to Rayna. Her expression was

grimly determined, and she showed not the slightest sign of being afraid of the weapon in her hand. Clearly she knew how to use the revolver and wouldn't hesitate to do so. Her hair had come unpinned in the struggle and was now a mane of molten gold flowing around her shoulders.

Despite his dislike of her, Meade couldn't help but admire the way she'd defended her sister, even if pulling the trooper's gun had been a damn fool thing to do. "Your sister has been released, Miss Templeton," he said calmly, careful not to make any sudden move toward her. "You may return Private Gless's gun to him now."

Rayna cocked her head toward Greenleigh. "Not until I have *his* assurance that Skylar won't be taken away."

Meade looked at the officer in charge. "Captain? I believe Private Gless would be grateful if you would apologize for the misunderstanding."

"There has been no misunderstanding, Major," Greenleigh said haughtily, glancing toward a soldier who had quietly sneaked up behind Rayna. Meade turned just in time to see the man lunge for the young woman, sweeping her gun hand into the air. The jolt caused the revolver to discharge harmlessly in the air, and before Rayna could recover from the shock, the soldier had wrenched the gun from her hand and pinned her arms to her sides.

"Let her go!" Raymond demanded, grabbing at the trooper who held Rayna, but another soldier restrained him while a third seized Skylar.

"Captain, please!" Collie shrieked, horrified by what was happening. "Stop this at once!" She tried to move to her husband, but Greenleigh waved his hand and a fourth trooper stepped forward to restrain her.

"Put that squaw into the wagon!" the captain ordered.

"Greenleigh, you can't do this!" Raymond shouted, straining against his captor. "You have no right! I have papers! She's my adopted daughter! Listen to—ah, ah—" Suddenly unable to breathe, Raymond clutched at a fiery pain in his chest and collapsed, nearly taking the soldier down, too.

"Papa!" Clawing at her captor, Rayna finally wrenched away and flew to her father's side. "Someone help him!" she screamed as she knelt, but Meade was already there.

"Corporal Lawton, get my medical bag!" The buttons on Raymond's shirt gave way as Meade ripped the garment open and began a hasty examination. "Is there a sharp pain in your chest, Mr. Templeton?"

Too racked with pain to speak, Raymond nodded.

"And down your arm?"

Raymond nodded again.

Meade looked over at Greenleigh. "Clear these men out of here, Captain. And have that man release Mrs. Templeton."

"You have no authority here, Major," Greenleigh argued.

"This is a medical emergency, and that gives me absolute authority. Now, do as I say! Get me a wagon so that I can take Mr. Templeton to the house. That's an order!"

Reluctantly Greenleigh detailed one of his men to fetch the Templetons' buckboard, which was tethered under one of the cottonwoods near the camp. As soon as Collie was released, she hurried to Raymond and knelt beside Rayna opposite the doctor.

"What's wrong with him, Major?" she asked, her voice surprisingly strong despite her fear.

"I believe he's having a heart seizure, ma'am," he answered just as the corporal returned with his medical kit.

"Will he be all right?" Rayna asked.

"I'll do everything I can for him" was all Meade could say. Stethoscope in hand, he continued with his examination. Collie opened her parasol to provide some shade for her husband until the buckboard arrived. Several soldiers were enlisted to carry Raymond to the buggy, and Collie never left his side.

Sickened with fear and still trembling from her scuffle with the soldiers, Rayna hung back, knowing there wouldn't be room for her in the buckboard. Stricken, she watched as the major climbed aboard and took the reins. Seconds later the carriage pulled away.

Knowing it would be futile to ask for the loan of a horse to
carry her to the house, she looked around for Skylar so that
they could go back to the house together. What she discovered made her blood boil anew. Greenleigh had used the moments of chaos after Raymond's collapse to have his men
shove Skylar into the wagon with the Mescaleros. The
wagon had been pulled some distance away, and a dozen soldiers now formed a close guard around it. With a hoarse cry
of anger and frustration, Rayna flew toward her sister, but
the soldiers blocked her way.

Tears were streaming down Skylar's face as her sister
struggled uselessly to get past the armed guards. "Rayna! Is
Papa dead?" she cried.

"No! No, he's not dead. He's not going to die!" She
shoved at one of the guards, but he used his rifle like a staff
to keep her at bay.

"That's quite enough, Miss Templeton," Greenleigh said
as he stalked toward her leading his horse. "You've created
enough trouble for one day."

Rayna whirled on him. "You bastard. This is all your
fault. Let my sister go!"

"Sister or no sister, that squaw is coming with us."

"But I told you, she's not a Mescalero. My parents got her
from Mexican slavers nearly twenty years ago. She was
raised as my sister," Rayna told him desperately.

"That doesn't change the fact that she's an Apache, and all
Apaches are to be confined to the reservation."

"But we have legal papers to prove that she was adopted."

"That's a matter you'll have to take up with General
Whitlock, miss. My orders are clear."

Rayna took a step back. Nothing she could say would
make a difference to this arrogant ass. "You really are enjoying this, aren't you, Captain?" she asked with disgust.

"Actually I am," he said with an unconscionable smile.

Rayna's hands knotted into fists. "And if my father dies
because you've kidnapped his daughter? Will you enjoy
that, too?"

Greenleigh's smile faded. "Your father's illness is regrettable, Miss Templeton, but his poor health is not the fault of the United States Army. If it's any consolation to you, I will be leaving Major Ashford here to tend to your father until another physician can be located. The major can rejoin the company as soon as it is convenient for him."

"How very generous of you," she said sarcastically. "However, you're overlooking one important detail: You're not leaving here with my sister."

"And just how do you propose to stop us? Any further resistance on the part of these Apaches or anyone on this ranch will be met with force." He fixed her with an arrogant gaze. "Now, do you want to be responsible for the resulting casualties?"

Rayna had never felt so helpless in her life, and that feeling fueled her anger even further. "I will get my sister back, Captain," she vowed. "And if one hair on her head has been harmed, you will pay for it personally, sir. Do you understand me?"

"Quite," he replied, completely uncowed.

The laughter in his eyes was almost more than Rayna could bear. At that moment she realized that she was fully capable of committing cold-blooded murder. Stiffening her jaw against the violent emotions flooding through her, she took another step back and squared her shoulders. "I'd like to speak with Skylar before you take her," she said, mustering all the dignity she could locate.

"I'm afraid that's not possible. We are pulling out."

"Please! Our father may be dying. At least let me tell her that he's being cared for."

Greenleigh gathered up his horse's reins and mounted. "Miss Templeton, that squaw's father is an Apache, and *your* father could probably benefit from having you at his side. Good day to you." He wheeled his horse around and galloped off, bellowing an order for the company to mount up.

Rayna darted back to the wagon, but there were more soldiers surrounding it now. Horses had been brought up, and

Rayna found that she couldn't penetrate the barrier of men and mounts. Her breath came in hot gasps, and tears scalded her eyes as the wagon began to inch forward.

"Skylar!" Her hoarse, agonized scream was drowned out by the creak of the wagons and the hooves of a hundred horses clattering into motion.

"Rayna! Rayna, stop them!" Skylar shrieked. "I have to see Papa! Rayna, help me!"

Inside the wagon, Tsa'kata plucked harshly at Skylar's arm, forcing her to look at the Mescaleros she called her friends. "You are an Apache, child," the old woman said sternly in her native language. "An Apache does not look back. The wild one cannot help you."

Tears streamed down Skylar's face. "My father may be dying. I must go to him."

Tsa'kata shook her head. "No. We are your family now. You are one of us."

Trying to muffle the sobs that welled up in her throat, Skylar looked toward her sister, knowing how much Rayna's inability to prevent this was costing her. She had always been Skylar's protector, her buffer against hatred and prejudice. With Rayna at her side, Skylar had always known that she would be safe.

Now Rayna was gone, and Skylar was alone. A deeply buried memory came back to her, and she felt more than remembered another time when she had been taken against her will. The smoke of her burning village hung in the stifling air, and her Apache sister placed herself between the five-year-old Skylar and the grinning Apache renegade who had slaughtered the entire population of their village.

"She will make trouble. Kill her," the renegade had said. He was standing over the bodies of her parents, and a shiny necklace dangled from his hand as he pointed to Skylar's sister. "The other one will come with us." He had turned his back as his order was carried out, and Skylar had screamed and screamed as she watched the renegades club her sister to death.

Skylar closed her eyes tightly, trying to shut out the hideous memory, but it stayed with her. When she opened her eyes again and looked out of the wagon, Rayna was gone. Skylar was alone.

All of her life she had wondered what her life would have been like had the Templetons not taken her in. She was about to find out. . . .

And she was terrified.

Rayna paced the courtyard, her fists clenched almost as tight as the knot of fear and uncertainty in her stomach. Major Ashford had been with her father for an hour, and he had banished everyone but Collie from the study that had been turned into a makeshift sickroom. Rayna hadn't seen either of her parents, and she had no idea how serious her father's illness was. For all she knew, he was dying, and she was powerless to do anything to help him—just as she'd been unable to help Skylar.

"Miss Templeton?"

Rayna turned and found the major at the study door. "How is he?" she asked, hurrying toward him.

"He's resting now," Meade replied, taking in the young woman's disheveled appearance with a single glance. After what she had been through today, it wasn't surprising that her clothes were torn and her face smudged. What astonished him was that her red-rimmed eyes gave mute testimony to the fact that she had been crying. Meade found it impossible to imagine this woman weeping and vulnerable, particularly when she was glaring at him so fiercely.

"May I see him?" she asked, her voice as tightly strung as a bowstring.

Meade nodded. "He's asking for you and your sister."

Rayna looked away from him as she struggled to control her emotions. "My sister is gone. Captain Greenleigh took her with him."

"What?" Meade couldn't believe it. "Greenleigh is gone?"

"That's right," Rayna said viciously. "But I'm sure you'll be happy to know that he left your horse and a trooper in case you needed assistance in locating the regiment. Private Baker is outside."

"Damn him," Meade swore, moving away from the study door. "How could he do that? I understood there were papers proving that Skylar was adopted."

"The captain wasn't interested in legalities," Rayna snapped, then tried to calm herself. Her father's life was in this man's hands, and there might be other ways that he could help, too. Though it galled her to beg for anything from a man in uniform, she managed to soften her voice and ask, "Can you do anything to get her back?"

Meade could see what it had cost her to ask the question. He wished he could give her a better answer. "I don't know, Miss Templeton. It's unlikely that Captain Greenleigh will listen to anything I have to say, but I can send a dispatch to General Whitlock explaining the situation and asking for your sister's immediate release."

"And that's all?" Rayna asked scornfully.

Meade's face hardened against his anger at his own impotence. "For the time being, yes," he said tightly.

"And what are we supposed to do in the meantime, Major? What do I tell my father when he asks why Skylar isn't at his bedside?"

Meade hadn't considered that, and it worried him. He wasn't sure that Raymond Templeton's heart could stand the strain of knowing his adopted daughter had been kidnapped. "It would be in your father's best interests to forestall giving him the news as long as possible."

Rayna felt her heart turn over painfully. "You mean the shock could kill him?"

"Yes."

She barely found the breath to ask her next question. "Is he going to die anyway?"

Meade found it difficult to look at her. "It is possible that he won't survive the night, Miss Templeton," he said as gently as he could. "However, if he can make it through the next few days, he might very well live to a ripe old age if he avoids strenuous physical activity."

Tears stung Rayna's eyes, and she turned away quickly before the major could see them. "Then I ask you again, what should I tell Papa when he wants to see Skylar?"

He thought it over. "Perhaps I could tell him it's in his best interests to have no visitors at all for the time being."

"Then I wouldn't be able to see him, either?" she asked, her voice strangled.

"I'm sorry, but it's the only way I can think of to keep him from questioning Skylar's absence."

Rayna thought about the coming night, knowing that her father might die without having seen either of his daughters. There would be no chance for her to tell him how very much she loved him, no chance to hold his hand or to gather strength from just being in his presence. But for his sake she had no other choice.

Choking back tears, she nodded mutely, then cleared her throat and turned to Meade, her eyes dry. "Very well. Tell him that Skylar and I love him very much, and we are praying for him."

Meade's admiration for her rose another notch. "I'm very sorry, Miss Templeton. I know what that decision cost you."

His sympathy was more than Rayna could stand. "Just deliver my message, Major Ashford. Save your sympathy for someone who needs it."

So much for his growing admiration. "Yes, ma'am," he said briskly, turning toward the study.

Rayna regretted her outburst before he'd made it halfway to the door. "Major, I'm sorry," she said, hurrying after him. "I do appreciate everything you're doing for my father."

Meade touched the caduceus on his collar. "I'm a doctor, Miss Templeton, and I take my Hippocratic oath very seriously. Considering how ineffectual I've been in other areas today, this is the least I can do."

For the first time, Rayna caught a glimpse of his self-loathing and realized that he was frustrated and angry, too. It made him seem a little more human to her, and she didn't like it. If she acknowledged that this wasn't Ashford's fault, she would no longer have anyone to vent her rage on; and at the moment, having someone specific to blame was oddly consoling.

"Major, Captain Greenleigh said that you were to rejoin the regiment as soon as another doctor could be brought out to take charge of my father."

He raised his eyebrows questioningly. "And?"

Rayna hesitated. "The nearest doctor is in Albuquerque, and he has made it clear in previous emergencies that he doesn't travel outside the city."

"Don't worry, Miss Templeton. I'm in no hurry to rejoin the regiment. I had already planned to stay through the night."

Rayna nodded and gave him the closest thing to a smile that she could muster. "Thank you. I'll prepare rooms for you and Private Baker."

"A room for Baker won't be necessary," Meade replied. "As soon as I've checked on your father again, I'm going to prepare a dispatch for the private to deliver to Fort Marcy."

"Thank you, Major."

"It's my pleasure, Miss Templeton." He turned again and disappeared into his makeshift hospital.

Somewhere in the house a clock had just struck midnight, and the full moon was almost directly overhead as Meade stepped into the courtyard and stretched his arms. He was getting too old for late night vigils like this one, but there was consolation in the knowledge that his patient was sleeping comfortably.

Exhausted, Meade dropped into the nearest chair and ran one hand wearily over his face. Lanterns suspended from the balcony made pools of warm golden light that contrasted sharply with the cool silver moonlight. In this lovely shadowed setting, it would take only a little imagination to envision elegant ladies in ball gowns dancing in the arms of their gallant escorts or strolling through the arcade into the garden.

But there was no music in the hacienda tonight, and Meade was afraid that gaiety had been forever banished from the Templeton home. An eerie silence pervaded the house, and with good reason. In the course of a single day the pleasant, peaceful life Raymond Templeton had carved out for his family had been irrevocably shattered. A decent, hardworking man was lying at death's door, his wife at his side, emotionally crippled by her husband's illness and by the heartless kidnapping of her adopted daughter.

Though Raymond had been kept in the dark about Skylar's abduction, Colleen had known something was wrong the first time she stepped out of the sickroom. Meade hadn't envied Rayna having to give her mother the news. Collie was carrying on as best she could, keeping up the charade for her husband's sake, but Meade knew she was too numb to truly comprehend what had happened.

And what of the lovely Skylar? What was she going through tonight? he wondered. From what little he'd gleaned this afternoon and evening, Miss Skylar Templeton had been rescued from slavery and raised in this genteel atmosphere, sheltered from many of the cruelties the rest of her people had been subjected to over the years. Meade had no doubt that eventually the Templetons would succeed in getting her released, but that could take days or weeks. In the meantime, the young woman would be living a nightmare. Ripped from her family, not knowing whether her father was dead or alive . . . Meade couldn't help but pity her. Tomorrow when he rejoined the regiment, he would be able to report to her on her father's health. He only hoped the news he had to give her would be encouraging.

As for Skylar's sister . . . Meade wasn't quite sure what to make of Miss Rayna Templeton. She was salt and vinegar, pepper and spice. She had a temper unlike any he'd ever seen before, but she also had a wellspring of strength and courage that kept her disposition from being childish or petulant. During the course of the evening he'd found out what a competent woman she was.

With her mother totally occupied with Raymond, Rayna had taken charge of the household—indeed, the entire ranch. More than once Meade had seen her conferring with the ranch foreman, giving orders and assuaging everyone's deep concern. Most of the house servants had been taken away, but Rayna's firm hand had turned chaos into order in the hacienda. At her bidding, the remaining servants had prepared meals and converted a small parlor near the front of the house into a bedchamber. As soon as he'd felt it was safe, Meade had moved his patient into the more comfortable surroundings.

Rayna had prepared a room for him, too, as promised, but Meade had yet to make use of it. He was considering doing just that when a noise on the upper balcony captured his attention. He looked up and saw a ghostly figure in diaphanous silver robes floating toward the stairs. Startled by the apparition, he was on his feet before he realized that his ghost was actually Rayna Templeton.

As she came down the stairs, her flowing robe turned from silver to gold when she passed through the light of a lantern, and by the time she reached him, Meade could tell that the dressing gown was actually an unrelieved white that reflected the colors around her. A high lace collar encircled her throat, and more lace spilled from her sleeves onto her hands, making her look as demure and fragile as a nun.

Her golden blond hair was tamer now. It fell in soft waves around her shoulders like a cape of molten gold framing a freshly scrubbed face that looked more vulnerable than Meade would have ever imagined possible. Her blue eyes, the color of priceless sapphires, were softer than before, too. The rage that had made them flash with fire had been drained from her by exhaustion.

Meade's heart went out to her, but his far more surprising reaction to her was a purely physical one. He felt his body tighten in an instinctive male response to her incredible beauty. Irritated with himself, he tried to tamp the feeling down. Miss Rayna Templeton might look like a vision from heaven itself, but she was no angel, and she was far too young for him. Just looking at her made him feel like a lascivious old man.

"Good evening," Rayna said quietly, puzzled by the strange look the major was giving her. Though she knew better, she thought she saw a flash of desire in his dark eyes. It must have been a trick of the moonlight. "Did I startle you?"

"For a moment," he replied, trying to get a grip on his unexpected emotions. Even her voice was different tonight—softer, like a lover's gentle caress. "When you appeared on the balcony, I thought I was seeing a ghost."

"There are no ghosts here, Major. Only the restless souls of the living."

"Understandably so," he replied.

He was still looking at her most strangely, and Rayna found his gaze disquieting. "How is my father?"

"Sleeping comfortably," he was happy to be able to tell her. "He's very weak, but I have reason to believe that the worst has passed."

Her eyes lit up with hope. "Then he'll live?"

"I'm sorry, Miss Templeton. I can't promise you that." The expectation in her eyes died, and Meade hated himself for having killed it. "I thought you had turned in for the night."

Rayna moved to one of the wrought-iron benches flanking the silent fountain that flowed only in the spring and winter. "I couldn't possibly sleep, Major. I have been packing instead."

"Packing?" Meade asked as he settled onto the bench next to hers.

"Yes." Rayna clasped her hands together and forced them to be still in her lap so that the major wouldn't see how they trembled. "I mean no offense, but I can't assume that the dispatch you sent to General Whitlock this afternoon will be sufficient to secure Skylar's release. I fear the only solution to this absurd dilemma is for me to go to Santa Fe to speak with the general personally and to show him Skylar's adoption papers."

"That's probably a wise course," Meade replied, not surprised that she would take the initiative. "I would be happy to write you a letter of introduction and reiterate my objections to Captain Greenleigh's action, if you think that would be of help."

"Thank you, Major Ashford. I would appreciate that."

"When will you leave?"

Rayna glanced away from him, hesitating, wondering what he would think of her decision. What dutiful, loving daughter would abandon her father, knowing full well that he might not be alive when she returned? This was the hardest decision Rayna had ever made in her life. "I plan to leave first thing in the morning. There is a train leaving Malaventura at ten o'clock that will put me in Santa Fe before nightfall."

"Have you any suggestion regarding what we should tell your father?"

Rayna was absurdly relieved that she detected no censure in his voice. "I've thought about that a great deal. I suppose you or Mother could tell him that Skylar and I were so encouraged to hear about his recovery that we felt it would be safe for us to go to Fort Marcy to see about getting the Mescaleros returned. He may be disappointed that we left without seeing him, but the shock won't kill him." Emotion clogged her throat, and it was a moment before she could go on. "I don't recall ever having lied to Papa before," she said softly.

Meade couldn't restrain himself from reaching over to gently place his hand on hers. "You've never had a better reason than this, Miss Templeton. It's for his own good, and this way he won't question your sister's absence."

The kindness of his touch and his voice were more than Rayna could handle. Her emotions were being held in check by a fragile thread that could be too easily severed. "Thank you," she said, slipping her hands away from his and rising.

Meade straightened abruptly, cursing himself. He had meant only to be comforting, but instead he had obviously betrayed his curiously tender feelings toward this woman. She probably thought he really *was* a lecherous old man. "My apologies, Miss Templeton," he said as he rose. "I didn't mean to be presumptuous."

Rayna had difficulty facing him, but she did so anyway. "You weren't," she assured him. "You've been far kinder to me than I deserve, after the way I treated you this afternoon, but kindness is something I'm not sure I can deal with at the moment."

Meade thought he understood what she meant, and he smiled. "You mean you'd be more comfortable yelling at me?"

Caught off guard by his candor, Rayna couldn't keep from smiling. "Precisely. It seems you know me too well already."

I'm learning, he thought, and at that moment he couldn't recall having wanted anything in his life more than he wanted to take this lovely young woman into his arms. Instead, he offered, "You may yell at me if you like. I don't bruise easily."

"Nor do I," Rayna replied, her smile fading. "Yet I seem to hurt all over tonight."

"That, too, is understandable."

A small silence fell between them. A cool breeze wafted through the arcade, rustling Rayna's gown, and Meade had to take a step back to prevent himself from taking two steps toward her. "Would you like to see your father, Miss Templeton?"

"Could I?" she asked, hardly daring to hope. "But you said—"

"He's sleeping now. If he should awaken, we can tell him that Skylar has already retired for the night."

It was a moment before she could answer. "Yes, I would like very much to see him."

The tears of gratitude that suddenly shimmered in her eyes were nearly Meade's undoing. He took another step back and gestured toward the parlor. She preceded him, moving like a wraith floating on a cloud of white silk. Meade's heartbeat quickened again, and he sent up a fervent prayer that morning would come quickly so that he could leave Rancho Verde and escape this misbegotten attraction to Rayna Templeton.

Chapter Five

SKYLAR COULD SEE very little difference in the landscape as the cavalrymen and the wagons moved slowly
through a pass in the mountains that bounded the Mescalero
reservation, yet she seemed to know instinctively when they
reached the land that had been set aside for this small tribe of
Apache.

For three days they had followed the winding trail alongside the Rio Grande before veering east across the northern
limits of the Jornada del Muerto, a section of desert aptly
named the Journey of the Dead. Water had been carefully ra-
tioned during the crossing, but it had escaped no one's notice
that the soldiers received the lion's share of the water from
the great barrels attached to the army supply wagon.

Skylar suspected that she should have been grateful to receive any water and rations at all, and she knew that Major
Ashford was responsible for the relatively decent treatment
she and her people—as she had come to think of them—had
received. The doctor had caught up with the company the
evening before they left the Rio Grande valley, and his first
act upon entering camp had been to seek Skylar out and report on her father.

Though he had not sugarcoated the news, he had encouraged her to hope that her father would survive. He had also
told her about Rayna's departure for Santa Fe. "If anyone
can secure your release, she can," he had said with a wry
smile. "Your sister is a most determined young woman."

"That she is, Major Ashford. I've never known her to fail

at anything she tried—well, almost anything," she had added with a shy smile.

Meade cocked his head to one side curiously. "And what might that be?"

"Her needlework is atrocious," she whispered, as though revealing an embarrassing secret. "And her biscuits have been known to choke a mule."

Meade laughed. "Why do I not find that difficult to believe?"

Skylar's smile faded as she thought of her family and how much she missed them already. "Rayna's strengths lie elsewhere, Major. She has a loving, loyal heart, and that's worth more than all the petit-point pillows and flaky biscuits in the world."

"Her sister has great strength, too," Meade had said with a tender look that had bolstered Skylar's flagging spirits.

Throughout the journey she had gathered a great deal of comfort from the doctor's presence. He was almost always on hand to act as a buffer between the soldiers and the Apaches, and he was always quick with an encouraging smile or word for Skylar in particular. Often she found herself searching for a glimpse of him. He became almost a talisman for her, the only tangible cord that connected her to her family.

After two days of searing desert heat they had reached the foothills of the Capitan Mountains and turned south; within another day they reached the reservation. The arrival of a full cavalry company caused a great stir in the small Apache camps they passed, and long before they reached the cluster of rickety wood and adobe buildings that housed the offices of the agency, Buck Newsome, the Indian agent, had been warned of their arrival.

It was apparently ration day, and a considerable number of Mescalero had gathered at the agency. They stood in long lines in front of two wagons at the end of the compound, and Skylar wondered how two small wagons could possibly hold enough food to feed so many people.

The cavalry line eventually veered away from the agency buildings, and the wagon jolted to a halt. Somewhere in front of the team, Skylar could hear Captain Greenleigh's voice, but his words were indistinct. Private Gless, however, was all too understandable as he stepped to the end of the wagon and unceremoniously ordered everyone out. Some of the old women moved too slowly to suit the trooper, and he took a perverse pleasure in hurrying them up by grabbing them roughly and all but slinging them onto the ground.

Throughout the journey Skylar had stayed close to Tsa'kata, and she did the same now, holding the old woman's arm to balance her as she moved to the wagon gate. They were the last out, and when Gless yanked at Tsa'kata's arm, Skylar tried to protest.

"Please, Private. There's no need to hurt her. I'll help her out."

"You just get out here yourself, squaw, and let me worry about the old woman," he growled.

"That's enough of that, Private. Let her go."

Skylar looked up and wasn't at all surprised to see Major Ashford, still mounted, scowling down at Gless. She flashed him a grateful smile. "Thank you, Major." Moving quickly, she jumped out of the wagon and helped Tsa'kata down.

"That will be all, Private Gless," Meade said as he dismounted. "I'll handle it from here."

Gless hesitated a moment, then joined his fellows some distance away. Skylar watched him go. "I'll be glad to see the last of him," she told Meade. "He enjoys hurting people."

"I'm sorry to say he's not the only such man in the army," Meade replied.

Skylar looked toward the agency and caught sight of Captain Greenleigh. "No, he isn't."

Meade followed her glance. "I'm sure you'll be happy to see the last of him, too."

Skylar's answering smile was gentleness personified. "That I will, but I shall regret your departure, Major

Ashford. I shudder to think how much more difficult this journey would have been without you along. You have been more than kind."

Meade smiled down at the young lady who had become a study in paradox to him. Except for her youth and beauty, she looked no different from any of the other Apaches, yet her manner rivaled that of any gently bred lady of his acquaintance. Even Libby, for all her quiet compassion, couldn't hold a candle to Skylar Templeton.

Unbidden, Meade thought of the other Miss Templeton and wondered how two young women raised in the same household by the same loving parents, given the same education, could be so different in personality and temperament. Given Skylar's brief Apache upbringing, he would have expected her to be the more aggressive of the two, and yet she was not. Rayna was fire, and Skylar was a draft of cool, soothing water.

But that wasn't his concern, he tried to remind himself. In a short while both the Templeton ladies would be out of his life forever. To his great irritation he suspected that Rayna would be more difficult to forget. She hadn't been far from his thoughts for a minute since he'd left Rancho Verde.

"Come," he said, offering Skylar his arm. "I think we should have a talk with Mr. Newsome, the agent. I want to explain your situation to him."

"Does he have the power to release me?"

Meade shook his head. "I don't believe so, but he should be made aware that your incarceration is unfounded and possibly even unlawful. It might secure better treatment for you and your friends."

"I wonder if that would be wise, Major," Skylar said with concern. "If we are treated differently, it might cause resentment among the other Mescalero."

"I don't believe talking to Newsome can hurt anything. From what I've heard about him, it's unlikely that he'll be more generous with your friends, but your sister made it clear to me that we were to leave the wagon and teams with you, and I want to be certain that Newsome doesn't try to confiscate them. I also want it made clear that you aren't to be mistreated in any fashion."

Skylar lifted her head, trying to replace fear with pride. "Once you are gone, Major Ashford, I fear nothing will guarantee that."

Meade didn't know how to respond, because she was absolutely right. Anything could happen. Encouraging words failed him, and all he could do was introduce her to Buck Newsome and hope for the best. With any luck, Rayna had already secured her sister's release and someone would arrive soon with the appropriate papers to get Skylar off the reservation and back where she belonged.

By the end of the day everyone on the reserve knew of the newcomers and of the wealth they had brought with them. Few braves on the reservation had horses, but the ones who called themselves Rancho Verde Mescaleros had fine mounts and good saddles. They also had a wagon, a team of mules, and a fine load of blankets and food. Few who were brought to the reserve came with such wealth, and it created suspicion among many.

In full view of the Apaches in the rations line, the Verdes—as they soon came to be called—were processed by the Indian agent and assigned tag-band numbers. To the astonishment of those watching, nearly all of them spoke the white man's language and could even write their names in Newsome's ledger. Once they had been given their meager share of agency rations, they were told to disperse and make their camp.

Normally the resident Mescaleros would have helped the newcomers find a place for a temporary encampment, but the Verdes were strange, and no one wanted anything to do with them. The others were all reserving judgment until they could study and understand the strangers. If they were truly Mescaleros, the Verdes would take the initiative to make themselves part of the tribe by presenting gifts to the elders and sharing their wealth. If they did not, they would be shunned and might very likely perish, for cooperation was the key to survival on the reservation.

Sun Hawk had collected his rations early that morning and had spent the afternoon hunting in the southern foothills of the Capitans. There was little game at this time of year, but he had snared several rabbits that would help feed one or two of the larger families whose rations did not go far enough to fill the hungry bellies of their children.

When he returned at dusk and began distributing his gifts, he was told about the Verdes at every camp he visited. By the time he reached his father's camp, it was old news, but he sat by the fire and listened as though hearing it for the first time.

"Ten horses and two mules?" he queried as though asking for verification that he had heard his father correctly.

"And a wagon," Naka'yen said with a nod of his head.

"Do you know the name of their chief?" Sun Hawk asked. This was one bit of information he hadn't yet learned.

"The name Consayka was overheard by your uncle's wife," Naka'yen replied, and Sun Hawk looked across the fire to Klo'sen.

"This is true," his mother's brother said with a nod.

"I have heard of Consayka and his people," Sun Hawk said. "They have not lived among us for many years."

"Consayka chose the white man's way long before you were born," Naka'yen replied. "It did not spare him their wrath. Now he must learn to be one of the People again."

Sun Hawk considered this for a moment. His own contact with the white man made it inconceivable that any Mescalero would want to live as they did. He could not escape a feeling of sympathy for them, though. Whatever their lives had been, they were no more, and he understood that only too well.

"Who among us greeted them when they arrived, Father?" Naka'yen seemed surprised by the question. "No one."

"You did not speak with Consayka or help his people find a place to build their camp?" Sun Hawk asked, astonished.

The old chieftain drew his shoulders back proudly. "I am the leader of all our people. It is Consayka who should come to me."

Sun Hawk hid a smile. "But, Father, if no one will speak to the Verdes, how is Consayka to know who you are and where you can be found?"

Naka'yen's weathered face wrinkled in concentration. Then he looked at his brother-in-law. "My son is right. Perhaps that is why Consayka has not come to me with presents."

"I could send my wife to speak with some of their women," Klo'sen suggested.

"That is not necessary," Sun Hawk told him. "I will go and say words of welcome to Consayka. If he has questions, I will answer them."

"They may not understand you, my son," Naka'yen warned. "It is said that they speak the white man's language so well that they have forgotten their own."

This was a surprise to Sun Hawk. He had not considered the possibility of a problem communicating with his own kind, but more than that, he was intrigued by the Verdes' knowledge of the white man's language. In this one thing he envied them. Though his father was the chief, Sun Hawk was often called upon to deal with the agent, Newsome, or with his assistant or one of the reservation policemen. Only the assistant spoke Apache, and that he did so poorly that Sun Hawk was never certain his words had been understood.

He had made an attempt to learn a few of their words, but when he used them, the white men often laughed at him. It was a constant source of frustration and humiliation to him that he could not deal with the Indian agent and other white men as an equal. Consayka's band would not have that problem. They would not be laughed at when they spoke to Newsome, and they would never have to fear that their words had been misunderstood.

Perhaps at least one good thing had come from Consayka's break with the People. Meeting Consayka,

which had before seemed like a duty to Sun Hawk, was now
something he anticipated with relish.

He listened patiently to a few words of advice from his father and uncle, then went off to find the Verdes' encampment.

Though Skylar was trying very hard not to be sad, it was
difficult for her to look around the pitiful excuse for a camp
she and her friends had made and not feel the tug of that
emotion. Their departure from Rancho Verde had been so
swift that they had not had time to dismantle the poles of
their lodges, and this afternoon they'd had no chance to
search for stout saplings to replace them. Instead, they had
constructed several brush-covered wickiups like those the
Mescaleros used when they traveled. There were not enough
shelters to accommodate everyone, but at least the elderly
would have some protection from the chill night air as they
slept.

The departure of Major Ashford with the other soldiers
had also saddened Skylar, but she tried not to dwell on his
absence. She had to rely on herself now that there was no
one to act as her protector, and she tried to imagine what
Rayna would do if their situations were reversed. Knowing
her sister as she did, she found it easy to visualize her taking
charge, telling people where to construct their wickiups and
deciding who should collect firewood and who should carry
water from the trickling stream nearby. And Rayna, in the
midst of the noise and confusion she had created, would be
doing as much work as anyone, if not more.

Skylar couldn't imagine herself taking over as Rayna
would, but she found it easy to take the initiative in one area.
Since she had never made a wickiup before, she knew she
would only get in the way if she tried to help Gatana, so
she focused instead on preparing supper. Foraging through
the supplies Rayna had sent, she found flour, sugar, beans,
dried beef, and even some rice, which she knew Tsa'kata
was quite fond of. Consuelo, the Templetons' housekeeper,

had even thought to send along cooking utensils to supplement those the Mescaleros had brought.

While Gatana and the others finished constructing the wickiups, Skylar prepared a fire and began cooking beans seasoned liberally with strips of beef. With Mary Long Horn's help, she rolled out tortillas, and by the time darkness fell, the Mescalero braves were seated around the fire eating. The women served their men in the traditional fashion, then retired to a separate fire, almost too exhausted to eat.

"You have done well today, Skylar," Gatana told her when they had finished the meal. "Your mother would be proud."

"Thank you," she replied, trying to smile. "I know my mother would be grateful to you for all you have done to help me."

"That is nothing," Gatana said with a shake of her head. "I wish I could do much more. You should not be here."

"Grandmother thinks otherwise," Skylar said with a nod toward Tsa'kata, who appeared to be nodding off to sleep but was probably listening to every word. "She believes it is time I learned what it truly means to be an Apache."

Gatana stroked Skylar's hair and gently touched her cheek. "If that is your destiny, so be it. Perhaps it was meant for you to journey in this full circle. No one can say what Usen has planned for you."

"Then I can only await his will."

Gatana smiled. "Good. You are already learning—but that has always been so, little one. From the time you were first brought to Rancho Verde you learned what was expected of you very quickly. Once you understood that you were in a place of safety, you were eager to please. You have done what you were told and behaved as you were expected to behave."

"I had no place to go, Gatana. I did not want to be sent away. The Templetons provided me with the same kind of warmth and security I remember receiving from my first mother and father. I would have done—and would still do—anything to keep from dishonoring them."

Gatana shook her head. "That would not be possible for you, child."

Tears stung Skylar's eyes. "I miss them, Gatana."

"I know. If Usen wills it, you will see them again soon. But my husband and I have talked and agreed that between now and then we should take you into our family until you can return to yours. If you will allow it, I will be proud to call you daughter for a little while."

"That would be a great honor."

Gatana smiled and wiped at the wetness on Skylar's cheeks. "Then dry your eyes, daughter. There is work to be done."

"Yes . . . *indé'cìmá*," she said. My Apache mother.

Gatana was pleased. After handing Skylar a bowl of rice and beans, she gestured to Consayka. "Here. Take this to your Apache father so that he can share it with the others. It will tell them all that you are his daughter and that you have his protection."

Though Skylar knew she had nothing to fear from the men who had worked as cowhands on Rancho Verde, she did as Gatana bade her, partly out of obedience, but primarily because it was comforting to feel that she was part of a family again. She loved these people very much, and being one of them would make her separation from her real family a little easier to bear.

She moved to the brave's fire, and with only a softly spoken *"indé'cìtà,"* acknowledging Consayka as her Apache father, she knelt and handed him the bowl. He glanced at her, his eyes smiling warmly, and for a moment Skylar was transported back in time to the nights on Rancho Verde when she had sat across a campfire from this kind old man, listening to the wonderful stories he told. She hesitated a moment, caught in a web of sweet memories of a time that could never come again.

When she finally realized that the other men were looking at her strangely, she stood, and it was everything she could do to keep from crying out as a huge shape materialized in the darkness just beyond the glow of the fire. It moved to the rim of firelight, stopped, and coalesced into an Apache brave.

Skylar's fright passed quickly, but she was assailed by other, more confusing emotions. She had never seen any man this handsome before. Tall, with broad shoulders and narrow hips, the half-naked brave would have been enough to make any maiden swoon. His coal-black hair, parted in the center, hung loose on one side of his face, flowing around his shoulder. A single braid hung from the other side, the end tipped with a feather that dangled onto the intricate bone breastplate that covered his chest.

His long legs were encased in buckskin leggings with broad flaps on either side, similar to the chaps worn by cowhands, and a small breechclout hung from his waist to cover the area that would otherwise have been exposed by the cutaway leggings.

The light dancing on his chiseled features made him seem like something from another world, like one of the fearsome Mountain Spirits Consayka had often told her about. Skylar could barely see his eyes in the darkness, but somehow she sensed that he was looking directly at her. She suddenly found it difficult to breathe.

"A friend might come to sit by the fire of other friends if he knows that he would be welcome," the brave said in deep-throated Apache.

"A friend would never be turned away from my fire," Consayka replied in kind. "Sit, my young friend, and share what we have."

Wordlessly the Apache moved to the fire, choosing a vacant space between two Verde Mescaleros who were dressed in white man's trousers and calico shirts.

"Daughter, give this to our friend," Consayka said. He held the bowl up to Skylar, but she didn't move. "Have you grown roots, daughter?"

The laughter of the braves brought Skylar out of her trance, and she took the bowl, chiding herself for her foolish-

ness. Their visitor was only a man, after all. He was not a
Mountain Spirit or any kind of a deity, despite his dramatic,
seemingly mystical appearance from out of nowhere. It was
only the stress of a long journey and the tension of this difficult day that quickened her heartbeat.

She skirted the circle and knelt beside the visitor. A true
Apache maiden would have bowed her head as she offered
food to a stranger, but Skylar's curiosity overwhelmed her
knowledge of Mescalero customs. Eager to dispel her image
of him as a handsome god, she looked into his face as he
turned to her and became instantly lost in a pair of eyes that
were as black as the night and as soft as the moon shining on
dark water. The eyes regarded her curiously; then a veil fell
over them, and he glanced away.

Expecting no thanks for her good deed, for it was not the
Apache way, she quickly rose and left the fire.

"Who is he?" Gatana asked as she returned to the wom-
en's camp.

It was difficult for Skylar to remember how to speak. "A
visitor who calls himself a friend," she said finally.

Gatana looked at her questioningly. "Daughter? What is
wrong? You sound strange."

"Nothing, *indé'cìmá*," she replied. "The brave appeared
so suddenly that he startled me. That's all."

"I see," Gatana said, smiling into the fire as she began
clearing away the remnants of their meal.

For the twelfth morning in a row, Rayna walked from her
rooms at the Palace Hotel down Washington Street to the
headquarters of the Military Department of New Mexico on
Palace Avenue. It was a short jaunt she could have made in
her sleep, but nothing about her bearing suggested anything
even remotely resembling somnambulation. Though this
daily routine was wearing thin, Rayna had lost none of the
ire that she had brought with her to Santa Fe. If anything, the
events of the last two weeks had increased her rage.

The moment she arrived in the city, she had gone directly

to General Whitlock's office and discovered that he was gone for the day. She had left a terse message requesting an appointment at his earliest convenience, and she had returned the following day, only to be pawned off on a dim-witted aide-de-camp named Bascomb who didn't know his hat from a hole in the ground. The aide had referred her to a Colonel Collingswood, the commander of Fort Marcy, who was not only unsympathetic but downright rude.

Rayna could have tolerated his brusqueness if there had been any chance that he could help her secure the return of her sister and the Rancho Verde Mescaleros, but even if he had wanted to, the colonel did not possess the authority to countermand General Whitlock's order.

After another day wasted, she had returned to department headquarters and threatened bodily harm to the next person who prevented her from seeing the general. Her threat had been to no avail. She was told that the general had left Fort Marcy and no one was certain when he would return.

It had taken nearly a week for Rayna to ferret out the information that Whitlock was on a holiday with several visiting dignitaries from Washington. While Skylar endured God only knew what on the reservation, the general was bear hunting in the Sangre de Cristo Mountains.

Rayna's first impulse had been to follow Whitlock's trail and track him down in the mountains, but she had quickly realized the folly of such an act. She could sooner find a needle in a haystack than a small hunting party in the mountains. Her only alternative had been to wait, making daily visits to his office and growing more frustrated with every wasted day.

She had, of course, called on all of her father's friends in the territorial government, including the governor himself. All had been sympathetic and supportive, but short of writing letters on her behalf there was nothing they could do to countermand General Whitlock's edict.

Telegrams from her mother reported that Raymond was weak but mending. Though Collie never said so directly,

Rayna inferred that he was growing suspicious about his daughters' long absence. When he had learned that the "girls" were waiting for General Whitlock to return from his hunting trip, Raymond hadn't understood why they didn't come home to wait. He had slipped into a state of melancholy, and seeing his daughters would have been a boon to his recovery.

Had Raymond known the truth, Rayna would have gone home for at least a day or two to see him, but she hadn't been willing to take the chance that learning of Skylar's abduction would cause him to have another heart seizure. So she had stayed in Santa Fe, sick with worry about her father and her sister.

And she was beginning to worry about her mother, too. Collie was such an innately honest person that it must have been difficult for her to lie to her husband. What was worse, though, was that Collie had no one with whom to share her deep concern for Skylar. Rayna had no doubt that her mother was keeping up the pretense, but the strain had to be taking a dreadful emotional toll on her. She prayed that on this, her tenth daily visit to Whitlock's office, she would finally find him there and put an end to this nightmare.

When she arrived, she found instead a kind of frenetic chaos, as though something had thrown everyone into a panic. Officers were moving quickly through the halls, doors were slamming, men were shouting orders. In Whitlock's outer office, his aide told Rayna that the general would certainly be back within a day or, at most, two days. For the first time, Rayna actually believed him, because it was clear that something had happened to upset the quiet routine of the military post. But of course no one would tell her what that was.

Frustrated, she left the office with a promise to return again that afternoon. As she left the building she was nearly bowled over by an officer bounding up the steps. He muttered a hasty but heartfelt apology, then disappeared inside. The parade ground stretched out in front of the building, and to the right of that were the officers' quarters, soldiers' barracks, and the office of Fort Marcy's commander, Colonel Collingswood. Far beyond that, at the top of the hill that formed the northern boundary of Santa Fe, stood Fort Marcy itself, a small walled fortress that acted as a guardian of the city.

What was it guarding today? Rayna wondered as she paused to study the fort in the distance. What had happened to set everyone in such an uproar? The most obvious answer was Indian trouble. Had Geronimo come out of his stronghold in the Sierra Madre, or had another tribe of Apaches gone on the warpath?

Despite the intense August heat, the question chilled Rayna to the bone. If there was trouble on the Mescalero reservation, Skylar could be in terrible danger, and there wasn't one blessed thing Rayna could do about it.

Immobilized by fear and frustration, she stood by the white picket fence watching an infantry drill on the parade grounds without actually absorbing any of the intricacies of the soldiers' movements.

Chapter
Six

SKIRTING THE EDGE of the parade ground, Meade
moved briskly toward the headquarters building, ignoring
the infantry drill taking place on his left. He'd seen the routine far too often to be impressed by the pageantry. He tipped
his hat to the ladies strolling along Palace Avenue and waved
away the cloud of dust that poured over him when a carriage
went careening down the street.

Halfway down the long block he glanced at the headquarters, and when he spotted the woman at the foot of the steps
he cursed his foolish imagination. He'd been back in Santa
Fe less than twenty-four hours, and already every fair-haired
woman he saw made him think of Rayna Templeton. This el-
egantly dressed lady in the slim-skirted walking suit and
feathered boater was probably the wife of a visitor or some
new officer. She was *not* the hot-tempered hellion who had
been plaguing his sleep for the last fortnight. Miss
Templeton was long gone, having most likely completed her
business with the general before Meade had caught up with
the men of Cavalry Company B on their way to the Mescalero reservation.

Unfortunately that near-certainty couldn't keep Meade
from glancing in the lady's direction again and again as he
progressed down the walk. By the time he reached the picket
fence that framed the headquarters building, he was surprised and irritated to discover that his heartbeat was quickening like that of a randy schoolboy in the throes of his first
bout with puppy love. The woman ahead of him gazing with

apparent concentration at the infantry drill was indeed Rayna Templeton.

Meade's first clear thought was that he should do an abrupt about-face and slink off like a thief in the night. His feet—and other parts of his anatomy—had other ideas, though, for his pace quickened rather than slowed. He managed to convince himself that curiosity fueled his haste, since he *had* been coming to headquarters in the hope of finding out how General Whitlock had resolved the injustice that had been done to the Templeton family.

"Miss Templeton?"

Startled, Rayna pulled her thoughts away from her dismal speculations about her sister and turned. When she saw the officer at her side, nothing could have quelled the flush of pleasure that coursed through her. "Major Ashford! Thank God you're back."

She grabbed his hands and squeezed them as though clutching a lifeline, and Meade was too shocked by her greeting to even consider pulling away. "I arrived last night," he informed her. "But I'm amazed to find you here, Miss Templeton. I assumed you were well on your way to the Mescalero reservation with an order to free your sister."

"General Whitlock left on holiday before I could get an appointment to see him. I've been waiting ever since," she said hastily, then with a touch of desperation asked, "How is Skylar? When did you last see her? Was she well?"

Meade smiled reassuringly. "I last saw her six days ago, and she was fine when I left her. She's understandably a little frightened and anxious to return home, but she was making a valiant attempt to keep her spirits high. I don't believe she's in any danger, if that's your concern."

"Are you certain of that, Major? Your military headquarters are in absolute chaos today, as though something dreadful had happened. Has there been another Apache outbreak?"

Meade chuckled. "As far as General Whitlock's staff is

concerned, something dreadful *has* happened, but it has nothing to do with the Apaches. At least not directly."

Rayna couldn't imagine anything that would be a subject for levity at a time like this, and she retracted her hands from his. "Then what is going on?"

"We learned today that the military departments of New Mexico and Arizona have been combined into the Department of the Border, and that new division has been placed under the control of General George Crook."

"You mean General Whitlock has been stripped of command?"

"Something like that," Meade replied. "It is expected that Crook will make his command headquarters in Arizona, nearer to the heart of the Apache conflict. No one knows for certain yet whether this office will be closed and everyone reassigned. Hence, the chaos you witnessed."

Rayna couldn't have cared less whether the insensitive officers she'd encountered were out of a job or not. Skylar was her only concern. "But will Whitlock have the authority to countermand his order and free my sister?"

Meade hadn't considered that complication because he'd assumed Skylar's problem had already been solved. "I don't see why not," he replied after a moment. "It was his order. He certainly has the power to remand it."

Rayna turned her profile to him, wishing she had someone to vent her frustration on. "Damn him, why doesn't he come back?"

"You may rest assured that he's already en route, Miss Templeton. A telegram was sent to him early this morning at the Montezuma."

Rayna whirled toward him. "The Montezuma? He's taking the waters at a luxury spa? I thought he was bear hunting."

"He hunted for only a few days, from what I gather," Meade replied. "Apparently his hunting party, which includes two senators and a European prince, got tired of roughing it in the mountains."

"Damn him to hell. And damn all those bloody clerks who've been telling me they had no idea where he was!" Furious, Rayna pivoted toward the steps, hiked up her skirt, and was halfway up before Meade caught her.

"What are you going to do?" he demanded.

"I'm going to give those bastards a piece of my mind!"

"No, you are not," Meade said sternly, taking her arm.

"Let go of me, Major! If Whitlock's aide had told me where the general was staying, I could have ended this ordeal days ago! Skylar could be home now!" She tugged at his grip, but Meade was unyielding. "Let go, damn you!"

"And what will that accomplish? If you storm in there and blast Lieutenant Bascomb, you'll only alienate him—if you haven't managed to do that already. Now calm down and think this through rationally."

Rayna stopped struggling and glared up at him, her jaw stiffened with rage. "I don't need your advice, Major, nor do I appreciate your low opinion of me."

"My opinion is neither here nor there," Meade answered, dropping her arm as though he'd been scalded. "What counts is getting your sister back into the bosom of her family. Giving Bascomb a piece of your mind might be a great comfort to you, but it won't help Skylar one iota. Bascomb is the keeper of the keys, so to speak. No one gets in to see the general without going through the lieutenant, and if you get Bascomb's dander up, you'll be twiddling your thumbs in Santa Fe well into the next century!" He took a step back from her. "Think that over, Miss Templeton, and then tell me you don't need my advice."

He turned on his heel and marched down the steps, leaving Rayna standing there, her cheeks flaming and her hands knotted into fists. He was right, of course. She needed Bascomb. Unfortunately Ashford was also right about her already having alienated the general's aide. So far, she had been none too diplomatic in her handling of any of the officers she'd encountered.

Major Ashford, on the other hand, had been kind and

courteous, despite his apparent dislike of her. The quiet moments they had spent in the courtyard at Rancho Verde had forged a kind of fragile truce between them, and Rayna realized she had just shattered it to pieces. He was the closest thing she had to a friend in the military, and it would be moronic to let him slip away.

Swallowing her pride, she hurried after him. "Major Ashford, wait!" she called, and added as an afterthought, "Please."

It was the "please" that stopped him. He waited a moment, then turned, wondering what expression he would find in her beautiful eyes. Contrition? Humility? Remorse?

Hardly. She was looking up at him with a mixture of defiance and defensive pride. This was a woman who didn't back down from anything, even when she was wrong.

Meade raised his eyebrows questioningly, waiting. "Yes?"

Rayna took a deep breath. "I'm sorry," she said tersely. "You're quite right. Telling Bascomb to go to hell won't do Skylar a bit of good."

Meade sighed and shook his head in amazement. "How can any woman look as sweet as you do and be so accursedly unladylike? Didn't your mother ever take a bar of soap to that foul mouth of yours?"

"I am not foul-mouthed," she snapped, getting her back up again. "Any man could use the words I've used and be called hail-fellow-well-met."

"Yes, but you're not a man. Good Lord, it's no wonder you're long past the age when most young women are married and you still haven't snared a husband. Who would want you?"

Rayna had suffered many insults in her life, but few as blatant as this. "Why you bas—"

"I assure you, *Miss* Templeton, my parents were married. It wasn't much of a union, but it *was* legal, so there's no reason for you to question the circumstances of my birth."

Rayna ground her teeth together to keep from spewing a

string of invective that would have turned the major's sensitive ears blue. It was a very long moment before she finally had enough control to speak without her voice quavering too much. "Since you find me so offensive, Major, I'll take my leave of you now. I wouldn't want to tax your delicate sensibilities any more than I already have."

She stalked off, and Meade watched her go, cursing himself and wondering what the blazes had come over him. He'd never been that rude to a woman in his life . . . but then, he'd never met anyone quite like Rayna Templeton, either. When he wasn't fighting the urge to turn her over his knee, he was wrestling with the far more powerful desire to take her into his arms.

It took only a moment for him to realize that it wasn't *her* he was disgusted with—it was himself. Rayna Templeton was too young and too headstrong for a man of Meade's age and temperament who wanted nothing more from his life now than to lead a quiet existence as a gentleman rancher. Yet he was drawn to Rayna like a moth to a flame. It was outrageous and totally out of character for him. Passions were something he had always controlled easily, but it seemed that he'd finally met a woman who turned that restraint upside down.

By far the best thing he could do was allow her to sashay away from him and consign her to the past where she belonged.

But of course he couldn't do that. Skylar Templeton was a gracious young lady who was suffering from a grave injustice, and Meade couldn't turn his back on her, no matter what he thought or felt about her sister.

With a resigned sigh he took off down the concourse. Despite the constraints of her draping, layered skirt, she was moving quickly. He finally caught up with her at the intersection of Palace Avenue and Lincoln. "Rayna, wait," he said, matching his gait to hers as she crossed the dusty street.

She was surprised that he'd come after her and even more astonished that he'd addressed her by her given name.

"What's wrong, Major? Did you suddenly remember some insult that escaped you a moment ago?" she asked without bothering to look at him.

Damn her sharp tongue! "No, I remembered that your sister needs help and that I may be able to provide it."

Rayna stopped dead in the middle of the street, looking up at him eagerly, her anger forgotten. "What can you do?"

"I can get you past Lieutenant Bascomb and arrange an audience with General Whitlock when he returns."

"You would do that?"

"Yes. If you don't get us both run over in the meantime," he said, taking her arm to usher her out of the way of an on-coming carriage.

"Thank you," she said when they were safely on the boardwalk in front of the old Spanish palace.

"For rescuing you from the carriage or for offering to help with the general?"

"The general," she replied, a strained smile wisping around the corners of her mouth. "I wouldn't have been in front of that carriage if you hadn't accosted me in the street."

Since she was teasing, Meade let the saucy remark pass and offered her his arm. "Come on. Walk with me through the plaza. I want to know what you've done so far to secure your sister's release. I can't imagine that you've spent all your time camping on the doorstep of the headquarters."

Rayna considered his crooked arm with a critical eye. "Are you sure your reputation can survive a stroll in the park with a desperate, foul-mouthed spinster? I might try to *ensnare* you."

"Yes, and I might be elected President tomorrow." He lifted his elbow another notch. "Now, shall we walk? I need to know how many feathers you've ruffled before I start smoothing them over."

Reluctantly she took his arm, and he led her across the street into the tree-lined plaza. "You really don't like me, do you, Major?" she asked, keeping her voice carefully neutral because she wasn't quite sure how she felt about his low opinion of her.

Meade considered the question and decided he should be honest with her. Well, partially honest, anyway. Since he had no intention of ever pursuing his inappropriate carnal interest in her, he saw no reason to reveal *that*. "Actually, Miss Templeton, I have a certain grudging admiration for you."

She looked up at him with surprise. "The key word being 'grudging,' I take it."

"Yes. I understand that this is a harsh land and it has yielded a new breed of Americans—a much rougher lot than those I was reared among back east. But a young woman of your background and breeding shouldn't be one of them, Miss Templeton."

"According to you," she accused lightly. "Who made you the arbiter of what's proper and what's not?"

"We are discussing my opinion, no one else's," he reminded her. "And you did ask."

"Hmmm. Tell me, Major Ashford, have you ever pulled a bog?"

His eyebrows went up. "I beg your pardon?"

That was all the answer Rayna needed, but she elaborated, anyway. "Have you ever pulled an irate, frustrated longhorn steer out of a waist-deep mud bog, only to have the animal turn on you once it was free, cuff the seat of your pants, and send you flying?"

It was everything Meade could do to suppress a smile as he visualized Rayna in the predicament she described. "No, I've never had that pleasure."

"Try it sometime, Major, and if you can accomplish it without muttering a single swearword, I will gladly mend my wicked ways."

He seriously doubted that it would be possible for her to live up to that bargain. "Miss Templeton, my point is that a real lady would never participate in the type of activity you described. Have your mother or sister ever . . . pulled a bog?"

"No," she admitted reluctantly.

"I rest my case. You were raised by a lady to *be* a lady, but for some reason, the lessons didn't take. You had the benefit of a genteel upbringing, and it's obvious that no expense was spared to educate you."

"You gleamed that from my refined speech, I presume?" she asked wryly.

Meade tried not to laugh. It wouldn't have surprised him if she'd added a "hell" or "damn it" after her question just to tweak him. "Let's just say I know a finishing school graduate when I see one."

"Well, I'm sure Mrs. Purdy would be happy to know that some of her training wore off on me."

"Actually I was referring to your sister. I just assumed that if your parents sent one of you off to school, they'd have sent both of you."

"I went reluctantly," she told him. "I was dragged away kicking and screaming. You'd have loved that sight, I'm sure."

Meade didn't rise to the bait this time. "You tolerated the experience for the sake of your sister, didn't you?" he asked quietly.

His insight into her personality caught Rayna off guard. "Yes."

"That's where my admiration for you comes from, Miss Templeton. I may not approve of your methods, but I admire devotion and loyalty. Here." He guided her to a bench beneath a shade tree, and they sat down. "Now, tell me how you've been keeping yourself busy these last weeks. And what word have you heard on your father?"

Rayna was grateful for his questions, because she had no idea how to respond to his compliment. What she did realize in that moment was that his opinion had somehow become very important to her. "Papa is still weak, but apparently there have been no more seizures," she replied, arranging her skirts around her.

"Does he still believe Skylar is with you?"

She nodded. "Mother has managed to keep up the charade, but I'm afraid it can't go on much longer. Skylar is an inveterate letter writer. Always before when we've been away from home, she's written our parents every day. If Papa hasn't caught the inconsistency yet, he will soon." A hopeful thought occurred to her. "I don't suppose Skylar gave you any letters to post, did she?"

He was sorry to disappoint her. "No. Writing materials weren't available to her on the trip, and I never thought to offer her mine. I'm sorry."

Rayna shrugged. "Well, that's Skylar for you. She wouldn't have asked for fear it would be an imposition. Sometimes I think my sister is too good for this world."

"Have you always been her protector?"

"Yes," she replied wistfully. "And she was my salvation. It was a more than fair trade."

Meade frowned. "Salvation?"

"I was six years old when Papa brought Skylar home to live with us, and when you're six, a ranch in the middle of nowhere is a very large and lonely place. When Skylar came, the loneliness went away."

Meade understood that only too well. When he was a child, Libby had been his salvation. Their father had been away pursuing his military career most of the time, and their mother had cared more for the social whirl than for her two children. Libby and Meade had felt isolated and alone long before their parents died. They had taken care of each other, forging a bond that could never be broken. If Rayna loved her sister half as much as he loved his, she was most certainly in agony now; and one thing Meade knew positively about Rayna Templeton was that she loved her sister.

"What happened to Skylar's Apache parents?" he asked.

"We're not completely certain," Rayna replied. "Skylar has very few memories of that time, and the Mexican slavers Papa bought her from were understandably loath to explain how she came to be in their possession. We do know that her entire village was massacred. Papa believed it was the slavers who committed the crime, but Skylar has a vague memory of other Apaches being on the scene."

Given Meade's knowledge of the history of the southwest territories, either version seemed completely plausible. Even before the arrival of the first white settlers, the Apaches had been preying on one another, and the hostilities between them and the Mexicans were legendary. It wasn't out of the realm of possibility that the culprits could have been a contingent of Americans, either. Senseless massacres of peaceful Apaches were still being committed by groups of "concerned citizens."

"She's very fortunate to have encountered your father," Meade commented.

"I know. I shudder to think what might have happened to her otherwise."

The sadness in her voice tugged at Meade's heart. "And what's happening to her now?"

Rayna nodded and looked away from him. "Yes."

"Why don't we go back to my original question?" Meade suggested, wishing he could banish her sadness. He liked it much better when she was prickly and obnoxious, because it was easier for him to erect barriers against her.

"What have I done to alienate everyone in Santa Fe? That question?" she asked with a hint of a smile.

"Yes."

Rayna thought back over the last two weeks. "To the best of my knowledge, the only people I've insulted were wearing uniforms similar to yours, give or take a few stripes and gewgaws."

Meade glanced down at the gold-rimmed stripe on the shoulder of his tunic. "I've never heard gold oak leaves described as gewgaws."

"Forgive me if I fail to show the proper degree of respect, but I don't have much respect for anything military these days."

"Perfectly understandable. Have you been able to gain access to anyone in the territorial government?" he asked, getting back on track.

"Of course. Believe it or not, I'm welcome in many of the best homes in the city."

"That makes sense. You have a wealthy and probably somewhat powerful father."

"Thank you for giving me the benefit of the doubt," she said dryly.

Meade grinned. "You're welcome. All right, go on."

Rayna shrugged. "I've spoken to every friend of my father's who might be even remotely able to help, but so far all I can boast of is a rather limited letter-writing campaign. Correspondence has been sent from several sources to the Bureau of Indian Affairs, senators, congressmen, the War Department, even the President himself. So far no one has responded."

"Letters take time, especially when you're dealing with the government."

"Really? I hadn't noticed."

"Don't be glum, Miss Templeton. We'll get Skylar back."

Rayna appreciated his confidence and his support. She was curious about one thing, though. "Why is it, Major, that you call my sister Skylar but refer to me as Miss Templeton?"

The question surprised him, and it took a moment to find an answer. "I suppose it's less confusing than referring to both of you as Miss Templeton, and addressing you thus is a form of courtesy and respect."

"Grudging respect," she reminded him.

Meade cleared his throat. Apparently she was never going to let him forget that comment. "Yes."

Rayna thought it over. "It's odd. Earlier you called me a foul-mouthed, unladylike spinster. Addressing me as Rayna seems almost deferential in comparison."

"Is that your roundabout way of inviting me to call you Rayna?"

"You did it once before and it didn't choke you to death," she reminded him, and was surprised when he began chuckling. "What's so funny? My comment was meant to be a clever barb, not a joke."

"It's not you," Meade assured her. "I was remembering something your sister—the other Miss Templeton—said to me."

"What?"

The laughter still sparkled in Meade's eyes as he informed her, "She told me that you are such a horrendous cook that your biscuits had been known to choke a mule."

Rayna glowered at him. "What else did she tell you about me?"

"That you're terrible at needlework."

Rayna threw up her hands. "Well, there you have it. All my dirty little secrets. You might as well take me out and shoot me now. I don't deserve to live."

Her rapid-fire delivery had Meade buckled in half with laughter that carried far across the plaza and caused passersby to stop and look. "You are a caution, Miss Templeton," he said, still chuckling as he straightened.

"A foul-mouthed—"

"Enough! Enough! I surrender," he said, straightening up and extending his hand to her. "Come on, I'll take you to lunch at the Palace and apologize."

Rayna looked at his hand, then directly into his eyes. "I don't want an apology unless you mean it sincerely."

"Do you want lunch?" he asked, raising one dark eyebrow.

She hesitated a moment. "Yes."

"Then take my arm, and we'll go. If you can manage to get through the meal without questioning anyone's parentage, I'll apologize sincerely over dessert."

"I should warn you, Major. I've never lost a dare," she informed him, slipping her hand into his as she rose. The innocent contact suddenly seemed very intimate to them both.

Their eyes met, questioning the odd sensation, and several seconds passed before Meade found the presence of mind to release her hand.

They began strolling toward the Palace Hotel, and neither of them could think of a single thing to say.

Chapter
Seven

SKYLAR WAS ACCUSTOMED to hard work, but her daily chores at Rancho Verde had not prepared her for the harsh realities of her new life. After a simple exchange of gifts with Naka'yen, the old chief had helped the Verde Mescaleros find a suitable location for a permanent camp, and since then the work had been unending. Alongside the other women, Skylar had cleared brush and helped erect sturdy lodges. From dawn to dusk she cooked, carried water, collected firewood, tended the livestock . . . and in her spare time she made clothes for herself from scraps of cloth and blankets given to her by her friends. Having had so little time to prepare for their journey, no one had much to spare. Mary Long Horn had given some of her clothing to Skylar, but her dress from the maiden ceremony and the calico skirt and overblouse Mary had given her wouldn't last long. It wasn't surprising to her that nearly everyone she saw on the reservation was dressed in oft-mended clothing that amounted to little more than rags.

Skylar knew that cleanliness was highly prized by the Mescalero, but under these conditions keeping clean was next to impossible. Water was scarce, and while the other women were able to make soap from the aloe plant, that skill had long ago been lost to the Verde Mescaleros. Even if one of them had known how, Skylar couldn't imagine when anyone would have had time to do something as mundane as making soap. Tending a camp was a full-time occupation.

As difficult as it was, Skylar didn't mind the work. Having so much to do helped distract her from her constant worry about her father and her desperate longing to go home. With every day that passed, that dream seemed to slip a little further away from her, though. She knew she had not been forgotten or abandoned, and that Rayna was doing everything humanly possible to secure her freedom; but at the end of each day when no one had come to take her home, she felt a little more hopeless and lost than she had at the start of the day.

Little by little she was learning about the other Mescaleros on the reservation. Like other Apache tribes, the Mescaleros were broken into small bands comprising several family units. Joe Long Horn, Mary's father, had found a few distant relatives, but so many of the Mescaleros had been exterminated over the last few decades that there were few other connections between the Verdes and the other bands.

Their chief was Naka'yen, and Skylar had eventually learned the name of the brave who had so startled her that first night. He was Naka'yen's son, and his name was a complicated phrase that had taken a considerable amount of study to translate. Skylar still wasn't sure she had it right. To the best of her knowledge, he was called Angry He Flies Like a Hawk into the Sun. She had also heard him referred to as Iya'itsa—Sun Hawk—and it was far easier for her to think of him by that name. To her great surprise, she thought of him often.

She had seen him many times since that first night, and each time she fully expected that the breathless jolt of excitement she experienced would dissipate. It didn't. Every time she caught a glimpse of him her heart began to race as it had when he appeared in the darkness.

The Verdes' camp was situated less than a half mile from Naka'yen's, and Sun Hawk often passed by, occasionally with other braves, but most of the time he was alone. If Consayka was outside his lodge, Sun Hawk would stop and speak with the old man; if not, he would pass by, rarely look-

ing at any of the women in the camp, for that would have
been bad manners.

Many times Skylar had caught herself watching for him,
and it always took considerable effort not to stare. He wasn't
just handsome, he was mesmerizing. His every move be-
spoke a quiet power that drew Skylar like a magnet. She had
never exchanged a word with him, but several times she
overheard parts of his conversations with Consayka, and she
knew that he was a man committed to peace.

To her great surprise she had found Sun Hawk watching
her several times when he thought she was not looking. Her
heart would quicken in those moments, but if she dared look
directly at him, his glance would dart away. She suspected
that his interest was merely curiosity, or perhaps even
amusement. It was obvious to anyone who cared to study the
workings of the Verde camp that Skylar was different from
the other women. She had learned many things about her
friends over the years, but she'd had little opportunity to put
her knowledge to practical use.

As a result, Skylar was clumsy and slow at almost everything she did. On the day she attempted to erect her own
lodge, Sun Hawk had been a witness to her ineptitude, and
the memory of it still made Skylar smile. She had been grap-
pling with the poles, trying to align them in an even circle
when Sun Hawk passed nearby. He had given no appearance
of being aware of anything taking place in the camp, but
when Skylar caught sight of him she had tripped over one of
the poles, causing the entire framework to come tumbling
down around her.

Embarrassed, she looked up and found Sun Hawk still
strolling along, but his shoulders had been jerking with what
could only have been laughter. It was clear that he had been
trying hard not to look at the spectacle openly, and despite
her exhaustion and frustration, Skylar had laughed, too—for
the first time since she had been abducted from Rancho
Verde. She had Sun Hawk to thank for that brief respite from

her despair, and her gratitude only increased her warm feelings for him.

Under other circumstances, Skylar might have been amused by her fascination with the brave. She had had schoolgirl crushes before. When she was thirteen, she had thought Gil Rodriguez's son was the handsomest man she had ever seen. Of course, the word "man" had been loosely applied, since Tomás was barely sixteen at the time. Rayna had teased Skylar mercilessly and threatened to tell Tomás of her infatuation with him, but blessedly Skylar had outgrown her crush and Tomás had married a few years later without every realizing that he had been the object of her childish affections.

There had been other infatuations in her life, and once she had thought herself truly in love. Skylar had been in school in Boston at the time, and she had met Stephen Dodd through friends of the Templetons whom she and Rayna often visited. There had been nothing particularly handsome about Stephen, but he had been a quiet, considerate gentleman who loved poetry and knew how to flatter all the young ladies of his acquaintance. Skylar had adored him, and had allowed herself to believe that he loved her in return.

Though she rarely thought of him anymore, Skylar liked to imagine that Stephen had loved her—in his own peculiar way. Unfortunately that way hadn't included marriage, at least not to a young woman of Indian blood, though he had been perfectly willing to offer her a position as his mistress.

After that crushing blow, Skylar had forced herself to face the reality of her situation: No white man was ever going to see her as a suitable wife. She had sworn never to open herself to such pain again, and so far she had kept that promise.

Sun Hawk was an unexpected—and decidedly unwanted—obsession. He was a *bija'n*, a widower, but that made no difference to Skylar. It was still foolish for her to long for a glimpse of him. He was a medicine man, greatly respected by his people, and since his father was a chief, he would likely be one, too, someday. He was a full-blooded

Mescalero warrior who would eventually take an appropriately reared Mescalero wife; Skylar was an educated, fully Americanized Apache who wanted nothing more than to get back where she belonged as quickly as possible. The only thing she had in common with Sun Hawk was the color of her skin.

On the fourteenth day of her captivity she was giving herself that very lecture as she walked to the stream where the Verdes drew their water. The sun was low, the day was nearing its end, and the mantle of depression that always settled over her at this time of day was coming again. When night fell, there would be no more work to do and hence nothing to distract her from the hopelessness of her situation. Night had become her least favorite time of day.

Using a cut-out gourd, she filled both buckets from the trickling stream and then paused, her head bent over the wooden pail. She caught a glimpse of herself in the dark surface of the water and sighed. The woman looking back at her was a stranger, someone she barely recognized. Had she not been so exhausted, she might have wept.

"Hurry, Rayna," she murmured sadly. "Please come quickly and take us away from here before I lose myself completely."

With a weary sigh she eased back onto her heels and discovered that her reflection had been replaced by another. Startled, she looked up and found Sun Hawk standing over her, his arrival as dramatically unexpected as the first time she'd seen him.

"Why do you speak to the water?" he asked without ceremony or introduction, his head cocked in curiosity as he looked from Skylar to the bucket and back again.

Though Skylar had discovered many gaps in her knowledge of the Apache language, it was easy for her to slip into speaking it because her friends rarely spoke English any longer. She also knew from long experience that the Apache rarely wasted time with pleasantries. They spoke their minds and expected others to do the same. Skylar was finding that more difficult to adapt to than the constant use of their language, and locating her voice and her wits with Sun Hawk towering over her made it even harder. "I was speaking to my sister," she replied after a moment.

Sun Hawk's dark brows went up in surprise. All of his people claimed kinship with various animals, but he had never known anyone related to water before. "The water is your sister?" he asked, crouching beside her.

"No," she answered, wondering how she could explain her way out of this when her mind had turned to muddled mush. "When I looked in the water, I thought of my sister, and the words in my heart were spoken aloud."

Sun Hawk nodded thoughtfully. "Why do you not say the words to her yourself rather than asking the water to do it for you?"

"Because she is far away."

"She is free? Living in the mountains?" he asked with a kind of envy that Skylar might not have understood a fortnight ago.

"She is free, but she lives on a ranch far above this place."

"Why was she not brought here with you and your father?"

Skylar was finding it increasingly difficult to remain still with Sun Hawk so close. His deep voice aroused feelings inside her that she didn't want to be having. He was dealing with her matter-of-factly, and she wanted to be able to respond with the same detachment. "Because my Apache father is not hers. My sister is not of the People."

Sun Hawk frowned. He had heard this woman call Consayka "my Apache father" once before, and this puzzled him. And now he learned that she had a sister who was not a sister. Odd. There was so much about the Verdes that he did not understand, and this woman was the greatest mystery of all. Since the night he had first seen her in the glow of the fire, her eyes as wide as those of a startled doe, Sun Hawk had watched her. She was as beautiful as a sunrise, and her people treated her with great deference, yet it did not seem to

Sun Hawk that she belonged here. He had learned that she was called Skylar, but the name was even more incomprehensible than she was.

That was why he had approached her when he saw her kneeling by the stream. He did not like mysteries. He wanted to understand her and the other Verdes so that he would know how to react if trouble sprang up between this woman's people and his. Gradually he was learning about the others through his conversations with Consayka, but the old man had never volunteered any information about his daughter, and Sun Hawk could not ask for fear that his curiosity would be misinterpreted.

The best course, it had seemed to him, was to talk to the woman called Skylar directly.

"Why do you refer to your father so strangely?" he asked.

Skylar wasn't sure how to answer him. "I have had three fathers," she finally told him, unable to hide her sadness. "The first was a White Mountain Apache, but I do not remember him very well. I was taken from my village and sold as a slave to a white man named Templeton who took me home and loved me as much as he did the daughter of his blood. Now I have been taken from that family, and my good friend Consayka has given me his protection by calling me his daughter. It is an honor I carry proudly."

Now Sun Hawk understood why she seemed so different. "You lived among the white men willingly?"

"I was only five years old, and these people were kind to me. What choice did I have?"

Sun Hawk nodded, but he did not think the white man Templeton had done this woman a real kindness. "Is it hard for you to be an Apache again?"

"You have seen that it is." She lowered her eyes. "I want very much to go home."

Sun Hawk looked down at her, studying the way her dark lashes brushed against her cheeks. She was beautiful and sad, but there was nothing he could do to help her. It surprised him to realize how deeply he regretted that, and how profoundly she touched him.

Perhaps I have been in mourning too long, he thought. The thought startled him so much that he stood up abruptly, drawing Skylar's questioning gaze up with him. Her eyes were soft, but Sun Hawk had been immune to soft eyes for nearly two years.

If it was indeed time for him to lay his beloved wife to rest, it could not be for this woman whose heart yearned to be far away.

Without another word he turned on his heel and departed, leaving Skylar wondering what had happened and why he had looked at her so strangely.

"If I didn't know better, I'd think you were nervous," Meade said, looking down at Rayna's hands. They were clasped together, resting demurely in her lap, but her knuckles were white and there was nothing serene about her posture. Her whole body fairly radiated tension.

"I am nervous, Major, and this isn't a good time to tease me about it," she said matter-of-factly as she looked across the room to General Whitlock's office door.

"I'm sorry. I didn't mean to make light of your dilemma," he said, then fell silent again. He really hadn't meant to be callous; it was just that he always had difficulty controlling his burgeoning feelings for her when she looked vulnerable like this. In the last two days he'd spent a considerable amount of time with her, and in that time he'd experienced more emotional ups and downs than he had at any other point in his life. One moment he wanted to strangle her; the next, she had him laughing out loud with her tart repartee. A single glance from her could reduce him to speechlessness. She could flay him alive with her razor-sharp tongue, and the absurdity was that he had begun to look forward to the lashings. It was insane.

General Whitlock had returned to Fort Marcy within twenty-four hours of learning that he was no longer the king of this particular hill. Meade had tried immediately to set up an appointment for Rayna, but to no avail. And it was just as well, he'd reasoned. Whitlock had arrived in a high dudgeon and had gone on an uncontrolled rampage, like a child whose favorite toy had been taken away. His bellowing and barking could be heard throughout the building as he took out his wrath on everyone who crossed his path. It wouldn't have been a good time to try to get him to admit that he or anyone in his command had made a mistake.

Fearing that the general's temper hadn't had nearly enough time to mellow, Meade had counseled Rayna to wait another few days before putting her suit to Whitlock, but naturally she hadn't listened. With or without Meade's help she had been determined to get an audience with the general at the first possible moment, and Meade had been too much of a gentleman to abandon her. He had pressed Lieutenant Bascomb to schedule an appointment and had demanded that Rayna allow him to accompany her to the meeting. To his amazement, she had agreed without a fight.

And now they were waiting in Whitlock's anteroom, Rayna with her hands turning white in her lap and Meade trying to ignore his sympathy for her—as well as other, stronger emotions.

"Then send *another* telegram, damn it! Get me an answer! Dismissed!" The general's booming voice shook the whole room, and a split second later a harassed-looking captain came out of Whitlock's office looking as if he'd gone ten rounds with a boxing kangaroo. He closed the door behind him, but it flew open a moment later and a florid General Whitlock stepped into the opening. "And I want that report by the end of the day, Captain!"

"Yes, sir," the officer said, making a hasty exit.

Whitlock turned away, but Rayna was already on her feet. "General Whitlock, a moment, please," she said, hurrying across the room. Meade had no choice but to accompany her.

"Yes, what is it?" Whitlock snapped.

"I have an appointment, sir," she said, careful to keep her

voice polite. "I've been waiting for two weeks, and it's a matter of great urgency."

"You're Miss Templeton, aren't you? From Rancho Verde?" he asked. "You're the one who's been plaguing my staff."

Rayna managed a strained smile. "Yes, sir. I fear I've taken my considerable frustration out on some of your men."

Whitlock nodded curtly. "Yes, I've heard all about it, and that was a damned fool thing to do."

A comment about the pot calling the kettle black sprang into her mind, but she had the good sense not to voice it. "I realize that, General," she said contritely, "but my family has become ensnared in a very desperate situation, and you're the only man in the territory who can possibly come to my aid."

Meade was astonished by the honey in her voice. He hadn't thought Rayna capable of the kind of feminine flattery she had suddenly slipped into. On any other day Whitlock might have been susceptible to it, but not today.

"If this is about those Mescaleros I ordered onto the reservation, I—"

"Only peripherally, General," she said hastily. She'd sensed an automatic rejection coming on, and she wanted to cut him off before he took a stance he couldn't back away from. "If you'll just hear me out, I believe the reason for my impatience these last weeks will become obvious." She removed a packet of letters from her reticule and extended them to him. "I have letters of introduction from the governor and a number of other officials who hold you in high regard."

Whitlock cleared his throat and took the letters. "Very well, Miss Templeton. Come in and we'll discuss this problem of yours." He looked sternly at Meade. "I take it you're with the lady, Major?"

"That's right, sir."

"What is your role in this?"

"I'm merely a friend of the Templeton family, sir. I attended Miss Templeton's father, Raymond, after his recent heart seizure."

Whitlock was clearly surprised. "Raymond Templeton had a heart seizure? I didn't know that. When did it happen?"

"When your Captain Greenleigh kidnapped my sister," Rayna replied, her pleasant tone slipping a bit. She'd told this story to everyone at the post who would listen and a few who wouldn't. Why in blue blazes hadn't anyone informed the general?

Whitlock's pudgy face reorganized itself into a scowl. "Kidnapped? What the devil are you talking about? Greenleigh would never do something like that."

"Oh, but he did," Rayna argued, and would have said more if Meade hadn't placed a restraining hand on her arm.

"General, please. If we could discuss this in your office?" he suggested mildly.

"All right. Come in, come in. I suppose I should clear this matter up before you damage the good name of one of my best officers." He marched toward his desk, leaving Meade and Rayna to follow.

As soon as the general's back was turned, Meade lowered his head to Rayna's ear. "Calm down, or we're sunk before we sail," he muttered, then placed his hand at her waist and ushered her into the office.

"Now, what's this about a kidnapping of your sister?" Whitlock demanded as soon as they were all seated.

Meade could see that Whitlock had gone on the defensive, and he decided it was time to take charge before Rayna could do her cause any more damage. "At the time Captain Greenleigh seized the Rancho Verde Mescaleros a grave misunderstanding took place, sir. Raymond Templeton has a legally adopted daughter of Apache blood who was participating in a ceremony with the other Indians when we arrived. She was dressed in Apache fashion, and Greenleigh understandably assumed she was one of the Mescaleros.

However, when the mistake was pointed out to him he refused to acknowledge the error."

"Well . . ." Whitlock was at a loss, but he seemed determined to defend his man to the very last. "As you said, Major, his mistake was understandable. Greenleigh had orders to round up *all* the Mescaleros."

"That's right," Rayna said argumentatively. "But my sister isn't a Mescalero." She handed him another set of papers. "Here are her adoption documents."

Whitlock looked them over reluctantly and handed them back. "Well, I'm no lawyer, but they do seem to be in order."

"It was a perfectly legal adoption, I assure you," she told him. "My sister is as much a citizen as you or I, sir, yet she is being forced to live on the Mescalero reservation against her will."

Whitlock frowned and pulled at his muttonchops. "Actually, Miss Templeton, the question of your so-called sister's citizenship might be debatable, since the Apache people have no legal standing in this country."

Rayna's composure slipped another notch. "General, my *so-called* sister is—"

"Is a gently reared young woman ill-equipped for life on an Indian reservation," Meade said placidly. "I had the good fortune of being able to speak with her a number of times on the journey to the reservation, and she wants very much to go home. Naturally she is deeply concerned about her father's health."

"Templeton is quite ill, is he?" the general asked.

Meade nodded. "Yes, sir. The strain of seeing his daughter taken away was too much for his heart to bear. From what I understand, he is slowly regaining strength, but I am deeply concerned about the effect this will have on him if Miss Skylar is not returned." He went on to explain the charade that was being carried out to protect Raymond from the shock of knowing Skylar had been taken away.

Whitlock was leaning back in his chair, plucking at his whiskers again, giving every impression of a man who had much better things to do with his time. Even before the general began to speak, Meade realized he and Rayna had been wasting their time.

"Well, that's all very unfortunate, Major, but I don't see how I can possibly be of any assistance to you," he informed them.

"What?" Rayna gasped, coming to the edge of her seat.

"You heard me, Miss Templeton. There's nothing I can do. Military control of this territory has been passed into the hands of General George Crook. All matters regarding the Indians of the new Department of the Border are to be referred to him. This is now his problem to deal with."

"You can't be serious!" Rayna was on her feet in an instant, her hands planted on the general's desk. "You caused this problem with your ridiculous order to incarcerate the Rancho Verde Mescaleros—now you can damn well solve it!"

"Rayna, calm down," Meade ordered, coming to his feet.

"I will not calm down! This pompous ass—"

"I beg your pardon?" Whitlock said, rising indignantly.

"You heard me. You're a pompous, unfeeling—"

"Rayna, shut up!" Meade demanded, grabbing her arm before she could do something stupid, like flying across the desk to punch Whitlock in the face. "General, please forgive her. As you can imagine, this ordeal has put an incredible strain on—"

"Damn it, don't apologize for me," Rayna snapped, jerking her arm away from him. "How can you possibly toady to a man like this?"

"I am not toadying!" Meade snapped as his perspective on the situation slipped away from him. "This is my commanding officer, and he is to be treated with respect."

"Well, you may have to kowtow to this petty martinet, but I certainly don't!"

"You do if you want Skylar back!"

"That's enough!" Whitlock thundered. "I have given you

my answer, Miss Templeton, and you will have to live with it. Now get her out of here, Major Ashford."

Meade managed to calm himself. "General, I beg you to reconsider. Since it was your order that resulted in Miss Templeton's abduction, surely you have the power to rescind it regardless of the reorganization of the department."

Whitlock glared at him. "Major, I gave you an order and I expect you to carry it out. I want this woman out of here. If she wants that Indian back, she'll to have to write George Crook. I believe he'll be arriving in Arizona shortly to take charge." He plopped into his chair. "Dismissed, Major."

It was everything Meade could do to force himself to offer the general a brisk salute. "Good day, General. Come on, Rayna," he said, taking her arm. "There's nothing more to be done here."

Rayna couldn't believe it. Whitlock was blithely dismissing her as though Skylar's welfare—indeed her very life— meant nothing. Epithets and accusations sprang to her lips, but Meade was bustling her out of the office before any of them could form. Trembling with barely suppressed rage, she allowed Meade to lead her out of the building.

"How could you let that happen?" she demanded, jerking her arm out of his grasp.

"Me?" Meade gasped. "If you'll recall, I'm the one who warned you to wait until Whitlock was in a better mood. Having his military command usurped by General Crook has been tantamount to being told that he's incompetent to handle the job of controlling this territory."

"Considering the decisions he's made, I'd say that's a pretty accurate assessment," she replied hotly.

"Oh, why don't you go back in there and tell him that? I'm sure that'll make him relent."

"Damn you, Meade Ashford, don't you understand what's happened here?"

"Yes, I do. Quite well, in fact. You're angry at Whitlock and you're taking it out on me."

"Well, who else am I going to take it out on?"

She had a good point. "You're right," he said calmly, spreading his arms wide. "Fire away."

His feeble attempt at humor was Rayna's undoing. Her failure and the devastating repercussions it was going to have, not only on Skylar but on their father as well, came crashing down on her. A sob of anger and anguish caught in her throat, and tears flooded her eyes. "Oh, God, Meade. What am I going to do? How do I tell Papa? What if he dies?"

"He won't die, Rayna," Meade said gently, pulling her into his arms as he'd longed to do so many times since he'd met her. To his surprise she didn't pull away but instead lowered her head to his chest and let the tears spill out.

He held her close, trying to ignore his body's intense and immediate reaction to having her pressed against him. The fact that he shared her concern and understood her sorrow only enhanced the sensations.

Be paternal, Ashford, he told himself sternly. After all, you are old enough to be her father. Well, nearly old enough. The twelve-year chasm that separated them was far too wide for either of them to cross. Unfortunately he couldn't make himself feel paternal or even brotherly about Rayna Templeton.

He crooned comforting words to her, and to his great relief—and disappointment—she quickly regained control of her emotions. She allowed him to hold her until her sobs had subsided; then she pulled away. "I'm sorry," she said, still not fully in command of her breathing. "I'm not normally a weepy female."

"I would never have mistaken you for one," he said charitably, hoping it would alleviate her embarrassment. For the first time, Meade noticed that a number of soldiers on the parade ground were watching them. He encouraged Rayna to allow him to walk her back to the hotel, and she didn't argue.

"What will you do now?" he asked as they moved down the walkway.

Rayna tried to collect her thoughts. "Go home, I suppose, and write to General Crook."

"I'll make some inquiries this afternoon and see if I can find out where he'll be making his headquarters."

"Thank you." She glanced up at him, but her eyes darted away quickly. She was too embarrassed about her ridiculous bout of weeping to hold his gaze.

"If you like, I'll write a letter to Crook that you can include in your packet to him. I campaigned under the general during his first tour in Arizona, and I'm certain he'll remember me."

Rayna sighed. She didn't deserve his kindness. "It seems that whenever I'm not cursing you, I'm thanking you. I am already deep in your debt, Major, but I won't refuse this favor." She fell silent a moment as they walked. "Do you think Crook will help me?"

"I'm positive of it, and you should be, too. General Crook is one of the most fair-minded men I've ever met. He'll be as outraged about this as Whitlock was apathetic. But, Rayna . . ." He hesitated until she looked at him expectantly. "This is going to take some time. Crook will act the moment he receives your letter, but there's no telling when your dispatch will catch up with him."

"Is that your way of telling me to be patient?" she asked without rancor.

"Yes."

"Patience doesn't come easily to me."

"Neither does restraint nor prudence, but you're going to need all three to get through this ordeal."

Rayna didn't have enough fight in her at the moment to be offended. Instead, she felt an overwhelming surge of guilt wash through her, and she averted her face, looking across the street without seeing anything that was transpiring there. "Is this my fault?" she asked, her voice small and far away.

Meade wanted to take her into his arms again. "No, Rayna. You mustn't blame yourself."

"But if I hadn't gotten angry—"

"It still wouldn't have made a difference," he insisted. "Nothing you could have said or done would have changed Whitlock's mind. He is a pompous ass even on the best of days. Calling him one didn't make it less than true, nor did it change the outcome of the meeting."

She gave him a weak but grateful smile. "You're only saying that to make me feel better, but I appreciate it."

If he had thought she'd believe him, Meade would have protested, but it didn't seem worth the effort. For the moment all of Rayna's fighting spirit had deserted her, but he knew she wouldn't stay down long.

"When are you leaving?" he asked. The hotel was just ahead of them, and he was already dreading their parting.

"Tonight. There's a train leaving for Albuquerque at six o'clock. I can stay there overnight and be home tomorrow."

"You have the train schedule memorized?"

She nodded. "I've had two weeks to plan my speedy, triumphant departure. I hadn't allowed myself to consider the possibility that I might return home in utter defeat."

"You're not defeated, Rayna. Merely delayed." Meade pulled a pocket watch from his tunic. It was nearly 2:00 P.M. "If you're leaving at six, I have plenty of time to write that letter to Crook and get it to you at the hotel. I have to stop by the hospital to check on a patient, but I can be back in two hours. Will that be all right with you?"

"Of course," Rayna said as they stopped at the entrance to the Palace.

"Then I'll see you shortly."

"All right. Thank you again, Major." She turned to the door.

"Rayna . . ."

She stopped and looked at him. "Yes."

"It really wasn't your fault. Believe that."

The gentle look in his eyes was almost more than she could bear. "I'll try," she said, then disappeared into the hotel.

Chapter Eight

BY THE TIME Meade's two hours had expired, Rayna's bags were packed and she had nothing to do but pace and think. She had considered sending a telegram to her mother, but delivering this dreadful news in that fashion seemed too cruel. Somehow she and Collie would have to find a gentle way to break the news to Raymond, for once she arrived home there would be no way to continue the charade.

Rayna wished desperately that Major Ashford could come back to Rancho Verde with her. Though she told herself it was only because she wanted a doctor on the scene when she told her father the news, she had to admit that there were other reasons as well. In the last two days the major had made himself almost indispensable to her. He had been kind and helpful, but he had also been a much needed distraction. Most of all, he had bolstered her flagging spirits and given her a strong arm to lean on when she had needed it most.

She knew that he was doing all of this only out of sympathy for Skylar, not because he had any particular affection for Rayna. He'd made his opinion of her clear on more than one occasion and he had a knack for making her angry, but she was going to miss him. Despite their constant bickering, she felt as though she was losing a friend.

At shortly after four he finally arrived with the letter he had promised. Though he was late, Rayna hadn't doubted that he would come. She admitted him to her suite, and once he had handed over the letter she invited him to sit, but Meade had a better idea.

"Let me take you out for a light supper," he suggested. "You won't have a chance to eat on the train."

"Thank you, but I'm afraid I couldn't eat anything right now."

"But you could use the distraction," he said wisely. "It's better than pacing in here or at the train station until time to leave."

"I suppose you're right."

Meade smiled at her. "I'm always right. Haven't you noticed that?"

He was trying to cajole her into smiling, and it worked. "I've noticed that you always *think* you're right. There's a difference."

"Why don't we debate this over supper?"

He raised his arm, and Rayna slipped her hand into the crook of his elbow. "Very well. 'Lead on, Macduff.' "

Meade's dark eyebrows went up. "You know Shakespeare?"

"I'm educated, remember?"

They adjourned to the Palace dining salon and ordered a light supper that Rayna knew in advance she would barely touch. Meade ordered a bottle of fine Bordeaux wine, and they sat back to await the meal.

"To the return of your sister," Meade said, raising his glass in a toast.

"Soon," she added, touching her goblet to his. They drank, and Rayna began playing absently with the stem of her glass. "Major, what would be my chances of getting a letter or package to Skylar?"

"Hmmm. I don't really know. I can't imagine that it's routine for any Apache to receive mail, so I suppose it would depend on how obliging Mr. Newsome wanted to be."

Rayna knew that Meade had made a point of explaining Skylar's situation to the Indian agent. "Perhaps if I sent the package in care of him with a letter begging him to see that Skylar received it?"

Meade couldn't imagine Rayna begging, but he had no

doubt that she would do anything for her sister—even beg, if it came to that. "A letter to Newsome is a good idea. However, I wouldn't put anything in the package that would tempt him to keep it for himself."

"I was thinking of sending her writing materials so that we could correspond," Rayna told him, her spirits sinking again. "But that would mean sending her postage stamps as well. Do you think Newsome would confiscate them?"

Meade reached out and covered Rayna's hand with his own. "Give it a try and see what happens. You might consider sending Newsome a small amount of money to compensate him for any inconvenience it causes him, since Skylar won't be able to leave the reservation to post her letters. And at the same time, I'd mention General Crook and the letters that have been written to everyone from the President to the head of the Indian Bureau. If he thinks there's a chance that this could come back to haunt him, he might be more inclined to deal fairly with you."

"I'll try it," she said, then leaned forward intently. "Meade, do you think he'd let me see her if I went to the reservation?"

Meade frowned at the thought of her making that hazardous journey. "Would that be wise, Rayna? Even if you didn't stay more than a day or two, the trip would take at least two weeks, possibly more. Discounting the danger involved, can you take the risk of missing General Crook's reply? Someone will have to arrange for Skylar's return once Crook acts, and your father is in no condition to handle any of this. Not to mention the stress it would put on him knowing that you were making that difficult journey."

Every one of his arguments was valid. Discouraged, Rayna sank back in her chair, her eyes closed to stave off the threat of tears. "You're right, of course. I really don't have any choice but to wait, do I?"

"I'm afraid not." Meade raised his glass again. "To patience."

Rayna halfheartedly joined him in the toast, and they fell

into a companionable silence that lasted through most of
their meal. Meade understood Rayna's preoccupation, and
though he wanted very much to pull her out of her melancholy silence, he also respected her right to be discouraged.

"I think this is what I will miss most about Santa Fe," he
said as he divided the last draft of wine between their glass-
es.

"What's that?"

Meade raised his glass. "The wine. I've been drinking
cheap rotgut for so long that I'd forgotten what a delight a
fine wine can be. I'll miss it when I go home."

Rayna was amazed to realize that she knew absolutely
nothing about Meade Ashford. At some point she had
gleaned that he was a bachelor, but that had made no difference to her. For the most part, she had regarded him as an en-
tity whose existence began the moment she met him, and it
had never occurred to her that he had a life that went beyond
being her liaison with the army. "Where is your home?" she
asked, genuinely interested.

"Arizona," he replied. "Or it will be as soon as I resign
my commission in a few months."

"You're not a career officer?"

"At one point I had planned to be, but I'm sick to death of
it. I can't wait to get out."

"Then why not resign now?"

Meade grimaced and explained the trade he had made
with the army—a course in surgical procedures for two additional years service.

"And what will you do when that time's up?" she asked.

"Become a gentleman rancher," he announced grandly,
and Rayna had to laugh. "What's so funny?"

"I'm trying to imagine you pulling a bog or culling
calves," she said, chuckling at the image. "I don't expect you
know a branding iron from a salt lick, do you, Major?"

Meade couldn't believe how good it felt to see Rayna genuinely amused. "I most certainly do. And as for pulling

bogs, I said I wanted to be a *gentleman* rancher, remember? I'll leave the pulling and culling to the experts."

"While you sip fine wine on the veranda?"

"Exactly."

"You'll be bankrupt within a year," she predicted.

"Not possible. What I don't know about ranching might fill an encyclopedia, but my brother-in-law, Case Longstreet, is a genius—in more ways than one," he added cryptically, thinking of the prediction Case had made several months ago. He had been absolutely right about Crook's impending return. Astonishing.

"So you're going into business with your brother-in-law?" Rayna asked.

"I already am. When Case married by sister, Libby, eight years ago, we jointly purchased a large plot of ranchland. Between the two of us—my capital and his know-how—the ranch has done very well. It's not as grand as Rancho Verde, but then, few places in the Southwest are."

Rayna's smile thanked him for the compliment. "What's your ranch called? Where is it located?"

"It's called Eagle Creek, and it's located just west of the White Mountain and San Carlos Indian reservations."

"Really?" she asked, impressed. "I'm amazed that anyone would deliberately choose a location adjacent to a reservation."

Meade finished off the last of his wine. "Actually, the choice of location was Case's." He hesitated a moment, then became a little angry with himself for being embarrassed to admit the truth. "You see, my brother-in-law is a full-blooded White Mountain Apache. He was orphaned when he was twelve or so, and he was raised by a frontiersman named Jedidiah Longstreet. Case always maintained his ties to his people, though. He's considered something of a legend among them, in fact."

Rayna's smile widened. "It seems we have something in common."

Meade could have gone on to tell her that he was very *re-*

luctantly related to an Apache, but it would have required more explanations than he wanted to delve into at the moment. "Apparently so," was all he replied.

She asked him other questions, general ones about the time he'd spent in the army and why he'd chosen the military over a practice as a private physician. She'd inquired about his sister and the remainder of his family. Though Meade's answers were somewhat superficial, what emerged was a portrait of an idealistic young man whose outlook on life had changed drastically, courtesy of the harsh realities of being an army surgeon. He had become a cynic who felt he had grown old before his time. His only real joy in life, it seemed, was his sister Libby and her small family.

"Why have you never married?" Rayna asked, hoping he wouldn't take offense at the personal nature of the question.

"Marriage is not an institution that appeals to me," he replied, then turned the tables. "And what of you? Why aren't you making some poor man's life a merry hell?"

She bit back a smile. "My opinion is much the same as yours, Major. It's not an institution that appeals to me, and I've yet to encounter a man I respected enough to make me change my mind."

"You mean you've yet to encounter someone stout enough to handle you."

"I don't want to be handled, sir. If I ever marry, it will be to someone who treats me as a partner and an equal. Frankly, I don't see that happening. I've worked alongside my father running Rancho Verde for as long as I can remember, and that is all I want from the remainder of my life. Thus far, the only men who have expressed a serious interest in me have been those who were anxious to become Raymond Templeton's heir."

"I find that hard to believe," Meade said, studying the graceful slant of her brow and the sculpted set of her jaw. "No young man could look at a woman as beautiful as you and see only land and cattle."

The compliment momentarily robbed Rayna of the power of speech. "Th-thank you," she stuttered after a moment.

Meade cursed himself for having given voice to his thoughts. "No thanks are necessary. I was merely stating the obvious. I just meant that if you've failed to attract the right sort of suitor, it's because of your personality, not your looks."

That was a subject that had become something of a joke between them, and he was obviously trying to lighten the mood because she'd taken his compliment too seriously. Had Rayna not been so emotionally vulnerable, the comment might have rolled off of her as so many of his others had, but in this instance she felt as though he'd slapped her.

"Excuse me, Major, but it's time I left for the train station," she said, slipping her chair back from the table.

"Rayna, wait, I'm sorry," he said, realizing that he'd hurt her. "I meant what I said as a joke."

"I know," she replied. "It just didn't come out that way."

"I apologize."

"No apology is necessary." She rose, and Meade stood up as well. "Thank you for supper, Major. And for all the other kindnesses you've shown me." She offered him her hand, but Meade refused to take it.

"I had planned to see you to the train station."

"You don't have to trouble yourself. You've done too much already."

"It's no trouble," Meade insisted. He couldn't possibly let her go like this.

Seeing that it was pointless to argue, Rayna waited while he settled the bill. In the lobby he hired a porter and sent the man on up to Rayna's suite to collect her bags while he ordered a carriage.

"If you don't mind, I'd like to make one more turn through my room to make certain I haven't forgotten anything," she told him.

"Of course." Meade stayed at her side as she went upstairs. They encountered the porter as he was coming out of the room, arms laden, and Meade instructed him to deliver Rayna's things to the carriage out front.

He waited near the door as Rayna walked through her quarters, and he noted that when she came out of the bed-chamber she was carrying a book. "Did you strike gold?"

She held up the volume. "Elizabeth Barrett Browning. I left it by my bedside."

"Browning?" Meade craned his neck to see the book. "You're a romantic after all, Rayna."

He was trying to be friendly and polite, but she was in no mood to be teased. "It's Skylar's favorite," she said defensively.

"But not yours?"

"Now, what would a woman with my prickly personality and prospects want with a book of romantic poetry?"

Meade sighed heavily and looked down at the floor. It was a moment before he looked up again. "I apologized for that, Rayna. I thought we had progressed beyond the point of con-tention on this issue, and I certainly didn't mean to hurt you."

"I'm not hurt."

"Yes, you are, and understandably so. I was callous." He took a step toward her. "Now, tell me you forgive me so that we can say good-bye at the train station like the good friends we have become."

His absolute sincerity disarmed her. He really did view her as a good friend. For some strange reason, that knowl-edge brought tears to her eyes. "I forgive you. I should never have taken offense in the first place."

"That's better," Meade said with a smile, tipping her chin up so that he could look into her eyes. "I wouldn't have let you go otherwise."

"Why not? It's unlikely we'll ever see each other again," she said, then felt a stinging, bitter sense of sadness when she realized what she'd said and how true it was.

Meade suddenly found it difficult to breathe. "That's pre-cisely why I wouldn't let you go away angry." He lowered his head, intending to give her a perfectly decorous, brotherly kiss on the cheek, but when Rayna tilted her head questioningly, her eyes sparkling with unshed tears, all his brotherly thoughts faded. His lips brushed hers lightly, and he was lost. Before he fully realized what he was doing, he had taken her into his arms.

Rayna was stunned by Meade's sudden display of affection, but nothing in the world could have made her shy away from his kiss. There was an urgency in the way his lips brushed against hers, and in the way she responded. A breathless ache blossomed inside her, and she pressed herself against him, wrapping her arms around his shoulders as the kiss deepened into something Rayna had never experienced before. It was sensuous and wonderful. It rocked her to the very core of her femininity and made her gasp with need. She moaned softly, a hoarse, breathy sound that caught in her throat and blended with a nearly identical groan from Meade.

And then suddenly it was over. His mouth was no longer slanted against hers; his arms were no longer around her. Meade stepped back, and it was everything Rayna could do to keep her knees from buckling.

"I'm sorry," he said hastily, mortified by his behavior. "That was thoroughly improper, Rayna. Forgive me."

It was a second before she recovered the power of speech. "I don't recall protesting, Meade."

The way she said his name made him ache to take her in his arms again. But he couldn't, of course. It was impossible. Ludicrous. "Well, you should have," he scolded. "Good Lord, Rayna. I'm old enough to be your father."

"No, you're not," she replied, feeling as though they were on the verge of another argument and not at all sure why. She certainly didn't want to quarrel, not when her blood was pulsating with the most pleasurably frustrating sensations she'd ever experienced. "Meade, you're not nearly old enough to be my father."

"Yes, I am, and you shouldn't be entertaining gentlemen in your room without a suitable chaperon."

He was chastising her as her father would have, but instead of being irritated, Rayna found herself amused. He was embarrassed because he'd kissed her. She couldn't help but smile. "Oh, really? In that case, would you like me to call up the porter or the chambermaid to be a witness to our next kiss?"

"There will not be a next kiss, Rayna," he said sternly.

"Are you trying to convince yourself or me?"

Meade felt a painful stirring in his loins, and it infuriated him. "Don't play the coquette. You're no good at it, and I'm in no mood for it." He moved toward the door. "Now, come on. You have a train to catch."

The reminder sobered Rayna, and the situation no longer seemed amusing or thrilling, for the truth was that this one kiss really would be their last.

"Well?" he prompted, holding the door open for her.

Not knowing what else to say or do, she let him escort her to the carriage. A few minutes later he put her on the train and turned away briskly with only a terse but fatherly goodbye.

Rayna had hoped to make a quiet arrival at Rancho Verde so that she could break the disheartening news to Collie before they told her father. Even that small boon was denied her. One of the hands saw her coming, and by the time she stopped the buckboard in front of the house, everyone—including Raymond—knew that she had returned. Though his daily exercise was confined to a few short walks through the courtyard, Raymond was on his feet and waiting for her at the door with Collie at his side doing everything she could to draw him back into the house.

"Rayna, honey!" He held his arms out to her, and she flew into them, hugging him tightly, her head buried in his chest. He was thinner and pale, but he was alive.

"Oh, Papa, it's so good to be home." She let him go long

enough to embrace her mother, but it was impossible for her to look Collie in the eye.

"Where's Skylar?" Raymond asked as Rayna slipped one arm around his waist.

"Come inside, Papa," she encouraged, trying to smile. "We have to talk, and I don't want you taxing your strength."

"Where's Skylar?" he repeated, digging his heels in like a stubborn mule when Rayna tried to guide him into the house.

"Papa—"

"Damn it, Rayna Louise, talk to me!"

"I will, Papa, but you have to come inside and lie down."

"She's right, Raymond. Please," Collie pleaded. "I couldn't bear it if you had a relapse. Please come inside."

He looked from his wife to his daughter and, for their sake, relented. "Skylar's not with you, is she?" he asked as he let them lead him into the house like a crippled old man. It seemed appropriate to the way he felt. "She never was in Santa Fe at all, was she?"

"No, Papa," Rayna replied.

"Damnation," he muttered. "I knew there was something damned peculiar going on when you left without saying good-bye. That bastard Greenleigh took her, didn't he?"

"Yes."

The fight seemed to drain out of him completely, and he didn't speak again until he was propped up in the bed in the downstairs parlor that had become his prison these last few weeks. The women sat on the bed, flanking him, and he demanded, "Now tell me what's going on, and don't leave anything out."

With Collie's help, Rayna explained how Skylar had been taken and that she had been delivered safely to the Mescalero reservation.

"Why in blue blazes didn't you tell me this before?" he asked, giving his wife an accusing glare.

"Because Major Ashford said the shock might kill you," Collie replied, holding her ground. "My daughter had just been stolen from me, and I couldn't have survived losing you, too. Lying seemed like the only way to save your life, and I'm not sorry I did it."

Raymond reached over and took his wife's hand. "All right. I can accept that. I wasn't exactly in any shape to go to Santa Fe and get her back." He looked at Rayna. "I'm sorry you had to bear the brunt of this, honey."

"You know I'd do anything for you and Skylar, Papa." Her voice broke, and tears threatened, and she had to look away. "But I failed you both."

Raymond wasn't accustomed to seeing his daughter like this, and it frightened him almost as much as the thought of Skylar living unprotected among the Apaches. "What do you mean, honey? What happened with General Whitlock?"

Collie felt a stab of fear, too. "Rayna, you did get to see him, didn't you? Surely he ordered Skylar's release?"

"I'm sorry, Mother. I did see him, but . . . he wouldn't do anything."

"Oh, dear God," Collie murmured, and Rayna hurried on to explain about the reorganization of the territories and Whitlock's insistence that her only recourse was to write General Crook. She also told them of the assistance Meade had given her.

"Before I left, Major Ashford asked around and learned that Crook is expected to make Fort Whipple his headquarters. I have letters from Meade, who once served under the general, and also a plea from Governor Denning. I wrote the letter to Crook last night and posted the whole lot from Albuquerque this morning."

"Then there's nothing to do but wait," Collie said.

"I'm going to send a letter to Skylar, too, so that she'll know what we're doing to secure her release," Rayna told them. "I thought if we sent her some writing materials we might be able to establish a correspondence that would help us all."

"That's a fine idea," her mother said brightly, but then her brave front collapsed and tears flooded down her face. "Oh, my poor Skylar. My poor baby," she sobbed.

"There, there, Collie. She'll be home soon."

Raymond pulled her to him, and they clung together. Though they never would have intended it, their closeness made Rayna feel like an outsider, and she quietly slipped out of the room. Standing outside the door, her teeth biting deeply into her lip to hold back her own tears, she listened to her mother's sobs and her father's hollow words of comfort.

From somewhere far away, Rayna seemed to hear her sister's voice calling to her, quietly begging her to come soon and take her home.

A sob she couldn't control welled up in her throat. "I'm trying, Skylar. I'm trying," she whispered.

Libby Longstreet stepped out onto the porch, and a shiver ran down her spine as she gazed at the tiny pinpoint of light up on Windwalk Mesa. Upstairs, Jenny and Lucas were fast asleep. The house was quiet; the night sky was full of stars. It seemed inconceivable that Libby's peaceful life was about to be turned upside down, but she knew the upheaval was coming just as surely as she knew the sun would rise in the morning.

George Crook had come to Eagle Creek today. Libby had been surprised and delighted to see him again, and Crook had greeted her warmly. He had crooned with grandfatherly pride over her two beautiful children and had even teased Libby about their first meeting eight years ago when she had shocked an assemblage of officers and their ladies with her liberal ideas about the Apaches. Crook had expressed his delight with her obvious happiness . . . and of course he had asked to see Case.

Libby was still cursing herself for not having comprehended the purpose of Crook's visit the moment she saw him approaching with a small escort of cavalrymen. She should have known instantly that he had come to recruit her husband. But she hadn't known, most likely because she hadn't wanted to know. She hadn't wanted to consider the possibility that Case might go away.

Now, though, she had no choice but to confront the truth. Case had spent hours talking to the general. Libby hadn't been present during the conversation, but she knew what had been said. If Crook was going to succeed in capturing Geronimo, he needed Apache scouts, and eight years ago Case Longstreet had been the best the Gray Fox had ever had. Crook trusted him, and the White Mountain Apache trusted him; if Case enlisted, the other braves would follow suit.

The thought of her husband going into battle against Geronimo struck terror in Libby's heart. It would be a difficult and dangerous campaign because Geronimo wasn't going to surrender easily this time. Many would die.

And of course Geronimo wasn't Crook's only problem. There was considerable discontent even among the Apaches who had not revolted. They had been living with poor rations and broken promises for too long. Many different Apache tribes—not all of them friendly to one another— were being concentrated on the White Mountain, San Carlos, and Rio Alto reservations, and this was causing even more trouble.

The entire territory was a boiling caldron that had been stirred up by Geronimo's escape and the brutal raids he had been making to the south. Libby had heard rumors that so-called citizens' committees were springing up in towns throughout Arizona. In the past, such groups had been responsible for some of the most hideous massacres that had ever taken place in the territory. They acted under the well-meaning guise of solving the Apache problem and were heralded in the press as heroes, but for the most part they were just mean liquored-up cowboys who wanted something to brag about.

Libby had often feared that one of those committees would strike at Eagle Creek because she and Case employed a number of reservation Apaches as ranch hands. Case was respected by their neighbors, but all it would take to cause trouble was one drunken bigot who didn't understand how much Case had done to keep the peace between the Apaches and the ranchers in the area. If Case went with Crook . . .

Libby didn't want to think about that. It was too terrible to comprehend. Yet she knew that she was going to have to face that fear eventually.

She looked again at the flickering light on the mesa and wondered what advice Case was receiving from the Apache spirits he was praying to up there. Would they tell him to go or to stay? He hadn't given Crook an answer today, but tomorrow or the next day he would ride to Crook's temporary headquarters at Fort Apache. At the end of that day he would either come home or be gone for a very long time—if he ever came home at all.

"Please, God, don't let him go," she murmured.

Pulling her shawl around her to ward off the chill of dread she couldn't escape, Libby sat in a rocking chair on the porch and waited until long after the light on the mesa vanished. When Case finally appeared out of the darkness, neither of them was surprised to see the other.

"Have you decided?" she asked quietly as he came up the stairs.

Case sat on the edge of the porch and leaned back against a post so that he could look at his wife. "Yes."

"Will you go?" Libby held her breath.

"Yes."

Libby looked down at her hands, fighting back a rush of tears. If he'd made his decision, nothing she could say would change his mind, and she wouldn't dishonor either of them by trying. From the moment she had met Case, she had accepted him as he was, and over the years nothing had changed that. Despite his education and knowledge of the white world, his heart was still fiercely Apache. He was brave, proud, and strong, a loving husband and devoted father. He was also a man who had walked in two worlds, but felt that he truly belonged to neither. Together they had carved a place for themselves that was their own, and if the time had come for him to leave, Libby knew he had good reason and it wasn't for her to question the rightness of it.

The brutal slaying of his parents when he was only twelve had set him on a path of vengeance that had led him into the White Man's world. With the help of Jedidiah Longstreet, Case had learned English—not only to speak it but to read and write it as well. He had studied manners and customs. He had visited cities in the East.

Guided by the mysterious visions that Libby still didn't understand, Case had maintained his ties with the Apache and had waited patiently until it was time to extract his revenge from the Chiricahua renegade who had killed his parents and stolen his five-year-old sister. Gato, the renegade, was dead now, and for eight wonderful years Case had been at peace.

Lately, though, Libby had sensed a restlessness in her husband. Now she understood why.

"You knew Crook was coming back, didn't you?" she asked, not looking at him. "You saw it in a vision."

"Yes."

"Why didn't you tell me?"

"Because I didn't understand everything that I saw, and I had no intention of scouting for him. My place is here with you."

She finally looked up. "Then why are you going?"

Case was silent a moment before he answered, "Morning Star."

Libby was astonished. It had been years since she'd heard him speak that name. "Your sister? What has she got to do with Crook and Geronimo?"

"I don't know, beloved, but there is a connection."

Libby moved across the porch and sat beside him. "What have you seen?"

Case frowned as he took Libby's hands. "It's not what I have seen so much as what I have felt." He shook his head. "I had given her up for dead years ago, long before I met you, even. After Gato kidnapped her, Jedidiah and I spent years looking for her, but we found no trace. Gato sold her to Mexican slavers, and the earth swallowed her up."

Libby reached out and gingerly touched the simple carved medallion that hung from a buckskin cord around his neck. It was so much a part of him that she sometimes forgot it was there. It was an unadorned version of the magnificent Thunder Eagle necklace that Gato had stolen on the day he murdered Case's parents. Case had made it to symbolize his love for his slain family, and even after the original necklace was restored to him, he had continued to wear the simple copy as a tribute to his missing sister. One eagle feather, representing her life, hung from the medallion.

"And now you believe she is alive?" Libby asked, praying that he was right. It had been nearly twenty years since Case had seen his sister, but she knew he still grieved for the lost child whose fate had been a painful mystery for so long.

"Yes, and somehow scouting for Crook will lead me to her, just as it led me to you . . . and to Gato eight years ago."

Libby took Case's hand and laced her fingers through his. "Then you have no choice but to go with Crook."

Case squeezed her hand and pressed his lips against her temple. "I knew you would understand, beloved," he murmured.

"When will you leave?"

"I will go to Crook tomorrow. I promised him I would act as interpreter when he speaks with the other Apache."

"When will the campaign against Geronimo begin?"

"Crook doesn't know, but it may not be for a while yet. I won't be leaving until the campaign begins."

Libby sighed with relief. It might take Crook months to prepare.

Case wrapped his arms around his wife. "When I go, I'll ask Jedidiah to come stay with you and the children."

"Good." She smiled up at him, pleased with the thought of having their old friend so close. Jedidiah's small cabin was only a few miles away, but he was spending more and more time in the mountains these days. "He stays away too long."

"And Meade will be home soon," Case reminded her. "You won't be alone, beloved. I'll see to that."

"I know you will."

He cupped her jaw and raised her face to his. "You are my life, Libby," he said softly. "If you tell me to stay, I will stay."

"I know that, too," she replied. "That's why I would never ask."

He gathered her close, and their long, tender kiss blossomed into the quiet passion that made them one spirit, one soul, one life.

Chapter
Nine

My dearest sister,

Even as I write this letter, I have no idea whether it will find you or not. I have begged Agent Newsome to deliver it to you, and I can only hope that he will take pity on us and place it in your hands along with the parcel I am including.

Father is alive and growing a little stronger with every passing day. I know he has been your deepest concern, but you may rest easy. He longs to be as active as he was before, but seems resigned to the changes his weakened heart has forced upon him.

Naturally his greatest concern is for your welfare, and we all ache for news of how you are faring. We love you, and we miss you, dear Skylar, and we are doing everything we can to secure your release.

How I wish I could say that would be soon, but it seems that we have become trapped in a sea of bureaucratic nonsense. General Whitlock in Santa Fe could not help us, and I have been forced to initiate a correspondence with . . .

THE TEARS IN Skylar's eyes made the words blur beyond recognition, and she had to stop for a moment. It was the second time she had read Rayna's letter since Agent Newsome had given her the packet less than an hour ago. She had devoured this one as well as the letter from her mother and the brief note from her father that proved he was indeed alive.

The joy of knowing that was more than enough to over-shadow the disappointing news that Rayna had related in the rest of her letter. Skylar could endure anything now that she knew her father was alive.

At long last she had a tangible connection to her family. Smiling through her tears, she touched the packet of writing materials Rayna had sent her. They were lying on the end of the wagon the Verdes' had driven to the agency to collect their supplies, but otherwise the wagon was empty. Her friends were standing in the long line awaiting their weekly rations, and Skylar knew she should join them, but she couldn't bring herself to move. She wanted to savor Rayna's letter, so she dried her eyes and read again how the military departments had changed, how Rayna had waited in Santa Fe for Whitlock's return, how kind and helpful Major Ashford had been.

She read Rayna's promise to write again soon, and she smiled. Rayna hated letter writing, but Skylar had no doubt that she would eventually receive another letter from home. When that might be was anyone's guess, of course, since this packet had taken nearly three weeks to arrive. Whether that was due to the inconsistency of the mail delivery service, the remoteness of the agency, or Newsome's neglect, Skylar couldn't have guessed and she didn't care. The packet was here, and that was all that mattered. Skylar could hardly wait to return to camp and begin a letter to her family.

When she finished reading Rayna's letter for the second time, she glanced up and noticed that Gatana was watching her. She couldn't delay going to the ration line any longer. Clutching the parcel, she hurried across the compound and was halfway there when she noticed a disturbance near the agency office.

Looking closer, she saw Naka'yen and several subchiefs. Sun Hawk was there, too, as was the assistant Indian agent,

Frank Hawley, who acted as Newsome's somewhat ineffectual translator.

Even from a distance Skylar could tell that Naka'yen was agitated. His voice was raised, but the words were indistinct. She didn't have to hear him to know that something was wrong, though.

"What has happened?" she asked as she hurried to Gatana.

"I do not know," the elderly woman replied, her face drawn into lines of concern.

Others had noticed the disturbance and had begun moving toward their chief. Skylar moved, too. Gatana tried to hold her back by placing a hand on her arm, but Skylar gently shook it off and joined the others.

"We will not go! This is our land," Naka'yen shouted at Newsome. "It is all we have left to us. The white man has taken everything else and left us with only this one small piece of land. Our hunting grounds are gone, and there is not enough food. We will not go!"

Go? Go where? Skylar wondered, desperately clutching the letters and papers to her breast. More murmurs went through the crowd as Hawley translated Naka'yen's words.

Quickening her pace, Skylar forced her way through the growing crowd until she was standing between Sun Hawk and Newsome. "What's happening?" she asked the agent.

"I'm trying to explain to your chiefs that this agency has been closed."

"Closed?"

"That's right," he said, clearly no more pleased with this than the Apaches were. "All of the Mescalero are being transferred to the Rio Alto agency in Arizona."

Skylar was appalled. "But that's absurd! Why?"

"Damned if I know," Newsome barked. "It's got something to do with the reorganization of the Indian Bureau. They're trying to consolidate all the Apaches into one area so that they can be controlled better."

"You mean the Apaches will no longer have their own

land? They'll be sharing a reservation with other tribes?" she
asked, trying to comprehend what was happening.

"That's right," Newsome answered. "They'll be on the
Rio Alto with the Tonto, the Lipan, and what's left of the
Chiricahua—those who didn't take off with Geronimo."

"Is the Rio Alto a large reservation?"

"No," Newsome said, growing impatient with her questions. "It's just a little bigger than this one."

"But that's insane," Skylar said. "*This* reservation is
barely big enough to support the Mescalero. You can't expect that many people to survive on a tiny reservation."

Newsome poked a finger sharply at his own chest. "*I'm*
not the one doing this," he said hotly. "These are the orders,
and I've got to obey them—just like all of you do."

Skylar discovered suddenly that all eyes were on her as
she conversed in English with Newsome. Sun Hawk's gaze
finally captured hers, and in Apache he asked her bluntly,
"What does he say to you? What do you say to him?"

Skylar realized with some embarrassment that she had
taken over the conversation and that many would think what
she had done was inappropriate. She couldn't refuse to answer, though, and she looked up at Sun Hawk hesitantly.
"We are to be sent to Arizona. We will live on the Rio Alto
reservation."

Sun Hawk frowned as more murmurs went through the
crowd. "Where is this Rio Alto?"

Skylar had no idea, and she looked at Newsome. "They
want to know where Rio Alto is located."

"It is below San Carlos near the Pinaleno Mountains," he
replied, and Skylar translated to Sun Hawk and the others.
There were more angry shouts, and Skylar felt herself being
jostled as the Indians pressed forward. Sun Hawk called for
silence and looked down at Skylar.

"Ask him who made this decision."

"It was the Indian Bureau," she told him.

"Can nothing be done to stop it?"

Skylar looked to the agent. "Is there any way to prevent this? Is there anyone we can talk to?"

He shook his head with disgust. "No. The Apaches are not going to like it, but they're going to have to live with it. Soldiers from Fort Travis will be here this afternoon, and they'll move out day after tomorrow."

"You expect them to be ready to leave in a day?" Skylar asked, aghast.

"That's right. Make that clear to them. As soon as they've collected their rations they should begin making preparations for the move."

Skylar looked at Sun Hawk and reluctantly told him what Newsome had said.

The crowd erupted into shouts of anger as they surged forward, but when Hawley brought up his rifle, everyone stopped.

"Get back, all of you!" he demanded in his less than perfect Apache.

Newsome drew his own pistol and took a step back. "Hawley, put an end to this at once! Tell them that if they make trouble, there will be no more rations distributed and they will have to make the trip without food!"

Hawley raised his voice again and spoke to the Indians, but what he said did nothing to quell the disturbance. More angry shouts rent the air, and it was easy to see why. Instead of repeating Newsome's threat in its entirety, Hawley had inadvertently told them that the rations were being cut and there would be no food for the journey.

The angry Apaches surged forward again, and Hawley raised his rifle, panic showing plainly in his eyes.

"Wait!" Skylar shouted, but she couldn't be heard above the chaos. Desperate to avert a tragedy, she grabbed Sun Hawk's arm. "Wait, calm the people! Make them listen. There *will* be provisions for the journey. The agent said it. I heard him."

"But that is not what this one said," Sun Hawk replied, gesturing toward Hawley.

"He spoke wrong. Calm your people and let me tell them what the agent said."

Sun Hawk raised his voice, counseled his people to step back, and managed to quiet them enough so that Skylar could be heard. Ignoring the anger and suspicion in their eyes, she translated Newsome's words accurately, then looked at the agent and switched back to English. "You should be careful, Mr. Newsome. Your assistant's poor command of the Apache language is going to get someone killed. He told them you were cutting off their supplies."

Newsome shot an angry glance at Hawley, then turned to Skylar again. "Then you speak for me," he demanded. "Tell them to disperse and go back to the lines to collect their rations."

She did as he asked, but no one moved. She looked beseechingly at Sun Hawk. "They respect you. Make them go back or there will be trouble."

Sun Hawk exchanged a troubled glance with his father; then Naka'yen ordered his people to go back to the ration lines. Slowly the crowd began to disperse until only Sun Hawk and the council of elders remained.

Relieved that the crisis had passed, for the moment at least, Skylar stepped back as well, but Sun Hawk stopped her. "No, you must stay. We want our words understood, and we want to hear his clearly so that there will be no mistakes. You will speak for us."

Klo'sen drew his shoulders back proudly. "I do not want a woman to speak for me! She is not even one of us."

Sun Hawk turned to him. "She has lived among the white men, uncle. She knows their ways and ours. We need her. If a woman can stop a tragedy from happening, I will listen to a woman. It does not make me less of a man."

With Skylar interpreting, Newsome went on to give his instructions: At daybreak the day after tomorrow, all the Mescaleros were to gather at the agency, ready for travel. They would be counted. Anyone who was missing would be considered a renegade and would be shot on sight.

Naka'yen argued, and the others made speeches, which Skylar dutifully translated, but there was nothing Newsome could do.

By the time the soldiers arrived, Skylar and the other Verde woman had returned to camp, but the braves had remained behind to listen to the soldier talk. The story Captain Haggarty told the Mescalero was considerably different from the one Newsome had related. According to Haggarty, the Rio Alto was enormous, water was plentiful, and food was abundant. He made the reservation sound like the most beautiful place on earth, but the Mescaleros had heard too many lies to be fooled.

When Naka'yen said his people would not go, Haggarty replied that if they did not go willingly, they would be taken in chains. He made other threats, too, which were much more severe. In the end, Naka'yen could do nothing but submit to the will of the army.

Many of his people did not agree with their chief's decision, and that night a war council was held. Consayka and the other Verde braves were invited to attend, and Skylar learned later that many braves favored joining Geronimo. Fortunately, Sun Hawk had not been one of them. Though the order to move was a terrible blow and an outrageous injustice, he had counseled peace.

Consayka believed that some of the braves would steal away in the night, taking their families with them, not caring if they were branded renegades. The younger ones whose blood ran hot were sick of being treated like dogs. To them, dying as warriors seemed preferable to dying as slaves.

Skylar knew that if the braves left, their people would suffer for it, and that saddened her. This move was all so unnecessary. It was also a great blow to her, but she tried not to dwell on the complications the move was obviously going to cause. This morning she had rejoiced because she finally had the means to communicate with her family, but already that fragile thread had been broken. Rescuing her from the Mescalero reservation was proving hard enough; how much more difficult would it be to get her off the Rio Alto, hundreds of miles away in the Arizona Territory?

Skylar waited until her friends had all retired for the night before she began the task of relating the events of the day to Rayna in a letter she dreaded writing. Newsome had promised to post it for her, but she had no assurance that the soldiers or the Rio Alto agent would do her a similar courtesy in the future. Knowing this letter might be the last her family would receive from her, she wanted to tell them everything that had happened to her and assure them she was surviving.

Sitting by the fire in front of her lodge, she wrote page after page. She would have a full day tomorrow striking camp, but she couldn't bring herself to conclude the letter. She wrote long descriptions of the people she had met and the conditions on the reservation. She confessed the difficulties she was having and poked fun at the many mistakes she had made.

"I think you would have been proud of me today, Rayna," she wrote. "When Agent Newsome made his announcement of our impending departure, I stepped to the forefront with the assembled Mescalero leaders and began asking questions. Naturally, my boldness was motivated by self-interest, for I was thinking only of how this move would take me farther away from you, Mother, and Papa.

"Presently, though, I found myself acting as interpreter when Newsome's assistant created a panic among us by inaccurately relaying one of his employer's messages. A tragedy was narrowly averted, and as I think on it now, I am amazed at myself. It is not like me to leap into the fray. That has always been your forte, and I have always been content to stand back and let you fight the battles, even the ones that involved me.

"Could it be that some of your fortitude has transferred itself to me? Truly, I often find myself thinking, What would Rayna do in this instance? My actions can be only a poor imitation of yours, at best, but I cannot deny that I am changing."

She wrote on, losing all track of time, but finally a sense that she was being watched drew her out of the word painting she was creating. Frowning into the darkness, she looked up and saw a dark shape just beyond the rim of firelight. Her pulse quickened, but not out of fear, when she recognized the visitor. Sun Hawk was standing there watching her. With a smile of welcome she beckoned to him, and he came to the fire.

"My Apache father and the other braves are asleep," she told him, keeping her voice low so that she wouldn't disturb anyone in the nearby lodges.

Sun Hawk crouched beside her, careful to keep a respectable distance between them. "I know this. It was you I came to see, but I did not want to startle you as I have in the past."

"I was not startled."

"I know this, too. You are learning."

Skylar found it difficult to hold his gaze and glanced at the fire. "Not quickly enough, I fear."

In the small silence that fell between them, Sun Hawk studied her profile in the dancing firelight and wondered if coming here had been a mistake. It had been a long time since he had spoken to her at the stream and she had solved the mystery of why she seemed so different from the other Verdes. With his curiosity satisfied, Sun Hawk had expected that his fascination with her would end. It had not. If anything, she called to him even more strongly than before.

He had made a pointed effort to stay away from the Verde camp, but that had not erased her from his thoughts. Her beauty haunted him, and the quiet dignity with which she carried herself in her daily struggle to survive touched his heart. Seeing her courageously stand up to Newsome and the others today had increased his respect for her, and he had found it impossible to stay away any longer.

Now, though, seeing her by the fire so composed and so lovely made his heart race and his loins tighten. He had been a fool to come, but he could not bring himself to leave.

Skylar knew he was watching her, and her face grew

warm. "Why are you here?" she asked when she could no longer bear the silence or his intense scrutiny.

Sun Hawk roused himself from his foolish reverie. "To tell you what a good thing you did today. Had you not spoken, some of my people might have been killed," he said, wondering if one of the deities would punish him for the half-truth he told.

"I was happy to do it," she assured him, pulling her gaze away from the fire to his face.

Sun Hawk nodded. He had said what he came to say, and now he should go. But he couldn't. Instead, he gestured toward the letter Skylar had placed on the ground beside her. "What is this?"

She handed him several of the pages. "It is a—" She struggled for an Apache word comparable to "letter," but since the Apache had no written language, there was none that she had ever heard. "A letter," she said finally in English.

"Let-ter," he repeated, looking at the strange marks on the parchment. He had seen paper, of course, and the white man's scratchings, since he was required to make a mark in a book when he received his rations. He had never seen so many scribblings all together, though.

He handed the papers back to her. "Why do you do this?"

"I am talking to my sister, telling her of my life here and that I will soon be at Rio Alto," she explained. "Newsome has promised to send my words to my family so that they will know I am well."

"I saw the agent give you a package today."

Skylar nodded. "This was in it, along with letters from my parents and sister."

Sun Hawk looked at her closely. "I saw it made you cry," he told her, watching for her reaction. "Were the words they sent you sad ones?"

"No," she said, smiling. "My tears were ones of happiness. When I was taken from Rancho Verde, the pain in my father's heart was too much for him and he became ill. When I learned that he had not died, I cried with joy."

Sun Hawk could see the happiness on her face, but strangely, it did not please him. This woman had ties to the white man's world that would never be broken. "Then your white father will come for you soon?"

Skylar's smile faded. "No. General Whitlock, the chief of soldiers, would not release me. Only General Crook can do that now, and my sister is waiting for his answer."

Sun Hawk recognized both names and was surprised by the second one. "Gray Fox has returned?"

"Yes. Do you know him?"

"I have not met him, but I have heard many good things about him. It is said he does not lie, and if he makes a promise he will keep it—even if the promise is made to an Apache."

"I have heard the same thing of him."

Sun Hawk's handsome face hardened into a scowl. "Was Gray Fox the one who said my people must move?"

Skylar thought it over and realized that it was unlikely. "I do not believe so. Newsome said it was the Indian Bureau's order, and Gray Fox has no control over them. He must live with their decisions just as we must." She was pleased to see that his face softened. Clearly he did not want to think ill of General Crook, and she could understand why. In a desperate situation it was a great relief to have at least one person who could be trusted.

"I was told you spoke of peace at the council tonight," she commented, hoping to learn more about his attitudes. She had guessed Sun Hawk to be about thirty years of age, and she was learning that it was unusual to find so much wisdom in one so young. "That was a good thing," she told him.

Sun Hawk looked into the fire. Her praise warmed him, but he was not altogether certain she was right. "Will you say that if our people perish at Rio Alto?" he asked quietly.

She caught a glimpse of his pain and confusion, and was

moved by it. "Do you have doubts about the things you said at the council?" she inquired, her voice soft with sympathy.

It was a moment before he answered. "My friends called me a coward and said I was like an old woman." He looked at her with a touch of defiance. "I am not."

"I know that," she assured him with a gentle smile. "You are wise to counsel peace. There are too many white men and too few Apaches. If you fight, eventually all the Apache will die."

He looked at the fire again. "Some say that dying is better."

"They are wrong."

"My cousin, Dull Knife, believes that if we stand against the soldiers we can drive all the whites out of our land."

"Dull knife is foolish," Skylar said firmly. "I have been to many places far away from here and seen the villages of the white man that stretch farther than the eye can see." She reached down and scooped up a handful of dirt. "Their numbers are many times greater than all the grains of sand on this reservation. For every soldier killed, two more will come to replace him, and four will replace those if they die. The Apache cannot win; they can only survive and learn to live as best they can."

Sun Hawk studied her face as he listened to her words. The images she created were frightening, but he did not doubt her, because the things she said matched his own beliefs. What was surprising was the way she spoke. It was good to find a woman who did not think of him as less than a man because he did not want to fight a battle that could not be won.

"You have much wisdom and knowledge for a woman so young," he told her.

Skylar smiled. "I had thought the same of you."

"I am not young," he replied, and then a teasing light came into his dark eyes. "I only look young to you because everyone in your Apache family is old."

She laughed lightly, and Sun Hawk felt a stirring of desire

so strong that it nearly took his breath away. His good humor vanished. "Where is your man?"

Skylar was astonished by the sternness in his voice. "My man?" she asked, frowning.

"You should have a husband and many children already."

Skylar felt as though she was being scolded, and it irritated her. "I have no husband or children."

"Why not?"

"Because I am an Apache, and no white man has wanted me as a wife."

That made sense. "And no Apache would want you because you have lived among the whites too long to know the things a good wife must know," he added crossly, following the thought to its natural conclusion.

He was right, of course, but Skylar was stung by his blatant rejection of her as a woman no man could possibly want. She knew it in her heart, but hearing someone say it—particularly *this* man—made her feel like the lowest creature that had ever walked on earth. Fighting back tears, she looked into the fire again. "As I said before, you are wise."

Sun Hawk saw the pain he had caused her and regretted it deeply. "It is not your fault," he said, softening his voice.

Skylar couldn't look at him. "Maybe you think it would have been better if the Chiricahua who slaughtered my people had killed me as well."

"Do you think that?" he asked quietly.

Skylar whirled to face him. "No! I have never thought that! Because I lived, I have known the love of very good people. I have laughed with joy, and when I cried there was always someone to comfort me. I have seen beautiful sunrises and thrilled to the sight of a coming storm. My life has been good, and if I must pay for that by living with the sorrow of never having a husband or children, it is a small price to pay for the gift of being alive."

Sun Hawk sat back, startled by her ferocity—and by the way her flash of fire made him feel. But the needs she aroused in him were unwelcome ones. They were not a betrayal of his wife, for he knew he had passed through his time of mourning, but they were wrong feelings nonetheless.

"Then may you live a long life," he said tersely as he rose. Without giving her a chance to respond, he turned and became one with the darkness.

Meade threw the letter onto the table and moved across the room to pour himself another drink. Damn it to hell, why was Rayna Templeton writing to him? He had enough trouble not thinking about her without her harassing him with these constant reminders.

Of course two letters in six weeks didn't exactly constitute harassment, he reminded himself bitterly. Rayna was just being polite, keeping him abreast of her father's continuing progress and her lack of the same in obtaining Skylar's release. Except for her polite expressions of gratitude, there had been nothing terribly personal in either of the letters. She certainly hadn't mentioned the kiss they'd shared.

Unfortunately that hadn't stopped Meade from thinking about it.

He took a long swig of whiskey, but he already knew from experience that it wasn't going to do any good. Eight years at Fort Apache hadn't turned him into an alcoholic, but the memory of that accursed woman just might. Why the devil couldn't he forget about her?

Simple, he told himself. It was because she was a damsel in distress and he was a gentleman who'd been conditioned to lend aid in a crisis. Nothing more. The problem of Skylar Templeton was still unresolved, and until it was, it would weigh on Meade's mind. It was a natural, logical conclusion.

Except that Skylar Templeton wasn't the one who'd caused him more sleepless nights than he could count, and thinking of her sister, Rayna, as a damsel in distress was nothing short of laughable. She was trapped in a mire of frustrating bureaucracy, but she was far from helpless. She was beautiful, yes. And she was fiery, spirited, unladylike, and damned infuriating at times, but helpless? Hardly.

Blast it all, he didn't even like the woman! he tried to tell himself, but of course it was a lie. He admired her spirit and her courage. He respected her loyalty and her deep commitment to her family. He even respected her ability to stand up for herself, and what was worse, he actually missed sparring with her. Too often he found himself smiling for no reason as he thought of something she'd said or of an impudent look she'd given him.

What he thought about at night, though, was the passionate kiss they'd shared. The memory made him ache with the most ferocious need he'd ever experienced. There were places he could go to assuage that need, of course, but Meade couldn't bring himself to seek the services of a whore. As a physician, he knew the hazards only too well, but if it would have obliterated his obsession with Rayna Templeton, he might have been willing to take the risk.

That wasn't likely, though, and Meade had deep distaste for the base behavior he'd witnessed in so many of his colleagues and subordinates. He'd heard too many men boasting of their prowess with the camp followers who plied their trade in wagons just outside Fort Apache. The thought of paying for sexual favors didn't appeal to him, and over the years he had disciplined himself to shut out unwanted desires.

But Rayna refused to be locked out of his mind, and she was wreaking merry hell on his body.

Angry and frustrated, Meade stalked across the room and retrieved her letter. "As you can imagine," she had written, "this long wait without word from General Crook has taken its toll on all of us, but in some ways I am more fortunate than Mother and Papa. I, at least, can busy myself with the daily concerns of running the ranch. Only the great volume of paperwork daunts me, for I much prefer riding the range to being confined in Papa's study. However, I'm sure this unladylike attitude comes as no surprise to you."

Meade could envision her teasing smile as clearly as if she had been in the room with him. She would have bowed her head slightly and slanted a glance at him. Her eyes would have sparkled with mischief as she tweaked him, and then she would have waited expectantly for his tart reply—which he would have given, if only to keep himself from kissing that delightful smile away.

Groaning with frustration, Meade stomped into the kitchen where the coals on the hearth were just beginning to wane. Furious at his lack of control, he threw the letter into the fireplace, but before it had even begun to singe, he snatched the letter back, folded it, returned to the parlor. His personal journal was on the reading table by his chair, and he jerked at the leather band that held it together and shoved the letter into the back . . . right alongside the first one Rayna had sent him.

Chapter Ten

"MY, MY, WILL ya take a look at that, gents?" Private Andy Norris said, giving his comrades his best hoity-toity impersonation. "I do believe I see me some rich Apaches comin' our way."

The small cluster of soldiers looked in the direction Norris pointed. What they saw wouldn't have been impressive anywhere but on a reservation. In the midst of the long procession of Mescaleros straggling in to the agency on foot was a group mounted on fine horses and riding alongside two wagons. One of the wagons was even covered with a canvas canopy that swayed drunkenly as it bounced along.

"Well, fancy that," Stan Talbot said. "Come on, boys, we'd better check this out. Lieutenant Zaranski said we was to make sure these heathens didn't bring in no moonshine or no"—he drew himself up in imitation of the snooty lieutenant—"contraband. Apaches this rich prob'ly got lots of that."

"Hell, Stan, you don't even know what conterband is," Norris snorted, poking his buddy in the ribs.

Talbot's grin betrayed the loss of his two front teeth. "That don't mean I cain't look for it, does it?" He turned to the other men in the detail that had been assigned to search the incoming "hostiles." "You boys stay here and keep lookin' through the bundles. Me an' Andy is gonna check out them wagons."

"Who died and made you general?" one of the men asked

irritably, but Talbot ignored him. He and Norris walked down the line of Apaches toward the slow-moving wagons.

"Whew, boy! Would you get a load o' that squaw," Talbot crowed when they'd gotten a little closer.

"Where?" Norris asked, looking around.

"Boy, you been in the sun too long. Your eyes is plum gone. Lookee there, sittin' up front on the first wagon. If that ain't the prettiest Injun I ever saw, I'll eat my boots."

"Yeah? What're you gonna use to chew 'em with?" Norris said, then guffawed at the good one he'd gotten off on his friend.

Talbot shot his friend a mean glance. "Jest fer that, I ain't gonna share when I get me a piece of that squaw."

"You're the one who's been in the sun too long," Norris said with disgust. "Ain't nothin' could make me dive 'tween the legs of no Apache."

"Boy, you don't know what you're missin'! A good squaw is about the best there is. No other woman in the world can buck like an Apache. You just wait an' see. After another week on the trail, they'll start lookin' real good to you."

Quickening his pace, he hurried the final distance toward the wagon. The riders flanking the wagon shied out of his way but stayed close enough to protect their women and belongings.

"Hey, you! Injun! Where'd you steal them wagons and horses?" Talbot shouted up at Joe Long Horn, who was driving the team.

"The wagons were not stolen. They belong to Miss Skylar, and the horses are our own."

Talbot hooted with laughter. "Well, how about that. Didja hear, Andy? We got ourselves an Injun who speaks English better'n you do."

"Zat right?"

"Yep." It took only a slow walk to keep pace with the wagon, and Talbot looked up at Skylar. "What about you, squaw? You speak English, too?"

It was broad daylight, there were several hundred Mesca-leros within shouting distance and at least half that many soldiers, but for the first time since she'd arrived at the reservation, Skylar was truly frightened. It wasn't a vague fear of the unknown or concern for her father or any of the other emotions that she had called fear in the past few months. She had seen this man and his friend coming; she had seen the way one of them looked at her. What she felt was a genuine fear for her life.

It was everything she could do to keep her voice calm and even. "Yes, Private. I do speak English. Mr. Long Horn was correct when he told you that these vehicles and animals be-long to us."

Talbot whooped again. "Whew, boy, don't you talk pretty. *Mr. Long Horn*, la-di-da. I guess that must make you *Miss Skylar*."

"That's right," she answered quietly.

"Well, tell this buck to stop the wagon, 'cause Norris an' me gotta search it."

"Why?" Skylar asked, but Joe pulled the team to a halt and whispered, "We must do as he says, miss. Let him search so that he can go about his business."

"Climb on down from there, you two," Talbot ordered as he circled to the rear of the wagon. "And tell these old women to get out, too!"

There was no need to translate, of course, and everyone began climbing down. Talbot ordered Norris to get in the wagon and search the bundles while he gave the women a cursory once-over.

"Nothin' in here but some food and clothes," Norris said as he glanced through the bundles.

"Well, keep lookin'. They gotta have some conterband somewheres." He moved back to the front of the wagon and leered down at Skylar. "Ain't that right, *Miss Skylar*?"

She suppressed a shudder. "We have nothing illegal or forbidden with us."

"I'd like to see that for myself if you don't mind," he said, grabbing her arm and pulling her roughly toward him. In an instant he was groping at her breasts under the pretext of conducting a search. As Skylar struggled against him, Joe tried to insert himself between her and the soldier.

"Let her go!" Joe demanded.

Talbot gave him a shove that sent him into the dirt. "Keep yer hands off me, you stinkin' Apache. Andy, get your butt down here and help me search this squaw!"

But his friend didn't comply. He was frozen by the sight of the dozen mounted Apaches who had closed in on the wagon. "Stan, you better quit that right now. We got trouble," he said as one ancient old man urged his horse toward Talbot.

"Let her go," Consayka ordered.

His voice was soft and cracked with age, but there was no denying the power of it. Startled, Talbot looked around and realized he was outnumbered. With one hand dug tightly into Skylar's arm, he whipped out his revolver and pointed at the old man. "You get yourself and these braves back, old man, or you're gonna be a dead Injun."

"When you let her go, we will move. You cannot kill all of us."

The commotion had drawn considerable attention from the other Apaches, and even more were gathering around the wagon. Talbot saw his life passing before his eyes, but he was too cussed stubborn to give in. He raised the gun and pointed it at Consayka's heart.

With a strangled cry, Skylar lunged for the gun, trying to shove it upward. Her movement set them both off balance, and Talbot fell heavily against the wagon. His gun discharged in the air, and the horses shied away. A second later Talbot heard the thundering charge of horses approaching, and he cast Skylar away from him, pushing her so hard that she fell to the ground.

"Make way! Make way!" someone ordered, and the Mescaleros scattered as a half-dozen cavalrymen charged

through them. Only Consayka and the Verdes held their
ground.

"Private, what's going on here?" Lieutenant Zaranski demanded, gun drawn as he glared down at the soldier.

"Norris and me was searchin' this wagon just like you ordered, an' these Apaches tried to bushwhack us."

"That's a lie," Skylar said, her voice trembling with anger
and the remnants of her fear.

"I beg your pardon?" Zaranski said, looking around to see
who had spoken.

Skylar stumbled to her feet and stepped toward him. "I
said that man is lying," she repeated. "He was using the
search of this wagon as an excuse to assault me. My friends
were only trying to protect me."

Zaranski stared down at her with a combination of be-
musement and irritation. If he hadn't known better, he'd
have thought himself in some grand lady's parlor in Phila-
delphia. "You speak English."

Skylar sighed heavily. "That's right, Lieutenant. And so
do all of the Mescaleros you see here."

Zaranski nodded. "Ah, you must be the Apaches from
Rancho Verde that Mr. Newsome was telling me about."

"That's right."

"And you're the one Newsome uses as an interpreter, isn't
that correct?" he asked.

"I have acted in that capacity, yes," Skylar replied.

"Well, we have our own interpreter, so don't expect any
special treatment," he said somewhat haughtily.

"We have asked for none," Skylar said tightly. "But we do
not expect to be singled out and abused, either."

Zaranski wasn't sure how to respond to that, so he looked
at Consayka. "Are you the chief of this band?"

"Yes."

"Well, get them loaded up and join the others. Everyone
with horses will be allowed to keep them, but you'll have to
be responsible for feeding and watering them yourselves.

When it comes to forage, remember that the army's livestock comes first. Understood?"

Consayka nodded. "We understand. Are you going to punish the soldier who attacked my daughter?"

Zaranski looked at Talbot, who had slowly edged away from the circle of Indians. "I believe Private Talbot has learned his lesson. Have a care in dealing with these people, Private," he warned lightly. "We don't want any more mis-understandings."

"Yes, sir."

The lieutenant looked at the soldier on his right. "Sergeant, get these people moving again." With that, Zaranski wheeled his horse and returned to the agency headquarters. The sergeant's command to load up came a little late, since the Verdes had all started climbing back into the wagon.

Still trembling from her disgusting encounter with Talbot, Skylar gingerly fingered the darkening bruises on her arm and tried to ignore the similar pain in her breasts. "That will happen again, won't it?" she asked Joe quietly, too embar-rassed to look at him.

He kept his eyes straight forward as he urged the mules into motion. "You should never go anywhere alone until we reach Rio Alto," he advised.

It was good advice, but it was less than reassuring. If Tal-bot or someone like him wanted to have his way with any of the Mescalero women, a witness or two wouldn't stop him. Any of the soldiers could kill an Apache, claim self-defense, and be heralded as a hero. Conversely, any Apache who tried to defend himself or herself would be shot without question.

Sickened by the injustice of a situation she couldn't change or control, Skylar glanced at the growing number of Mescaleros gathered at the agency. When she saw Sun Hawk looking at her, his face set into a hard, unreadable mask of marble, she looked away, too humiliated to hold his gaze.

She didn't see that his hands were clasped in barely con-trolled rage.

* * *

It took most of the day to count the four hundred Mescaleros and get them on the trail. Captain Haggarty, commander of the cavalry detail charged with moving the Apaches, was anxious to get on his way despite the fact that more than a dozen braves and several of their women were missing. He wasted no time looking for them, since they were undoubtedly long gone, probably making their way to Mexico.

Before they moved out, Skylar was able to place her letter to her family in Newsome's hands, and he promised to post it as soon as possible. What she considered truly miraculous, though, was that he had quietly given her the balance of the money Rayna had sent to him as a consideration for handling Skylar's correspondence. It wasn't much, but it could come in handy.

They were less than ten miles from the western boundary of the reservation when they made camp for the night. Some of the soldiers erected tents, but there was no shelter for the Mescalero. They spread out as much as the soldiers would allow and built their fires.

The huge sea of humanity hemmed in like animals in a pen sickened Skylar, but she did her share of the work as always. Though fetching water was considered woman's work, Joe Long Horn and the other braves accompanied the women to and from the nearby stream. No one commented on it, but Skylar knew they were hoping their numbers would prevent a repeat of this morning's attack. Fortunately the soldiers kept their distance, and Skylar was relieved that she didn't spot Talbot all evening.

When darkness came, the camp fell silent, the quiet punctuated only by the occasional wail of an infant or the abrupt bark of a laughing soldier. Conversations around the campfire were hushed, and nearly all of the Mescaleros laid out their blankets early and tried to sleep.

Skylar made her bed alongside Gatana, but before they could retire, a shifting shadow that Skylar recognized instantly as Sun Hawk approached stealthily and crouched in front of Consayka.

Skylar studied his face in the light of the fire and found it
as unreadable as it had been moments after Talbot's assault
on her.

"For your daughter," Sun Hawk said, handing a long
leather-bound object to Consayka.

The old man examined it and pulled on both ends. A flash
of steel glinted in the waning firelight.

"Enju," Consayka said. It is good.

He handed the gift to Skylar, and she realized that it was a
wicked-looking knife in a Mescalero-made leather scabbard.
Long laces, presumably to be tied around her waist, dangled
from the sheath.

Astonished by the gift, she looked up and found Sun
Hawk's eyes boring into hers.

"For the next soldier who touches you," he said, his voice
hard and hushed.

Before she could reply, he was gone.

The next morning when they broke camp and moved out,
their train formed a wide, straggling line more than a mile
long, with soldiers in the front and the rear, and a number
who rode back and forth in pairs among the Mescaleros. As
before, the Verdes on horseback flanked the wagons, but
Skylar noticed that today Sun Hawk's family was traveling
close to hers.

Coincidence? she wondered. Or did the brave's presence
have something to do with the knife hidden beneath her long
overblouse? He never seemed to look in her direction, but
was always in view.

There could be no doubt that he was concerned about her;
otherwise he never would have given her a means of protecting herself. After his brutally honest assessment of her by
the fire, his show of concern was both surprising and touching. In one way, Skylar took great comfort from his nearness, but it also worried her. Was he planning some timely
rescue of her if Talbot came back? If so, he was signing his

own death warrant, and the same would be true of anyone else who might try to help her.

Fortunately the first day passed without incident, but by the end of it, Skylar was more exhausted than she had ever been in her life. Knowing that food and water for their animals would be scarce, the Verdes walked more often than they rode, hoping to tax the mules and horses as little as possible. The elders took turns riding in the wagon, but Skylar stayed afoot most of the day. By the time they made camp for the night her moccasins were in shreds and her feet were bruised and bleeding. Before she could retire for the night, she had no choice but to repair them.

With so many others in similar straits, Skylar removed the canvas canopy from the wagon and divided it among her friends. She put aside one large piece, and after mending her moccasins, she quietly made her way to Naka'yen's camp, adjacent to that of the Verdes. Not caring about the propriety of her act or the questioning eyes that bored into her, she approached Sun Hawk and handed him the canvas.

"One gift deserves another," she told him, meeting his surprised gaze boldly.

A pleased smile teased the corners of his mouth. "Your kindness will be remembered."

"As will yours," she replied, then turned and went back to her Apache family.

Puzzled by the exchange, Naka'yen watched her go. He glanced at Sun Hawk and frowned. He had not seen such a tender expression on his son's face in a very long time.

"We traveled with the Verdes today," the old man said matter-of-factly.

Sun Hawk forced himself to look away from the Verde camp. "Yes, we did."

Naka'yen searched his son's face. "Why did you insist on it?"

His father's scrutiny embarrassed him. "We had to walk someplace. That seemed as good as any."

"It had nothing to do with the white soldier's attack on Consayka's daughter?"

"No."

"Are you sure?"

Sun Hawk sighed with exasperation. "You ask too many questions, Father."

Naka'yen shook his head. "And you do not ask enough. You are not thinking with your head. That girl is not one of us."

"But she is learning, Father," he argued, wondering why he was defending her.

"This is true. She is a hard worker, and she does many things to take care of her elders. It is clear she has a good heart, but you told me that she longs to return to the whites who raised her."

Sun Hawk clenched his fists, collecting a handful of useless dirt. "Why do you say these things to me? I do not care if she goes back to her people."

Naka'yen fell silent a moment, looking him over, and Sun Hawk prayed that the discussion would end. It did not.

"Where is your knife?" the old chief asked, looking down at the sheathed blade at his son's waist. "Not that one, but the one you took many years ago in your first battle against the Mexican soldiers?"

Disgusted, Sun Hawk tossed away his handful of dirt and jumped up. "I told you, Father, you ask too many questions," he said harshly, then gathered up his belongings and moved to the opposite edge of the camp, as far away from his father—and the Verdes—as he could get.

The next day, Skylar saw Talbot again. He was riding with Norris as part of the detail that swept through the Mescaleros several times a day to hurry them along and make certain no trouble was brewing.

Skylar knew that it had to be a tense job for them, outnumbered as they were by so many Apaches, but she couldn't bring herself to feel sympathy for any of them—particularly

Talbot. She was easy for him to spot because she stayed close to the wagon, and with his first pass through the slow-moving crowd, he drew his horse alongside her and stared down at her for a short time that seemed like hours to Skylar. She didn't acknowledge him with so much as a glance, and he didn't say a word. There were no threatening gestures, no posturing . . . but he made his presence known and his intentions clear.

He sought her out on his return pass and twice again that afternoon. The tension he created was almost more than Skylar could bear, for it went beyond her own jangled nerves. Whenever Talbot approached, all the Verdes became watchful, alert for any sign of trouble. When he passed on, Skylar invariably saw that Sun Hawk, too, had drifted a little closer to the wagon, but he never made an effort to speak with her or even acknowledge her presence.

The encounters with Talbot became a daily ritual, but repetition didn't make them any less unnerving.

By the end of the first week as they reached the rugged trail that led through the Caliente Mountains, the forced march had become a grueling test of endurance. The heat was fearsome, rations were scarce, and water was even more so. On the seventh day, word circulated among them that an old woman had died. A detail of soldiers stayed behind while her family buried her in a shallow grave along with all her worldly possessions. In less than an hour the mourners rejoined the main body of the procession.

That night they made camp near a tributary of the Gila River, and for the first time since they had crossed the Rio Grande, there was enough water for all to drink their fill and ample grazing for the animals. There were even trees for firewood in the glade where they made camp. Captain Haggarty announced to Naka'yen that they would stay there for two nights to allow them to "recuperate" before they began the difficult trek through the Calientes.

The Mescaleros were too weary to rejoice, but Skylar noticed a subtle difference in their demeanor that night. They were able to build fires for the first time in days, and the next morning the women took advantage of the opportunity to wash clothing and bathe. This they accomplished by entering the cool, swift river fully clothed, for soldiers had been assigned to patrol up and down the irregular banks because the rugged terrain hid the river from view of the camp.

Even the men had a great deal to do that day, but Joe Long Horn and several others took the time to escort the Verde women to the river near midday. They were all keenly aware of the isolation on the trail, but once they reached the hill overlooking the stream, the number of women grouped in small pockets up and down the banks made Joe feel it was safe to leave Skylar and the others alone. They left with a promise to return shortly.

At first, Skylar felt perfectly safe, but as she and Gatana picked their way through the rocks to the edge of the stream, she realized that the area was more isolated than it had appeared from above. The soldiers were widely scattered, and occasionally she heard one of them in the distance shouting to the women in the water. Once, she looked upstream and saw a soldier standing on a rock overhead, holding out a string of beads. She couldn't hear what he was saying, but his posture and his crude gestures made it clear that he was trying to trade sexual favors for the paltry trinket.

Thoroughly disgusted, Skylar returned to her bathing. Despite the restriction of her clothes, the water felt better than she had imagined anything could feel. It was shallow and swift in many places, but she found a pool deep enough to sit down in, and she let the current wash over her, cooling her skin and rinsing away the stench of the journey. She longed to strip off her overblouse and skirt, but nothing in the world could have made her do something so foolish. Instead, she lived with the limitations, enjoying every second of this respite from weariness.

Unfortunately her pleasure died a violent death when she looked up and saw Talbot and Norris conversing with the soldiers who had been patrolling this section of the stream when Skylar arrived. After a moment the first two disappeared back up the trail, leaving Talbot and Norris alone on a craggy shelf above the stream.

The changing of the guard? Skylar wondered, fighting down a sense of panic. Or had her tormentor merely traded places with his comrades because he'd seen her coming down the trail?

It really didn't matter. Skylar knew that she could be in for trouble. To her surprise, Talbot made no effort to climb down to the stream. What he did, instead, proved almost as bad, though. Like the other soldiers she'd heard upstream, he began shouting lurid comments at her. While she was in the water, he shouted in vivid detail the things he wanted to do to her. Skylar never acknowledged him with so much as a look, and certainly none of the soldiers paid any attention—if they heard him at all.

Skylar scrubbed her dress as best she could with it on her, but eventually she had to return to the bank to get the other clothes she had brought to wash. Gatana stayed with her as they knelt on the rocky bed near the shore, and Talbot finally came down from his perch above. Norris stayed where he was, taking advantage of his bird's-eye view of the river, but the two men still talked back and forth. Or perhaps "argued" would have been a better term for it, since they were debating the issue of sex with white women versus sex with Apaches.

Though Norris was opposed to the latter, Talbot took great pleasure in proudly relating tales about the Apache women he had "had." The word "rape" was never used, of course, because taking an Indian against her will wasn't considered a violent attack and an offense to human decency. Apaches weren't human, so where was the harm?

Though Skylar tried to shut out his words, which she knew were directed totally at her, she had no language barrier to insulate her from his disgusting barrage. His constant verbal assault made her feel nauseated and weak, and the harder she tried to ignore him, the more abusive he became.

Soon her hands were shaking so hard that she couldn't hold the calico overblouse she'd been trying to scrub against the rocks.

"I cannot stand this any longer," she said softly to Gatana. "I've got to get out of here. Perhaps if I complained to Captain Haggarty . . ."

Gatana kept her head low, not looking up from her washing. "It would do no good, daughter," she replied. "Finish what you are doing and we will go back to the camp. Joe will come for us soon."

Collecting her wits, Skylar did the best she could with her clothes and wrung them out. She had volunteered to wash Tsa'kata's things as well, so the bundle she gathered up when she had finished was a large one. Gatana assembled her own clothes and Consayka's, and they looked around for Joe, but he was nowhere to be seen. Desperate to escape, they looked for someone else who was ready to walk back to camp and spotted Naka'yen's wife and two daughters gathering their things.

Moving downstream, fighting the slippery rocks and current, they tried to hurry toward them.

"Done so soon?" Talbot asked, splashing into the water to catch up with them. "But you didn't take a good an' proper bath, *Miss Skylar*."

"Stan, don't," Norris called after him, but the river swallowed his voice.

The water deepened, forcing Skylar and Gatana onto the shore, and Talbot stayed with them as they moved along the jutting inlets and crags that bordered the stream.

"What's your hurry, squaw?" Talbot asked, leering down at Skylar. "I been waiting a long time for this."

"Leave us alone," Gatana ordered, but Talbot only laughed and ignored her.

"I'll bet them clothes is heavy, ain't they, Miss Skylar? Here, let me give you a hand." He snatched at the bundle in her arms, deliberately knocking it to the ground. "Oh, ain't that too bad."

"Stop it! Get away from me," Skylar demanded as she knelt to pick up the clothes. Gatana stooped to help her, and Talbot squatted beside them.

"I'm sure sorry, ma'am. I am a clumsy oaf. That's what my mama always used to tell me, an' she was right," he said, plucking the garments out of her hands as quickly as she could pick them up.

Trying to quell her trembling, Skylar looked downstream to where Naka'yen's family had been moments ago. There was no one in sight now, and panic washed through her.

"If you're lookin' for help, squaw, ain't none gonna come," he said gleefully.

"Get away from me, you foul-mouthed pig!" she said angrily, darting a glance over her shoulder, looking for anyone who might come to her aid, but a huge boulder blocked them from the view of the women and soldiers upstream.

"Ooh-ee, I found me a squaw with a mean temper," he crowed, grabbing her as she tried to rise.

"Let me go!" she screamed. "Someone help—"

Talbot clamped his hand across her mouth, and Gatana lurched toward him, pushing with one hand on his shoulder while using the other to try to pull Skylar out of his grasp. She shouted for help, but her cry was silenced abruptly when he planted his fist in Gatana's face. She fell back, cracking her head against a rock, and lay still.

"Gatana!" Skylar struggled to reach her, but Talbot's hold was unbreakable. "You pig, let me go. She's hurt!"

Talbot slapped her across the face, bringing tears to her eyes, but somewhere inside her a wellspring of courage bolstered her and she glared at the private. "You're not going to hurt me here, you bastard. There are too many people."

"What people?" he asked, digging his fingers into one of her breasts. "Ain't none o' them Apaches gonna come to help you, an' none o' my buddies is gonna stop me, either, squaw. They all want a piece o' you, too."

Frantically, Skylar groped for the knife beneath her

blouse, but it eluded her as Talbot began struggling to get to his feet, jerking her up with him.

"Come on, squaw. You and me are going to find someplace quiet. I got me a nice little spot already picked out in them rocks up there."

He pulled her up, and the movement freed Skylar's right hand. Too panicked to think, she groped for Sun Hawk's knife again, and this time she found it. It slipped loose from the scabbard, and as soon as she had sure footing on the rough ground, she slashed at Talbot's arm.

With a yowl of pain and surprise, he let her go and whirled toward her. "You dumb bitch squaw! You cut me!"

Keeping the knife extended between them, her eyes wild with fear, she began backing away. "If you come near me again, I'll kill you."

"Why you—" His wounded hand moved toward his revolver, and Skylar realized that if he reached the gun, he would kill her.

"No!" She lunged forward, slashing at him with the knife, and Talbot instinctively made a grab for her arm. When he missed, she slashed again, and this time he went for his gun. Desperate, she thrust the knife at him, and Talbot lurched back, losing his footing in the rocks. As he grappled for balance, he pitched forward and knocked Skylar to the ground.

She cried out in pain as his weight forced her down, pinning her on the jagged rocks. A wave of nausea coursed through her and she pushed at him while her feet clawed at the rocks, seeking purchase that would help her escape. She shoved at his shoulders, and when he finally fell away, she scrambled back.

But Talbot didn't move. A dark, wet stain was spreading across his shirt, radiating from the knife, which had been driven to the hilt into his heart.

Sun Hawk looked around the Verde encampment, frowning. Consayka and the braves were there, but he saw only a few women. Obviously they had gone to the river.

Sun Hawk cursed himself as he moved off along the trail that led to the water. He should not be worrying about Skylar. If her family did not feel obliged to protect her, neither should he, but he couldn't keep himself from going after her despite the other problem that weighed heavily on his mind.

Hacké'tisan's wife had become ill, and her husband had asked for prayers to be spoken over her. Sun Hawk had not been able to refuse, but he doubted the song he had sung to drive the fever out of her body was going to work. He had seen the fever before; it was the same one that had killed his wife, his sons, and many others. If he was right and the fever was spreading through camp, hundreds of his people might never live to see Rio Alto.

His concern for Hacké'tisan's wife warred with his fear for Skylar's safety, but that was foolish. She was not even one of his people. He should not be thinking about her at a time like this. He had sent Klo'sen to fetch the soldiers' medicine man, and Sun Hawk knew he should have been scouring the camp for others who might be ill. He had no time to chase down a woman who was not his and whose life and welfare were not his problem.

That didn't stop him from hurrying down the trail.

He was only halfway up the hill when the first group of soldiers appeared above him, dragging Skylar between them. Her wrists were bound, her face was wet with tears, and blood stained the front of her dress. A few paces behind, more soldiers were carrying the body of Talbot.

Skylar was speaking desperately to her captors, but Sun Hawk couldn't have understood her words even if he had been close enough. He didn't need to know what she was saying. It was clear to him that she was telling the soldiers that Talbot had attacked her and that she had defended herself. But Talbot's friend was also there, shouting her down, pointing and accusing.

If Skylar and the cavalryman told different stories, as it

appeared they did, Sun Hawk knew the soldier would be believed.

Knowing he could not help her, Sun Hawk vanished into the trees and rocks, making his way back to the camp. His mind was racing, and his blood burned with rage.

Skylar was an Apache. She had killed a soldier. There wasn't a doubt in Sun Hawk's mind that the white men would take her life for it.

And he was the one who had given her the knife.

Chapter Eleven

THE DARK CLOUDS gathering over the Datil Mountains
warned Rayna of an approaching thunderstorm. The weather
was always fickle in New Mexico; clouds promised rain and
then evaporated like will-o'-the-wisps, but late September
was the worst. The summer drought ended, and when the
rains came, they were torrential downpours that turned
streams into rivers, flooded dry creek beds, and transformed
certain ravines into death traps.

Dead Man's Wash was one of them, and it was Rayna's
misfortune to have found a knot of skittish cattle in the arroyo as she'd been making her way back to the ranch. For
her own safety, she wanted to beat the storm home, but she
couldn't leave the small herd to perish. Kicking Samson into
motion, she used her coiled lariat to hurry them along, determined to get the stubborn cows to safety before they died of
their own stupidity and took her with them.

Long before she reached higher ground thunder was rum-
bling and lightning was dancing in the distance. Dark clouds
were spreading like spilled ink, and she could already hear
her father teasing her about not having the sense to come in
out of the rain. Finally, though, she reached a gently sloping
bank and managed to guide the herd up it. She scattered
them with a loud "Eee-ya!" and urged Samson into a gallop
toward home.

A few minutes later she was charging into the ranch yard
with lightning nipping at her heels. Gil Rodriguez was outside the stable, grinning at her.

"You are still trying to outrun the thunder, Señorita Rayna?" Gil asked with a smile as she dismounted. "I thought you had stopped playing that game."

She grinned at him. "I like to keep in practice every now and then."

Gil reached for Samson's reins. "Here, Señorita. I will take care of him."

"That's all right, Gil. I lathered him up, I can cool him down."

His smile faded. "Let me, please. You must go to the house now. Your mother has been asking for you."

Rayna's heart tripped in alarm. "Is Papa—"

"No, no," he assured her hurriedly. "But Flint went into Malaventura to pick up supplies this morning and there was a letter from Señorita Skylar."

"Thank God," Rayna murmured, her face wreathed with a brilliant smile as she tossed Samson's reins to Gil and dashed to the house. She was too excited to wonder why Gil hadn't been happier about the news, but the chaos she found inside dashed her buoyant spirits.

"Raymond, you can't! I forbid it!"

"Damn it all, Collie. I'm not sitting still for this any longer. By God, I'm going to take Sam Whitlock apart piece by piece if he doesn't do something about this!"

The voices were coming from the upper balcony, and Rayna looked up to find her father stalking down the gallery and Collie scurrying after him as they moved toward the room they had shared before his illness. Just the fact that he was up there was terrifying, for he was still too weak to be navigating the long flight of stairs.

"Papa, what's going on?" Rayna demanded, taking the stairs two at a time.

"I'm going to Santa Fe!" he roared, almost drowning out the rumble of thunder overhead.

"You can't do that!" she protested.

"The hell I can't!"

Rayna ran down the gallery and caught up with them just

as they entered the room where only Collie had been sleeping for the last two months. "Tell me what's happened, damn it! Gil said there was a letter from Skylar. What did she say? What's wrong?"

"Hellfire, Collie, where are my shirts?" he snapped, throwing open the armoire. "And get me a carpetbag."

"I will not! I'm not going to let you kill yourself!"

"Damn it! Tell me what's going on!" Rayna roared, startling both her parents.

Collie looked at her daughter. "Skylar isn't on the Mescalero reservation any longer."

Rayna knew that what should have been good news actually wasn't. "Where is she?"

"The goddam Indian Bureau closed the reservation and is sending the Mescaleros to the Rio Alto agency in Arizona," Raymond answered.

"Oh, my God," Rayna muttered, her heart skipping a full beat. "When? When is she going?"

Collie wrung her hands together. "She's already gone. Her letter was posted a week ago, the day after she left the reservation." She dug into the pocket of her skirt and handed a thick packet to her. "Skylar wrote letters to us all."

Rayna took the packet of letters gingerly, as though it was something precious to be treasured and handled with the greatest care. As, of course, it was. "Is she well?"

"Yes," her mother replied. "The work of daily living is very hard, but she is surviving. Consayka and Gatana have taken her under their wing."

That wasn't at all unexpected. As much as Rayna wanted to devour Skylar's letter, there was a more important consideration now that she had the facts. Her father was still tearing through his wardrobe and had already tossed his best suit carelessly onto the bed. "Papa, you can't go to Santa Fe."

"Oh, but I can and will, missy," he argued. "I'm going to get my little princess back if it's the last thing I do in this world."

Collie moved to him. "If you go to Santa Fe, that's exactly

what it will be." She grabbed his arm and looked up at him imploringly. "Raymond, please. General Whitlock has already said there's nothing he can do."

"Well, maybe I can change his mind. Crook certainly isn't helping us. It's been six weeks, and we've written him three letters in that time!" He shook off Collie's hand. "I'm sick and tired of waiting around here like a crippled old maid. I'm going to see Whitlock, and there's not a damned thing you can say to change my mind. Now, where the hell is that carpetbag?"

As Rayna and Collie exchanged helpless looks, Raymond charged across the room to his wife's armoire. He snatched the bag from the floor, but as he straightened and whirled around, the room began spinning faster than he did. A gray film blurred his vision, a prickle of pain spread through his chest, and before he fully understood what was happening to him, his wife and daughter were flanking him, leading him to the bed. He sat heavily, his breath coming in heavy pants.

"Dam . . . nation," he gasped as Collie gently guided him back onto the pillows. Rayna lifted his feet and pulled a coverlet over his legs. "Hang . . . it all, I'm not . . . cold," he groused.

"Be quiet," Collie said sternly, torn between anger and fear. "Just rest. This will pass. Please, God, let it pass."

"Papa, you have to take care of yourself." Rayna slipped around the bed and sat next to him.

"But Skylar—"

She took his hand. "I'll handle it," she vowed solemnly. "I'll go to Whitlock again and get down on my knees and beg if I have to, but I *will* find a way to get Skylar back."

Raymond closed his eyes tightly, and the tears that pooled in the corners nearly broke Rayna's heart. "My poor princess," he muttered, his strength fading to nothingness. "She's so far away."

"But not for long, Papa," Rayna promised. She patted his hand and let it go, then hurried out of the room and down the gallery to her own. The storm had arrived, and sheets of rain were washing through the courtyard like waves pounding onto a beach, but Rayna ignored the downpour. Hastily she removed her own carpetbag from the wardrobe and began selecting clothes.

Whitlock wouldn't be able—or willing—to help her. She already knew that, but she would try for her father's sake. It was the first and most logical step to take. And when that failed . . .

A plan had already begun forming in Rayna's mind. It was only a vague shape with rough edges, but it was a plan nonetheless. It was dangerous. It was probably even foolhardy. But if no one in the United States Army would help her, she had no choice but to take matters into her own hands.

Though she ached to read Skylar's letter, she packed first and then washed away the trail dirt she had accumulated that morning. By the time her mother came looking for her, Rayna was dressed for travel and the storm was beginning to abate.

"How is he?" she asked as Collie came into her bedchamber.

"Sleeping."

"Is he in pain?"

Collie swallowed hard. "He says not, but I don't know that I believe him."

Rayna went to her, and they hugged each other tightly. "It will be all right, Mother. I'll talk to Whitlock and make him see reason."

"And if you fail?"

Rayna released her and stepped away. This was going to be the hardest part. "Mother, if Whitlock won't do anything . . . I'll go to Arizona and find Crook myself."

Collie was stunned. And frightened. "Rayna, that's too dangerous. You can't make a trip like that alone," she said desperately.

"I don't care!" Rayna retorted as her temper flared again. "I'm sick to death of being helpless, and by God if Crook won't do anything, I'll snatch Skylar away from that damned reservation myself!"

Flanked by two soldiers, with four more stationed around the perimeter of the command tent, Skylar stood in front of Captain Haggarty's desk fighting back hysterical laughter that had nothing to do with humor. She was frustrated and terrified because no one believed her story. She had killed a soldier, and Haggarty wasn't the least bit interested in hearing the truth. In his mind, he had captured a dangerous renegade, and as near as Skylar could tell, his only concern was whether or not he would eventually be able to persuade his superiors to hang a woman.

The soldiers had been at this for hours, dragging her in front of Haggarty for questioning, then shackling her to a wagon outside while the captain thought up new questions. The one he had just asked her—why she had ambushed Talbot—was an old one, though.

"I have told you again and again, Captain, I did not ambush him. He attacked me and dragged me into the rocks, where he made it clear that he intended to rape me. My only thought was to keep him at bay until I could escape, but he lunged at me and fell on the knife!"

"That's not the story Private Norris tells," Haggarty replied. "According to him, you enticed Talbot away from his post and attacked him without provocation."

"Norris is lying!"

"He is a valued member of the United States Army," the captain said arrogantly.

Skylar shook her head. "That doesn't change the fact that he's lying to protect the reputation of his friend—and to save his own skin. Talbot attacked me, and Norris did nothing to prevent it."

"So you've said before," Haggarty replied with a dismissive wave of his hand. "Tell me, where did you get the knife you used on Talbot?"

This was a new question, but it was one Skylar didn't

want to answer. "That type of weapon is not forbidden to us, Captain," she said evasively. She was in enough trouble as it was; bringing Sun Hawk into the picture wouldn't do anyone a bit of good. "A knife is considered essential to survival on the reservation."

Haggarty picked up the bloodstained knife and the leather sheath they had taken off Skylar. "True enough. A brave needs a knife for killing and skinning game. But as I recall, you were searched thoroughly when you came into the agency, and nothing like this was found."

Skylar could hardly deny it. "That's true."

"Then where did you acquire the knife? This is an exceptionally fine weapon—certainly not Apache made. Ergo, it must have been stolen."

"Have any of your soldiers reported a knife missing that matches the description of that one?" she challenged.

He paused a moment, his weathered face furrowed into a frown. "No," he finally admitted. "I've had the men check, and no one reports anything of this nature missing."

Skylar raised her head defiantly. "Then how can you accuse me of stealing it?"

"It had to come from somewhere," he argued stubbornly. "Now, who gave it to you?"

"It wasn't *given* to me, exactly," she said hesitantly, feeling her knees about to buckle. "The morning after Talbot's first attack on me at the agency, I woke up and found it on the ground beside me."

"You're lying."

"Prove it," she flung back at him.

The soldier on her right slapped her soundly across the face, splitting her lip and knocking her to the ground.

Haggarty came to his feet. "Get her up," he commanded, coming around the desk. The soldiers pulled her roughly to her feet and supported her until she could shake off their hands. The captain took a stance directly in front of her and glared down at her. "You murdered one of my men, and before we reach Fort Stanford, you'll confess the deed, squaw! I don't care what it takes!"

"I did not murder him!" Skylar shouted desperately. "Why would I?"

"Because you were offended by his search of you at the agency," Haggarty replied, giving every appearance of being convinced of the accuracy of the conclusion he had drawn. "You didn't like the manner in which he performed his duty, and you wanted revenge. When you caught him unaware at the river, you saw the perfect opportunity."

Skylar felt nauseated, but she managed to hold her ground. "That's one version of the truth. Personally, I have another."

"I would be delighted to hear it."

"I think that having one of the soldiers under your command accused of attempted rape would be bad for your career."

Skylar saw his blow coming, but before she could react, Haggarty backhanded her across the jaw. This time the soldiers grabbed her before she could fall. "Get this squaw out of here at once! Place her in irons and withhold all food and water. I want her under twenty-four-hour guard. Is that clear?"

"Yes, sir," Lieutenant Zaranski said, stepping forward from his post at the tent door. "Come on, men. Get her back to the wagon."

Though Skylar's wrists and ankles were already raw from the shackles, she was relieved to be taken away. Her head was spinning from Haggarty's blow, and she could taste her own blood in her mouth, but she squared her shoulders proudly as she trudged between the soldiers. It wasn't until they threw her to the ground at the base of a wagon wheel and reattached the heavy irons that she finally gave way to her anguish. With her shoulder leaning heavily against the wheel, she drew her knees up, wrapped her arms around her legs, lowered her head, and let the tears come.

Such behavior was decidedly un-Apache, but she didn't

care. The soldiers were the only humans within a hundred miles who even saw her as an Apache. Sun Hawk and his people knew better. Certainly Skylar knew better. She was a dismal failure as a white woman and as an Indian.

Skylar had always known that there was no real place for her in the world, but she had never imagined that her life might end in this fashion, chained to an army wagon, accused of a murder that was, at the very least, a case of self-defense.

But die she would. She had no doubt about that. If she could survive long enough to reach a military tribunal at Fort Stanford, she might have a slim chance of convincing her judges that she hadn't committed cold-blooded murder. Having a natural compunction against hanging women, they would probably only sentence her to spend the remainder of her life in some filthy Indian agency jail. If that happened, Rayna and her parents might have a chance to effect her release and eventually take her home.

But Skylar knew she wouldn't live long enough to reach a tribunal at Fort Stanford or anywhere else. Haggarty would see to that. He would try to starve a confession out of her, and when that failed, he would have his men beat it out of her. If she somehow managed to survive the beatings, he would have her shot "while trying to escape," so that no one would ever learn of her abuse or of Talbot's assault.

There was certainly precedent for such an occurrence. Skylar couldn't count the number of stories she'd heard about Apaches who had foolishly tried to flee from their captors. In not one of those accounts did the army ever admit to having been at fault. Haggarty had already tried and convicted her. Somehow he would see that a sentence he considered appropriate was carried out.

Going without food that night was no problem for her. Even the smell of the evening mess brought bile to her mouth and increased her nausea. The blood on her dress was dried and crusted, and residue of it on her hands made her even sicker. It reminded her of Talbot's bloody corpse and the way he had touched her.

Oddly, despite her desperate straits, she couldn't summon any remorse for his death. She had never killed anything before, but Talbot had been a pig who deserved to die. She believed that with every fiber of her being. This was his fault; he'd brought it on himself. The only tragedy was that Skylar was going to suffer for it.

As the evening wore on, a steady procession of soldiers began finding excuses to stroll past the wagon on the perimeter of the camp. With her armed guard looking on, smiling, they jeered and cursed her. They spit at her. They made threats. Occasionally one would squat beside her and grab her breasts or roughly try to shove his hand up her skirt. Skylar fought them as best she could, but her efforts were useless and her screams were ineffectual. Her only salvation was that her guard seemed to draw the line at out-and-out rape, but by the time the camp fell silent for the night, Skylar already wished she were dead.

The defiant words she had flung at Sun Hawk about the beauty and value of life came back to haunt her. Tomorrow's sunrise was one she never wanted to see.

There was no moon that night, which was good. The pitch blackness would make what Sun Hawk had to do easier. He had said nothing to his father before stealing away after everyone had fallen asleep. If he was not dead when the morning came, Naka'yen would know what he had done.

The thought of leaving his family behind saddened Sun Hawk, but he refused to dwell on it. His family was large; he had many sisters with fine husbands who would see that his mother and father were cared for. The soldier medicine man had looked at Hacké'tisan's wife and decided that the fever was one caused by bad meat, not an epidemic that would sweep through the camp like wildfire. Though Sun Hawk trusted the word of no white man, the fact that the medicine man had not separated the woman from the rest of the camp convinced him that his people were safe from that horror.

They would survive without him. Skylar would not.

Leaving the camp without being detected had been simple. Throughout the journey, braves had been stealing away with their entire families under the cover of darkness. The soldiers had noticed the absence of some and sent details out to look for them, to no avail. However, many of the absences were as yet undiscovered. Sun Hawk knew he would not be one of those, but it didn't matter. By morning he would be a renegade.

The wooded hillsides made it easy for him to circle around the camp to a place above the wagon where Skylar was chained. Like all the Apaches, he had studied the routine of the soldiers during the past week, so he knew that they stationed guards at intervals around the camp and that those guards changed twice during the night. All afternoon one guard had stood over Skylar at the wagon.

Biding his time, Sun Hawk crouched near one of the outer guards. Sometimes the man sat on a rock and dozed, and at other times he meandered around while he smoked a fire stick of tobacco. Presently another guard came to replace him, and Sun Hawk knew it was almost time. He waited until the newness of the soldier's job had worn off and he had relaxed; then Sun Hawk slipped silently away and began working his way toward the wagon.

When there were trees and boulders for cover, he used them. When there was only open ground, he crawled, never moving quickly, but never stopping unless a noise reached his ears. Some soldiers had made their camp between the hillside and the wagon, but they were not an obstacle. Their snores told him they were sound asleep, and he crawled among them, making no more noise than the gentle breeze wafting over the sand.

He reached the back of the wagon and smiled with satisfaction. The tiny red glow of a fire stick made the guard easy to find. Crouching low, knife in hand, Sun Hawk crept around the wagon until he was behind the guard, and then he sprang. With one hand he covered the man's mouth, and before the guard could utter a single strangled sound, drove his knife between the soldier's ribs.

After dragging him beneath the wagon, Sun Hawk quickly searched the soldier's pockets until he found the key to Skylar's shackles. Then he removed the soldier's revolver and cartridge belt. He secured them around his own waist and crawled out from under the wagon. He could barely make out Skylar's form, but the angle of her head as she leaned against the wheel convinced him she was asleep. Knowing no way to prevent her from being startled, he clamped his hand over her mouth.

Skylar came awake instantly and began struggling, her eyes wide with fear as she strained to see her captor's face.

"Be silent," Sun Hawk whispered with his mouth next to her ear, and she stopped struggling at once. He removed his hand from her mouth and unlocked her shackles. The rusty hinges creaked, and he paused, listening, but the only sounds he heard were the uninterrupted snores in the distance.

It was incomprehensible to Skylar that Sun Hawk was really here. Her mind was still drugged with sleep, and she wondered if she was still dreaming. He had no reason to take such a terrible risk for her. "You must not do this," she whispered. "The guard—"

"Dead," Sun Hawk told her as he moved past her to grab the soldier's rifle, which was leaning against the wagon. He turned back to her and pressed his mouth to her ear again. "Do as I do and make no sound." He yanked her toward the opposite end of the wagon, then let her go as he fell onto his stomach.

Questions soared through Skylar's mind. Why was he doing this? Did he realize the terrible consequences of his act? Where would they go? What would they do? How would they survive when the soldiers came after them?

But of course she couldn't ask the questions, and she couldn't refuse to go with him. If she stayed, she would die anyway. Beyond that, Sun Hawk had killed a man to save her life. If they were discovered, there would be no long day of questioning for him as there had been for Skylar. The soldiers would fall on them like a pack of wolves until nothing was left but their bullet-riddled corpses. The die had been cast, and Skylar could only follow the man who was risking death for her.

Mimicking his position, she crawled slowly beside him, painfully aware of every rustle of her skirt and the scrape of every pebble that was dislodged by her body. When they came to the sleeping soldiers, she knew it was all over. She could never pass among them without waking them, but Sun Hawk slipped ahead of her and they crawled between the soldiers in single file like a long-bodied snake.

No one stirred.

They reached a crop of boulders well away from the soldiers and paused. "We will go to the trees," he whispered into her ear. "When you are there, walk lightly or we will not get past the guards."

Skylar couldn't see the trees, much less the guards, but she trusted Sun Hawk. If he said they were there, they were. But she had much less faith in her ability to navigate as silently as he could. The crack of one broken twig could kill them both, but they crept forward until they reached the trees and the ground began to slant upward. And then, after what seemed like a lifetime, Sun Hawk stood up, took Skylar's hand, and began to run.

Chapter
Twelve

OVER HER MOTHER'S protests, Rayna left for Malaventura and barely arrived in time to catch the evening train to Albuquerque. The eastbound from Los Angeles arrived shortly before midnight, and a few hours later she was in a room at the Palace Hotel once again. She felt no sense of nostalgia at her return, but she did manage to catch a brief nap before going to the Military Headquarters office early the next morning.

Fueled and ready for a fight with Whitlock, Rayna quickly had the wind knocked out of her sails when she arrived and discovered that the general was no longer stationed at Fort Marcy. He had been transferred to the Department of the Platte, and in his place sat a colonel with less rank, less authority, and much less personality than his predecessor. Colonel Duncan McLeash was a pleasant, round-faced, placid man who listened patiently to Rayna's tale of woe, clucking his tongue and nodding in commiseration.

Unfortunately there wasn't a blessed thing he could do to help her but nod and cluck. His greatest contribution to the conversation was to inform her that General Crook was indeed in Arizona and that he was making his headquarters at Fort Apache, at least temporarily.

This wasn't news to Rayna. Several weeks after she left Santa Fe, Meade Ashford had written a letter to her father passing along that information.

It was the first and only time she'd heard from the major despite the two letters she'd sent to him. She certainly hadn't expected him to fall on his knees in gratitude for her effort, but she hadn't anticipated being ignored, either. The insult was just one in a growing list of grievances she had been trying to catalog against him. He was a pretentious, irascible, weak-kneed milksop. And that was only the beginning of her inventory. At the bottom of it was a small notation that somehow outshone the rest: The thought of the way he'd kissed her made her own knees weak.

Since Rayna detested weakness, particularly in herself, it wasn't something that counted in Meade's favor. That was why she found it incomprehensible that after her meeting with Colonel McLeash the first thing she did was head for the post hospital.

On her last day in Santa Fe, Meade had told her he would be leaving the army soon, but she didn't even entertain the idea that he was already gone. Despite the way he'd ignored her letters, she knew in her heart that he wouldn't have left New Mexico without contacting someone at Rancho Verde to inquire about Skylar, if nothing else.

At the desk in the front hall of the hospital, she asked about him and was told that Major Ashford was in the wards. A solicitous young corporal ushered her into a Spartanly furnished consultation room off the hall, and after she refused his offer of a cup of tea, he disappeared.

Corporal Engberg hurried upstairs and located Meade as he was about to enter the officers' lounge. "Major Ashford! A moment, please."

Meade stopped and looked at the corporal. "Yes?"

"There's a lady to see you downstairs, sir. She's waiting in the consultation room."

"A lady?" Meade asked, unable to imagine who would be calling on him. "Did she give her name or give you her card?"

"Oh, no, sir," Engberg said hesitantly. "I forgot to ask." He started to add that she was a very *beautiful* lady, but he didn't think the major would approve of his comment.

"It's all right, Corporal. Return to your post. I'll see to it."

As he made his way downstairs, buttoning his tunic as he went, Meade decided that his mysterious guest was probably the wife of the soldier he'd been treating. A supply wagon on its way from Fort Waring had overturned, crushing the man beneath it. By the time he'd been brought to the hospital, gangrene had set in, and Meade was being forced to discharge him; the army had little use for one-legged sergeants. His wife had been sent for, naturally, and had undoubtedly arrived.

With that explanation fixed in his mind, Meade was understandably taken aback when he opened the door and found Rayna standing at the window. The morning light spilled in, creating a golden halo around her, and Meade suddenly found it difficult to breathe.

Damn it, why does she have this effect on me? he thought irritably, and on the heels of that question came another: And what the hell is she doing here? In a few days he would be out of New Mexico completely, with hundreds of miles between himself and Rayna Templeton, which would, logically, leave him no choice but to forget about her. Now she was here, probably because she'd remembered that he was leaving the army and she just wanted to stir him up again for spite.

When Rayna turned at the sound of the door, it finally occurred to Meade that something could be wrong. He hurried toward her, wishing he could read the odd expression on her face. "Rayna, has something happened? What are you doing here?" he demanded.

It wasn't the greeting she had hoped for, but she knew better than to take offense at his brusqueness. His attitude did help her quell the impulse to fly across the room and embrace him, though. "That kind young corporal obviously mistook me for a lady and offered me a place to wait while he went to find you."

He sighed with relief. If she was joking with him, nothing could be drastically wrong. "I meant what are you doing in Santa Fe? Is Skylar home yet?"

Rayna's face fell. "No. Things have gotten worse. Have
you heard that the Apaches on the Mescalero reservation are
being transferred to the Rio Alto?"

"Oh, good Lord," Meade muttered, lowering his head in
disgust. Would the idiocy of the Washington bureaucrats
never end? He raised his head. "No, I hadn't heard, but I've
been exceptionally busy. I presume Skylar is on her way
there now."

"That's right. And I'm going to Arizona to get her."

"I beg your pardon?"

"You heard me. Crook hasn't answered any of our letters.
I can only assume that they have gone astray or he just
doesn't give a damn."

"If he had received your letters, he would have done
something," Meade assured her.

"That's neither here nor there," Rayna replied tersely.
"I'm sick of waiting. As soon as I leave here, I'm heading
for Fort Apache. Colonel McLeash says that to the best of
his knowledge, Crook is still there." She didn't go on to say
that if Crook refused to help her, she had plans of her own.
She trusted Meade after a fashion, but he was a military man.
He'd probably see it as his duty to report her.

"Rayna, you can't possibly make a journey like that," he
argued. "The train can take you only as far as Holbrook, and
then it's ninety miles through some of the most ungodly
mountain terrain you've ever seen."

Rayna nodded. "The Calderos. Yes, I know."

"And do you also know that there's no stagecoach route
through the mountains because there's nothing south of them
but reservation land? The only trails are ones that were
forged by army supply wagons, and those are dismal at
best."

He was treating her like an idiot, and she didn't like it. "Of
course I know it. I plan to hire a guide in Holbrook."

"Oh, that's delightful," Meade said grandly. "Trust your
welfare—not to mention your virtue—to a complete stranger."

"I can take care of myself, Meade. I've been doing it for years."

"Yes, in the bosom of your nurturing, loving family on a ranch where your father is king and no one would dare lay a hand on his royal offspring. If you go to Holbrook, you'll be totally alone, and no one's going to care one jot that your father owns one of the largest ranches in the New Mexico Territory."

Rayna fought down her exasperation. "Meade, a ranch is not a convent, and I have been off the property once or twice. It might surprise you to know that before the railroad arrived, I participated in a number of cattle drives on the Goodnight Loving Trail." Well, *one* drive, actually, but she didn't want to retract her statement.

Meade was appalled. "You're not serious."

"Oh, but I am. Believe me, I'm perfectly capable of taking care of myself."

"Be that as it may, you can't make a trip like this unescorted. It's unthinkable."

"Then what do you suggest? Shall I let my sister rot on the Rio Alto?"

"Write another letter!"

"I am sick to death of writing letters. My father's sick of it, too. He collapsed yesterday when we learned the news about Skylar."

Meade took another step toward her in concern. "Is he all right?"

"I believe so. I *pray* so. But the point is, our family can't take any more of this, Meade. I have to do something."

Meade turned away, more impatient with the situation than with Rayna. She was right. Something had to be done, but he couldn't let her risk her life on a dangerous trip like this. After a long moment he turned back to her, knowing he was going to regret his impulsive decision.

"All right. Can you wait two days before beginning?"

"Why should I? I can be in Arizona long before then if I take the next westbound train."

"I know, but tomorrow is my last day as an officer of the United States Army, and I have already booked passage to Holbrook Friday morning. I'm going home, and I see no reason why you can't make the trip with me."

Rayna was stunned. "Friday? You were planning to leave the territory on Friday?"

She looked . . . hurt, Meade realized, but he tried to insulate himself against it. "That's right. As I told you weeks ago, I'm anxious to get home. Why do you ask?"

Rayna turned away and moved to the window. "No reason," she replied, trying for a cavalier attitude. "I was just surprised that you'd be leaving so soon."

Meade accepted her answer because he didn't want to believe that she might have been disappointed that he had planned to leave without seeing her again. "Well, I am, and it's to your benefit. I know the route to Fort Apache, and I'm offering to act as your guide. What do you say?"

Considering the circumstances, Rayna found it difficult to believe that he'd made the offer, but she knew better than to question it. Though she had doubts about how much help this tenderfoot would be to her on the trail, at least he knew how to get her to where she was going. If worse came to worst, she could take care of *him*. "Very well, I accept your generous offer."

He paused a moment. "You do?"

"Yes."

"No argument? No protestations that you can get along without my help?"

"But I do need your help. I don't know the route to Fort Apache and you do. You are known to me, and since you're going to that area anyway, you'll be far less expensive than a hired guide."

Meade bit the inside of his lip to keep from smiling. "Perfectly logical, reasonable, and economical," he decreed.

"My thinking exactly."

He sighed. "Very well. We'll leave day after tomorrow. Are you staying at the Palace again?" When she answered in

the affirmative, he said, "I'll call for you at eight o'clock on
Friday morning."

"I'll be ready."

"Good."

Their business concluded, there didn't seem to be anything else to say but a polite round of good-byes. Even after
they had been said, though, neither of them moved. They
looked at each other for a moment; then Rayna finally put an
end to the tension by moving to the door.

"Rayna?"

She stopped and turned. "Yes?"

"You had already made up your mind to go to Fort
Apache when you got here. Why did you bother coming to
me at all?"

A flush of humiliation washed through her. Did he really
have to ask? "I thought you might be interested in knowing
what had transpired. What other reason could I have had?"

"None, I suppose," he replied, sorry he'd asked the question.

A thought occurred to Rayna and she frowned. "I had no
idea you were leaving Friday, if that's what you're thinking.
I didn't come here to rope you into taking me—"

"No, no," he assured her hastily. "That thought hadn't
crossed my mind."

"Well, good." She edged toward the door again. "Good
day, Meade. I'll see you on Friday."

"Yes."

She turned and grasped the door handle, then stopped.
Without looking at him, she asked softly, "Would you really
have left New Mexico without—" *Seeing me again*, she
wanted to say, but she quickly replaced that phrase with "in-
quiring about Skylar?"

Meade wasn't fooled by the substitution, but he didn't
think it was wise to admit how many times he'd talked himself out of the sentimental notion of stopping at Rancho
Verde on his way home. "I had planned to write your father
once I reached Eagle Creek."

Well, that certainly made his feelings—or lack thereof—plain enough. She said good day again without looking at him and left.

Sun Hawk began covering their tracks not long after they cleared the camp, but except for a few brief pauses to allow Skylar to catch her breath, they never stopped moving, climbing higher into the mountains. At daybreak they stopped at a trickling mountain spring, and Skylar collapsed beside it to drink greedily. Sun Hawk knelt at her side but waited until she had drunk her fill before cupping his hand in the water.

It was the first chance they'd had to talk, but only one question came to Skylar's mind once she'd quenched her intense thirst. "Do you know this country?" she asked.

Sun Hawk didn't look at her. "Not as well as some, but I know it. Before the whites came, my people were free to hunt wherever we wanted. I have been in these mountains."

"Good."

"Rest. Don't talk," he instructed. "We must move on soon." He stood up, and Skylar grabbed his hand.

"Where are you going?"

Sun Hawk looked down and saw the panic in her eyes. It was only to be expected, he supposed. "You need food, and I must scout the area. You will be safe here for a little while."

He had to do what was best for both of them, and Skylar reluctantly released his hand. He studied her for a moment, then reached for the revolver strapped to his waist. He extended it to her, and their eyes held as they remembered the last gift he had given her.

Skylar's hand was trembling as she took the gun. Sun Hawk turned away and jumped lightly across the stream.

"Why did you do it?" The question was out before she even realized she was going to ask it.

Sun Hawk stopped and looked at her. "The soldiers would have killed you."

"Why should that matter to you?"

His handsome face hardened into a scowl. "You ask too many questions, even for a woman. It is done. We cannot turn back now." He spun away from her and a moment later disappeared into the rocks above.

At precisely eight o'clock Meade arrived at the Palace Hotel and found Rayna waiting for him in the lobby with a single carpetbag at her feet. At least she hadn't overpacked for the trip. If nothing else, he could count on her to be practical once they left civilization behind. Probably.

He took off his broad-brimmed hat as he approached her, and realized that she was looking at him strangely. Knowing that spending the next few days with her was going to be sheer hell, it seemed hypocritical to wish her a good morning, so instead he questioned her odd look. "What's wrong?"

"Nothing." She waved her hand up and down, gesturing to his clothing. "It's just a shock to see you out of uniform, and that's not what I would have expected you to wear."

Meade frowned down at his serviceable black trousers, casual white shirt, and open vest. "What's wrong with the way I'm dressed?"

"Not a thing."

"What were you expecting? A cutaway and bowler?"

Rayna chuckled. "Actually, yes."

Meade snatched up her carpetbag. "Well, I'm sorry to disappoint you, but I sent them on ahead last week with the rest of my personal belongings. Shall we go? I have a carriage waiting."

She dutifully took her place beside him. The doorman took the bag and placed it in the boot while Meade handed Rayna into the carriage. Once they were settled, she shot him a sidelong glance. "Do you really have a cutaway and bowler?"

Meade wanted to order her not to look at him with that delectable teasing smile, but instead he looked straight ahead and replaced his hat. "No, I don't. Disappointed?"

"Disillusioned," she countered. "Although I must confess that I do prefer your cavalry hat to a stuffy bowler."

"So do I," he said, tugging on the downturned brim in front. "I've spent several years training it to my head, and it's the only piece of military equipment I've ever grown attached to."

"That's understandable. It makes you look quite handsome."

"Thank you." Meade was uncomfortable with the compliment, but he felt obligated to give one in return. "You look quite . . . nice yourself today. Though I am a little surprised by the traveling suit."

Rayna smoothed her skirt. "I thought I should carry one appropriately feminine costume along for my meeting with General Crook."

"That's probably wise." Meade fell silent and dusted at an imaginary spot of dust on his trousers. Good Lord, how was he going to survive the next week? Already she was wreaking havoc with his senses, turning him into a blathering, anxious schoolboy. How much worse would it be once they reached Holbrook and set out alone for Fort Apache?

He didn't want to consider it. He'd offered to act as her escort so that she'd be protected, but if he didn't get a firm grasp on his emotions, Rayna would need someone to protect her from *him*.

They completed the ride to the station in silence and discovered that the train had already arrived. Fighting the crowd, they made their way through the depot to the platform where a porter took their baggage and pointed them to the Liberty Pullman. Rayna allowed Meade to take her arm, and they fell into the stream of passengers moving down the length of the train.

Ahead of them, a young stable hand and a baggage man were approaching, leading a spirited-looking gray Arabian stallion toward the stock cars. As the crowd made way, Meade stepped aside and paused. "Magnificent animal," he

commented, studying the horse's features. "Look at the con-
formation . . . the perfect arch of the crest."

"Yes, he's a real beauty," Rayna said lovingly, surprised
by Meade's knowledge of horses. She shouldn't have been,
of course. He was a cavalryman, after all, but as she recalled,
the horse he'd been riding at Rancho Verde had been undis-
tinguished. She couldn't fault him for that, though.

"I imagine he has incredible speed and endurance," he
said appreciatively as the horse drew alongside him. Unfortunately, at that moment the train whistle shrilled loudly,
spooking the horse, which had already been unnerved by the
crowd and hubbub of the train yard. The stallion reared,
clawing the air with his hooves, and as the passengers
screeched and scrambled for safety, Meade grabbed Rayna
to pull her out of the way.

Naturally Rayna had other ideas. The frightened horse
reared again, straining against its lead rope, and the stableboy lost his hold. Before the wild-eyed Arabian could bolt,
Rayna sprang forward and grabbed the lead.

"Easy, boy, easy," she crooned, pulling down hard on the
hackamore. The animal shied away, but Rayna held on. The
battle between the lovely young lady in the beige traveling
suit and the powerful stallion should have been a woefully
one-sided one, but it wasn't. When the horse tried to rear
again, Rayna applied all her weight against the rope, tighten-
ing the hackamore around his nose, and the stallion quieted.

"Good boy. Easy, boy. There's a good fellow." A spatter-
ing of applause swept through the crowd, and Rayna stroked
the stallion's nose to keep him quiet.

Feeling like an ineffectual fool, Meade watched Rayna
turn the spirited Arabian into a docile pet. Why on earth had
he bothered trying to protect her? "Strong, beautiful, skittish, and mean-tempered, to boot," he muttered churlishly as
he moved toward Rayna and the horse.

"He's not mean; he's just high-spirited," she said lightly,
stroking the animal's nose. "That's the price you sometimes
have to pay for a horse this well bred."

"Well, I wouldn't pay a greenback dollar for him."

Rayna shot him an exasperated glance, then handed the lead to the stableboy. "Keep a firm hand on this from now on," she advised.

"Yes, ma'am. And thank you." The crowd applauded again as the boy led the Arabian away.

"If you're finished performing feats of derring-do for your grateful public, could we go now?"

Rayna frowned at him as they began moving briskly toward the Pullman car. "What is wrong with you? I very likely averted a serious accident, and you're treating me as though I'd done something wrong."

"You could have been killed," he snapped as he took her arm and helped her up the steps to the car. "That animal obviously needs a great deal of training and gentling before he'll be fit for anything but showing off."

"Don't be ridiculous. It wasn't Triton's fault the engineer blew the whistle."

"Triton?" Meade frowned as they moved into a coach that looked more like a drawing room parlor than a train car.

"The horse," she replied, glancing around for a seat. "The name is a mythological reference to—"

"I know what it refers to," he snapped. "How do you know what he's called?"

Rayna settled onto a reasonably comfortable padded sofa. "I know his name because I'm his new owner. I bought him yesterday."

Meade glared down at her. "You what?"

She looked up at him innocently, truly unable to imagine where his animosity had come from. "I bought him from a breeder who lives just outside Santa Fe," she explained. "Papa and I buy a great deal of our stock from him." Meade was still staring at her. "What on earth is wrong? You didn't think I was going to walk to Fort Apache, did you?"

"No, but I expected—" A fellow passenger jostled Meade, and he joined Rayna on the sofa, lowering his voice. "I expected that we'd find a couple of serviceable trail horses in Holbrook. I didn't know you'd go out and pay a king's ransom for a man-killing stallion."

"He is not a man-killer, and you're being contrary for no reason, Meade," she said, finally losing her patience.

"That's because you make me angry with the ridiculous things you do," he flung back at her.

"If that's the case, why the devil did you offer to escort me to Fort Apache?" she snapped.

"Because you needed help and it was the gentlemanly thing to do."

"Then why don't you start acting like a gentleman?"

"I will when you start acting like a lady!"

Every head in the coach swiveled toward them, but that didn't keep Meade from wanting to wrap his hands around Rayna's lovely throat and strangle her.

Calming herself, she fixed him with her most determined gaze and lowered her voice. "Meade, I didn't ask for your help, and I certainly didn't ask to be snipped at, condescended to, and scolded like a child at every turn."

"I'm sorry. You're absolutely right. How you conduct yourself is your own business." Despite his apology, he didn't sound the least bit remorseful.

"Remember that, or I'll go back to my original plan and find another guide in Holbrook."

"Perhaps you should."

"Perhaps I will!"

They glared at each other until finally Meade turned away in disgust, wondering if he would ever be able to get the last word in on Miss Rayna Templeton.

Chapter
Thirteen

DESPITE THE TRAGIC complexities of her situation, life became very simple for Skylar over the next few days. It was an endless, exhausting cycle of sleeping and moving on. Knowing the soldiers would expect him to go south to join Geronimo, Sun Hawk headed north instead, leading Skylar through the most rugged parts of the mountains so that they would be more difficult to track. On the third day they came down to the northern foothills of the Caliente range. A storm blew up, and they took shelter beneath a rock shelf, sleeping through the afternoon so that they could cross the long valley under the cover of darkness that night. The next morning they crossed the Manosa River and slipped into the southern foothills of the White Mountains.

She knew that having her with him made traveling more difficult for Sun Hawk, but she never complained and he never commented on their slow pace. When she reached the limits of her endurance, Sun Hawk seemed to know it instinctively and would find an excuse to stop. Though scavenging for roots and other food sources was woman's work, Sun Hawk provided for their needs without complaint. Until they were farther away, building a fire was out of the question, so he made no attempt to snare rabbits or other small game. They lived on piñon nuts, pine bark, and gooseberries, if they could be found. Skylar had never been so hungry, but she gratefully ate whatever Sun Hawk brought.

Late on the fourth day he found a valley sheltered by steep

cliffs on three sides, and announced that they would make camp there for several days. He was convinced no one had followed them, and the entrance to the high valley had a commanding view of the area they had just traversed. No one could approach without his knowledge, and there was fresh water in a pool fed by a mountain stream and the recent rains. He led Skylar up to a shallow cave in one of the cliff walls and left, after promising to return as soon as he had found food.

Too exhausted to question his decision even if she had wanted to, Skylar lay down in the cave and fell asleep. When she awoke the next morning, Sun Hawk was still gone and there was no indication that he had returned during the previous afternoon or night. Though the thought of being completely alone was frightening, it never occurred to her that she had been deserted. Sun Hawk hadn't risked everything just to leave her in the mountains to die, and he was too skilled to allow himself to be captured.

Secure in the certainty that he would return soon, Skylar climbed down from the cave and tried to think about what she should do. Making decisions, even simple ones, wasn't as easy as it should have been. For days, Sun Hawk had directed her every movement, and escape had been her only clear, reasonable thought. Everything else had been shoved away from her consciousness.

She tried to imagine what Sun Hawk would do and realized that her priorities were, first, to make certain the valley was still safe and, second, to learn everything there was to know about it. Quietly backtracking to the mouth of the valley, she studied the rugged terrain they had covered the day before. She stayed there a long time, examining all possible routes that might lead someone to her location, but nothing stirred.

Once she was convinced she was still safe, she returned to the valley and began memorizing every crack and crevice on the cliffs. She found places to hide and even located another way out. She collected what food she could find, but she gathered little of it, for she was not nearly as astute as Sun Hawk in judging what was edible and what wasn't.

It was midmorning by the time she finished, but there was still no sign of Sun Hawk, so she made her way down to the pool and removed her overblouse. Shutting out the significance of the encrusted bloodstains, she knelt on the bank and scrubbed the dress. When she had finished and laid it in the sun to dry, her hands were nearly raw, but the stains were only faint circles, much dimmer than her memory of how the blood had gotten there. She washed her skirt, too, and then slipped into the cool water to bathe.

She stayed there for a long time, savoring the feel of the water on her skin, and when she was as clean as it was possible to get, she floated on the surface and forced herself to think about her situation.

It was obvious that she and Sun Hawk could not hide in the mountains forever, but what were the alternatives? Turning themselves in at one of the forts in the territory was unthinkable. In the eyes of the whites, she and Sun Hawk were both murderers, and there was no reason to believe that they would receive better treatment than Captain Haggarty had given her.

Of course, if Sun Hawk would agree to help her get to Rancho Verde, there was a chance that her father could sort out this mess. If she had to go on trial for killing the soldier, at least she would have the benefit of a lawyer, and she would have her family around her. Testimony could be presented to point up the fact that she had not been raised as an Apache, and if she appeared in front of the tribunal dressed in a fashionable tailored dress with her hair upswept, speaking eloquent English as she related what had really happened with Talbot, there was a chance the judge and jury might believe she had acted in self-defense.

But there was a vast difference between what she had done and what Sun Hawk had done to help her escape. Perhaps they could convince a military court that he had acted because he knew the soldiers were going to kill her, but that wouldn't change the fact that he was an Apache who had killed a soldier in cold blood. They would hang him. Skylar could go back to her placid life as the spinster daughter of Raymond Templeton, but she'd never be able to forget that she had purchased her freedom with Sun Hawk's life.

Of course he didn't have to turn himself in. He could deliver her to Rancho Verde and disappear . . . and Skylar would never see him again. The thought brought her almost as much pain as the thought of seeing him hang. Selfish considerations aside, though, she had to consider what his life would be like from now on. He was a renegade who could never return to his family. He had nothing. Quite simply, he had given up everything . . . for her.

Skylar still didn't understand why, but one thing was clear to her. Whatever decision she made about her future had to include what was best for Sun Hawk. She owed him her life, and that was a debt she would repay with her own, if necessary.

She also realized quite clearly that she was in love with him. Her childish infatuation had evolved into a deep respect for the man he was and for his commitment to his people. She wasn't sure when that respect had turned to love, but it had happened long before he unshackled her from the army wagon. That act had merely bound them together with a bond of blood that could never be broken.

Skylar floated in the pool, reaching no decisions because none could be made without Sun Hawk. Until she knew what he wanted or what he had planned, she could only go on as they had been, surviving as best they could.

Though her future was as blank as the sheets of writing paper Rayna had sent her, Skylar felt no panic. Perhaps she was more Apache than she had imagined, after all. They lived one day at a time, adjusting and adapting to whatever fate threw at them. She could do the same—as long as she had Sun Hawk's strength to sustain her.

Skylar opened her eyes and started when she saw Sun Hawk on the rock shelf that bordered one end of the pool.

She couldn't guess how long he had been there, but she quickly righted herself and began to tread water, wafting her arms gently back and forth to keep herself afloat. He was frozen like a statue as he stared at her, his expression hard and unreadable. At his feet were several sacks, but Skylar's thoughts were too muddled for her to wonder what was in them or where they had come from. She was too overwhelmed by the tension in the air and the sweet, sensual ache that pulsed through her body.

She could think of nothing to say to him. In fact, she could think of nothing at all.

And then he moved. He climbed down the rocks to the pool and placed his rifle near the edge of the water. Never taking his eyes off Skylar, he removed his clothes and stood on the bank naked.

He was elemental, powerful, and frightening. He was also the most beautiful thing Skylar had ever seen. She had lived on a ranch too long to be ignorant of the meaning of his jutting manhood, but she knew instinctively that Sun Hawk would never take her by force. That was why he was waiting at the edge of the pool. It was his way of offering her a choice.

But why did he want her? she had to wonder. Did he think that because he had saved her he had a right to her? Had he simply seen her naked as she floated in the water and become aroused? Was this merely an animal instinct that he longed to gratify? Or did he truly love her?

Most important, did the answer really matter?

Yes. It mattered very much.

When Sun Hawk finally dived into the water and surfaced at the opposite end of the pool, desire coursed through Skylar, but instead of swimming toward him, she made her way to the bank and slipped out of the water. She glanced over her shoulder and discovered that he had turned away. If disappointment or hurt was etched on his face, Skylar couldn't see it.

Quickly she dressed and hurried back to the cave without

acknowledging his presence. Keenly aware of every sound below her, she listened as he bathed and scrubbed his clothes. Then the noises stopped, and a few minutes later Sun Hawk climbed up to the cave wearing only his breech-clout and carrying the sacks he had brought. They clattered when he dropped them at her feet, but his eyes never met Skylar's.

"We have good food now, and other things we need. I will make a fire below so that you can cook."

"As you wish."

He left abruptly and Skylar began opening the sacks. In one she found tins of meat and bags of flour, meal, and sugar. In another she found blankets, a cook pot, and several knives and other utensils. The third held sacks of dried beef and boxes of rifle cartridges, a sewing kit and soap, scraps of material, a shirt, and even a long skirt and other articles of clothing.

What he had brought her, supplemented by what they could forage from the mountains, would keep them alive for weeks. But at what cost?

Her heart tripping with dread, she hurried down the rocky bluff to where Sun Hawk was carefully creating a fire that would make hardly any smoke at all.

He knew she was there, but he didn't look at her, even when she quietly asked, "Where did the provisions come from?"

"A small ranch many miles to the west."

Skylar knelt beside him, terrified of hearing the answer to her next question. "You didn't—" She hesitated, and finally he looked at her with cold, lifeless eyes.

"I did not kill to get the food, if that is what you want to know. It was not necessary."

Skylar's relief was overshadowed by the knowledge that her doubts had hurt him. "I'm sorry. It is only that I don't want anyone else killed because of me," she said, reaching out to touch his arm, but her jerked away from her.

"I will do what I have to do to keep you alive," he said harshly.

"But I would rather die than know I had caused the death of another innocent person."

He continued laying wood for the fire. "You think the soldier I killed was innocent," he said flatly.

"In a way, he was," she replied. "But I know that if you had not silenced him, I would be dead now."

"Then what I did was right."

Skylar didn't know how to debate the moral implications, and she didn't want to. It had been done, and there was no way to turn back time. "What you did saved my life, and I am grateful."

"It is not your gratitude I want," he snapped.

"Then what do you want?" When he remained silent, a vision of him as he had stood naked at the pool flashed into Skylar's mind. "You have given up everything for me, but I do not understand why. You made it clear long ago that I am not fit to be the woman of an Apache warrior."

Sun Hawk paused in his work. "That is true."

Skylar swallowed hard and summoned all her courage. "Then why did you come to me at the pool?"

He looked at her then, and the veil of coldness fell away from his eyes. The tender expression that remained told Skylar everything she needed to know. She reached out and gently touched his face. "If you had ever spoken of love, I might understand better why you risked so much for me," she said gently.

"Do you *need* me to speak of it?" he asked hoarsely, moved by her touch and the soft lights in her eyes.

Skylar nodded. "Yes. I do."

Abruptly Sun Hawk pulled away and stood. Irritation replaced tenderness in his eyes. "My wife has been dead a long time, but I did not imagine that when it came time to select another one, my heart would choose someone like you."

Skylar wondered if that was as close to an avowal of love

as she would ever get from him. He loved her, but clearly he didn't want to. "Are you asking me to be your wife?"

He drew his shoulders back proudly. She had humiliated him once with her rejection at the pool. He didn't want to give her the chance to do it again by speaking foolish lovers' words to her. "We have both killed white soldiers," he said flatly. "Neither of us can go back to our people and live as before. It makes sense that we should live together because we have no one else now."

He was offering her a marriage of convenience? The very idea was ludicrous, since nothing about their situation was even remotely convenient. Obviously he had not considered the possibility that her white family might be able to clear her of the charges, but there was no reason why he should give the possibility any credence. His treatment at the hands of white men had been vastly different from hers.

Would he take her to Rancho Verde if she asked him to?

Possibly. But Skylar couldn't bring herself to ask it. Instead, she told him, "I will think on what you have said because you have saved my life and taken care of me."

"As I told you, I do not want your gratitude," Sun Hawk said angrily. "Do not come to me as a wife because you owe me a debt."

"Then do not come to me as a husband because it is a practical thing to do," she flung back. "If you want someone to cook for you and see to your needs, you have only to ask and I will care for you as a sister would care for a brother."

"I do not want a sister, I want a wife!"

"And I am the only woman available? That is not enough for me, Sun Hawk." Skylar came to her feet and placed one fist against her breast. "What I feel in my heart for you is more powerful than anything I have ever known, but I will not be your wife unless I know your heart feels the same."

Torn between salvaging his pride and the joy her confession brought him, he studied her angry face. "Why do you think I saved your life?" he asked, gentling his voice.

"I have asked you before to tell me, and you would not."

"If your heart is as strong as you say, it should tell you the reason."

Skylar did know. She had known it, most likely, from the moment he had given her the knife almost a week ago. "I need to hear the words from you."

He hesitated a moment. "I love you. Why else would I give up everything to keep from losing you?" he asked quietly.

There. He had said it and there was no turning back. Skylar felt no elation, no flush of longing, only a strange sense of inevitability. All she was certain of was her own love for him and his for her. She had to stay with him now, to go where he went, give up her dreams of being reunited with her family, and spend whatever was left of her life as his wife.

"Very well." She nodded slowly and turned away.

Sun Hawk took a single step after her. "Where are you going?"

"To get the food. A wife's first duty is to cook for her husband."

At that moment Sun Hawk could have argued with her, but he didn't. She had agreed to be his wife. There would be time for proving his love later. For now he had to finish laying the fire so that his wife could cook for him.

Case rode into Fort Apache unable to imagine why General Crook had summoned him again so soon. Only yesterday Case and a cavalry detail led by the general had returned from a month-long campaign hunting down a band of Chiricahua who had left San Carlos and were attempting to join Geronimo. Luck had been with them and they had captured part of the band, but the others had escaped and were probably already in Mexico. Geronimo's followers were growing in number, and Crook estimated the total number of braves, women, and children to be nearly a hundred by now.

That seemed like a small number in light of the superior forces Crook was amassing against Geronimo, but it was more than enough to wreak havoc and create panic among ranchers and townspeople throughout the southern half of the territory.

Unfortunately, Crook had been unable to move against Geronimo directly. Faced with administrative problems of pacifying the reservation Apaches and cutting through the red tape involved in persuading the Mexican government to allow his troops to cross the border, the general had been completely stymied.

That was why Case was so puzzled about the reason Crook had sent for him. Even if authorization to move into Mexico had come, it would take at least a week to mount an expedition.

Quelling his curiosity, Case presented himself to the general's aide and was ushered in immediately.

"Case, thank you for coming so quickly," Crook said, inviting him to sit by pointing to a chair. "Please convey my apologies to Mrs. Longstreet for dragging you away from her so soon."

"Libby understands."

Crook smiled, betraying his fondness for Case's wife. "I'm sure she does. She's quite a remarkable lady."

"I agree, General," Case replied solemnly. "But you did not ask me here to discuss my wife."

"Quite right." Crook's smile was replaced by a frown as he looked down at the enormous stack of correspondence and dispatches that had been awaiting him on his return. "It seems there's been some trouble with the Mescaleros who were being transferred to the Rio Alto."

"How many refused to go?" Case asked, understanding the source of the irritation in Crook's voice. The general had learned of the transfer yesterday almost the moment he arrived at the fort, and he had been furious. Crowding the Mescaleros onto the Rio Alto was absurd, and Case had no doubt that the commander of the Department of the Border had already lodged a complaint.

Crook looked at the dispatch from Captain Haggarty.

"Forty-two in all, including those who disappeared before the forced march began and those who have vanished during the march."

This was bad news, but not unexpected. "They will join Geronimo."

"Of course they will, but until I can get down into the Sierra Madre to root Gerry out, there's nothing I can do but twiddle my thumbs and handle problems like this one." He tapped Haggarty's report. "It seems that one of the captain's soldiers was knifed to death without provocation by a Mescalero woman named Skylark."

It was clear from Crook's tone that he didn't believe the military version of the account. Case didn't either. That was not what captured his interest, though. "That's an odd name for an Apache. I've never heard anything like it before, even among the Mescaleros."

"One story at a time. I'll get to that one in a minute," Crook grumbled, leaving Case mystified as to what he meant. "It seems that after the woman was caught and questioned, one of the braves helped her to escape, seriously wounding one of the guards."

"Only one guard?" Case questioned lightly.

Crook's mouth twitched at the corners. "My sentiments exactly. The brave was obviously a prudent man whose only thought was to get the woman away from her captors. I know Captain Haggarty, and I shudder to think of the kind of treatment this Skylark would have received at his hands."

"I know Haggarty, too," Case replied. The captain was an arrogant imbecile with an ugly sadistic streak, but Crook didn't need Case to tell him that. "The brave probably saved the woman's life."

"Agreed. Certainly I can't sanction what the brave did, but I can't say I blame him, either. At any rate, a thorough search of the Caliente Mountains where the cavalry was camped yielded no trace of either of them, and Haggarty is requesting that I launch a full-scale expedition to track the couple down. In lieu of that, he asks for permission to do it himself once he gets the Mescaleros to Rio Alto."

"We both know that would be a waste of time. They're probably across the border in Mexico already."

"Quite possibly. Unfortunately there is a horrible complication to what should be a simple story." Crook picked up a packet of letters. "This was also waiting for me when I arrived. It is a petition for the release of a Miss *Skylar* Templeton from the Mescalero reservation. It seems that the young lady is a full-blooded Apache by birth, but she was raised by a white family in New Mexico, educated, and legally adopted."

Case felt his heart turn over in his breast and he hardly dared to breathe. Was this what his dreams about his sister had been leading him to? "The two women—Skylark and Skylar—are the same," he said, trying to keep his voice from betraying the hope that blossomed inside him.

"I would guess so," Crook replied, "though Haggarty made no mention of the fact that the one he called Skylark was an anglicized Apache."

Without realizing it, Case fingered the simple medallion that hung around his neck. "If Skylar Templeton has a white family, how did she end up on the reservation?"

Crook glanced through the letter he'd received from Miss Rayna Templeton and gave Case the pertinent details, then threw the paper onto his desk in disgust. "This is a complete travesty. That poor girl was ripped away from her family and is now living a nightmare, thanks to Sam Whitlock. He didn't need my permission to countermand his own order. He could have put an end to this two months ago, but he was too peeved with the reorganization to do it. He ought to be horsewhipped."

Case couldn't have agreed more, but the reasons why this had happened were less important than righting the wrong. Knowing Crook as he did, Case understood now why he had been called here. "You want me to find them, don't you, sir?"

Crook smiled at him. Case's insight was only one of the things that made him so valuable. "Yes, I do. I know that you've only just returned, but I'd appreciate you handling this. If anyone can pick up their trail, you can."

Case nodded. If the couple had joined Geronimo, this would be a very dangerous mission. Even if he could locate the band in Mexico, the renegade might kill him without allowing him to explain the purpose of his mission. But the danger meant nothing to Case. The odds against Skylar Templeton being his sister were enormous, but he could not rest until he knew the truth.

"Their trail will be too cold to follow," he told Crook.

"I know that, but you can go where I can't and find information that would never be available to any white man, let alone a soldier." He handed Case the packet of documents he'd received from Rayna. "Look these over. They contain information that might be useful to you. Frankly, if I were Miss Skylar Templeton, I'd be far more interested in returning to my home in New Mexico than going on the warpath with Geronimo. It could be that she's headed home even as we speak.

"Now, I've already dispatched some communiqués requesting information on this brave"—he consulted Haggarty's report—"Sun Hawk. If I can track down the former Indian agent for the Mescalero reservation, he may be able to give us some valuable information about the man that would help you in your search."

"It would be better to speak with Sun Hawk's people," Case replied. "If you'll give me the necessary papers, I'll catch up with Captain Haggarty and ask questions among the Mescalero. If they know I'm trying to help Sun Hawk, they may be honest with me." Case stood, then hesitated. "*Am* I trying to help him, General?"

Crook looked at him blankly, not grasping his meaning. "I beg your pardon?"

"What will happen to the brave if I find him?"

Crook thought it over. He'd been so focused on the problem of the young woman that he hadn't thought much about the Mescalero brave. "I'll launch a full investigation into all of this and see if I can find the truth. If the soldier he wounded survives, I can assure you the man won't be hanged."

"But he will be punished."

"As I said, Case, it all depends on the circumstances. Find him for me so that we can get at the truth and get Miss Templeton back to her family."

Case almost smiled. It would have been so easy for Crook to offer a hollow assurance of leniency, but he never made a promise he wasn't certain he could keep. That was the reason Case and the other Apaches trusted him so much. "I'll do my best, sir," he said respectfully.

"I know you will. Here." He gave him Haggarty's report as well. "See what you can glean from this, too. Come back tomorrow morning before you set out, and I'll have the passes for you. I'm told that a number of citizens' committees have started forming again, and I don't want anyone mistaking you for a hostile."

It was a problem Case had faced too often to take lightly. "Neither do I, sir."

"Do you want to take some scouts with you?"

Case thought it over. "Yes. My uncle, Angry Coyote, and his son will come with me."

"Very well. You inform them, and I'll arrange their passes as well. And then I must write to the Templeton family and tell them what's happened," Crook added with a bewildered shake of his head.

Having been raised in two worlds himself, Case had a fair inkling of what Skylar Templeton was going through—and what her family was suffering. "I prefer my job to yours, sir."

"As well you should, my friend." Crook stood and offered Case his hand. "Good luck."

"Thank you, sir."

Case left a moment later, tucking the papers Crook had

given him into his shirt. He longed to study them for any scrap of information that might tell him whether or not Skylar Templeton was his sister, but he wanted to get home to Libby and share this with her as soon as possible. She would be upset that he was leaving again so soon, but she would not try to discourage him. Her heart would bleed for the plight of poor Skylar, and even if the girl was not Sonsee-a-ray, Libby would want her found.

As soon as Case arrived home, he explained the situation to Libby, and his assumption about her attitude was completely correct.

"Oh, Case, what that poor thing must have suffered," she said quietly, looking over Haggarty's report while her husband studied the letter from Skylar's sister. "Do you think this Private Talbot was trying to assault her?"

Case didn't want to think about it. "Such things have happened before," he replied, trying to remain impassive. There was no proof this girl was his sister, but there was no denying that his heart had already assigned her that station.

Though Case had made no mention of Morning Star, Libby knew what he was thinking. "Is this your sister, Case?" she asked, leaning close to place her head on his shoulder.

Case touched her face lovingly and pressed a kiss to her brow. "I do not know."

"But you think it, don't you? You told me that your visions were trying to lead you to her, and now this has happened."

He took Haggarty's report from her. "The captain said the girl was a Mescalero about twenty years of age. Morning Star would be nearer twenty-five."

Libby raised her head. "Haggarty could be mistaken."

"True, but how could a White Mountain Apache child like Morning Star come to be raised by a white family near Santa Fe? It is much more likely that this Skylar is indeed a Mescalero."

Libby couldn't help but smile. Case wanted very much to

believe that this girl was his sister, but he was afraid of being
hurt by a disappointment that would bring him immeasur-
able pain. He had kept Morning Star's memory alive since
the day she had been taken, but now that there was a chance
that he might be reunited with her, he was trying to think
with his head and not his heart.

"Will you be able to find her?" she asked.

"I don't know."

Libby placed her head on his shoulder again and wrapped
her arms around his waist. "If she is Morning Star, the eagle
will lead you to her. Your guiding spirit has never failed us
yet."

Case wrapped his arms around her and pulled her close.
Sometimes he wondered if his wife had a deeper Apache
soul than his own.

"I pray you are right, beloved."

Chapter
Fourteen

SKYLAR AND SUN HAWK filled the afternoon with practical tasks. While she cooked, he began gathering the things he would need to replace the valuable weapons he had left behind with his people. After they ate, while Sun Hawk carved and cured a stout mulberry branch into a bow, Skylar mended their clothes.

They worked quietly, seldom murmuring a word, but their minds were both keenly attuned to the tension that filled the air.

In her youth, before reality had intervened, Skylar had often imagined being married in a beautiful cathedral. In the fantasy, she wore a magnificent dress, and Rayna was standing beside her, smiling happily as the bride and groom exchanged their vows.

The face of her husband-to-be had been a blank then, but it was no longer. Skylar had pledged herself to a man whose handsome face was forever emblazoned on her memory and in her heart. There would be no cathedral or expensive gown. Rayna might never know of her betrothal, and there would be no priest asking her to recite the vows. The wedding ceremony tonight would be very simple. When Sun Hawk went to his bed, she would join him. He would take her body and, in so doing, bind them together for as long as they lived.

Skylar was terrified.

"What does your name mean in our language?"

His soft voice startled her, and it took her a moment to focus on his question. The valley was growing dark, and Sun Hawk had banked the fire so that it was only a red glow in the twilight. She looked across the embers at him and found that he had laid his bow aside and was studying her intently.

It took her another moment to find a suitable translation for her name. "It means 'one who studied,' " she told him, feeling a flush of heat crawl up her cheeks. "It is a name that my white mother cherished because it belonged to her own mother who died many years ago." It was the simplest way Skylar could think of to explain how Collie's maiden name, Schuyler, had been transformed into her own. "Why do you ask? Does it displease you?"

The depth of tenderness in his eyes nearly stole her breath. "No, it does not displease me. I only wanted to know it in the language we share so that I can whisper it to you in the night."

An ache of need like the one she had experienced in the pool flooded through her, and she looked back at her sewing, unable to comment.

"Do you still miss your white family?" he asked.

She couldn't look up. "Yes. I always will, just as you will miss the family you left behind."

"I am sorry you will never see them again."

"So am I." She glanced up and met his gaze. "For both of us." Another silence fell between them as darkness gathered in the valley. "What will we do when we can no longer stay here?"

Thus far Sun Hawk had been acting on instinct and had no particular plan in mind. He might not have confessed his indecision to anyone else for fear it would make him look weak, but he knew he had to be honest with his wife. "I am not certain, beloved."

Skylar gathered the endearment to her heart and held it close. "Will we join Geronimo?"

"There may be no other choice," he replied sadly. "We will travel north for a while longer until the soldiers stop searching for us, but when the snows come, we must go south. Only Geronimo and his people are in the south, and we cannot survive alone."

"Geronimo's raids have already killed many people who did him no wrong," she reminded him. "Will you be able to kill if he says it must be done?"

"I will do whatever I must to keep you safe and alive," he repeated.

"We will not be safe with Geronimo."

"Then we will find a safe place," he promised her, though he knew it was a promise he could never keep.

Skylar knew it, too, but for this one moment it didn't matter.

It had grown too dark to see the rents and tears in the leggings she was mending, and when Sun Hawk began laying out his blankets next to the fire, Skylar put her sewing away. A knot of fear and anticipation formed in her throat, but she swallowed it down.

This was the course she had chosen. No other was open to her, and though she would have given the world to change the circumstances, she could not regret having met Sun Hawk or having grown to love him. Fate had ripped her from her life of security and replaced it with the love of this man. Whatever event fate planned for her next she would share with Sun Hawk.

He slipped between his blankets and turned his back to the fire, offering Skylar one final chance to change her mind. She wouldn't, of course, but she had no notion of what she should do next. What she had learned of Apache customs from the Mescaleros had not included the tutoring of a bride for her wedding night.

Clearly, though, it was she who must make the first move, so she cast all thoughts of embarrassment aside, removed her moccasins, and stood. She slipped out of her dress, closing her mind to the way the cool night air felt to her feverish skin as she circled the fire. When she knelt beside Sun Hawk, he turned to her.

A small moan sounded in his throat as he looked at her naked body silhouetted by the red embers of the fire. Reverently he reached out and placed his hands on her waist, then moved them up slowly, savoring the feel of her skin. He came to his knees in front of her, and as he filled his hands with the globes of her breasts he pressed his lips against her throat.

Skylar gasped at the dual sensual assault and wrapped her arms around his shoulders. Her head fell back, offering his seeking mouth whatever it wished to take, and his hands moved lower, sliding down her flanks until he cupped her buttocks and pulled her to him. Skylar felt the hard ridge of his manhood beneath the breechclout pressing into her belly and it brought a fresh ache of desire to her. She gasped as his mouth found her breast, suckling one, then the other, until her gasps became whimpers.

She wove her hands into his hair as he lowered her to the blanket, and when his knee slipped between hers, Skylar opened herself to him. Poised above her, he looked into her eyes and whispered her name in a lover's voice as he joined their bodies into one.

"You are mine now," he said hoarsely again and again as he pressed into her, carrying her past the first jolt of pain to the place where there was only searing heat, blinding light, and a bond of love that could never be broken.

The difference between the pseudo-ladylike Rayna who had boarded the train with Meade on Friday and the woman who met him in the lobby of the Holbrook Hotel on Saturday morning was the difference between night and day. Gone was the demure traveling suit with lace at the collar. In its place were boots, Levi's, and a mannish shirt and vest. Her hair was drawn away from her face into a thick golden braid that fell almost to her waist. What startled him most, though, was the Colt revolver strapped efficiently around her hips.

Rayna was conscious of him watching her as she came down the stairs, but she couldn't decide if his expression was one of shock or disapproval—or equal parts of both.

"Which do you object to more, the pants or the Colt?" she asked tartly before he could say so much as a good morning.

"Can you use the Colt?" he asked.

"Probably better than you can."

He let the insult roll off him. "Then I don't object to either. Frankly, I didn't expect you to ride Triton sidesaddle."

She smiled at him. "Good. That will save us another argument when I go to buy a saddle. Now, shall we purchase our provisions? I'd like to be on the trail as soon as possible."

"By all means." He gestured toward the door, and she preceded him out of the hotel and down the street to the mercantile.

If all went well, which was certainly not guaranteed, the trip would take the better part of four days, but they kept their rations and cooking supplies simple. Amazingly enough, they found nothing to argue over in the selection. At Rayna's insistence, they split the cost of the supplies, and then she purchased a saddle and a simple felt hat. What surprised Meade was that she also selected a Winchester repeating rifle that matched the caliber of her Colt.

She shot him a defiant look as she paid for the lot, but Meade made no comment because he was thinking of the horse she had purchased and what it had cost to ship the animal to Holbrook. Then there had been her train fare, her room at the hotels in Santa Fe and Holbrook, and now this. Their journey had barely begun, and already she had spent an outrageous amount of money without showing any concern that she might run short of funds.

He shouldered her new saddle as she picked up the burlap sack of provisions and moved toward the door. "Rayna, exactly how much money are you carrying on you?" he asked, keeping his voice low.

"Enough to see me through this trip."

"Where is it?"

She shot a startled look at him as she thought of the narrow money belt strapped beneath her shirt. "That's none of your business!"

"It is if I'm going to be protecting a king's ransom as well as your virtue."

"Rest easy, Meade. I'll protect my own virtue and whatever else I have about my person. You just get us to Fort Apache," she advised as he held the door open for her. They left the store without noticing the two men who were playing a game of checkers over the cracker barrel near the door.

They didn't notice the broad, malicious smiles the men exchanged, either.

It took longer than Meade had expected to find a horse for the trip. The owner of the livery stable sold him a serviceable packhorse, but he had no riding stock that looked suitable for the difficult journey ahead. Ultimately he and Rayna were forced to ride to a ranch eight miles out of town where Meade finally found a sturdy, surefooted bay named Chicory.

By noon they were on their way south, following the course of the Little Colorado River. They made excellent time on the high plateau, but Rayna couldn't say that Meade was the most invigorating companion she'd ever traveled with. He rarely spoke, and by the time they made camp for the night the tension in the air was as thick as a cloud of swamp mosquitoes—and just about as irritating.

They shared the camp chores and as soon as they had eaten, Meade spread out his bedroll, said a terse good night, and lay down with his back firmly turned to his companion. Rayna followed suit, but it was a long time before sleep finally found her.

By noon the next day the formidable Caldero Ridge was in view. When approached from the north, it didn't look particularly threatening as mountain ranges went. There were no towering peaks to speak of but its incredible width made it impressive indeed, as it stretched a hundred miles to the east and west in a seemingly unbroken line. However, its most intimidating feature wasn't at all visible from the north. The Ridge was the dividing line between the high plateau and the basin that cut across the south central part of the territory. Going into the Ridge was no problem. Getting out of it—or *down* from it—would be a different story.

They camped that night at the base, and the next morning began the most hazardous part of their journey. The rutted wagon trail they'd been following became more difficult to detect as Meade led Rayna up a series of winding switchbacks, then down a narrow escarpment and back up the next peak. Occasionally they would come across an area where a landslide had obliterated the trail, and they had to find another, even more dangerous route.

As they navigated the treacherous course, Rayna watched Meade closely and discovered that he wasn't quite the tenderfoot she had expected him to be. He rode exceedingly well and never once betrayed any hint that the perilous trail unnerved him.

"How long will it take us to get through this?" she asked when they stopped near noon to eat.

"If all goes well, we'll be clear of the mountains by mid-morning tomorrow," he said, then fell silent again as he had so much of the trip.

When they were riding, it didn't bother Rayna much, particularly now that handling Triton on the difficult terrain had become a full-time matter of life and death. But when they were stopped like this with nothing to do, the silence was oppressive. It seemed to Rayna that Meade was determined to ignore her, and she was getting fed up with it. This wasn't a good time to pick a fight with him, but she was too keyed up to sit quietly.

"You ride very well, Meade," she told him, hoping a deserved compliment would spark a little conversation. "I'm impressed."

He didn't bother looking at her. "What did you expect? My father was a cavalry officer for twenty years, and I've spent half that much time as one myself."

She tried not to take offense at his churlish tone. "Yes, but you told me once that you spent most of your career as a post surgeon and you didn't do a lot of campaigning. You don't need exceptional horseback skills to run an army hospital."

He shot her an exasperated glance. "Would it make you feel better if I fell off Chicory every once in a while?"

Rayna gasped. "Damn you. I was only trying to make conversation. In case you hadn't noticed, I paid you a compliment."

"Well, thanks a lot, but your so-called compliment suggested that you had anticipated I would be less than competent to begin with."

He had a point. "You're right, I was concerned, but I was wrong. At least *I'm* not too petty to admit I made a mistake," she said, more as an indictment than an admission of error.

Meade glared at her. "And what mistake have I supposedly made?"

"You called Triton a troublemaking man-killer, but you were wrong, weren't you? He's been an absolute angel."

"So far," he admitted reluctantly. "But if you don't mind, I'll reserve judgment on him until we're out of here. This is the easy part."

Easy? If this was easy, Rayna didn't want to think about what lay ahead, and she didn't want to think about Meade's surliness, either. Falling silent, she chewed on a tough strip of jerked beef until Meade announced it was time to mount up again.

They headed up another narrow switchback with Meade in the lead, and as they neared the summit where the trail seemed to disappear into thin air, Meade called back to her, "Brace yourself."

"For what?"

"You'll see," he replied as he reached the summit. With the packhorse in tow, he disappeared around a sharp curve.

Rayna had heard about the Caldero Ridge of course, but nothing in the rugged New Mexico landscape had prepared her for the dizzying sight of the mountain falling dramatically away as she rounded the curve. The sheer drop-off just a few feet to her right plunged down a thousand feet or more, making the basin below seem a hundred miles away. Numerous small mountain ranges dotted the basin, but from this vantage point, they looked like insignificant anthills. Rayna had never seen anything quite like it, or even half as breathtaking.

"My God, Meade, it's magnificent," she called to him. "I feel as though I've reached the end of the world."

"In many ways you have," he said, turning in the saddle to look back at her. The glorious smile on her face made him wish he hadn't. Why wasn't she frightened out of her wits by the daunting spectacle? Why in hell wasn't she cringing with dread at the thought of having to make her way down to the valley below? Why did she take everything in stride, even his foul, unfair bouts of temper?

Because she was the singular Miss Rayna Templeton, that's why, Meade thought, answering his own questions. It seemed that nothing in the world could frighten her. Except, of course, the thought that she might not get her sister back. The sympathy that was mixed with his irritation and his attraction was a potent combination, and Meade righted himself in the saddle. Being with Rayna twenty-four hours a day was a thousand times harder than he'd imagined it would be, and he just wanted to get to Fort Apache and be rid of her.

"Come on. We can't sit here gawking all day." He urged Chicory into motion down the steep escarpment. Then the trail doubled back and the mountains swallowed them again.

An hour later they stopped in a wide gorge to rest the horses, and Meade strolled around the area studying what appeared to be a set of fresh tracks made by two riders on horseback.

"What's wrong?" Rayna asked as she caught up with him.

"Someone has moved through here recently," he replied, frowning.

Rayna studied the imprints. "Yeah, I noticed those same markings earlier." She knelt and pointed to the irregular ridge left by one of the horses' shoes. "See the cleft there?

We've been following whoever is riding that horse for quite a while."

She was so proficient at everything else that Meade wasn't too surprised she'd picked that up. "Did you also notice that they stop frequently, and every so often one of the riders doubles back?"

Now Rayna was frowning. "No, I hadn't noticed that." She rose to begin her own survey and discovered that he was right. Near the mouth of the gorge, the horse with the cleft shoe had made three sets of prints. "They're not in too big a hurry, are they?"

"Or maybe they're waiting for someone," Meade suggested thoughtfully.

"Us, you mean," she replied.

Meade studied her expression and found concern but no fear. "Could be. Or it could be that some of my brother-in-law's instincts are wearing off on me. Somehow this just doesn't feel right." He started back to the horses with Rayna at his side.

"What kind of terrain do we have coming up?" she asked.

"The kind I'd rather not be traveling through right now," he answered, wishing the skin on the back of his neck would stop prickling. "This gorge snakes around for another mile or so, then narrows into Denning Pass, a swath of canyon that's barely wide enough for a wagon."

Rayna took a deep breath and expelled it slowly. "Great ambush country, huh?"

"Exactly. During the early years of the Apache wars, that pass was the site of more ambushes than I care to count. In fact, it got its name from a party of settlers who were massacred there. Road agents have made use of it, too," he added grimly.

"Is there another way through?"

Meade looked at her. "Nope."

Nodding thoughtfully, Rayna looked up at the steep walls of the gorge. "If they're going to attack us, they'll have to go into the cliffs eventually. I don't see that we have much choice but to keep going until we lose their trail."

Regrettably, Meade didn't see any choice, either. "Let's lead the horses awhile," he suggested.

"Agreed." She removed her Winchester from its scabbard on Triton's saddle, and Meade followed suit. Moving cautiously, with one of them always keeping an eye on the cliffs above, they followed the trail left by the cleft-shod horse. In sections where the ground became too rocky to show sign, they stopped and Meade scouted ahead until the tracks resumed.

They rounded a bend that led southward, and the gorge began to narrow before it snaked off to the east again.

"They stopped here," Rayna commented, and Meade crouched beside the prints.

"Yes, but neither of them dismounted."

Rayna felt her pulse pounding steadily harder with every foot they traveled, and when the tracks disappeared on a rocky shelf of ground, her heart nearly thudded out of her chest. She waited while Meade searched ahead for fresh sign, and when he returned to her, his expression was grim.

"Come on," he said, taking Chicory's reins from her and turning the horse in the direction they had just come.

Rayna had no choice but to follow. "What's wrong? I didn't see anyplace where they could have hidden the horses or led them into the cliffs. Didn't the prints resume?" she asked.

"Yes, but good old Cleft Shoe's prints don't look quite as deep as they did before."

"You think his rider went up into the cliffs and the other one went ahead?"

Meade shook his head in frustration. "I don't know. Maybe I'm just being an alarmist, but I don't want to take any chances. You stay here while I check this out more thoroughly."

It was a gallant sentiment, but Rayna didn't care much for heroics. "Meade, how long have you known me?"

He frowned. "I don't know. Just over three months, I suppose. Why?"

She smiled at him. "What do you think the chances are that I'm going let you leave me here with the horses?"

He sighed with disgust. "Damn poor, I presume."

"That's right."

"Rayna . . ."

His stern look didn't intimidate her. "Meade, we can argue, or we can get this over with."

Her stubborn jaw was firmly set, and he knew it was pointless to try to reason with her. "If I go alone, you'll just follow me, won't you?"

She nodded.

"All right. I guess I'd rather have you where I can keep an eye on you."

"Where we can keep an eye on each other," she corrected.

Meade shook his head as he tethered Chicory to a stout scrub near the base of a cliff. "God, but you're stubborn." He replaced his rifle in its scabbard and advised Rayna to do the same. "If we have to climb, the rifles will only make it more difficult," he explained, and she couldn't argue with his logic. Once the canyon narrowed, they wouldn't need long-range weapons, anyway.

Rayna just hoped they wouldn't need them at all.

With the horses secured a good distance away, they returned to the rock shelf where Cleft Shoe's tracks became shallower. They studied the ground and finally found a clear boot print near the east wall of the gorge. Loosened rocks showed them where someone had started climbing, and Meade abandoned all hope that his imagination had just been working overtime. They went up and found a ledge that ran parallel to the trail, then moved along it with as much stealth as they could manage.

A few feet after the canyon curved sharply to the left, the ledge ended and they began climbing again, following the trail of dislodged rocks and an occasional boot print in the soft red clay. Ahead, Rayna could finally see the mouth of

Denning Pass, and she was grateful to be on the cliffs rather than trapped in the bowels of the narrow arroyo.

"Okay, this is as far as you go," Meade whispered when they stopped to rest beneath a sheltered overhang that hid the mouth of the pass from view.

"Meade, we agreed—"

"We agreed that you wouldn't stay with the horses. I'm going to follow our clumsy friend and see if I can get the drop on him from behind."

"And what about *his* friend? You know . . . the one who went ahead through the pass. Remember him?"

"Of course I do. Unless I miss my guess, he's already left the horses somewhere on the other side and has climbed into the cliffs, too."

"Then we should both go."

"No," he said as adamantly as he could and still keep his voice low. "You stay here and keep an eye out. That's an order."

"But—"

"Rayna, for God's sake, just shut up and for once do as you're told," he said, then ducked out of their little hidey-hole.

Concerned that she might stupidly follow him, Meade spent nearly as much time looking over his shoulder as he did concentrating on the shelf he was climbing. After a few minutes, though, it became obvious that she had done the sensible thing, and he devoted all his attention to following the difficult trail left by the brigand who was waiting somewhere ahead in Denning Pass.

Back in her hiding place, Rayna wasted very little time fuming over Meade's dictatorial command. She could never have followed without him seeing her, but that wasn't the logical thing to do, anyway. What they needed was a bird's-eye view of the pass, and the only way to get it was to go straight up.

After backtracking to a likely spot, she began free-

climbing with the same steady skill that she and Skylar had
learned when they were thirteen years old and had been
trapped in Diablo Canyon by a flash flood. It was a difficult
but not impossible climb, and within thirty minutes she had
reached the top, where a surprisingly flat mesa awaited her.

Keeping away from the edge, where she might have been
spotted from the opposite side of the canyon, she hurried toward Denning Pass. When the opposing rock walls finally
narrowed to a point where she could easily have tossed a
stone across to the other side, she dropped to her stomach
and crawled to the edge.

The rock face below her was by no means sheer or completely vertical, but she had a commanding view nonetheless. Unfortunately, she didn't see any sign of the man she
knew had to be lying in wait somewhere down there. She
crawled on, ignoring the rocks that cut and bruised her el-
bows, until she finally caught a glimpse of Meade. He was
less than a dozen yards below her, crouched on a ledge.

Rayna moved on, knowing that the would-be robber had
to be somewhere ahead of Meade, and finally she saw him.
He was stretched out as flat as a lizard, and Rayna might
have assumed he was napping if she hadn't seen the movement of the rifle he had trained on the mouth of the pass.

Obviously he expected his quarry to arrive at any second,
and considering the length of time Meade and Rayna had
spent stalking their assassins, he was probably even beginning to worry that something had gone awry.

She drew her Colt, and her assumption was confirmed
when the man suddenly propped himself up and looked up at
the cliff opposite him. Rayna followed the direction of his
gaze, but saw nothing until the man called out, "Damn it,
Hobie, you seen anything from up there yet?"

The words echoed off the canyon walls, and a moment
later a ragged gray hat popped up from behind a boulder on a
wide ledge. "No, I ain't," came the barely discernible
hushed reply. "And I won't, neither, if you don't shet up."

Gray Hat ducked back down, and the Lizard stretched out

again. Trying to figure out what to do next, Rayna glanced at Meade and saw him looking around, obviously trying to determine where the second voice had come from. He was well above Lizard's hiding place, which led Rayna to conclude that he had probably gotten a glimpse of the bushwhacker and had been trying to get above him.

Unfortunately, Meade's ledge had ended, and the only way off it was to go back or climb higher.

With so many crags and boulders, nooks and turns, it was hard for Rayna to judge whether or not Gray Hat would be able to see Meade when he began climbing. Calling out a warning to him would only betray both of them, so she remained quiet and worked her way along the mesa until she had a little better view of Gray Hat's hiding place. His hat and part of his shoulder were all she could see, but it was enough for the time being.

But what should she do next? She knew she could easily kill the Lizard with one shot, but could she live with the knowledge that she'd murdered a man in cold blood? No, she couldn't see herself as a back-shooter. In fact, she had to wonder if she could kill a man at all. Since she'd never been in a situation remotely similar to this one, it was a moral and ethical question she'd never been forced to face. She had always assumed that if a time came when she had to defend herself or someone she loved, she could do it without a second thought.

But principle was considerably different from reality, she discovered.

A clatter of rocks echoed loudly down the cliff, and Rayna's heart leapt into her throat as she looked for Meade. He had gained solid footing on a shelf above the Lizard, but the cost was going to be too high. Lizard scrambled to his knees, raising his rifle as he frantically searched for the source of the disturbance, and Gray Hat cautiously peered over his boulder.

"Throw the rifle into the gorge!" Meade shouted, his revolver trained steadily on the man beneath him.

"Now, lookee here—" Lizard said indignantly, but Meade cut him off.

"Do it or you're dead!"

"All right, all right." Reluctantly the Lizard held the rifle out over the ledge and released it. It clattered on the rocks and then was silent.

"Now your gun belt," Meade instructed.

"See here, mister, you ain't got no call—"

"Do it!" he roared.

Considering the circumstances, Lizard's protestations were laughable, but Rayna wasn't amused. As soon as Meade had spoken, Gray Hat had disappeared. Assuming that he was crawling around the cluster of boulders to get a better shot at Meade, she scrambled back the way she'd come, frantically searching for a glimpse of him.

She heard Meade order Lizard to drop his gun belt, but there was no time to look to see if he would comply, because Gray Hat chose that moment to come out of hiding. He rose just enough to take careful aim at Meade, and Rayna discovered that her moment of truth was at hand.

Centering him steadily in the sight of her Colt, she shouted, "No! Over here," hoping to startle him, and that was exactly what happened. Gray Hat instinctively swiveled the rifle toward the sound of her voice, clipping off one frantic shot that thundered through the canyon. Before he could draw the hammer of his repeater or even think about ducking, Rayna pulled the trigger and Gray Hat fell back heavily.

A split second later another shot rang out, and she looked down to find that the Lizard had used her distraction to draw on Meade. He wasn't successful. Meade's bullet caught him square in the chest, and he went toppling into the ravine.

Trying to forget the fact that she'd just killed a man, she glanced at Meade just as he looked up and spotted her head and shoulders leaning out over the cliff. They watched each other for a full minute, letting the heat of the moment pass, and then Meade shook his head.

"I thought I told you to stay back where it was safe," he said without rancor.

"Aren't you glad I don't know how to take orders?"

His smile started slowly, but by the time it was completely formed, it was magnificent. "Very glad." He glanced across the serrated edge of the cliff. "Now, how the hell do you plan to get down from there?"

Chapter
Fifteen

REPRESSING THE CHILL that ran down her spine, Rayna peered into the darkness beyond the golden circle of light from the campfire. Five horses were tethered out there, and she could barely make out the blanket-wrapped bodies strapped over the saddles of two of them. She was keenly aware of their presence, though. Over the years, she had heard Consayka's people talk about the ghost sickness that afflicted anyone who stayed too long around the body or property of someone who had died. She hadn't understood the superstition until now. Gray Hat's malevolent spirit was out there somewhere, watching her, pointing an accusing finger.

After the brief, intense confrontation, she and Meade had carefully made their way back down the cliffs. Rayna had gone back for their own horses while Meade searched for those of their would-be assailants. By the time she returned, Meade had wrapped the Lizard in his own bedroll, secured his body to a horse, and started climbing the cliff to retrieve Gray Hat's body.

The men's personal effects told them nothing. Who they were and why they had set their sights on Meade and Rayna were mysteries that might never be solved. But it really wasn't important. Knowing their names, where they came from, and whether or not they had families wouldn't change the fact that Rayna had killed a man.

The day had taken a terrible toll on her, and she knew she should try to sleep. Her bedroll was already laid out by the fire, but she couldn't imagine being able to rest—not with Gray Hat's ghost keeping watch over the camp.

"Here, drink this," Meade said, handing her a cup of coffee that he had liberally laced with whiskey.

He was standing over her, and Rayna looked up at him as she accepted the cup. "Thanks." She took a sip and found no reason to complain, though she would have preferred the shot of whiskey alone.

She peered toward the horses again, and Meade sat on the log next to her. "You did what you had to do, Rayna," he said quietly. "You didn't force them to bushwhack us. If I had to guess, I'd say they'd done this before. They knew those cliffs too well for this to have been a spontaneous act."

Rayna nodded and forced herself to look away from the bodies in the shadows. "You're probably right. That doesn't make knowing I killed him any easier, though."

"If you hadn't, I'd be dead now," he reminded her.

She turned a sad, rueful smile on him. "Drat. You mean I missed the perfect opportunity to get rid of my churlish traveling companion?"

That's better, Meade thought. Her humor and fighting spirit were starting to return. He'd been watching her all evening and hadn't been able to bear the haunting sadness in her, although he understood it only too well. "I have been a real ogre, haven't I?"

"Yes, you have."

"I'm sorry," he said sincerely.

The tender look he was giving her only confused her jumbled emotions even more. She didn't want him to feel sorry for her, and that was obviously all his comforting words and kind looks amounted to. Wishing things could be different between them, Rayna looked into the fire to avoid his soft hazel eyes. "Why do you dislike me so much, Meade? I know I'm too obstinate and I lack certain desirable ladylike traits, but I'm not really a bad person. I'm kind to children and animals."

He smiled, captivated by the way the light danced over

her face. "I'm sure you are. And you're also absolutely fearless, loyal, and devoted to your family. As the Apache would say, you have a strong heart."

"Then you don't detest me as much as you pretend to?"

"I don't detest you at all, Rayna," he said softly.

She looked at him. "Then why do we fight all the time?"

"You make me angry with all the brash, reckless things you do."

Like killing Gray Hat? she wondered. No, that hadn't been brash. Following Meade after he'd told her to wait had been reckless, but killing Gray Hat to save Meade had been a matter of harsh necessity. "Have you ever killed anyone before?" she asked after a moment.

"Not with a gun."

She looked at him, puzzled by his cryptic remark. "What does that mean?"

Meade shrugged. "I'm a doctor."

His answer confounded her even more, but the weariness in his voice made her heart ache for him. "That doesn't make sense, Meade."

"Army doctors lose many more lives than they save," he told her. "There's too much we don't know, and the military is finding new ways to kill faster than we can learn how to cure."

"Not being able to save a wounded man isn't the same thing as killing him," she said gently.

This time he was the one who looked into the fire. "That's not how I feel when I watch someone die or see a one-legged man drink himself to death because I couldn't find a less brutal way to save his life."

"That's not your fault, Meade. You can't blame yourself for the cruel realities of life."

"Can't I?" He looked at her, and the bleakness in his eyes nearly brought tears to Rayna's.

"No, you can't. You just *care* too much." Unable to stop herself, she reached out and lightly caressed his face. "No one could fault you for that."

The combination of her soft hand gently touching his face and the compassionate light in her eyes was too potent for Meade to bear. He took hold of her wrist, but didn't force her hand away. "Don't . . . do that, Rayna," he said softly, his breath hitching in his throat.

She searched his eyes and found a different kind of torment had entered his gaze. "Why not?"

"Because I want very much to kiss you," he answered before he could stop himself.

She let her hand slide into his. "Then why don't you?"

"Because . . ." He took a deep breath, trying to shut out the need that coursed through him more strongly than ever before, but it wasn't going to go away as long as her hand was in his and her lips were close enough to kiss. He stood abruptly, but couldn't summon any conviction when he told her, "Because what we're . . . feeling right now is just a reaction to what happened today."

Rayna didn't believe that any more than he did. She rose and stepped closer to him. "We hadn't been nearly ambushed when you kissed me in my hotel room," she reminded him.

Meade knew he should move away from her, but he couldn't. "But you were feeling vulnerable that day."

"What were you feeling, Meade?"

"More than I should have."

They stood looking at each other, not touching, and yet feeling each other's presence more devoutly than either had imagined possible.

My God, Rayna thought with amazement, I'm in love with him. It defied all logic, but it was true. Meade Ashford wasn't the type of man who fit into the image she had of her life or what she wanted from it, and she certainly didn't fit into his; he'd made that abundantly clear. But that didn't change what she felt—or what she wanted.

Without considering the consequences, she took another step closer, cupped his face in her hands, and brought her lips up to his. The feather-light touch sent a jolt of desire through Meade that he couldn't deny any longer. Pulling her to him roughly, he deepened the kiss, probing the sweet recesses of her mouth with an urgency that robbed them both of thought.

With a hoarse moan, Rayna pressed against him, then gasped with delight when Meade cupped his hand around the underside of her breast. He pressed wild kisses across her face and down her throat, and when he claimed her mouth again, Rayna thought she might die from the white heat of his fevered kisses. She ran her hands over his shoulders and down his back, clutching at him as though that alone would bring them closer and quench the ache that was spreading through her.

Unable to bear the torture of the clothing that separated them, Meade worked at the buttons of her shirt and pulled it free from her shoulders. As he filled his hands with her breasts and teased the crests to hardness, she cried out in breathless pants and ground her hips into his, inflaming the long, hard ridge of his manhood.

With a rasping moan, Meade tugged at the buckskin cord holding her hair, pulling it free. He dug his fingers into the thick golden braid until it fell loose, and then he pulled her down to the bedroll, kissing her as passionately as she was kissing him. He blazed a fiery trail of kisses down her shoulders to her breasts and rejoiced in the sensuous, writhing movements Rayna made as his lips teased the crests. She dug her hands into his hair and cried out, begging for more.

Exactly what "more" was, Rayna couldn't have said. She knew only that the fire raging inside her had to be extinguished. The ache had become so deliciously painful that she couldn't think. Rational thought had deserted her, leaving only instinct and need. She had never done this before, never felt such intense passions, but as in everything she did, she held nothing back. She gave completely, and if it was wrong, she would live with the consequences, whatever they might be. Her eager hands danced over the muscular ridges of his torso trying to give back every pleasure she received from him.

Somewhere in the dim, clouded recesses of his mind, a voice was telling Meade this was wrong, but he was beyond caring. He had wanted Rayna for too long, and his need was too great. She had penetrated the barrier he'd built around his passions, and that wall had come tumbling down the moment she kissed him. It was much too late to erect it again, even if he had wanted to.

They undressed each other hungrily, every touch fueling their passions even higher, until finally they were naked and Meade was poised above her. Acting purely on instinct, Rayna wrapped her legs around Meade's hips and arched up, taking him into her with one swift stroke. Her gasp of pleasure and pain was lost in Meade's mouth as it closed over hers fiercely.

Overcome by the dizzying sensations he created, she met each thrust eagerly. As the pleasure spiraled and grew, it seemed as though it would go on forever, carrying her higher and higher. And then the fire that coursed through every part of her body exploded in a blinding flash of heat. Meade buried his lips in her throat as she cried out his name again and again and, with a hoarse cry of pleasure, finally found his own release. His body constricted, and then he slumped against her, too spent to move, too overwhelmed to speak or even think.

"Oh, Meade . . ." she whispered, running her hands down the taut muscles of his back. "I feel—"

"Hush," he said, claiming her mouth in a languid, drugging kiss. "Hush, sweet."

Wrapping her in his arms, he buried his face in her silken hair and let the comforting pulse of her heartbeat lull him to sleep.

When first light broke in the sky, Meade came awake abruptly and discovered Rayna in his arms, her naked body pressed intimately against his. Her scent was everywhere,

even on his own skin, and her golden hair spilled in wild pro-
fusion around her head like a breathtaking sunrise. The
memory of every sensation, every touch, every sigh they had
shared came flooding back to him, arousing him fully again,
but it wasn't night any longer. Meade wasn't lost in his own
needs, and Rayna wasn't the vulnerable creature who had
looked so sad and beautiful in the firelight.

Quite simply, one gloriously passionate encounter hadn't
changed who they were. Rayna was still a hellion, the antith-
esis of everything he thought a woman should be; and he
was still a retired army officer who craved only peace and
quiet from the rest of his life. What he had done last night
was reprehensible.

Appalled by what he had done—and craved to do again—
Meade gingerly untangled his legs and rolled away from her.
He slipped into his trousers and boots, separated his clothes
from hers, took his canteen, and slipped away to perform his
morning ablutions.

Rayna was still sleeping with the deceptive innocence of
an angel when he returned. He wanted her to stay that way so
that he wouldn't have to look her in the eye, but eventually
they would have to get on the trail to Fort Apache. His anger
at his own weakness made him clumsy as he began making
breakfast, and the clatter of the coffee pot finally roused her.

Still half asleep, Rayna yawned and arched her back,
stretching like a contented kitten. The sensuous movement
caused the blanket to fall away from her torso, and Meade
groaned as her magnificent breasts were revealed to him. He
could still feel the weight of them in his hands and the taste
of them in his mouth. His loins constricted with a jolt of remembered pleasure, and he swiveled away.

"For God's sake, Rayna, cover yourself!" he barked.

The rough command brought her fully awake, and Rayna
grabbed the blanket and pulled it up between her breasts as
she rose up on one elbow. She didn't have to wonder how
she came to be completely undressed. The memory of their
lovemaking was the sweetest thing she had ever awakened

to. A contented smile spread slowly over her features as she looked at his back. "And a merry good morning to you, too," she said teasingly.

"Get dressed while I fix breakfast," he said gruffly.

Rayna felt too good to be offended by his tone. "Oh, good, my grouchy companion is back. I was afraid last night might have mellowed your disposition."

Good Lord, how could she joke about it? "Rayna, we don't have time for sarcasm this morning. Now get dressed so that we can get on the trail."

Rayna couldn't imagine why he was being so waspish. Was lovemaking different for men? Didn't he feel as wonderful as she did? Hadn't he experienced the same incredible sensations she had? The sweet words he had whispered to her and the fevered moans she could still hear led her to believe that he had. So why was he being mean?

"Meade, look at me," she said huskily. She wanted to see his face when she told him how much she loved him.

But Meade didn't want to see her. He could imagine only too well how she looked, lounging there with her bare shoulders and glorious mane of hair, her blue eyes still cloudy with sleep and the afterglow of passion. Just her husky voice was playing havoc with his senses.

"Meade . . ." she said more insistently, and he finally turned, steeling himself against the sight of her.

"Damn it, Rayna, get dressed. This is not a whorehouse, and I'm not your first customer of the day."

Her tender emotions and her desire to confess her love died a violent death. Barely holding on to her temper, she wrapped the blanket around her and came to her knees. "Why are you behaving this way, Meade? What in God's name would possess you to say something that cruel to me?"

Meade was ashamed of himself, but he needed his anger. It was the only protection he had against what his tangled emotions were doing to him. "I'm sorry," he said tersely. "It's just that I've never deflowered a virgin before, and this is something of a new experience."

Rayna almost laughed. "Speaking as the virgin in question, I can say it's a new experience for me, too, but I don't feel 'deflowered.' "

"Well, you should. What I did last night was reprehensible. You should hate me for it, Rayna."

She couldn't imagine how anything so wonderful could be reprehensible, but she was undeniably hurt that he thought it was. "Would you feel better if I threw something at you and called you a cad?" she asked sarcastically.

"Damn it, Rayna. Take this seriously."

"All right, I will. Why should you be so angry? I'm the one who's been ruined, not you."

"That's hardly true. Spending the rest of my life married to an uncontrollable wildcat was not in my plans!"

Insulted and deeply hurt, Rayna sat up straight and nearly lost her blanket. "When did marriage enter this argument?" she asked mulishly.

Her face was set into its most stubborn mode, and Meade realized he was making a bad situation even worse. "Don't be obstinate. It's obvious that I have to marry you now."

"My, how romantic. Why, Dr. Ashford, I do believe that's the sweetest proposal any girl ever received."

"Romance has nothing to do with this, Rayna," he snapped. "What if you're pregnant?"

She hadn't considered that, and didn't want to. "Heaven forfend. If such a *blessed* event occurs, I'll be sure to write and let you know," she said furiously, struggling to get to her feet without losing the blanket.

"That's not good enough."

"Well, it will have to be," she retorted as she began gathering up her clothing, "because marriage to a stuffed shirt like you is far too high a price to pay for one night's pleasure."

"Fine. You remain single and if you ever do go to a marriage bed, be sure to have a good excuse ready for why you're not still a virgin!"

"Go to hell, Meade," she said viciously as she disappeared behind a clump of bushes.

"I probably will," he muttered, then wondered if perhaps he'd already arrived.

The remainder of their journey was even more tense than the first part had been. Where before, Rayna had been eager for conversation to relieve the boredom of the trail, now she wanted nothing more than for the earth to open up and swallow Meade whole. It was her great misfortune to have fallen in love with a man who was determined to deny whatever tender emotions he felt for her simply because she wasn't enough of a lady to suit him. He wanted to marry her, but only out of guilt and a sense of honor that caused Rayna more pain than if he'd cavalierly taken her virginity and left her without so much as a farewell.

For his part, Meade was almost as furious as Rayna, but his anger was directed inward. His emotions were tangled in knots so tight he didn't think they'd ever unravel. He couldn't think straight when Rayna was anywhere near him, and though he hated the thought of what marriage to her would do to his life, he couldn't imagine letting her go. He had taken her virginity; the only honorable thing to do was marry her. That conclusion should have been simple, but Rayna was just too stubborn to see it. While he fumed and tried to sort out the mess he'd made of both their lives, she fumed and did an excellent job of ignoring him completely.

Once they traversed the Caldero Mountains, the going became much easier despite the encumbrance of the two additional horses they were leading. Their encounter with the thieves had cost them a great deal of time, and despite the grueling pace they set, they didn't reach Fort Apache until midday on Wednesday.

The regimental flags that signaled Crook's presence were flying over the fort, and as Rayna neared the outpost, her anger at Meade began taking second place to her anxiety at the thought of meeting Crook. She had been disappointed by too many military men to have any faith in Meade's earlier assurances that Crook would release Skylar. As they rode between the two headquarters buildings at the entrance to the fort, Rayna would have loved an encouraging word from her companion, but she was much too proud to ask for it.

Their unexpected arrival caused a considerable stir on the parade ground as former colleagues and subordinates called to Meade in welcome, but only one man came to greet them officially when they dismounted in front of Crook's headquarters.

"Major Ashford! Welcome back," Lieutenant Neville Franklin said effusively, pumping Meade's hand. "When did you return to the territory?"

"It's just Dr. Ashford now, Neville, and I've only just arrived," Meade answered. "This is our first stop."

Franklin glanced at the blanket-draped bodies. "I see you two fellows had a spot of trouble."

Fellows? Meade thought. How could any man be so blind as not to realize instantly that Rayna was a woman, despite her mannish clothes? "Yes, we did. These two tried to bushwhack Miss Templeton and me in Denning Pass."

He nodded. "Denning Pass, you say? We've had a number of ambushes there in the last few months. Maybe you've—" Meade's words finally soaked in, and Franklin swiveled toward Rayna, who was tethering her horse to the rail. "Oh, I beg your pardon, ma'am. I didn't mean to be rude. Welcome to Fort Apache."

"Thank you, Lieutenant. Could you tell me, please, whom I should speak to about arranging an interview with General Crook?"

"Um, that would be Lieutenant Cary, ma'am."

"Thank you."

Meade could see that Rayna was anxious to go, and understandably so. "Neville, would you take care of these bodies, please? They'll have to be buried at once, but I'd like to know if anyone recognizes them."

"Of course, Maj— er, Doctor. I'll see to it at once." He

unleashed the reins from Meade's saddle horn and led the horses away, tipping his hat to Rayna as he departed.

Meade looked at her. "Would you like to freshen up and change before we meet the general?"

She shot him an exasperated glance. "Why? Are you afraid he'll mistake me for a man, too? Heaven forfend I should embarrass you with my attire."

Meade bit down on his tongue and sighed before reminding her, "You're the one who mentioned something in Santa Fe about wanting to be appropriately dressed when you met Crook. If you want to waltz into his office reeking like a horse and looking like an itinerant saddle bum, far be it from me to object."

"Good, because I want to get this over with," she replied.

Meade gestured toward the stairs to Crook's headquarters. "After you, dear lady."

He was right behind her as she bounded up the steps, but once they were inside, Meade took charge of arranging an appointment with Crook. He'd never met the general's aide, and he anticipated having to wait awhile to see the commander, but the mere mention of Rayna's name sent the aide scurrying into Crook's office. Less than a minute later they were being ushered inside.

If George Crook was startled by Rayna's appearance, he gave no indication of it as he greeted her with a warm but restrained smile, then turned to Meade. "Good to see you again, Dr. Ashford. I heard you had decided to retire."

"Yes, sir."

"Well, it's a very grave loss for the army."

"Thank you, sir," Meade replied, genuinely warmed by the compliment. Crook never said anything he didn't mean. "May I take it from the way the lieutenant rushed us in here that you have some inkling of why Miss Templeton has come?"

"Yes, I do." Crook came around the desk and pulled a second chair away from the wall. "Please sit down. I'm afraid this isn't going to be easy, and I certainly hadn't anticipated being able to discuss this problem with you in person, Miss Templeton. In fact, I've been trying to draft a letter to you and your family."

What did he mean, it wasn't going to be easy? Rayna's heart thudded heavily as she took the chair. "You received my letters, then, General?"

"Yes, and you have my heartfelt apologies for the suffering the army has caused you and your family."

"Then you *can* help me rectify this injustice?" she asked, almost afraid to hope.

"I am doing my very best," he said solemnly.

Rayna frowned. "What does that mean? My sister is now on the reservation at Rio Alto. Surely freeing her is a simple matter of signing a form ordering her release."

"I wish it were that simple, Miss Templeton."

Meade knew that Crook wasn't completely at ease in the company of women, but his discomfort was out of proportion to the behavior Meade had witnessed in him in years past. "General, has something happened that Miss Templeton and I are not aware of?"

Crook couldn't look at either of them. "I'm afraid so."

"Oh, God," Rayna breathed, clenching her hands into fists. "What's happened to Skylar? General, tell me, please!" she begged, coming to the edge of her chair.

Crook was forced to look up from his desk. "The details are as yet unclear, Miss Templeton, but it has been reported to me that a young Apache woman named Skylark killed a soldier before their caravan reached the Rio Alto. She was placed under arrest, interrogated, and subsequently removed from captivity by a Mescalero brave named Sun Hawk. Both have vanished."

"Dear God." Rayna's words were no more than a hushed whisper. Tears sprang into her eyes, and she rose abruptly, whirling away from Crook so that he couldn't see them.

Meade was at her side instantly, drawing her into his arms. "I'm sorry, Rayna. I should have found a way to help you sooner."

Rayna didn't return his embrace, but she didn't reject it, either. She needed Meade's strength right now to bolster her own.

"I am deeply sorry, Miss Templeton," Crook said. "This never should have happened. General Whitlock should have ordered her release the moment you brought the situation to his attention."

Rather than comforting her, his apology pierced through her fear for Skylar and found a home at the core of her rage. A flash of blinding anger gave her all the strength she needed to pull out of Meade's arms and turn on Crook. "Don't talk to me about what should or should not have happened, General, and don't expect me to stand still for a mouthful of polite apologies," she spat out viciously. "I want to know what the hell you're doing to get my sister back!"

Crook sat back in his chair so quickly that it nearly toppled over. "I'm doing everything I can, Miss Templeton, I assure you," he told her when he finally found his voice. "But this is a very complex and complicated matter. I've ordered a full investigation into the death of the soldier—"

"That's absurd! Skylar couldn't kill anyone even if her life depended on it. The charge is obviously a lie!"

"I believe you're wrong about that, miss," Crook said, taking a stern tone with her. He understood her anger, but a lady found better ways of expressing her displeasure. "According to the report I received from the commander of the detail, your sister admitted killing the soldier."

"Damn it, I tell you that's not possible!"

"Rayna, that's enough. Sit down and listen to what the general has to say." Meade placed his hand on her arm, but she jerked it away.

"Don't tell me what to do!"

He took her arm more forcefully and all but threw her into the chair. "I said sit down and shut up!" he commanded, startling her into momentary silence. He turned toward Crook. "Please forgive Miss Templeton, sir," he said with very little apology in his voice. "You can't possibly imagine what she and her family have suffered because of the army's insensitivity. Perhaps if you gave us more details of this incident, we might be able to piece together the truth of the matter."

Crook looked at Rayna as though waiting to see if she had any objection.

"I'm sorry, General," she apologized sincerely. "Please tell us everything you know about what happened to Skylar."

With a nod, Crook recounted the scant details from the report he'd received.

Despite the sketchiness of the report, Meade thought he had a clear picture of what had happened, and it sickened him. "Who is in charge of the Rio Alto detail?" he asked.

"Captain Luther Haggarty."

Meade knew him and didn't like him one bit. "And the soldier who was killed?"

"Private Stanley Talbot."

Meade knew him and liked him even less. Now he understood exactly what had happened to Skylar. "General, I have met Private Talbot and know him to be a degenerate swine who openly brags about the Apache women he has molested." Meade heard Rayna's despairing gasp, but he continued. "If Skylar did indeed kill him, she was only defending herself from rape."

"That is my assumption as well," Crook replied, then glanced at Rayna and found that she was as pale as a sheet. "Are you all right, Miss Templeton?"

The tears she had conquered before were stinging her eyes again. "How can I be all right, General? My sister may have been raped, and she is most certainly living a nightmare. I don't know where she is or how to get her back or what she is suffering at this very moment."

Meade reached out and covered her hand, but she balled it into a fist and twisted away from his comforting touch. "Don't," she commanded. "I don't want or need your sympathy. I just want Skylar back."

Meade retracted his hand and looked at Crook again. He knew the general too well to believe that he hadn't taken some sort of action to rectify this problem. "What have you done to locate Skylar, sir?"

"I've turned the matter over to Case Longstreet," Crook replied. "He's taken his uncle and nephew with him, and by now they should have intercepted Captain Haggarty's detail. His plan was to question Sun Hawk's family in the hope that learning more about the brave would give him an idea of what he might do or where he'd go."

Meade felt his first ray of hope dawning. "That's good news, General. If anyone can find Skylar, it's Case Longstreet."

"My thinking exactly." Crook looked at Rayna again. "I know my apologies are meaningless, Miss Templeton, but my promises *never* are. And I promise you that I won't rest until you and your sister are reunited."

Rayna believed him, and she finally understood why the Apache people trusted and respected him so much. His clear eyes and resolute mien demanded respect. She was only sorry she hadn't seen it in him earlier. Crook was an honorable man who would do everything in his power to right this injustice.

Unfortunately, that knowledge did nothing to assuage her fear for Skylar's safety.

Chapter Sixteen

CASE CAUGHT UP with Haggarty's party at Fort Bowie, where they had been camped for two days to allow for provisioning the soldiers and collecting much-needed rations for the Mescaleros. In two more days the Apaches would be safely ensconced at Rio Alto.

Haggarty hadn't been happy about giving Case the complete run of the camp, but considering the wording of Crook's directive, he hadn't had much choice. Case inquired about the wounded soldier who had been sent ahead to Fort Bowie along with the dispatch that had eventually made its way to Crook. He learned that the soldier was expected to recover. Case considered that very good news for Skylar and Sun Hawk.

He wasted no time questioning Haggarty about the events that had led up to Skylar's escape, because he knew the captain would resent being interrogated by an Apache—even one who was so close to General Crook. Haggarty would only lie, and Case thought it best not to stir up trouble. He would leave getting the truth from the soldiers to Crook and instead concentrate on what he could learn from the Mescaleros.

Not surprisingly, Case was greeted with looks of suspicion as he made his way to Naka'yen's campsite. His heart bled for the pitiful condition of the Mescaleros who had been uprooted from their reservation. He couldn't understand why the government was so intent on stripping an entire race of people of everything they had—including what was left of their pride.

When he finally found Naka'yen, the old man was the perfect example of the kind of damage the white man could do to an honorable old man. Naka'yen had kept his people at peace for years and all he had received in exchange were broken promises, and now a broken heart. The old chieftain barely had the strength to sit upright when he saw Case approaching.

Case had had the foresight to bring gifts of food and cloth for Naka'yen. He knew he could never buy the man's favor, but at least he could show him the respect he deserved. "I offer a gift of friendship," Case said, placing the bag on the ground between them.

Naka'yen's sad eyes studied Case, looking him up and down suspiciously. "You are an Apache, but you wear the clothes of the white man, and I have seen that you have power over the soldiers. Why should you want to be my friend?"

"Because I have come to help your son."

Life sparked in the old man's eyes for the first time, and he sat up a little straighter. "What do you know of my son?"

Case sat facing Naka'yen. "I know that he is in terrible trouble, but that what he did was done for a good reason."

"He is in love with the girl," Naka'yen told him. "It was done for her."

Case wasn't particularly surprised by the news. He had assumed there was a bond of some sort between Sun Hawk and Skylar. Otherwise the brave would never have taken such a desperate chance to free her. "Do you know where he has taken her?"

Naka'yen's gaze became shuttered and unreadable. "He said nothing to me before he left. I do not know where he is."

"Would you tell me if you knew?"

The old man regarded Case suspiciously. "Why should I trust you?"

"Because I have been sent here by the Gray Fox, who

wants to help your son and the woman called Skylar. He knows that a great wrong has been done to her, and he wants to set it right. He wants to return the girl to the white family who raised her."

"And what of my son?" Naka'yen asked. "He will be killed for what he did."

"Not if the soldier lives," Case assured him. "And I have already been told that the soldier will not die."

A glimmer of hope sprang into the old man's eyes. "My son will not be punished?"

"I cannot promise that," Case answered. "But the Gray Fox has given his word that if Sun Hawk's actions were justified, he will come to no harm. The Gray Fox has never broken his word to us."

Naka'yen took the promise seriously, but there was nothing he could say to help this stranger. "I do not know where my son has gone."

Case believed him. "Would he join Geronimo?"

The old chief shook his head. "Only if he had no other choice. He does not believe that Geronimo's ways are good for our people, but this long journey may have changed his mind. He counseled our people to peace and urged them to go with the soldiers. We both wanted to believe this would be good for our people, but I think we were wrong. Even before he left, my son had begun to doubt his wisdom."

"If he counseled peace, he is infinitely wise, as are you, old grandfather," Case said respectfully. "The Gray Fox has made no promises about this, but he is already trying to send you back to your own reservation. He does not believe it was right to send you to Rio Alto. He is a powerful man, and many will listen to him. Speak of peace to your people, grandfather, and pray that you can go home soon."

Naka'yen nodded, and Case began asking questions about Sun Hawk and about the hunting grounds they had visited before their confinement to the reservation. As he'd suspected, this band like many others had ranged from the plains to the north and east, south to the Mexican deserts, and west as far as the White Mountains. As a boy, Case could remember many encounters with Mescalero bands. Occasionally there had been disputes over their rights to hunt game in the territory claimed by Case's people, but most of their relations had been friendly. He even knew of marriages that had taken place between the separate tribes.

If Sun Hawk was as skilled as his father boasted he was—and Case had no reason to doubt it, considering the efficiency with which he had engineered Skylar's escape—he was going to be a formidable adversary. Quite simply, he could be anywhere.

"One final question, grandfather," Case said. "Do you think your son would take Skylar back to her white family at the Rancho Verde?"

Naka'yen's surprise suggested that he had not considered that possibility. "Why would he? She killed the soldier who attacked her. My son would never believe that even the Gray Fox would care so much about a single Apache maiden that he would send someone to help her rather than punish her."

Case stood. "You have been generous with me and I will remember it, old grandfather."

He turned to leave, but Naka'yen stopped him. "If you seek to know more about the woman, you should talk to her people."

"Her people?" Case asked.

"The Verdes. If you find their wagon, you will find her Apache father and mother."

Case nodded, feeling his spirits plummet as he turned away. Had Skylar somehow been reunited with her real parents? If so, it was not possible that she was his sister, Morning Star. He looked around and located the wagon Naka'yen had referred to. The old man who greeted him in English seemed to have been expecting him. He invited Case to sit and introduced his wife, Gatana, who had a deep gash on her forehead that had barely begun to heal.

Once again, Case explained the purpose of his visit and

assured them that he was trying to help Skylar. Any information they could give him would be to her benefit.

"We know very little, Mr. Longstreet," Consayka told him. "After Skylar killed Talbot, the officers took her to their camp and questioned her for many hours. They questioned others as well about how she had come by the knife, but Skylar told them nothing." He shook his head sadly. "She paid for her silence dearly. We all heard about the bruises on her face and the blood that ran from her mouth."

"Where did she get the knife?" Case asked, trying to shut out the image of his sister—if she *was* his sister—being so violently abused. In his mind, Morning Star was still five years old, and his instinct to protect her was still strong.

Consayka hesitated a moment, then shook his head, and Case realized that he was protecting someone, just as Skylar obviously had.

"Can you read?" Case asked, pulling a packet of papers out of the pouch that hung from his waist.

"Yes."

"Then look at these papers and you will know that what I have told you is the truth." He handed Consayka the passes Crook had written that authorized Case to take custody of Skylar and Sun Hawk and release them to no one except Crook himself. It also stated that Skylar was an Americanized citizen and was to be accorded the respect and rights due her.

Consayka inspected the papers carefully, and any doubts he might have had about Case disappeared. "Sun Hawk gave her the knife the night we left the reservation. Talbot had attacked Skylar as we came into the agency that morning, and he wanted her to be protected."

Case felt a sudden surge of anger. "Did Captain Haggarty know about that attack?"

Consayka nodded. "There were many witnesses including the man, Norris, and Haggarty himself was there, though he refused to believe Skylar's word over his soldier's. But we were all a witness to what he did that day, and my wife was wounded when Talbot attacked Skylar at the river."

Case stifled the urge to whip Haggarty to within an inch of his life. He certainly deserved no less. It was unconscionable that there had been not one but two attacks and the captain still placed the blame for the entire incident on Skylar. But that was in the past, and Case had the future to deal with— and his dimming hope that she was his sister.

"I was told you are her parents," Case said quietly.

"When we were taken from Rancho Verde, my wife and I assumed responsibility for Skylar so that she would have the protection of a family. She is a kind and gentle young woman. We were proud to call her our daughter for a time."

"Do you think you can find her?" Gatana asked.

"I don't know," Case replied. "Would she try to make it home to Rancho Verde?"

"I do not know where else she would go," Consayka replied. "I think she would trust that her father or Señorita Rayna would be able to help her."

It was a natural assumption, but Case didn't want to jump to a hasty conclusion. There were too many variables involved. "Is Skylar in love with Sun Hawk?" he asked.

Consayka looked at Case blankly, but Gatana spoke up at once. "Yes, she is. I think she is confused about her feelings, torn between loving him and wanting to go home, but I know her feelings are strong. Love is in her eyes every time she looks upon him."

"Thank you for being so honest," Case said. "I want very much to help her."

Gatana searched his face. "I believe you do."

Consayka glanced at his wife, then at Case. "Would you like to take her things? She has very little, but if you find her, I know she would want to have them back."

Case needed to travel as light as possible, but he couldn't resist the offer. "Yes, thank you."

Gatana went to the back of the wagon and pulled out a bundle. She offered it to Case and he accepted it, never imagining the intense effect it would have on him. For a moment he was transported back in time to the day his parents and his eleven-year-old sister were murdered. He had been showing his father the arrows he had made when his mother returned to camp with her two daughters. One Who Sings was shy and quiet, but little Morning Star was a bold child, full of life, with sparkling eyes and a laugh that Case had never been able to forget. On that day, she had run to her father clutching several sticks that she had insisted were arrows.

Gray Wolf had taken her onto his lap, and Morning Star held the arrows out for Case to inspect. He took them from her, praised them highly, and returned them to her. It was his last happy memory of his family, and the sights, smells, and emotions were suddenly as clear to him as if it had happened yesterday rather than twenty years ago.

He had never felt closer to his sister than he did as he held the bundle Gatana had handed him. Unable to imagine what had sparked such an intense memory, he opened the burlap sack and removed a ragged buckskin dress that had probably been quite beautiful when it was new. There was a parcel of writing paper, a pen, and a bottle of ink, but nothing that might tell him if the girl called Skylar was really his sister.

Keenly disappointed, he picked up the dress. As he placed it in the bag, an object fell out of one of the buckskin folds and dropped to the ground. Case looked down at it, barely able to believe his eyes. It was the Thunder Eagle necklace that his father had given his mother thirty years ago and that Case, in turn, had given Libby. Pushing the bundle aside, he reached for the necklace, and it nearly seared his hand as he picked it up.

No, it wasn't the same, not exactly. The arrangement of turquoise and silver on the choker was different. There were no feathers, and the medallion was crudely carved. But the similarity was unmistakable.

"This was Skylar's?"

"Yes," the old man replied. "She made it many years ago

when she was a young girl. In wintertime I would tell stories around the fire, and Señorita Skylar would sneak out of the house to listen to me. Her favorite was the story of Willow and Gray Wolf. Do you know it?"

Case could barely breathe. "Yes, I know it," he managed to say.

"That necklace represents the one Gray Wolf gave to his bride. It had great meaning to Skylar."

"She remembered," Case whispered, clutching the necklace in his hand as he pressed it to his heart.

Consayka studied his intense reaction. "You wear the same symbol," he said, looking at the plain medallion on Case's chest.

Case took his own necklace and Skylar's in the same hand. "I wear this for my sister, the daughter of Willow and Gray Wolf, who was stolen from me when our parents were murdered." He looked into Consayka's eyes. "I have been looking for her for twenty years, and now I know she is alive. Tell me everything you know about my sister. . . . Please."

Consayka did as Case asked.

The news Crook gave Rayna changed everything. She couldn't go directly to Rio Alto now and liberate her sister by legal means, and there was obviously no reason to plan a daring escape. Sun Hawk had already done that, and no one had a clue as to where Skylar and the brave were or when they might be found. Even Rayna wasn't foolhardy enough to think she could initiate her own search, but she couldn't bear the thought of returning to Rancho Verde without Skylar. And she knew her parents would want her to remain in the Arizona Territory until this insane predicament was resolved.

Since she had nowhere to go, Meade insisted that she come to Eagle Creek with him, and Rayna wasn't in a position to refuse. She accepted his offer but made it clear that she would make other arrangements for accommodations as soon as possible.

"Fine. We can argue about it later," he told her. "For the time being, I just want to get home."

It took two hours of hard riding to reach Eagle Creek Ranch, but with each passing mile Rayna could see Meade's excitement growing. When finally they came over a rise and saw the ranch house in the valley below, he stopped and took a moment just to feast his eyes.

"The ranch doesn't look like much, does it?" he said, but his broad smile betrayed his pride.

"I think it looks wonderful," Rayna replied. And it did. The house was a simple two-story frame building with a wide porch running along two sides. Cottonwoods and syca-mores shaded the yard, and the stock pens, corrals, bunkhouse, and stable that sat away from the house testified to the fact that this was a thriving working ranch. Though it bore little resemblance to Rancho Verde, Rayna was none-theless struck by a deep pang of homesickness.

When two children darted out of the barn and began run-ning toward the house, Meade's smile widened even more. "That's Jenny and Lucas," he said happily, spurring his horse into motion. He went charging down the hill, and Tri-ton, who had grown accustomed to following Chicory, tried to match the breakneck pace as soon as Rayna signaled him to move. As they neared the ranch house, though, she forced the stallion into a more sedate pace so that Meade could ar-rive ahead of her. The family she would be intruding on de-served at least a moment alone to welcome Meade home.

The children saw the riders in the distance long before they reached the house, and by the time Meade thundered into the yard, Libby was on the porch with Jedidiah Longstreet at her side. Jenny and Lucas raced to see who could reach Uncle Meade first, but the seven-year-old boy, with his longer legs, won out over his very determined five-year-old sister.

From a distance, Rayna watched in amazement as Meade

practically threw himself off Chicory in his haste to greet the children. He gathered the boy to him and a second later was nearly knocked down as Jenny threw herself into his arms, wrapping her arms tightly around his neck. He kissed them both soundly, then stood as his sister ran into his arms with more decorum but no less enthusiasm than her daughter had displayed.

By the time Rayna rode up, the man on the porch had come down to the yard and was shaking hands with Meade, beaming happily, and telling him how good it was to have him home.

Sadly Rayna wondered how long it would be before she could take Skylar home to this kind of warm and loving welcome.

"Libby, I want you to meet someone," Meade said, finally remembering that he'd brought a guest. Still holding on to her brother with one arm around his waist, Libby looked up at the visitor she'd been too excited to wonder about before. As Rayna dismounted, her golden braid fell over one shoulder, and Libby was stunned to realize Meade had brought home a woman! How wonderful! Judging from her appearance, she didn't seem like the type of woman Libby would have expected her brother to marry, but despite her attire it was easy to see that she was exceptionally beautiful.

"This is Miss Rayna Templeton," he told her. "Rayna, this is my sister, Libby Longstreet, her children, Jenny and Lucas, and our good friend Jedidiah Longstreet."

"It's a pleasure to meet you all," Rayna replied with a subdued smile as the children looked her over with curiosity and Jedidiah murmured a surprised "How do you do."

Her name registered on Libby immediately, and she realized she had probably jumped to an erroneous conclusion. However, she wasn't disappointed. "You're Skylar Templeton's sister," she said, slipping away from Meade to greet Rayna properly.

"That's right," she replied.

Libby glanced cautiously from Rayna to Meade. "You've been to Fort Apache?"

Meade nodded. "Yes. We know what's happened." Little Jenny impatiently tugged at Meade's trousers, and he bent to pick her up.

"Your brother has been a great help to me in my efforts to free Skylar," Rayna told Libby. "And now I fear I'm about to draw your family into this travesty even further. He's offered me your hospitality until I can make other arrangements."

"Oh, that's wonderful! Of course you'll stay with us until Case finds Skylar. I wouldn't have it any other way," Libby replied, taking Rayna's arm and drawing her toward the house. She had a hundred questions about Skylar and about how Meade had become acquainted with Miss Templeton, but they could wait until she'd made her guest comfortable.

Jedidiah had far less patience. After the brutal murder of his friends Willow and Gray Wolf, the frontiersman had traveled throughout the Southwest with Case looking for the little girl who had been kidnapped in the wake of the attack. Morning Star had always held a special place in Jedidiah's heart, and he had never given up hope of finding her. "We're anxious to learn more about your sister, Miss Templeton," he told Rayna.

She glanced at him, taking in the anxious look in his clear blue eyes. He was a big man, with a wild mane of silver hair and a beard to match, and though he was well into his sixties, he looked as vigorous as any man of thirty. Rayna liked him immediately. "I can imagine that you would be curious about Skylar. I know it can't be easy for either of you, having Case away from home searching for her like this."

"Oh, if she can be found, Case'll find her," Jedidiah said almost dismissively. "But that's not what I meant. Is—"

"Jedidiah, please," Libby said, reaching out to silence him by placing her hand gently on his arm. "There will be plenty of time for questions later. Miss Templeton's had a long and difficult journey. I'm sure she'd like to clean up and rest a bit."

Jedidiah stayed behind as Libby led Rayna into the house, and Meade divided a curious glance between his sister and his friend, wondering what to make of the strange undercurrents he was picking up.

"What did you bring me, Uncle Meade?" Jenny asked, drawing his full attention by placing her hand on his cheek and turning his face to hers. "You promised me presents," she reminded him.

"Can I take care of your horses, Uncle Meade?" Lucas asked before he'd had a chance to respond to Jenny.

"Yes, thank you. And I have presents for *both* of you."

Jedidiah moved to the horses. "I'll give Lucas a hand."

"Thank you," Meade said, puzzled by Jed's subdued mood. He kissed Jenny. "Why don't you go help Lucas and Jed, little one? If you bring in the bags off the packhorse, I'll probably be able to find a present or two inside."

She started squirming even before the last word was out, and when Meade put her down, she was off and running after her brother as quickly as her legs would carry her.

Meade followed Libby into the house and almost wished he hadn't, because he was pressed into service immediately. While Tessa, Case's cousin who lived on the ranch with her husband and helped Libby with her household chores, drew water for Rayna's bath in the kitchen, Meade was assigned the task of moving Jenny's belongings into Lucas's room so that Rayna would have a room of her own.

Rayna protested that Libby was going to too much trouble on her account, and Meade was thoroughly delighted to hear Rayna finally lose an argument. Rayna might be tempestuous, but Liberty Ashford Longstreet was unstoppable once she set her mind to something.

It wasn't until after supper that the Longstreet household finally settled down. Jenny hadn't been willing to wait that long for her present, of course, and the porcelain-faced doll Meade had brought her was given a place of honor at the table while they ate. During the meal, Meade explained how he had made Rayna's acquaintance, and Rayna, in turn, told them of the steps she had taken to procure Skylar's release.

As they talked, Libby began to notice the strange, strained politeness that Meade and Rayna exhibited toward each other. They rarely looked at each other, and when they did, one or both looked quickly away. Theirs wasn't the behavior of even the most casual friends, and Libby wasn't quite sure what to make of them until she caught Meade looking at Rayna and Jenny as the little girl forced their guest to examine her new doll for the hundredth time. While Rayna patiently cooed over the newly christened "Matilda" and admired the doll's starched white petticoats, Meade betrayed his feelings utterly by watching Rayna with an intense hunger Libby hadn't believed he was capable of.

Obviously her original assumption about Meade and the woman he'd brought home hadn't been wrong, after all, though Libby suspected that her brother was a long way from admitting that he had finally fallen in love. And what of the lady in question? Libby wondered. She hadn't known Rayna long enough to truly like her or even to determine whether she reciprocated the feelings Meade was obviously trying to hide.

Only one thing was completely clear to Libby: There was a great deal more to the story they had related about their acquaintanceship than either of them had admitted over dinner.

Libby finally rescued Rayna from Jenny and put both children to bed. Jedidiah, who had been even more taciturn than usual, seemed relieved when Libby came back downstairs carrying a carved wooden box. He fixed her with an impatient look.

"Can we get to it now?" he asked.

Meade frowned. "Get to what?"

"If you feel up to talking about it, we'd like to know more about Skylar," Libby said to Rayna, throwing an impertinent look at Jedidiah as she sat on the sofa beside Rayna and placed the box between them. "In particular, how she came to live with you."

Rayna thought it an odd question, but she didn't mind answering. "My father rescued her from a trio of Mexican slave traders while he was buying cattle in Sonora." She went on to explain how Raymond had brought the frightened little girl home and ultimately adopted her.

"When did he get her from the slavers?" Jedidiah asked.

"When she was about five, nearly twenty years ago."

"So she's twenty-four now," Jedidiah said anxiously, coming to the edge of his seat. "Do you know anything about her Apache parents? The report we read that Captain Haggarty wrote said she was Mescalero."

Rayna frowned. Their questions and their responses to her answers seemed entirely out of proportion with casual curiosity. "Actually, Skylar remembers very little about her life before she came to us, but her clothing seemed to indicate that she was from the White Mountain tribe."

"My God," Jedidiah breathed, finally allowing himself to hope for the first time that he might be close to finding the child he'd called his pretty little princess.

Libby touched Rayna's arm. "Does she remember anything about her family?"

"Only that they were massacred by a band of renegade Indians she thought might have been Chiricahua. For years she had horrible nightmares about the death of her parents and older sister."

"Does she remember a brother?" Libby asked anxiously, but before Rayna could reply, Jedidiah topped her question with another.

"Did she speak any English?"

Rayna was getting dizzy looking back and forth between them. "Yes, as a matter of fact, she did," she replied, remembering her very first encounter with her new sister. The memory brought a lump of emotion to her throat, and she had to clear it before she could answer, "She . . . knew two words quite well. She could say, 'Princess pretty.' " Tears were suddenly coursing down her cheeks, and Rayna wiped them away with embarrassment. Her shame faded, though,

when she glanced at Jedidiah and saw tears on his face as
well.

Stunned, Rayna glanced at Meade, who seemed as mystified as she was, then looked at Libby again. "I don't understand what's going on here, Mrs. Longstreet."

"Nor do I, Libby," Meade added. "I think it's time you
started answering questions instead of just asking them."

"I'm sorry," she told them, unable to repress her smile.
"It's just that we've waited so long for this."

"For what?" Meade asked.

Libby opened the box and removed the Thunder Eagle
necklace from its velvet cushion. Before she could begin her
explanation, Rayna gasped.

"That's Skylar's—or very much like it," she told Libby,
reaching eagerly for the necklace.

Libby was shocked. "Your sister has one like this?"

Rayna nodded as she examined the necklace. "It's not
nearly as fine as this. She made it herself from a description
our Apache storyteller used to relate about . . ." She paused,
unable to think of the names.

"Willow and Gray Wolf?" Libby supplied.

"That's right."

"Then she does remember," Libby said softly, smiling at
Jedidiah.

"Libby, what in blue blazes are you talking about?"
Meade demanded to know.

She looked at him. "Morning Star."

Meade frowned and searched his memory. "You mean
Case's sister? Oh, but, Libby, surely you don't think Skylar
could be—"

"She *is*," Jedidiah said adamantly. "Miss Templeton just
gave us the proof of it."

"You mean the necklace?" Meade asked.

The old frontiersman shook his head and tapped his fist
against his heart. "*I* taught Morning Star how to say 'Princess pretty.' No other Apache child could have known those
two words." Tears were still glistening in his eyes as he

looked at Rayna. "Your sister is the daughter of Willow and Gray Wolf. She's the sister of Case Longstreet"—his voice broke completely—"and she's my pretty little princess."

Waving one hand in the air as though to shoo away his tears, he rose abruptly and stalked out.

Rayne felt her own tears returning. She could barely comprehend the enormity of what these people were telling her, but all she could think about was how happy Skylar would be to know she had another family who loved her this much.

Meade was having a little more difficulty accepting the truth. "Libby, this is too coincidental," he said skeptically.

"No, it's not, Meade," she replied calmly. "It's fate, and perhaps the mysterious workings of Case's guiding spirit. Case never gave up believing his sister was alive, and he's had a number of visions recently that led him to believe he might soon be reunited with Morning Star."

Meade lowered his head and looked at her cynically. "More visions?"

Libby smiled patiently. "He was right about Crook's return, wasn't he?"

Reluctantly, Meade admitted that he had been.

Rayna was growing more confused by the minute. "I don't understand any of this. Visions? Guiding spirit?"

Libby took her hand and patted it gently. "Let me explain. It's a story I love to tell, and God willing, it will soon have a happy ending."

Chapter Seventeen

THE NEXT MORNING Rayna forced herself to perform the most difficult task she'd ever done. After breakfast she escaped to the solitude of her borrowed room and began drafting a letter to her parents. Crook had been conspicuously relieved to have the dreadful burden of conveying the news removed from his shoulders, and Rayna knew that it would be better for her parents to learn it from her than from a stranger—even a well-meaning one like Crook.

She softened the details of Skylar's ordeal as much as she could, but she made no attempt to lie. It could be weeks, possibly even months, before Skylar was located, and neither Raymond nor Collie would believe a fabrication about bureaucratic complications. They would open the letter expecting to read that Crook had helped her or that he hadn't. Rayna knew she owed them the truth.

And she also had the amazing job of telling them that she was staying in the home of Skylar's brother.

Rayna wasn't sure how she felt about that particular twist of fate. Skylar would be overjoyed—if they ever found her—but finally having a link to Skylar's past was strangely disturbing to Rayna. As selfish as it sounded, it seemed almost as though she'd lost some special, ineffable quality of her relationship with her sister. Rayna had had Skylar to herself for so many years, and now she was going to have to learn to share her with a brother neither of them had known existed.

Rayna suspected that their mother would feel much the

same way. That certainty made writing the letter that much more difficult.

"Rayna, are you finished with the letter?" Meade asked, tapping lightly on her door before stepping inside.

She pulled herself out of the confused reverie she'd slipped into. "Very nearly."

"Good," he said, feeling the same quickening of his heartbeat that he always felt when he saw her. She was dressed as she had been last night, in the skirt and blouse of her traveling suit, and the sun that poured in on her through the window gave her a radiance he could hardly bear to see. "I don't mean to hurry you, but if we're going to make it back from town by dark, we need to leave soon. Unless, of course, you'd rather wait until tomorrow to post the letter."

Rayna shook her head. "No. I want to get this behind me, and I know Mother and Papa are anxious to hear something."

"I wish we had better news."

"So do I."

They looked at each other for a long moment; then Meade started backing out of the room. "I'll let you finish while I hitch up the team."

"I won't be long," she promised, returning to the letter.

Meade turned at the door, but something seemed to pull him back. "Rayna . . ."

She glanced up. "Yes?"

"We're going to have to talk eventually."

She knew what he was referring to, but it wasn't something she felt equipped to deal with. "I don't think we have anything to talk about, Meade. Why don't we leave it in the past where it belongs?"

He searched her face. "Can you really do that?"

Of course she couldn't. What had happened between them on the trail was so much a part of her she didn't think the memory would ever fade. Her pride wasn't about to let her admit it, though. "I don't see why not," she replied, drawing her shoulders up a little straighter. "You made your feelings clear, and I believe I did, too."

"But neither of us was thinking straight."

"I was. And I think you were, too. You offered to marry me out of a misguided sense of honor, and I refused. If what happened between us was a mistake, I don't plan to spend the rest of my life paying for it."

If it was a mistake? Wasn't she sure? Meade wondered. He knew very well that he'd been wrong to give in to his need to make love to her. The least she could do was hate him for it. Any proper lady of breeding would have. But then, Rayna didn't know the meaning of the word "proper." She was a force unto herself who bowed to no rules except her own.

"Very well," he said after a moment. "If that's your final word . . . ?"

"It is," she replied, hoping she had effectively covered her disappointment that he hadn't told her it *hadn't* been a mistake. "Now, may I finish this letter so that we can go?"

"Of course, your majesty," he said sarcastically, bowing his way out of the room.

Trying to shut Meade out, Rayna looked over the long letter she'd written and added one final assurance that she would do whatever had to be done to guarantee Skylar's return. As she signed the letter and sealed it with wax, she tried not to think about the effect this news was going to have on her father's weakened heart.

After stowing the letter in her carpetbag, she checked Jenny's room to be certain she'd left nothing behind, then put on her jacket and went downstairs. Libby was waiting to see her off, and Meade was just returning from having brought the wagon around. As he came through the front door, he glanced up the stairs at her and frowned.

"What are you doing with your bag?" he asked crossly.

"I'm taking it into town."

"Why?"

Rayna thought her reasons should be perfectly obvious. "There's no telling how long the search for Skylar could take, and I can't impose on your family indefinitely. I think it's best that I take a room in Bannon."

Libby stepped forward and met her at the bottom of the stairs. "I do wish you'd reconsider, Rayna. Having you here is certainly no imposition," she assured her.

"And besides," Meade added, "do you really think you can bear the suspense of not knowing whether we've heard from Case? What are you going to do? Ride out here every day to see if we've had word?"

Rayna hadn't considered that. "Well, of course not," she said hesitantly. "I suppose I just assumed someone might be able to notify me if—"

Meade cut her off with an exasperated glance. "Rayna, Eagle Creek is in the middle of the fall roundup. I don't see how we can spare someone to go traipsing into town every day to give you a report."

"I don't expect daily reports," she said tightly.

"Then don't insist on doing something stupid like staying in Bannon."

Libby was appalled at the way he was talking to their guest. "Meade! That's uncalled for."

"Believe me, Libby, you wouldn't say that if you knew what she's really like. All you've seen is a rare glimpse of her best behavior. She is the most stubborn, headstrong creature I have ever met, and—"

"And she's standing in this room," Rayna said hotly. "She'll thank you not to talk about her as though she were in New Mexico."

Libby whirled to her. "Rayna, I'm sorry. I know Meade doesn't mean to be rude."

"Oh, yes he does," she replied. "He's very good at it, too."

Meade's smile was sarcasm personified. "I've had lots of practice, thanks to you."

Libby looked back and forth between them. "I swear, you two are worse than Jenny and Lucas," she muttered in amazement. "Rayna, despite Meade's rather heavy-handed invitation to you, I wish you'd reconsider. You can't imagine how nice it would be for me to have you around the house for a while. I love the ranch and my children, but I do get lonely for another woman to talk to."

Meade let out a scornful snort of laughter, and Rayna threw him a look that dared him to express his thoughts aloud. In the face of her challenge, he couldn't resist. "Oh, by all means, Rayna, stay. I know you and Libby will have a lovely time discussing the latest fashions and exchanging recipes."

Libby placed a hand on Rayna's arm. "Don't pay any attention to him. He's only teasing me because he knows how much I hate superficial woman-talk about fashion and such nonsense."

Rayna looked down at the lovely, petite lady and wondered if perhaps they might have more in common than she'd thought last night, after all. Actually, it did make sense that she stay, but only on certain conditions. "Libby, I would be happy to accept your hospitality if you'll allow me to earn my keep around her. If you treat me like a pampered guest, I'll go crazy within a week."

Libby hadn't been certain before, but she was now: She liked Rayna Templeton. Anyone who could get Meade this fired up and hold her own against his sharp tongue was definitely a woman worth getting to know. "Very well. From this moment on, I shall consider you a part of the family and treat you as such. Tessa and I will be more than happy to have someone to help with the household chores."

Meade laughed outright this time and looked to Rayna. "Do you want to explain the facts of life to my sister, or shall I?"

Libby frowned in confusion, and Rayna told her, "What Meade is so graciously trying to insinuate is that I'm not very domestic. I've been helping my father run Rancho Verde for a very long time, and I'd much rather help with the roundup than with the dishes, if you don't object."

Libby was surprised, but not totally shocked. "Of course.

Whatever you like. Case took his uncle and nephew with
him, so we've been a little shorthanded, anyway."

"Good," Meade declared. "Now that that's settled, shall
we head into town?"

"Very well." Rayna removed the letter from her valise and
made her way outside to the carriage while Libby gave
Meade the list of supplies she needed him to pick up in
Bannon.

As they rode away, Libby stood on the porch watching
them. She noted their stiff backs and the more than respectable distance between them on the wide wagon seat. They
didn't speak; they didn't look at each other.

Libby smiled happily. If she'd had any doubts last night,
they were gone now. Her stubborn brother, who'd spent
most of his life insisting he didn't believe in love, had fallen
hard. He wasn't happy about it, and he had no idea how to
cope with his intense emotions, but he was in love all right.

It seemed that in the space of a single day, Libby had discovered not one sister-in-law but two. Of course, Case still
had to find Skylar, and Meade had to admit he was in love,
before they could all truly be a family, but it would happen.
Libby was confident of that. There was nothing she could do
to help Case, but Meade was a different story.

Humming a merry tune, Libby went about her morning
chores.

After a very practical shopping spree in Bannon's only
general mercantile store, Rayna waited in the wagon while
Meade finished filling the supply list. She had purchased
enough clothes to get by on and had impulsively picked up
presents for Jenny, Lucas, and Libby.

The ride home was as uncomfortably silent as the ride into
town had been, and the raw tension between them became
the cornerstone in the foundation of their relationship for the
next two weeks. They spoke to each other only when necessary and managed to keep their arguments to a minimum for
the sake of Libby and the children.

Six area ranches had joined forces for the roundup, and Jedidiah was ramrodding the Eagle Creek contingent. Once he realized what an excellent cowhand Rayna was, he made full use of her services and very quickly came to respect her. She got along well with the other hands and there was no job she considered beneath her. From sunup to sundown, she was on the range searching for small herds and driving them to the holding pens where they were separated into various herds according to their brands and earmarks.

She could cut a single cow out of the herd as well as any man Jedidiah had ever seen, and she was absolutely fearless. In fact, the only problem he had with her was that he couldn't pair her up with Meade, who was also helping with the roundup. In the beginning, Jedidiah had tried to keep both of them close to him because he knew Meade had a lot to learn and Rayna needed evaluating.

The three had ridden out together every morning, but Jedidiah quickly learned the folly of that. The first time Meade had seen Rayna charging at breakneck speed through the brush and over a hill after a stray, he had left the herd to go galloping after her. Long before he caught up with her, Rayna had reappeared on the rise with the docile steer trotting in front of her. The argument that ensued had spooked the cattle and kept Jedidiah's ears burning for the rest of the day. The next morning he had wisely paired Meade with one of the other hands.

The arrangement had worked out to the satisfaction of everyone except Libby. She had tried to persuade Jedidiah to force her brother and Rayna to stay together as much as possible, and when he asked her reason, Libby had finally confessed that she was playing matchmaker. Though Jedidiah loved Libby like a daughter, he seriously questioned her judgment—and her sanity. Never in his life had he seen a less likely couple than Rayna Templeton and Meade Ashford, and he was too busy with the roundup to dabble in playing Cupid for a totally lost cause.

The result of the working arrangement was that Rayna

and Meade usually saw each other only at breakfast and supper. They were generally so exhausted from their labors that they turned in early, having barely spoken to each other the entire day.

Though the work kept Rayna busy, she had plenty of time to worry about how the roundup at Rancho Verde was faring without her, and far too much time to fret about Skylar. Every day that passed without word from Case Longstreet drove another spike into the coffin of fear that imprisoned her. And the situation with Meade wasn't adding to her peace of mind. He wore his disapproval of her like a badge for all to see, and kept any kinder feelings well hidden behind a suit of armor that nothing could penetrate.

Despite her exhaustion, the frustrating combination of emotions made it increasingly difficult for Rayna to sleep at night. She was tired of fighting with Meade, and she resented him because he couldn't see that she needed his strength, not his disapproval. She needed his love, not his intractable hostility.

Only Libby seemed to understand what she was going through. Meade's sister was kind and encouraging. At odd moments Rayna would catch a glimpse of her concern for her husband, but her faith in his ultimate success was unshakable. Rayna needed desperately to believe that all would be well, and though she didn't quite have Libby's conviction, her new friend's faith kept Rayna going.

Two weeks to the day after she'd arrived at Eagle Creek, Rayna lay in bed tormented by fitful memories of her night with Meade and fearful imaginings about what Skylar was suffering. Everyone else had long since turned in, too, and the quiet house closed in on her. Finally she gave up pretending to sleep altogether, put on her robe, and silently made her way downstairs.

The instant she opened the front door, she realized that she'd been wrong; not everyone had turned in for the night. The faint smell of Meade's cheroot filled her senses, and her first instinct was to close the door and return to her room before he noticed her. The thought of spending another hour alone, tossing and turning, changed her mind. She saw him silhouetted in the moonlight as he stood leaning against the pillar at the top of the porch steps.

"Couldn't sleep, either?" she asked as she moved onto the porch.

Meade turned and stifled a groan at the sight of her. He'd come out here to escape the tormenting sound of her tossing and turning in the room next to his. He didn't need yet another reminder of her nearness. "No . . . I couldn't sleep. Too tired, I guess."

He faced the yard again, and Rayna sat on the steps. When he made no attempt at conversation, the silence became too much for her. "It's not exactly life as you had it planned, is it?"

The question startled him. Surely she wasn't referring to his obsession with her. "What do you mean?" he asked with a scowl.

"Your image of yourself as a gentleman rancher. It's not all sipping fine wine on the veranda, is it?"

Meade remembered their conversation in Santa Fe when they'd discussed his plans. That was the first time he'd seen Rayna genuinely amused, and he'd been deeply affected by her smile and the sparkle in her eyes. He shored up his armor against the return of those feelings. "Frankly, I didn't expect it to be. I'm not afraid of hard work, if that's what you're insinuating."

Rayna sighed regretfully and stood up. "Sorry to disappoint you, Meade, but I'm weary of arguing with you. I'll find some other place to sit, and let you enjoy your cigar in peace."

She started down the stairs, but Meade couldn't let her go. "Rayna, wait," he said, stopping her with a hand on her arm. "There's no reason for you to leave. Sit down."

She hesitated a moment, but when he lowered his long frame onto the top step, she joined him.

"I'm sorry," he told her. "I suppose striking the first blow has become a habit."

Rayna found a tired smile. "You could always just duck and run."

"You're not serious? I wouldn't give you the satisfaction. In fact, one of these days, I plan to get in the last word."

"Good luck."

Meade chuckled. "I'll need it."

They looked at each other and became ensnared in the web of emotion that always trapped them the moment they lowered their guard. Meade was the first to look away, and Rayna felt a sting of disappointment.

"How long do you think your brother-in-law will be gone?" she asked, moving the conversation to neutral territory.

"I've been wondering that myself," he answered. "I know Case won't give up until he finds Skylar, particularly since he suspects she might be his sister. He *will* find her."

Rayna heard the respect in his tone, nor was it the first time she'd heard it. "Libby told me you didn't approve of her relationship with Case when they first fell in love."

"Most emphatically not."

"Because he was an Apache?"

Meade nodded. "I feared my sister was walking into a living nightmare, and I wanted to protect her from making a grave mistake. I'm not particularly proud of some of the things I did to keep them apart."

"But you're very fond of Case now, aren't you?" she asked. "I can hear the respect in your voice when you talk about him."

"He's made Libby happy," Meade replied, betraying a little of the surprise he still felt. "It hasn't always been easy for them, but their love has given them enough strength to withstand the prejudice. And Case is an easy man to respect. I don't think I've ever met anyone more honorable or more trustworthy."

"I'm looking forward to meeting him," Rayna commented.

"You'll like him. Anyone who can see beyond the color of his skin does."

They fell silent a moment, both a little stunned by their ability to have a normal conversation. They'd had so few of them.

"I like Libby very much," Rayna finally said. "In a way, she reminds me of Skylar. They both have a certain air of quiet refinement and a gentleness of spirit that I envy."

She sounded so sad about it that Meade nearly suggested she try to emulate them, but he suddenly realized what a tragedy such an undertaking would be—and how futile. "You can't change what you are, Rayna. Not every woman can be a Libby or a Skylar."

"I know that," she said, looking at him with love and very painful regret. "But if I were more like them, maybe—" Maybe you could love me, she wanted to say, but couldn't. She had too much pride to beg him to love her. Abruptly she stood up. "I should turn in now. We have to get an early start in the morning."

Puzzled by her sudden change in mood, Meade stood up and cut her off before she reached the door. "Maybe what, Rayna?" He searched her face, unable to escape the feeling that he was standing on the edge of a very important moment in his life. "What were you going to say?"

"Nothing." She tried to go around him, but Meade blocked her way.

"Then why are you leaving?"

"Because it's late."

Meade placed his hands on her arms to keep her from moving away again. "I don't believe that. You're the one who's trying to duck and run now."

Rayna looked up at him imploringly. "What do you want from me, Meade?"

"I want to know why you think you should be more like Libby."

"I don't," she said firmly, wanting desperately to escape him before she did something foolish.

"But you said—"

"I was wrong." She shook off his hands and took a step back. "I can't change who I am for any man. Not even you."

Meade was stunned. "I haven't asked you to change, Rayna."

"No, but you disapprove of everything I say, everything I do," she reminded him, feeling the sting of unwanted tears. "One moment you're kind, and the next you're cruel. You snap and growl at me, and just when I think you despise me totally, you do something completely incomprehensible, like making love to me. What am I supposed to make of that, Meade? How can I not be confused?"

"Have you considered that perhaps I'm confused, too?" he asked crossly. "When I'm not possessed with the desire to wring your lovely neck, I want nothing more in the world than to kiss you."

"But I'm the one who gets punished for your confusion, Meade." She looked up at him defiantly. "Which would you rather do right now? Kiss me or kill me?"

Meade felt a familiar, painful swell of desire. "Kiss you," he answered honestly.

"Then why don't you?"

"Because it wouldn't lessen the confusion for either of us."

"So be it," she said, swallowing her disappointment. "Sleep well, Meade. If you can." She darted around him and disappeared into the house, leaving Meade on the porch to grapple with the intense emotions he didn't want to acknowledge.

Chapter Eighteen

RAYNA HAD ALREADY left with Jedidiah by the time
Meade came down for breakfast the next morning. Lucas
was in the barn tending to his chores, and Jenny was tagging
along, doing her best to pester him.

"You look terrible," Libby told her bleary-eyed brother as
she served him a plate of griddle cakes.

"I didn't sleep well," he grumbled.

Libby nodded wisely. "That seems to be a common ail-
ment. Rayna didn't rest too well, either."

Meade glared at his sister. More and more she was wearing a look that suggested she knew something he didn't
know, and it infuriated him. "Rayna has a lot on her mind,"
he reminded her.

"So do you."

"Is it any wonder? The roundup is almost completed, and
Case still isn't back. Jedidiah's going to have to start moving
the herd to the depot in Prescott in a day or two, and I'll have
to decide whether to go with him or stay here with you. That
won't be an easy decision to make. Jedidiah needs all the
help he can get, but I don't want to go off and leave you and
the children all alone."

Libby tried to hide her smile. "I can understand why that
would cause you sleepless nights," she said solemnly.

Meade sighed heavily. "Damn it, Libby, if you've got
something to say, just come out with it. I've never known
you to pussyfoot around like this before."

"All right, I'll tell you what's on my mind," she said, pulling out a chair so that she could sit beside him. "You're in love, and you're too stubborn to admit it."

Meade frowned and shoved his plate away. "I am not in love." His chair scraped loudly against the floor as he pushed back from the table and stood up.

"Really? Then what do you call what you feel for Rayna?" she called after him as he stalked to the door.

"I don't know, but it's not love," he said emphatically, shoving his hat onto his head.

Libby waited until he had flung the back door open to tell him, "That's too bad, because she's in love with you."

Meade stopped in his tracks and turned. "She's not."

Libby nodded. "Oh, yes, she is. It took me a while to be certain, but I am now. I can see the hurt in her face every time you growl at her. She's vulnerable, Meade, and she needs your love and support to get through this ordeal, but all you're giving her is your own stubborn defensiveness."

Meade returned to the table and planted his hands on the rail of the ladderback chair opposite Libby's. "Rayna Templeton doesn't need anyone, and neither do I." He turned away in frustration, then swung toward her again. "My God, do you really think I want to be saddled with a hellion like that for the rest of my life?"

Libby smiled. "Yes."

Meade's scowl deepened. "You're wrong. And besides, it might surprise you to know that she already refused my offer of marriage. What does that do to your theory that she's in love with me?"

Libby hadn't imagined in her wildest dreams that Meade had already proposed. "I don't know," she said with surprise. "Is that why you're so obnoxious to her? Are you trying to punish her for refusing you?"

"Of course not."

She shook her head in bewilderment. "Well, I certainly can't imagine why she wouldn't agree to marry you. It's so obvious that she wants your love, I just assumed you'd been too stubborn to confess it to her."

Meade looked distinctly uncomfortable. "Actually, I didn't come right out and tell her that I loved her," he admitted, and Libby repressed a smile of satisfaction. At least he was no longer denying the feelings.

"Then what did you say when you proposed?"

"Well . . . it wasn't so much a proposal as . . ." He hesitated, realizing that Libby had trapped him into a discussion that was too personal to discuss even with her.

"As what?" she prompted.

He squared his shoulders and started for the door again. "It's none of your business, Libby. Just stay out of it, all right?"

He stormed out the door, leaving Libby alone to speculate on exactly what was so private that he couldn't tell her about it. Surely he hadn't . . . He and Rayna hadn't . . .

Or had they?

Too practical and nonjudgmental to be prudish, Libby considered the possibility that Meade and Rayna had already consummated their relationship. The trip from Santa Fe to Fort Apache had been a long and hazardous one. Two people who were obviously in love but determined to deny their emotions . . . It could have made for an explosive situation.

Libby had a hard time imagining her staid, cynical older brother succumbing to his passions, but then, he'd never really been deeply in love before, and he'd certainly never encountered anyone like Rayna Templeton.

It was entirely possible. In fact, the more Libby thought about it, the more convinced she became that she was right. It made a great deal of sense. It was easy to imagine what Meade's proposal had been like, considering his reluctance to acknowledge his love for Rayna. They had made love, and then he'd probably bluntly told her he was going to do the honorable thing and marry her.

Libby was sure it hadn't been the avowal of love every woman dreamed of, and knowing Rayna as she now did, she assumed that the response Meade received was probably even blunter than his proposal had been. Just the thought of it kept Libby chuckling merrily throughout the morning.

Obviously they didn't need her matchmaking after all. If Meade had already made love to Rayna and still felt passionate about her, he wasn't about to let her get away from him. He didn't realize it yet, but he'd get her to the altar if he had to drag her there kicking and screaming.

And Rayna would let him.

Meade spent the entire day thinking about his conversation with Libby, unable to believe he'd all but confessed that he was in love with Rayna. It was preposterous, unthinkable, outrageous . . . and totally undeniable. Thorns and all, he loved her. And while he couldn't imagine what life with her would be like, he couldn't imagine being able to live without her, either. That was why he'd gotten so angry when she tried to insist on staying in Bannon, and why his heart leapt into his throat every time she pulled some damned-fool dangerous stunt. He couldn't bear the thought of losing her.

Every instinct he possessed called for him to protect her and keep her safe from harm. That was what a man did for the woman he loved, wasn't it? But the idea of protecting Rayna Templeton from anything was ludicrous. He'd learned that she could do virtually anything a man could do, and when it came to ranch work, she did it a damn sight better than he did! Even if Libby was right and Rayna did love Meade, what could she possibly *need* him for?

He would never be able to control her. She'd laugh in his face if he tried to coddle her. Their life together would be an endless series of arguments, most of which he'd lose, because no matter what he might dictate to the contrary, Rayna would always do as she damn well pleased.

But on the other hand, she made him feel more alive than he'd ever felt before. Just one of her mischievous smiles had the power to wipe away all the cynicism Meade had spent the last ten years building into a crusty exterior designed to keep anything from affecting him. She made him feel young again, and she inspired a passion in him that he hadn't even known existed.

With or without her, his life was going to be hell. But if their one night of lovemaking was any indication, there could be glorious glimpses of heaven, too.

All he had to do was convince her of that.

By the end of the day Meade felt that he was almost ready to tackle the job. He was disappointed when he returned to the ranch and discovered Rayna wasn't back yet. While Jedidiah went to the bunkhouse where he'd been staying since Meade's return, Meade went into the house fully prepared to tell Libby that she'd been right about his feelings for Rayna. She had seemed so positive that Rayna loved him, and he needed a little reassurance to bolster him.

He found Libby in the parlor just completing her daily school lessons with Lucas and Jenny. But when she sent the children out to play, Meade could tell something was troubling her. He'd always been keenly attuned to her every mood, and he knew something was wrong now.

"Libby, what is it? Have you heard from Case?" he asked as soon as the children were out of earshot.

"No, it's nothing like that," she replied, then added wistfully, "How I wish it were."

"Then what's wrong?"

Libby frowned as she collected Lucas' primer and slate. "I'm not really sure. I had a very strange visit from Black Rope early this afternoon."

Case tried to place the White Mountain Apache brave. "Isn't he one of Case's distant cousins or uncles, or something?"

"No, he's just a member of his mother's clan. He and Case have never been particularly friendly. I think there was some bad blood between Black Rope and Gray Wolf before Case was even born. He never comes here."

"No one can carry a grudge like an Apache," Meade said with a grin that Libby wasn't quite able to respond to. "What did Black Rope want?"

"He wouldn't tell me. My Apache is only fair, but I under-stood him to say that he wouldn't talk to anyone but Case. When I told him Case wasn't here, he left, and an hour or so later Lucas was out riding and found Black Rope making a camp about a mile east of the house."

"Maybe he came to ask for a job."

"Possibly, but he has to know that Case has been gone for weeks. With so much of Case's family still living on the res-ervation, news like that is known to everyone there."

"Do you want me to ride out and have a talk with him?" Meade asked.

Libby shot him a droll look. "Meade, you speak about three words of Apache, and even those you manage to man-gle beyond recognition. I don't think it would be much help. And besides, Black Rope has never been the friendly sort."

"Maybe his arrival is a good omen," he suggested.

"What do you mean?"

"Maybe Black Rope has had some sort of special—I don't know—premonition that Case is going to be home soon."

Libby chuckled at that. "We're going to make a believer out of you yet, Meade."

"Don't start, Libby," he warned lightly. "I'm just trying to do what you do—look for the bright side of everything."

"In that case, I hope you're right," Libby replied. "It would be wonderful if Case came riding into the ranch to-night with Skylar."

Meade had to agree, but when Case did indeed come home a short time before sunset, he was alone.

Libby and Meade were waiting supper for Rayna when one of the hands coming from the barn sent up the cry of "Rider comin' in!" Libby flew to the porch and recognized her husband in the distance. She ran across the yard, and the rider urged his horse into a gallop, then flung himself down and gathered Libby into his arms. Case barely had time to kiss his wife properly before Jenny and Lucas caught up with her. He hugged them, and together they made their way to the house, where Meade was waiting on the porch.

"Welcome home, Meade," Case greeted him as they shook hands.

"The same to you," he replied. "We've been very anxious about you."

Case nodded. "I just came from Fort Apache where General Crook told me that you had brought Rayna Templeton here. I need to speak with her. Where is she?"

"She's been working the roundup, and she's not back yet," Meade told him, a frown of worry furrowing his brow. "I'm starting to become concerned."

Case was surprised to learn that their guest had been put to work, but he didn't question it. At that moment Jedidiah appeared and greeted his surrogate son warmly.

"Has Libby told you yet?" Jed asked, beaming from ear to ear. "Rayna told us some things about Skylar that—"

"That prove she is my sister," Case said, finishing Jedidiah's sentence for him. "Yes, I know." He reached into his pouch and withdrew Skylar's Thunder Eagle necklace. "She made this herself from her memory of our mother's necklace. The Mescaleros gave it to me along with the other belongings she left behind. Once I saw it and touched it, I knew she was Morning Star."

"Have you found her?" Meade asked. "Do you have any idea where she might be?"

Case's face took on the inscrutable look of stone that had driven Meade insane in the old days. "No. I went south into Mexico, but I found no trace of them."

"Did you encounter Geronimo?" Jedidiah asked, as they moved into the parlor.

"It would be more accurate to say that he encountered me, as I knew he would. Once I reached the Sierra Madre, two of his scouts intercepted me and finally agreed to arrange a face-to-face meeting," he explained. "Geronimo swore that he knew nothing of Sun Hawk or Skylar, and I believed him. He had no reason to lie to me."

Meade sat on the arm of the sofa. "Did you take advantage of the opportunity to invite him to return to the reservation?"

"After a fashion," Case answered. "I told him that the Gray Fox would be coming for him soon and he should come in now."

"To which he replied . . . ?"

Case shook his head. "He is determined to fight to the death this time. He is raiding in Mexico and across the border, and he seems to think he can elude the Mexican authorities forever. He won't be easy to root out of the mountains—if Crook ever gets permission to go after him," he added.

"So you're no closer to finding Skylar than you were three weeks ago," Libby noted sadly.

"No. Although Crook did tell me that there have been several raids on ranches to the east of the San Carlos and White Mountain reservations. The locals in those areas are blaming reservation Apaches, and they could well be right—or it could be Sun Hawk trying to avoid having to join Geronimo." He went on to relate the things he had learned about Sun Hawk from the brave's father, and he explained the events surrounding the death of the soldier, Talbot.

"One very good thing has happened," he told them. "General Crook sent John Bourke, his adjutant general, to investigate Talbot's death. After questioning Gatana and the other Verde Mescaleros, he interrogated Private Norris, the one who had sworn Skylar acted without provocation."

"Did Norris recant?" Meade asked expectantly.

Case nodded. "Armed with the facts Gatana had given him, Bourke was able to break down Norris's story in a matter of minutes. He confessed that Talbot had been obsessed with Skylar from the very beginning of the march. He didn't see the actual confrontation between them because Talbot dragged Skylar behind an outcropping of rocks, but he admitted that she had not ambushed Talbot without provocation."

"Then there are no charges against Skylar?" Libby asked.

"None."

"Rayna will be very relieved to know that," Meade said. "But what about Sun Hawk?"

"Since the soldier he attacked didn't die, Crook is inclined to be lenient," he answered, his eyes taking on a shuttered facade that masked his anger. "Bourke and I both gave the general the accounts of several Mescaleros who swore that my sister was beaten and abused. Crook knows that Sun Hawk was right to fear for Skylar's life. If he turns himself in, I doubt that he'll spend more than a few days in the guardhouse."

It was fully dark, and Libby had lit the lamps by the time Case finished, but Rayna still hadn't returned. Meade was growing more anxious by the minute, and finally he couldn't sit still any longer.

"Excuse me, Case," he said as he stood. "I think I'll check with the hands and see if anyone knows what's keeping Rayna."

As he left, Case looked curiously at Libby. "What's wrong with your brother?"

"We've had a strange time of it here while you've been gone, beloved," she told him. "Rayna Templeton is not a usual woman, and my brother has finally fallen in love."

Case's surprise showed plainly on his handsome face. "This is the same brother who so often told you he didn't believe that love existed?"

"The very same."

A slow smile spread over his features. "I think I will enjoy meeting Miss Rayna Templeton even more than I had expected."

Meade made it only as far as the back porch when Rayna and her trail partner, Luis Santiago, came riding in toward the stable. By that time he was so worried about her that all his judicious notions of taking just the right kid-glove tone with her had been quashed.

"Where the devil have you been?" he asked as he charged toward the stable.

Rayna slid down from Triton and began dusting off her Levi's with her hat. "We were rounding up the last of the strays around Windwalk Mesa and delivering them to the holding pen. Where do you think we've been?"

"Come into the house," he commanded.

"I have to take care of Triton first."

Meade took the reins out of her hands and tossed them to Luis. "Would you mind taking care of Miss Rayna's horse, Luis?" he asked the man.

"I can take care of my own horse, thank you very much."

He looked down at her and said bluntly, "Case is back."

All the fight left Rayna, and she hardly dared to breathe. "Is Skylar with him?"

All of her emotions were shining in her eyes, and Meade hated having to crush the hope that blossomed there. "No."

Rayna closed her eyes tightly and covered her face with her hands. "Damn! Damn . . . damn . . . When is it going to end!" she screamed, her voice strangled by all the pain that came bubbling to the surface.

Unable to bear seeing her anguished, he placed his hands on her shoulders gently, and she looked up at him with tears streaming down her face. "When, Meade? When is it going to end?" she asked softly.

He gathered her into his arms. "I don't know."

She clung to him for a while, gathering the strength and control that had momentarily abandoned her, then pulled brusquely away and marched off to the house to meet her sister's Apache brother.

Case Longstreet was everything Rayna had expected and more. He was a large man, very tall and imposing, with broad shoulders; but more than that, he had a commanding presence and an aura of peace surrounding him that was mesmerizing. His dark eyes were often unreadable unless he was looking at his wife, and then he held nothing back. Libby was a lucky woman indeed.

Case repeated to Rayna everything he had told the others and assured her that he had not given up. His next move, he said, would be to investigate the raids east of the reservation. Rayna, in turn, told him what little she knew about Skylar's early years. The information was important to Case, but he needed no reassurance that Skylar was his sister. The knowledge in his heart was unshakable, and he was much more concerned with knowing about Morning Star's life with her adopted family.

They sat down to supper, but all of them, including Lucas and Jenny, were too keyed up to pay much attention to the meal. After supper, Case put his children to bed, and it wasn't until Libby heard a noise on the porch that she finally remembered her strange encounter with Black Rope.

She could only guess that word of Case's return to Fort Apache had spread through the reservation, and Black Rope had come looking for him. She went to the door and wasn't surprised to find the Apache standing at the top of the porch steps.

"I have come for Longstreet," he said in his own language.

"I will get him." Knowing Black Rope wouldn't come inside even if she invited him, Libby left the door open and she hurried upstairs to tell Case he had a visitor.

As puzzled by Black Rope's appearance as Libby was, Case made his apologies to Rayna as he slipped out onto the porch.

"You are always welcome," he told the brave in greeting.

Black Rope's response was hardly congenial. "I did not want to come."

"Then why are you here?" Case asked bluntly. He didn't want to be rude, but Black Rope wasn't a friend or a relative, and Case was eager to get back to Libby and their very special guest. There was still much he wanted to learn about Morning Star from Rayna Templeton.

What Black Rope had to tell him, though, more than made up for the inconvenience.

"What did he want?" Libby asked a few minutes later when Case returned.

He paused a moment as he captured Rayna's eyes. "He came to tell me where our sister is," he replied.

Chapter Nineteen

THE ROOM ERUPTED into chaos.

"How on earth could Black Rope know about Morning Star? Where is she? How long has he known? Why didn't he go to Crook? Why—"

The questions came rapid-fire from everyone in the room, and Case shook his head at the barrage and stood silently until the interrogation stopped. "Everyone on the reservation knows about Sun Hawk and the woman he helped escape," he told them once he had their undivided attention. "And they also know that Crook sent me to find them."

"Where is Skylar?" Rayna asked insistently.

"Black Rope told me that two days ago he came across a camp in the Nagona Valley. It had been vacated quickly, as though whoever had been camped there had known someone was coming. The signs he found told him it was a man and woman, but when he tried to follow them, their trail disappeared."

"Where is this Nagona Valley?" she asked. "Is it far from here?"

"Not too far," Case replied. "It's in the White Mountains above the Fort Apache Reservation."

Rayna couldn't sit still any longer. Her mind was racing, and she felt as though she'd had Skylar in her arms for a precious moment and then lost her. "If Black Rope scared them off, they could be anywhere by now, couldn't they? For God's sake, why didn't Black Rope go to Crook the moment he suspected he'd found them?"

Meade looked up at her. "Rayna, the Nagona Valley is off the reservation. If Black Rope was there, it's very likely that he was off the reservation without permission."

"Meade's right," Case said. "Black Rope couldn't go to Crook without risking punishment. We're lucky that he even came to me."

"Why did he, do you think?" Libby asked.

"Because he feared that our people would be blamed for harboring renegades if Skylar and Sun Hawk were found anywhere near the White Mountains."

"Is there a chance they're still in the area?" Rayna asked hopefully.

"Possibly, but even if they're not, I should still be able to pick up their trail."

"Black Rope couldn't," Rayna reminded him, then frowned when everyone else began to smile.

"Rayna, Black Rope isn't Case Longstreet," Libby told her serenely. "Case will find her."

Rayna couldn't argue with her assessment of her husband's skills because she needed to believe in them as much as Libby and the others obviously did. "Are you leaving in the morning?" she asked him.

"Yes."

Rayna squared her shoulders and prepared for a fight. "I'm going with you."

Case frowned as he thought it over. "That's not wise, Miss Templeton. I can travel faster alone."

"I won't slow you down," Rayna argued.

"Perhaps not, but if Sun Hawk was astute enough to realize that Black Rope was in the area, he'll bolt at the first hint that he's being followed."

"Then that's all the more reason for me to come along. Skylar doesn't know you. She and Sun Hawk will see you as another threat. But if she sees me, she'll know she's safe."

If the situation hadn't been so serious, Meade might have smiled. Rayna hadn't uttered a single "hell" or "damn" since she'd started arguing with his brother-in-law. "She's right,

Case. Skylar would never run from Rayna, and you don't need to worry about her slowing you down. Believe me, I know." He stood and faced him. "We're both going with you."

Rayna turned toward him, wondering what to make of his offer and startling defense of her. "You don't have to do that, Meade."

"I want to. I was there in the beginning, and I'm going to be with you till the end. It's only fitting, don't you think?"

He was looking at her so strangely, so . . . tenderly, that she couldn't hold his gaze. "I suppose so."

Meade looked at Case again. "Then it's settled?"

Case knew he could refuse. If nothing else, he could slip off in the night and leave them behind. It would certainly simplify his job of tracking Sun Hawk without running the risk of being discovered.

But then he touched the medallion on his chest, and a strange sense of peace came over him. It was as if his spirit, the eagle, had spoken to him, telling him what he must do.

"It is settled," Case said with a nod. "We leave together at dawn."

Skylar was sorry that she and Sun Hawk had been forced to leave the Nagona Valley. The time they'd spent there had been one of the happiest periods of her life. Sun Hawk had felt it safe to stop traveling for a while, and Skylar had built a simple brush wickiup for them. Water had been plentiful, and Sun Hawk had been able to find enough game to feed them and to supply them with several much-needed deer hides. He had patiently taught her how to scrape and tan the hides so that they could make them into moccasins and warm clothing to ward off the autumnal chill of the mountains.

She and Sun Hawk had worked hard, but there had also been time for play, and every night in their tiny home, they had made love with the same sweet passion as the night he had taken her as his bride. He proved his love for her every

day in small ways that Skylar had never imagined could be
so important.

Though he tried to protect her from his worry about what
lay ahead for them, she knew he thought about it a great
deal. But strangely, what troubled Skylar most was that he
also worried about the connection she still felt to the
Templeton family. He knew instantly whenever her thoughts
went to Rayna or her parents. He would see a glimpse of sadness in her face, and it would make him angry—or at least
that was how it had seemed to Skylar at first.

It had taken her a while to realize that what he felt was
fear, not anger. He wanted so much for her heart to be with
him and nowhere else that he was afraid he would someday
lose her to the white world she had been raised in. Skylar had
tried to assure him that such a thing could never happen because her life was with him now, but she knew that his
doubts persisted.

As one day blended into another, time lost all meaning for
Skylar. On the reservation she had carefully kept track of the
days, ticking them off one by one on a mental calendar,
counting down to the day she would return to Rancho Verde.
Now she had no goal other than surviving and learning how
to be a good Apache wife. She had no future, and the past
was a memory that seemed to slip farther away every day. All
that was left to her was the present, and each day she reveled
in the simple joys that Sun Hawk brought into her life.

She knew their mountain idyll couldn't last, of course.
There were hard times ahead. Winter was coming, and they
couldn't live in the high mountains once the snows came.
Before long they would be forced to turn themselves in or
join Geronimo in the Sierra Madre. Neither choice boded
well for their future, but Skylar resolutely kept those
thoughts at bay. She gathered and stored every precious moment with Sun Hawk because she knew that once the happy,
tranquil times were gone, they might never come again.

That was why she had been so sorry to leave the Nagona.
When Sun Hawk had spotted the White Mountain brave

hunting in the mountains, they had broken camp quickly and disappeared without a trace. But where before they had gone north each time they moved, this time Sun Hawk had led her south. The brave had tried to follow them, but Skylar and her husband had been careful to leave no trail; thanks to Sun Hawk's patient teaching, that was one thing at which she had come to excel.

They had traveled for two days and made camp again, but Skylar knew they wouldn't be here long. There was no guarantee that the brave who had spotted them would keep the information to himself, and staying in one place made the risk of discovery too great.

Each evening, no matter where they were, Sun Hawk carefully scouted the area before they settled in for the night. He was gone longer than usual that evening, and when he finally returned to camp, Skylar studied him with concern. His moods were difficult to read at times, and she was never quite sure what he was thinking.

"Is there trouble, beloved?" she asked as he sat next to her. "Should I put out the fire?" Skylar hoped he wouldn't say yes. It was the first they'd had since leaving the Nagona, and the nights were getting much, much colder.

But Sun Hawk shook his head. "No, there is no one about. We will be safe here tonight."

"Then why do you look so serious?"

Sun Hawk glanced at her, then stared into the fire, knowing she wasn't going to approve of the decision he had made. "I was thinking of tomorrow."

"Will we move on again?"

"No."

Skylar sighed patiently and cupped his jaw in her hand, forcing him to look at her. "Then what is wrong? If you do not share your thoughts with me, I will be frightened."

He gathered her into his arms, and Skylar nestled her head on his chest. "There is a ranch far to the west. Tomorrow I will go there, and when it is dark, I will take two of their horses. When I return, we will journey south again."

Skylar didn't have to be told the meaning of his decision. "We will join Geronimo," she said quietly.

He was silent for a long time, and when he finally spoke, his voice was laced with regret. "We have no other choice. I am sorry."

Skylar raised her head and looked into his eyes. "When you took me as your wife, you promised that you would do whatever it took to keep me safe. If you think this is best, I will go where you go."

Warmed by her words, Sun Hawk gazed into her eyes and gathered into his heart the love he saw there. There was no other woman like this one. She accepted the hardships of their life with gentle smiles. When he failed her, she never accused. She found joy in the simplest of things and brought him a kind of happiness he had never known. If it had been his to give, he would gladly have made a present of the world and placed it in her hands.

That could never be, though. The world that had once belonged to all the Apache had dwindled to a few pitiful pieces of land, and even these were places he could not take his bride. He knew what lay ahead for them, and it frightened him.

But not as much as the thought of losing Skylar. If the only way to keep her was to join Geronimo on the warpath, he would do what he had to do and pray that his beloved would forgive him for it.

Rayna stood in the center of the deserted campsite, taking in the forlorn little wickiup and the cold circle of ashes in front of it. Part of her felt lost and totally alone as she imagined Skylar living in such isolation, but another part of her felt closer to her sister than she had in months. There was no proof that the Apaches who had made this camp were really Skylar and Sun Hawk, but Rayna was as positive of it as Case had been last night after Black Rope's visit.

They had left Eagle Creek before dawn that morning and had pushed their horses hard to reach the Nagona Valley in one day. When they arrived nearly an hour ago, Case had wasted little time studying the immediate area. Instead, he left Meade and Rayna to set up camp while he used what was left of the daylight to look for the trail Black Rope had lost.

"Are you all right, Rayna?" Meade asked as he dropped another load of firewood into the pile he'd been collecting.

His return startled her out of her reverie, and she turned to him. He was giving her that strange, tender look again, and she still didn't know what to make of it. It almost seemed to her that he had something on his mind that he couldn't quite bring himself to say. The change from his usual combative stance to this new one unsettled her because she didn't know what to expect next. Of course, there was really nothing unusual about that.

"I'm fine," she told him. "I finished grooming and watering the horses, and I was just . . ." Her voice trailed off as she looked at the wickiup again.

"Trying to visualize Skylar in this place?"

She nodded. "Silly, isn't it?"

"Not at all. I've been doing much the same thing myself. I saw some small footprints on that hillside, and could almost see her walking ahead of me. I can only imagine how much stronger those images must be for you."

He crouched by the cold remains of Sun Hawk's campfire and began constructing a new one.

"They must have stayed here for quite a while," Rayna commented as she bent down to help him.

"A week or more, I'd guess," he replied.

A small silence fell between them before she asked, "Did you notice there's only one wickiup?"

Meade stopped and looked at her. "Yes."

"And there's no sign that either of them slept on the ground outside it. Do you think . . ." She couldn't bring herself to ask the question that had been plaguing her since she'd first learned of Skylar's abduction.

But Meade knew what she was thinking. "Rayna, contrary to what is printed in the eastern press, rape is almost unheard of among the Apache. If they were . . . lying together, it wasn't because Sun Hawk forced her."

Rayna appreciated his reassurance. "I hope you're right."

"According to Case, your friend Gatana believes that Skylar is in love with Sun Hawk," he reminded her.

"I know," she said with a confused shake of her head. "But I find that so hard to believe. Sun Hawk is obviously a very courageous and skillful warrior, but he's—" She realized how bigoted her thoughts were and stopped.

"But he's an Apache?" Meade supplied. When she nodded, he told her, "That's very much the way I felt when Libby fell in love with Case."

"Yes, but Case had lived most of his life with Jedidiah. You told me yourself that he was educated and almost courtly in his manner. But Sun Hawk, for all the fine qualities he might possess, has never known any way of life but that of the Apache."

Meade could understand her confusion, but he had also recently learned that love wasn't always logical. "That doesn't mean she couldn't fall in love with him, Rayna. Apparently love is something we mere mortals have no control over."

We? Was Meade including himself in the category of people who had fallen in love? Rayna wanted desperately to ask him that question, but she couldn't. And he didn't seem inclined to say more.

Meade went back to laying the fire, and Rayna began unloading supplies from their bags of provisions. She went to the stream to fill the coffee pot with water, and by the time she returned, the campfire was blazing. She made the coffee, then set the pot on the rock rim of the fire to heat while she began filling a skillet with salt pork.

"I never did thank you for convincing Case that I should come along," she said quietly. "I appreciate it more than you can know."

A smile creased the corners of his mouth. "I was just trying to spare my brother-in-law the brunt of your wrath."

She looked up sharply, but instantly realized he was teasing her. It had been a long time since they had been able to joke about her temperament. "I wouldn't have damaged him too much," she assured him. "A few broken bones, one or two cuts and bruises . . ."

Meade chuckled, but the sound died away as he fell under the intoxicating spell of her wistful smile. "This is the way we should always be, Rayna," he said.

More confused than ever, she tilted her head inquisitively. "What do you mean?"

"Making each other smile. We do that very well."

"We also make each other impossibly angry," she reminded him, terrified that something was going to break the fragile thread that was holding this moment together.

"I know. But I'd rather live with the fights than have to survive without the smiles."

"Meade . . . ?"

A noise somewhere behind Rayna signaled Case's return, and the thread broke. Meade and Rayna both stood abruptly and peered into the gathering darkness. A moment later Case appeared.

"Did you pick up their trail?" Rayna asked anxiously as she came back to the reality of their situation. She wasn't here to dally with Meade; she was here to find her sister.

"I found the same trail Black Rope found, heading to the south, but I lost it, just as he did," Case replied, crouching by the fire. "Sun Hawk is very good."

"So what now?" Meade asked.

"Tomorrow we will ride down to Littlefield's."

Rayna hated the fact that she knew virtually nothing about this part of the country. "Where's that?"

"It's the only ranch for thirty miles in any direction."

"Surely you don't think Sun Hawk would take Skylar to a ranch house," Rayna said in amazement.

"No, but if I were Sun Hawk, I would be thinking that it's time they stopped traveling on foot. He can get horses for them at Littlefield's."

Rayna hadn't considered that, and she frowned. "If Sun

Hawk was responsible for the raids on the ranches to the east of the reservation, why didn't he steal horses then? Why travel on foot for so long."

It was Meade who answered her this time. "Because horses are easier to track, and they sometimes create more trouble than they're worth."

"Because they have to be fed and watered?" she questioned.

"Yes, and because a rancher is more likely to pursue a horse thief than someone who just stole a few supplies."

Case agreed. "Sun Hawk has been very careful until now to do nothing that would call attention to him."

Libby frowned. "Why would he change that pattern now?"

"Winter is coming," Case replied. "He has to go south. It's been more than a month since he and Skylar escaped from Haggarty, and he can be relatively certain that any intensive search for them has stopped. He'll take horses to make the traveling easier, and so that he won't have to go to Geronimo empty handed."

That wasn't something Rayna wanted to hear. "Why would he go to Geronimo? Didn't his father tell you Sun Hawk didn't like him?"

Case could see how much the news upset her, but he wasn't about to lie. If everything Libby had told him about Rayna was true, she could bear to hear the truth. "That doesn't matter, Rayna. Sun Hawk can't stay in the mountains after the snows come, and there are too many ranches in the valleys. Geronimo's stronghold in the Sierra Madre is the last safe place for any Apache off the reservation."

"Safe?" Rayna said with a gasp. "Between the Mexican government, the citizens' committees, and Crook, who's just waiting for permission to pounce, Geronimo's people don't have a prayer of surviving. How can you call that safe?"

"It is all a matter of perspective," Case replied calmly.

"You mean Geronimo is the least of several evils."

"Yes."

"Then what are we supposed to do?" she challenged.

Case gestured toward the skillet of salt pork that sat beside the fire. "We eat and sleep, and tomorrow we ride hard and pick up their trail at Littlefield's."

"You make it sound so simple," Rayna said, irritated by his calm confidence.

Case picked up the pan and held it over the fire. "It is."

Despite everything she had been told about Case Longstreet's incredible prowess as a tracker and about the visions that supposedly guided him, Rayna had serious doubts about his plan to go directly to the Littlefield ranch. Granted, Sun Hawk's trail out of the Nagona Valley *had* led south, but it could have been nothing more than a decoy—a feint south before he covered his trail and led Skylar farther into the mountains to the north. And, too, there was no reason to suspect that Sun Hawk knew of the existence of the ranch Case was leading them to.

If Case had considered those possibilities, he had discarded them without discussing them with Meade and Rayna. His belief that Sun Hawk would eventually make his way to Littlefield's was unshakable, and Rayna had no choice but to trust him.

There was one advantage to his plan if he was right, though. They had started their trip at least three days after Skylar and Sun Hawk had left the Nagona Valley, but the fugitives had been on foot and had little choice but to keep to the mountains or risk discovery. Case's party had no such liabilities. They could take easier trails and cover the same distance in one-third the time it would take Sun Hawk and Skylar.

Despite her skepticism, Rayna allowed herself to hope that Case was right, and by the time they reached the ranch, she had concocted a glorious fantasy about having arrived ahead of Sun Hawk. They would lay a simple trap to ensnare him, and once he was caught, he would lead them to Skylar, who was waiting for him a short but safe distance from the ranch.

It was a delightful fabrication, but nothing more. When they rode up to the ranch house, Hugh Littlefield was on the porch, shotgun in hand, to greet them. He didn't lower his guard until he recognized Case, and even then he was in no mood to extend much in the way of hospitality. He had been robbed, it seemed. A huge band of marauding Apaches had raided his place the night before and taken all his horses.

His story might have been more credible had Rayna not known that one brave alone had raided the ranch and had she not seen the four horses in the corral beside the house. When she glanced curiously at the calm cow ponies, Littlefield recanted slightly, admitting that actually only three horses had been stolen. The others had just been run off, but he'd had a "devil of a time rounding them up!" he told them self-righteously.

As they rode away from the ranch, Case seemed neither surprised nor dismayed by the news. It was, in fact, what he had expected and hoped for. Now he had a fresh trail to follow and they were less than a day behind Skylar and Sun Hawk. An hour after they had left Littlefield, Case picked up Sun Hawk's trail despite the effort the brave had made to conceal it. At dusk he led them to the remains of a recently vacated camp, and all Rayna's doubts about Case's prowess as a tracker evaporated like a drop of water on the desert.

That night, for the first time in months, she slept soundly because she knew she was about to be reunited with her sister.

Chapter
Twenty

AT FIRST IT was instinct alone that told Sun Hawk they were being followed. When the feeling refused to leave him, he stopped early and found a sheltered area in which to hide Skylar. Then he climbed to a bluff to look over the area they had just traversed, and waited. It had been two days since he took the horses, and he and Skylar made good time through the mountains despite the precautions he took to mask their trail. But his efforts hadn't been good enough.

In the distance, too far away to be seen clearly, he finally spotted the movement of three, perhaps four, riders. They were less than half a day behind. There was a chance, of course, that they were merely travelers or a small hunting party of Apaches from the reservation to the west, but Sun Hawk knew better than to discount the threat they posed.

When he returned to Skylar, she knew at once that something was wrong. "What did you see, husband?"

"You can make camp here, but we cannot have a fire tonight," he told her. "I am sorry."

Skylar fought down a stab of fear. "Did someone follow us from the ranch where you got the horses?"

"It is possible, or they could be a hunting party. I cannot swear that they are following us, but I must find out."

"How many are there?"

"Three, four, maybe. They are still too far away for me to be sure. I must go back to look at them."

He had left her before, and Skylar had always known he would return as surely as the sun would rise. Now, though, something had changed. She had a strange feeling in the pit of her stomach, and she couldn't make it go away. "Be cautious," she begged him, though she knew it was an unnecessary request.

"I will return when I can, beloved." He looked at her for only a moment longer, touching her face in his mind, gathering her close to his heart, and then he left.

By the time night fell and Skylar finally drifted into a restless sleep, he still had not returned. It was not the first night he had been gone this long, but it was the first time since Sun Hawk had rescued her from the soldiers that Skylar had been truly frightened.

From a hilltop overlooking the narrow valley where the party was making camp, Sun Hawk studied the odd group below him. There were three of them, and he knew for certain now that they were following the scant trail he and Skylar had left earlier. He had seen them looking for sign, and despite the cold, they made no attempt to light a fire when they stopped. That could only mean they did not wish to betray their presence.

But Sun Hawk could not figure out who they were or why they would be searching for him and Skylar. Before he took the horses, he had studied the ranch and the people there carefully, and had seen only an aging rancher and his wife. None of the three men below him had been on the ranch, he was certain, and their behavior was most strange.

One of the tall ones wore the hat and the heavy cape of a soldier, yet he did not seem to be in charge. The second man, smaller than the others, was bundled in a heavy cloth coat and wore a light-colored hat. Clearly he was not a soldier.

The third man was the one who troubled and puzzled Sun Hawk the most, for he was obviously an Apache. Yet for some reason he was the leader of the group. The others looked to him often, and appeared to do things as he directed them to be done.

Two white men—one of them a soldier—accepting orders

from an Apache? Sun Hawk could not fathom it, but he had to believe what his eyes told him. He watched until it grew too dark to see them well enough to learn more about them, and he briefly considered working his way quietly down to their camp to study them closer. Had they been three white men, he would have done it, but the Apache made him change his mind. He was a skilled tracker or he would not have been able to follow Sun Hawk's trail. Until it was proven otherwise, Sun Hawk had to believe that his enemy was skilled in other areas, too.

Knowing that the risk of discovery was too great, he returned to the horse he had left a considerable distance away and began the long ride back to Skylar. She was sleeping fitfully when he arrived, but he did not awaken her. She would need all her strength for what was ahead of them.

Wrapping himself in blankets, he lay down next to her and forced himself to sleep. A few hours later, long before dawn, he awoke and roused Skylar. He held her in his arms as he told her what he had seen, and then they began what would be the longest day of the many they had spent on the run.

Leading the horses, they covered as much ground as they could before it became light, but at sunrise they mounted up and started traveling fast. Sun Hawk abandoned all attempts to hide their tracks and kept to the easiest routes available. Speed was all that mattered, and they stopped only when it was necessary to rest the horses.

But late that afternoon their three shadows were still there.

"We cannot stop tonight," Sun Hawk told Skylar at sunset when they stopped to water the horses and let them forage. "The Apache who leads them is too clever, and he knows this land better than I. We will have to walk the horses much of the night, but we can escape them only if we travel while they sleep."

"Then we will walk tonight," Skylar said stoically as she knelt by the trickling brook to drink.

Sun Hawk knelt beside her. "Can you do so much? It will be hard, and you are already tired."

She looked at him and her heart swelled with love as she took his face in her hands. Skylar had no concern for her own fate, but if something happened to this man, she would not want to live. "I love you," she told him, a strange sense of urgency coloring her voice. "And your love for me has made us both strong. I will walk forever if you ask it of me."

Sun Hawk gathered her into his arms and held her as tight as he dared. It was not appropriate for a brave to feel fear; it was an emotion that blocked out reason and made a man careless. Fear was to be controlled, mastered, and relegated to a place where it could not cause damage.

But when he felt Skylar's heart beating heavily next to his and he imagined never knowing that joy again, he was afraid. More afraid, in fact, than he had ever been in his life.

"We can make camp just ahead there," Case told Meade and Rayna as they stopped at a brook Skylar and Sun Hawk had crossed only a few hours earlier. He dismounted and studied the ground, finding the places where their horses had grazed and the spot on the bank of the brook where they had knelt to drink. It bothered Case greatly that Sun Hawk was no longer making any attempt to cover his trail.

Rayna reluctantly dismounted and let her horse drink. Though she was exhausted from their hard ride, she hated the thought of stopping. Case was right, though. It would soon be too dark to read the signs, and the little canyon they were in was a likely spot to make camp.

"We're not gaining on them, are we?" Meade asked as Case returned to the stream.

"Very little, but that isn't surprising," he answered. "Sun Hawk knows we're following him, and he's forsaken stealth for speed. If we continue like this, it will simply be a matter of whose horses wear out first."

"Then what are we going to do?" Rayna asked, arching her back and rubbing at the aching muscles.

"*We* are going to do nothing," he said cryptically, and Rayna frowned.

"What does that mean?"

Case took a deep breath and prepared for a fight. Over the last few days he had developed a healthy respect for everything about Rayna—including her formidable temper and her iron will. "I want you and Meade to stay here and rest tonight. I'm going on ahead."

Rayna shook her head adamantly. "No. If you go, we all go."

"I'm sorry, Rayna. I don't want to wound you with my bluntness, but I will never be able to catch Sun Hawk and Morning Star with you and Meade along."

Rayna started to protest, but Meade spoke up before she had the chance. "They won't stop tonight, will they?"

"I wouldn't, in Sun Hawk's place."

Rayna didn't have to be told that one of the things that made the Apache so hard to track and catch was their uncanny endurance and their ability to travel day and night. But Skylar wasn't accustomed to such rigors, and Rayna reminded Case of that, using a little bluntness of her own.

"I know," he replied patiently, "but we are a threat to them, and Morning Star will do whatever she must to escape. Even if it means traveling all night."

Rayna wasn't sure what bothered her more, his calm, dictatorial manner or the fact that he always referred to Skylar as Morning Star. It was so hard to think of him as Skylar's brother. "Then that's all the more reason for me to go with you, Case," she argued. "If Skylar sees me—"

Case was shaking his head. "Rayna, Sun Hawk won't let us get that close. Unless we have absolute surprise on our side, he'll hide Skylar and then turn on us and fight. That's a corner we don't want to force him into."

She knew he was right, but Rayna couldn't bear the thought of staying behind. As she stood indecisively, trying to force herself to let go of her instinct to continue the pursuit, Meade moved closer to her and placed his hands on her shoulders, turning her to him.

"Trust him, Rayna," he said gently. "He's been right about everything else."

He wasn't ordering her to stop fighting; he was merely giving her the reassurance she needed to let go. All the combativeness flowed out of her, leaving only weariness in its place. She nodded and turned to Case. "All right. You go ahead, and we'll follow your trail tomorrow."

"Thank you." Case collected his horse and a few moments later was gone.

Rayna stood quietly, watching him leave, and Meade stood quietly, watching her. "You're not thinking of doing something foolish, like sneaking off after him tonight, are you?"

Somewhere inside her she found the remnants of a weary smile and gave it to him. "Sorry to disappoint you, but I'm not that impetuous. Unlike Case, I can't track even with a nearly full moon, and I know nothing about this country. I'd be hopelessly lost in an hour."

"By God, I think there may be hope for you yet."

His teasing grin was Rayna's undoing. If he'd been harsh or abrupt with her, she could have found the strength to fight him, but kindness stripped her of everything—even her defenses against her own fears. She searched his face and finally abandoned every last shred of her pride. "I need you, Meade," she said softly.

It was the one thing Meade had never expected to hear her say, and it was what he *needed* to hear most. "I'm here," he told her, enfolding her in his arms.

She clung to him, and they stood there for a long time, giving strength and taking it, renewing hope and calming fears. It wasn't a passionate embrace, but when they finally stepped apart and began making camp, they both knew that everything between them had changed.

Case no longer needed to see the trail to follow Sun Hawk and Morning Star. His quarry was taking the path of least resistance out of the mountains, but even that made little difference to Case.

For twenty years the spirit of the eagle had guided his way. It had led him to Gato, the renegade who had murdered his parents, and had given him back the necklace that Gato had taken from his mother. It had warned him of danger and shown him visions that had never failed to come true. It had even given him Libby, the greatest gift of all.

Now the eagle was leading him to Morning Star, and he had never seen the way ahead more clearly than he did that night.

If Case was right, and Meade had no reason to believe otherwise, it was finally safe to build a fire. They had done without one the last few nights, and despite the fact that they were coming gradually out of the higher elevations of the mountains, the weather was turning beastly cold.

Without Case there, Meade and Rayna fell into the old habits they had formed on the trail from Holbrook to Fort Apache. He gathered wood while she unpacked supplies for supper; and while Meade cooked, she tended the horses.

Sitting on opposite sides of the fire, they ate, talking very little but gathering a strange kind of comfort from the silence. Meade didn't have to wonder what Rayna was thinking about, and he wished he had more to offer her than the tired refrain he'd recited to her so often.

"He'll find her, Rayna," he said confidently.

She looked up from the deep blue flame she'd been staring at in the center of the fire. "I know he will."

"Then why are you so pensive?"

She shrugged. "Because I've let myself believe it was over too many times. I believed it just before my first meeting with General Whitlock, and again before I saw Crook. I wanted to believe that Case was going to come riding into Eagle Creek with Skylar. When we reached the Littlefield ranch, I just *knew* it was nearly over." She shook her head. "I'm afraid to believe again, Meade. And mostly, I'm just plain afraid."

He held her gaze for a long moment. "Would it help any if I told you how much I love you?"

The words took Rayna's breath away. She knew she should have been surprised or shocked, maybe even a little distrustful. She felt none of those things because she'd known that he loved her as she'd stood earlier in the comforting circle of his arms.

"When did you figure that out?" she asked quietly.

Meade gave her a gentle, wistful smile. "When did I *know* it, or when did I admit it to myself?"

"Both."

"I think I knew it somewhere inside myself the night we sat in the courtyard at Rancho Verde. You came down the stairs in a white dressing gown, and your hair spilled around your shoulders like an angel's halo. You were so vulnerable that night, but you weren't at all defeated. And you were too proud to let a stranger see you cry." He nodded as he recalled the moment. "Yes, I'm quite certain of it. That's when I fell in love with you. Of course I wouldn't admit it to myself until a few days ago."

Rayna remembered that night at Rancho Verde and the way he'd tried to comfort her. "I think I envy you."

"Why?"

"Because you can recall the exact moment," she told him. "I'm not sure when I fell in love with you. It just seems to me that all of a sudden the certainty was there."

Meade felt his heart constrict with a joy so intense it was almost painful. "But you do love me?"

Rayna looked into his eyes with the same intensity as she'd gazed into the fire, only this time she wasn't looking for answers; she was giving her heart. "More than I ever imagined possible."

"Do you love me enough to marry me?" He held his breath, waiting for her answer.

She tilted her head to one side. "Loving you won't change who I am, Meade," she warned him.

"I hope not. The world would be a dismal place without at least one Rayna Templeton Ashford around to stir things up from time to time."

"Rayna Templeton Ashford . . ." She murmured the name and a delicious warmth spread through her. With a single word she could soon be Mrs. Meade Ashford. She would marry and raise a family. Neither had been part of Rayna's vision of her future, but now she couldn't imagine anything more wonderful.

Unable to bear the distance that separated them, she moved around the fire and slipped into Meade's arms as though she'd been doing so all her life. "I'll marry you if you promise me one thing, Meade," she said, reaching up to caress his face.

"What?" he murmured, mesmerized by the loving light in her eyes.

"When we wake up in each other's arms tomorrow morning, promise me you won't have any regrets this time."

"No regrets," he promised as his lips closed over hers.

A series of valleys and ridges marked the beginning and end of the White Mountains, and by dawn Sun Hawk and Skylar had traveled across and over the first ridge. Before they moved into the next valley, Sun Hawk knew he had to be certain he had lost his enemy. He found a safe place for Skylar to hide and rest, then returned to the highest point of the ridge and surveyed the wide open valley, praying he would see nothing but sage and cactus.

What he discovered instead was a lone Apache rider pushing his horse to its limits in an attempt to reach the shelter of the ridge. Sun Hawk's heart thudded heavily in his chest. There could be no escape this time, for once he and Skylar began to cross the next valley, the tenacious Apache would spot them when he reached the top of the ridge.

Alone, Sun Hawk knew he could eventually escape the

brave, but Skylar had reached the limits of her endurance. His desperate maneuver had failed, and he had no choice but to stand and fight. For Skylar's sake he would do his best not to kill their pursuer, but the brave had to be stopped or Sun Hawk would never be able to get his wife to safety.

Knowing his enemy would follow the trail Sun Hawk had left, he worked his way along the ridge and down. He lost sight of the brave, but it didn't matter. He knew just the place to lay his ambush. He and Skylar had ridden through a ravine that cut the ridge in half, and his enemy would have to transverse it, too. He approached it from above, and found a good hiding place with an excellent view of the entrance. Readying his rifle, intending only to kill his enemy's horse, he waited.

Patience had always been Sun Hawk's friend, but as the minutes crept by, he began to realize something was wrong. The brave could not have made it through the ravine before Sun Hawk arrived, but he should have arrived soon after. But nothing stirred. Everything was silent. There was not even a hint that anyone was approaching.

"You do not want to kill me, Sun Hawk, or I would already be dead."

The voice was close, and Sun Hawk sprang into a crouch and whirled. His enemy was on a ledge above him, not close enough to touch, but close enough to kill or be killed. The fact that Sun Hawk was still alive told him a great deal, as did the realization that his enemy had drawn no weapon. He stood boldly in view, waiting to see how Sun Hawk would respond.

Slowly he came to his feet. "And you could have killed me, my enemy, but you did not. Why?"

"Because we are not enemies."

"Then why do you follow me?"

Moving very slowly, Case crouched at the rim of the ledge and looked questionably at Sun Hawk. The Mescalero brave nodded, and Case jumped down. For an instant he was completely vulnerable, and they both knew it.

The show of bravery impressed Sky Hawk. "How did you know I would not kill you then or when you first spoke?"

"I know many things about you, my friend," Case replied. "Your father told me you are a wise man who believes in peace. I trusted his faith in you."

Sun Hawk frowned, not certain whether to believe him or not. "When did you speak with my father?"

"Two days before your people arrived at the Rio Alto reservation. He was very sad because he did not know what had become of you."

Sun Hawk shook his head. "My father would not have sent you and two white men to find me."

"No, he did not."

"Then why do you follow me?"

"You have something I want, and I have something you must know," Case said, alert to every nuance of Sun Hawk's stance and expressions. His distrust was obvious, and it deepened even before Case told him, "The woman who travels with you will not be punished for killing the soldier, Talbot."

Sun Hawk frowned. "Why should I believe this?"

"Because the Gray Fox himself sent me to tell you this. The soldier who accused her of murder confessed that he lied, and now everyone knows she was only protecting herself. She is free to do whatever she wishes. She has no reason to hide."

One part of Sun Hawk rejoiced in the news, but another part of him withered and died. If Skylar was truly free, she could go back to her white family, now. "What of the soldier I killed? Will she be punished for that?"

Not will *I* be punished, but will *she* be punished. Case knew then that Morning Star had found a wise and brave warrior who loved her above all else. When this nightmare ended, he would gladly rejoice in the love she had found, but for the time being, he was grateful to be able to tell Sun Hawk, "The soldier you attacked did not die. He is alive, and the Gray Fox knows that you took Skylar from the soldiers because you feared for her life. He cannot turn away from the fact that you wounded one of his warriors, but he has promised your punishment will be small. You can soon be free to return to your own people."

"Do you have proof that Gray Fox has sworn this?" he asked, afraid to believe it could be true.

Case briefly considered giving him the papers Crook had written so that he could show them to Morning Star, but they might do more damage than good. The pass for Sun Hawk and Skylar had been created for the benefit of any soldiers who might question Case's authority, and it said only that Case was to take them into custody and deliver them to Crook. Skylar might assume them to be nothing but arrest papers.

"I have nothing but my word with me," Case finally told him, "but I can bring proof to you."

"What can you bring?" he asked suspiciously.

"One of the people who traveled with me until last night is the white sister of the woman you know as Skylar." Case was finding it increasingly difficult to read Sun Hawk's reactions, but when the young brave's face turned to stone, Case feared he had made a grave mistake.

"I saw no woman with you when I looked at your camp," he said accusingly.

Case wasn't surprised to know that Sun Hawk had been close enough to study them. "She dresses like a man, but she is a woman. She has traveled far and risked much to see her sister." *As have I*, Case thought. But this was not the time to try to explain something so complicated. "If you will let them meet, Rayna Templeton will tell Skylar that everything I have said to you is the truth. Rayna would not betray her sister."

As Sun Hawk considered his words, Case carefully reached into his pouch and removed the necklace Skylar had made. He held it out to Sun Hawk. "This belongs to Skylar. The Verdes gave it to me because they knew they could trust me."

Edging forward cautiously, Sun Hawk took the necklace and examined it. He had seen Skylar wear it many times on the reservation, but she had left it behind with her Apache parents. If nothing else, this finally proved that his enemy had truly spoken with his father and that the Verdes trusted this man enough to give him something precious that had belonged to Skylar.

Sun Hawk nodded slowly. "I will give it to my wife. I know it has great meaning for her."

"And will you let her see her sister?"

Sun Hawk's face was completely unreadable. "Where is she?"

"Perhaps half a day behind us."

Sun Hawk was silent for a moment before he said, "Bring her to this place at sunset."

Case nodded. "Very well. We will meet you here."

They stared at each other warily for a moment; then Sun Hawk turned and began climbing out of the ravine. Case watched him until he disappeared over the top before making his own way down to the floor.

It didn't occur to him as he went that Sun Hawk had never agreed to bring Skylar back there. He had only told Case to bring her sister.

Chapter
Twenty-one

EVERY INSTINCT SUN HAWK possessed told him he should use the time he had purchased to spirit Skylar away. The Apache was no longer following them; he had ridden off across the valley, presumably to get Skylar's sister. Knowing the brave could be laying a trap, Sun Hawk wanted nothing more than to bury the necklace, return to his wife, tell her nothing of what had been said, and ride with her like the wind until they were far away. That course of action was his only hope of keeping Skylar. Whether it was a trap or not, Sun Hawk had seen the sadness in his wife's eyes when she thought of her white family. Her heart grieved for them, and if her sister was truly here to take her home, Skylar would go with her. Though he believed his wife loved him, Sun Hawk could offer her so little, and she had lived among the whites for too long. He had to take her away, or he would lose her.

But of course he couldn't do it. If there was a chance that Skylar could be freed from a life as a renegade, he had to give her that chance. Anything less would be a selfish betrayal of the love he felt for her.

Knowing it was going to cost him the woman he loved more than his own life, Sun Hawk returned to the place where he had left her.

She was asleep when he arrived, but he could see the small place where she had paced back and forth before exhaustion had claimed her. He knelt beside her, studying her face, memorizing every perfect line. He thought of every word they had exchanged, every touch they had shared. He remembered the way she had come to him as his wife, and all the nights since when she had slept with her head on his shoulder and his cheek pressed against her brow.

Their life together had been too short, and now their future was compressed into the span of a single day. By nightfall his life would be over, but until then she was still his.

After removing his clothing, he lifted the blankets that covered her and lay down beside her. As he pulled her into his arms, Skylar slowly came awake. Her mind felt drugged, but she gladly left her fretful dreams behind for the security of her husband's embrace. She had no sense of time or place, only the sweet pleasure of his kisses on her throat and her face. He touched her intimately, pulling away her clothing until their bodies pressed together without restriction.

His mouth found her breasts, and Skylar sighed with pleasure. Some part of her mind realized that it was daylight, and another remembered that they had traveled all night to escape a grave danger. But that danger had passed, or Sun Hawk would not have awakened her with sweet kisses. After so many days of fear, it was easy for her to give herself over to passion, to touch her husband as intimately as he touched her, to let his need become her own.

They came together with an abandon that took her breath away and robbed her of her senses, but when the glorious pleasure finally subsided, she realized that this one time had been different. There was a desperation in the way Sun Hawk held her long after the moment of release had passed. When he finally shifted his body off of hers and wrapped her in his arms, Skylar knew something was wrong.

"Why do you look so serious, husband?" she asked, gently caressing his face, trying to smooth away the strange hardness she saw there. "I know those who followed us are gone now, or you would not have awakened me so sweetly."

Sun Hawk closed his eyes and pressed his lips into the palm of her hand. "They are gone, but they will be back."

Skylar's eyes widened in alarm, and she started to rise. "Then we should go quickly."

"No." He pulled her back into his arms. "There is time. We have until sunset."

She frowned. "To do what?"

"Be together."

Skylar didn't like the sound of that. "And then what will happen?"

Sun Hawk didn't want to tell her yet. If she knew her sister was near, she might not want to wait. She might ride after the brave who had gone to get her, and Sun Hawk couldn't bear to see her go a moment before it was time. "Then we will meet the Apache who tracked us so skillfully. He has words you should hear."

"How do you know this?"

"He said the words to me, but I was not sure it was wise to believe him. He has promised to bring proof that will make you know what he says is the truth."

"Husband, what did he say?" she asked anxiously, unable to imagine what it could be.

When he told her of the promises Gray Fox had supposedly made, the most magnificent smile Sun Hawk had ever seen spread over Skylar's face.

"This is wonderful!" she exclaimed as happiness suffused every part of her body, cleansing it of the fear she had experienced in the last few weeks. "There is no reason to hide in the mountains or join Geronimo. We can be free now!"

"Free . . ." He nodded solemnly. "Yes, we can be free."

Skylar felt the first flush of her exuberance fade. "Why are you not as happy as I? If the Gray Fox promised you will not be punished, then you can believe it. You will see your family again very soon."

And you will see yours, he thought grimly. "I cannot be happy until I have the proof."

Though she clung to hope as tightly as she could, she trusted Sun Hawk too much to discount his opinion. "You think it is a lie designed to trap us?"

He pulled her more tightly into the circle of his arms. "For your sake I hope it is not," he said fervently.

Overwhelmed by the intensity of his emotions, Skylar rested her head on his shoulder and could feel the strong, steady beating of his heart. It was a long while before she finally asked, "If it is a trap, should we not take precautions, beloved?"

"Yes, but there is still time," he said in a voice that sounded very far away. "I wish to hold you as long as I can."

Before it was time to go to the meeting place, Sun Hawk made love to Skylar again with an intensity and sadness that made her weep. They dressed then, and her tears had only barely dried when he finally gave her the necklace. As she clutched it lovingly to her heart, Sun Hawk explained how the brave had come by it.

"If Gatana and Consayka trusted him, he must be telling the truth," Skylar told her husband, trying as hard to convince him as she was herself.

"Perhaps."

Skylar looked down at the necklace and traced the lines of the crude carving on the medallion. "Do you know what this is?"

"The Thunder Eagle," he replied. "It is a symbol of importance to the White Mountain Apache."

She smiled at him. "No, I meant the whole necklace. Have you ever heard the legend of Willow and Gray Wolf?"

"Yes. Gray Wolf was a powerful warrior who defied the traditions of his people and married the daughter of his enemy."

"And he gave Willow a necklace to prove how much he loved her."

Sun Hawk glanced from Skylar's radiant face to the piece of jewelry in her hands. "Is that the necklace?" he asked, betraying his skepticism.

"No," she said with a wistful shake of her head. "But that story has always had great meaning to me. I can remember hearing Consayka tell it many times at Rancho Verde, and I remember it from before, too."

"Before?" Sun Hawk believed in legends and the power they had to direct people's lives, but that was not what enraptured him about Skylar's memories. She was sharing something sweet and sad with him, and he wanted to treasure the moment.

"Before I went to Rancho Verde," she replied, her smile fading. "Before my parents were killed."

She had already told him that she remembered very little of that part of her life, and Sun Hawk was glad she had this one pleasant memory. "Where did the necklace come from, and what has it to do with the legend?" he prodded her gently.

"I made this necklace long ago from Consayka's descriptions of the one that Gray Wolf gave to Willow."

"It is very beautiful."

Skylar looked down at the medallion as she tied the choker around her neck. "Not as beautiful as the real one Gray Wolf gave Willow," she said sadly.

"How can you know that?"

She brought her gaze up to his. "I'm not sure. I just *know*."

Sun Hawk nodded and rose reluctantly. "It is time to go now."

She offered him her hand, and he pulled her to her feet. "I love you, my husband," she said, gazing deep into his eyes. "Whether this is a trick or not, we will still have our love to make us strong."

"I pray you are right, beloved."

"I know that I am."

He pulled her into his arms and held her close for what his own heart knew was the last time.

"Come," he said finally, pulling away, his voice rough with emotions he could not control. "We must hurry if we are to arrive before them."

He turned away from her so abruptly that Skylar felt bereft. She didn't understand his strange moods, but she helped him collect their belongings and break camp. He led her to a ravine that she vaguely recalled, having passed through it in the early hours of the morning, and once he was satisfied that the area was safe, he helped her up the rocky hillside to a place where she had a commanding view of both ends of the ravine.

"I will take the horses to the mouth of the ravine and hide them. Then I will come back. We will watch the Apache and the ones with him as they come in from the north. If they are being honest with us, they will ride in together without fear."

"And if not?"

Sun Hawk looked around him. He had chosen this spot because there was nothing above it, and no one could approach without being seen. The brave would not be able to surprise him again; Sun Hawk had never in his life made the same mistake twice.

"If they mean to trap us, I will have no choice but to kill them." He waited expectantly for her to protest, but what he saw in her eyes instead was calm acceptance.

"You have the rifle and the many fine arrows you made at Nagona." She held out her hand. "I will take the revolver."

Sun Hawk was astonished. "Could you use it to kill a white man?"

Skylar nodded. She had thought about this often in the last few weeks. Talbot's death had been a horrible accident, but she knew now that if she had to, she could kill with purpose. "I would do anything to protect what I love most."

Sun Hawk removed the revolver from its holster and gave it to her, then left to tether the horses in a spot that would be easy to reach. When he returned to Skylar, they settled into their hiding place and began the long wait.

"Are you sure he'll be there?" Rayna asked Case for what might have been the hundredth time.

"I'm sure," he said without looking at her. The three of them were riding abreast, and it seemed to Case that their pace quickened every time Rayna asked the question. If she didn't let go of her anxiety, they would be riding at a full gallop by the time they reached the mouth of the ravine.

"But if what you told us about your conversation with Sun Hawk is accurate, he didn't actually give his word that he'd bring Skylar," she reminded him irritably. "It could have been a trick to delay you and give them a chance to escape."

"It wasn't," he replied.

"But—"

"Rayna! That's enough," Meade commanded, throwing her an exasperated glance. "If Case says Sun Hawk will be there with Skylar, you can believe it."

"I'll believe it when I see it," she said tartly, then fell silent and tried not to think about what could go wrong. When Case had intercepted them at midday, the story he related seemed too fantastical to be believed. Terrified that she was being led into another devastating disappointment, she had refused to accept anything Case said at face value. She had looked for flaws in his plan and tried to quell her anger at him for having allowed Sun Hawk to walk away.

He should have forced Sun Hawk to take him to Skylar, at gunpoint if necessary, instead of confronting him unarmed. He said he had released Sun Hawk to earn the brave's trust, but it seemed like ridiculous manly bravado to Rayna. If Case's actions cost her the only chance she might have to find Skylar, Rayna would find a way to make him pay for it.

Meade's attempts to calm her down and reason with her hadn't worked, and some of her anger with Case had spilled over onto him. He had made love to her last night with a passion that was heartbreakingly tender at times and at other times breathtakingly tempestuous. He had kept his promise to wake up with no regrets, but the sweet words they had exchanged that morning didn't change the way she felt that afternoon.

As they neared the ridge, Rayna caught Meade looking at her a number of times, but she ignored him. If she looked at him, he would probably give her a tender look of understanding that would disarm her completely, and she wasn't ready to be disarmed. She needed her anger if she was going to survive another disillusionment.

They reached the base of the ridge, but before they began climbing, Case stopped and dismounted.

"What are you doing?" Rayna asked.

"The horses need rest," he told her.

She started to protest as she patted Triton's lathered neck, but she bit back the ridiculous complaint. As usual, he was right, and even that irritated her. She climbed down and joined Case and Meade. "How far to the ravine?"

"Thirty minutes, maybe a little less," Case replied. "We don't want to arrive too early, or Sun Hawk may suspect that we're there to lay a trap."

She wanted to ask again what made him so positive that Sun Hawk would even be there, but she restrained herself. No matter what he replied, she wouldn't believe it, so it was pointless to question him. She slipped her canteen off the saddle horn and drank, then let Triton have some water, too. The men followed suit, and Meade looked over at Case.

"Do you think one of us should take to the hills just in case Sun Hawk decides to try an ambush?"

"No. If he doesn't see all three of us coming in, he'll think we're the ones setting a trap. We'll leave the horses at the mouth of the ravine and walk in. It's the only way."

Meade accepted his decision and was surprised when Rayna didn't take the opportunity to argue. "All right. We'll do it your way."

Case looked at Rayna. "There is one thing you must do, though."

She squared her shoulders and faced him belligerently. "If you're going to tell me I have to wait behind or stay in the background like a good little girl, you can just go—"

"Take off your hat and unbind your hair," he said, cutting her off. "From a distance Sun Hawk thought you were a man. I want him to see that I didn't lie, and the sight of your hair will make you much easier for Skylar to recognize."

It was a reasonable request, and she was happy to comply. She was less happy about having to apologize because she suddenly felt ashamed of her cantankerous behavior. "I'm sorry I snapped at you, Case." She sighed heavily. "I know I haven't given you much reason to believe this, but I do appreciate everything you've done for my sister."

"She's my sister, too," he said calmly.

Rayna felt her ire rising again as a burst of uncontrollable jealousy swept through her. "So you keep reminding me."

Case frowned slightly, regarding her more with curiosity than with displeasure. "Why does knowing that Morning Star is my sister trouble you so much?"

"Because I don't know any Morning Star. I only know my sister, *Skylar*."

"And you've never had to share her with anyone, have you?" he asked quietly.

Rayna felt unwanted tears stinging her eyes, and she hated the weakness at a time when she needed all the strength she possessed. "No, I haven't, and I'm not sure I like the idea," she said crossly. "You have a blood tie to her that I can never share."

Case nodded slowly. "And you have had her love for twenty years. You have seen her smiles and heard her laughter. You know what makes her cry, what she dreams of, and where she goes when she is sad. I have nothing but a memory of a bright-eyed little girl who made arrows out of sticks and brought joy to the hearts of all who knew her." He paused a moment when he saw the twin tears that carved a path down Rayna's face, but he couldn't stop himself from adding, "It is I who should be jealous of you."

"Damn you," she whispered as a sob escaped her control. "Damn you." The tears came in a rush and nearly buckled her over, but Meade was there to hold her up. She turned to him, resting her forehead on his chest until she conquered the tears. Case's words made her feel selfish and small. Resenting him for loving Skylar as much as she did was so wrong.

When Rayna finally collected herself and turned back to Case, her resentment of him was gone.

"Skylar goes to a place called the Enchanted Mesa to

weave her dreams," she told him, her voice as soft as a sigh. "And she feels sad only when she tries to touch the memory of the family she lost but can't quite reach it. If I am jealous, it's because you can give her back those memories, where I've never been able to."

Case smiled at her. "You have given her everything else. Don't begrudge me that."

"I don't," she said with a little shake of her head. "All I've ever wanted is her happiness."

"As have I," Case replied.

Meade placed his hands on Rayna's shoulders and looked at his brother-in-law. "I think we've reached an understanding."

"Yes," Case said.

Rayna nodded, then glanced over her shoulder at Meade. "Yes, we have. But if he's wrong about Sun Hawk being at the ravine, he's still going to have to reckon with me."

Both men laughed, and Rayna smiled at them. "Can we go now? I don't know about the horses, but I've had all the rest I can handle."

"Mount up," Case said, and they did.

The confrontation with Case had released a number of Rayna's emotions, including the ones that had been shielding her expectations. She felt raw and vulnerable as they approached the ravine, and when they dismounted and left the horses, her heart began beating so hard that it nearly leapt out of her chest. Sandwiched between Meade and Case, she walked over the rocky ground on legs that seemed barely strong enough to hold her up. And then they reached the mouth of the arroyo, and Case stopped.

"Go," he told Rayna. "Walk ahead."

"No, Case," Meade protested. "It's too dangerous."

"It's not," Case replied, looking down at Rayna. "Our sister is in there. I feel it. Call to her and she will come to you. Now, go."

Balling her hands into fists, Rayna stepped away from them and walked slowly into the arroyo. It was sunset, and darkness had begun to gather, making contorted shadows of every rock and stunted tree. The fear she felt had nothing to do with the ghostly landscape.

She stopped and opened her mouth to call out, but nothing came. She tried again, whispering, "Please, God, please," before the name she needed to say was ripped from her very soul.

"Sky-lar!" Her cry echoed off the walls, and before the sound had died, she shouted it again, *"Sky-lar! Sky-lar!"*

A strangled cry blended with the echo, and from above her, stones tumbled as Skylar came running down the hill. When Rayna looked up and saw her, she began running, too, and somewhere on the shadowed hillside they fell into each other's arms.

Chapter Twenty-two

LAUGHING AND CRYING with unrestrained joy, Skylar and Rayna held on to each other as though they would never be able to let go. Eventually, though, Skylar's questions began spilling out one on top of the other as she and Rayna stumbled down to the floor of the ravine.

How did you get here? How did you find me? How is Father? The questions came too fast to answer, but when Rayna hugged Skylar to her again, she told her that when she had seen their father last, he was well. It didn't seem like the proper time to explain that she had heard nothing from their parents since she had written them of Skylar's ordeal. If something had happened to their father, they would at least be able to share their grief this time.

Cherishing the sight of her sister, Skylar stroked Rayna's golden hair lovingly. "I had given up all hope of ever seeing you again." She smiled wistfully. "I should have known you would come for me."

"Yes, you should have," Rayna agreed, not caring that tears were still streaming down her face, because they were tears of joy, not weakness. "I'm only sorry I didn't find a way to protect you from the horror of what you've suffered."

Skylar shook her head. "It was not all suffering, Rayna. My journey took me away from you, Mother, and Papa, but it took me *to* something I had never imagined I would find."

Rayna searched her sister's face and discovered a strength and serenity in her eyes that had never been there before. "You've changed, Skylar."

"Yes, I have. In ways I don't even understand myself yet."
A movement caught her eye, and she looked beyond Rayna
to the two men who were moving toward them. A happy
smile lit up her face as she recognized Meade. "Major
Ashford!" She flew toward him and embraced him. "What
are you doing here? Oh, how good it is to see you."

"It's a great pleasure for me too, Skylar," he said fondly.
"I'm so happy to know you're finally safe."

"I *feel* safe." She turned toward her sister. "Rayna, did the
major tell you how kind he was to me on the way to the reservation?" She looked up at Meade again. "I will never forget that kindness. It sustained me more than you can know."

"I should have been able to do more," he said regretfully.

But Skylar shook her head. "No, Major. Nothing could
have changed what has happened to me. It was a journey I
had to make, and I gained much more than I lost."

Rayna placed a loving arm around her shoulders. "Even
more than you know, Skylar. There is someone else you have
to meet," she said, drawing her toward the third member of
the rescue party. "This is Case Longstreet."

Skylar smiled and extended her hand to him graciously.
"You are the one who confronted Sun Hawk this morning."

Case had been watching her, devouring every word and
gesture. He had always known his little sister would grow
into a lovely woman, but he had not expected this. Her
clothes were ragged and her face was stained with smudges
and tears, but she was poised and eloquent. Her manner was
graceful, and her eyes held a serenity that warmed his heart.
His sister had grown into everything he had dared hope she
would be, and much, much more.

Though he longed to gather her into his arms, Case could
only take her hand and press it between both of his. "Yes, I
gave Sun Hawk the promises General Crook made to both of
you."

Skylar didn't doubt for a moment that the promises were
good ones. "You risked your life, following us as you did,"

she told him. "If it had been necessary to protect me, Sun Hawk would have killed you."

"I know."

"Thank you."

"I had good reason to risk so much," he told her as he slowly unbuttoned his coat. Beneath it was the Thunder Eagle necklace. "Do you recognize this?"

The sight took Skylar's breath away, and she gingerly reached out to touch the medallion. A flood of memories came rushing back to her. Images that had always been nothing more than phantoms took shape in her mind. She saw that necklace on a beautiful woman and remembered running into that woman's arms. She remembered touching the beads one by one and hearing her mother laugh because Skylar's hand was tickling her throat. She saw a tall, handsome man who made her feel safe and loved as he put his arms around both of them. She saw her dark-haired sister and remembered the face of the brother who had teased and adored her.

For the first time, Skylar saw past the hideous memories of her parents' death to the pleasures of her earlier life. Images flashed one after the other, and with them came a knowledge that filled the dark void in her heart where only shadows had lurked . . . until now. She looked up at Case with a kind of wonder. "You are my brother."

A coil of happiness constricted around Case's heart. "Yes."

Skylar felt tears on her cheeks. "I remember loving you," she said, her voice tremulous.

"And I have never forgotten loving you," he told her as he opened his arms. She stepped into his embrace and felt as though she had come home.

From his hiding place atop the hill Sun Hawk watched his wife embrace the golden-haired woman, then the soldier, and finally the Apache. Their words reached his ears, but meant nothing to him. He knew only that they were happy words. Skylar was where she belonged, where she wanted to be. These people would take care of her now. She no longer needed him.

He watched until his heart could bear no more. Then he quietly made his way along the top of the ridge and down toward the horses.

It seemed like a long time before Case let Skylar go, yet it didn't seem nearly long enough, either. They couldn't make up for the lost years in a single moment, but there would be time to discover each other in the years ahead.

Standing in the little circle that Meade, Rayna, and Case had formed around her, Skylar shook her head in amazement as she looked at her sister. "I have so much to tell you."

"I know," Rayna said, and found her gaze drawn to Meade. "I have a lot to tell you, too."

"You must meet my husband, Rayna." Skylar's radiant smile took on a rapturous glow. "He has changed my life."

Until that moment, Rayna hadn't been able to believe that Skylar was in love with Sun Hawk. Now she knew it was true. "If you love him, he must be very special indeed."

"He is," she replied, then glanced around, looking for Sun Hawk. It took her a moment to realize that he had not followed her down the hill. She could hardly blame him, since he had no reason to trust these people as she did. She looked up at Case. "The promises General Crook made . . . you believe them, don't you?"

"Yes."

"And Sun Hawk won't be punished for rescuing me from the soldiers?"

"If there is punishment, it will be very light," he assured her. "Perhaps a few days in the stockade at the most."

Skylar moved away from him and looked up toward the place where she had left Sun Hawk. *"Ciká!"* she called out in Apache. When there was no answer, she called, "My husband!" again and told him it was safe. "The promises of the Gray Fox are good ones. We have nothing to fear."

The words echoed, but no one answered. A stab of fear pierced her as she recalled how fiercely Sun Hawk had made love to her and the strange, sad looks he had given her afterward. With a sickening sense of dread, she realized that he was gone.

"Ciká!" she screamed again as she began running toward the mouth of the ravine, but Rayna caught up with her quickly and grabbed her arm.

"Skylar, what are you doing?"

"Let me go," she demanded, tugging against Rayna's hold on her. "Sun Hawk doesn't understand. I have to find him!" Her eyes wide with panic, she wrenched free and ran.

"Skylar!" Afraid of losing the sister she'd only just found, Rayna started after her, but Meade held her by the shoulders.

"Rayna, don't," he commanded.

"What are you doing? Let go!"

"No, Rayna, you let go! Skylar is doing what she has to do."

"But she's going after him! What if he takes her away again?" she asked desperately, struggling to get out of his grasp.

Meade gave her a hard shake, and she stopped struggling. "Rayna, if Skylar goes with him, it will be because she wants to go, not because he forced her. She loves him."

Case moved closer to them. "And he loves her very much. Believe me, he won't do anything to put her in danger now."

"Then why didn't he come down here? Why did he slink away like a thief in the night?" she demanded hotly.

"Because he has no reason to trust us."

Rayna looked after her sister, but she had already disappeared from view. "Oh, God, don't let me lose her again," she whispered.

Her heart pounding with desperate fear, Skylar ran out of the ravine to the place where Sun Hawk had tied the horses. All three were still there.

Trying to control her breathing, she fought for rational

thought. Would he have gone on foot, thinking that he could disappear more easily that way? It was possible. In fact, it was very likely.

Feeling her life slipping away from her, Skylar sank to her knees, unable to stop the tears that had turned from joy to sorrow in the space of a single heartbeat. "Why could you not trust me, husband?" she whispered. She closed her eyes, but it didn't shut out the pain.

She knelt there for what seemed like an eternity, unable to think, feeling only an aching sorrow and a growing anger. How could he leave her? She could never have walked away from him, and yet he had left without even a good-bye. She had thought their love was strong, but it wasn't. It was like a web shining with diamonds of morning dew—beautiful but too fragile to touch.

When she heard a restless movement among the horses, she looked up, and some of the pain slipped away. Sun Hawk was silently untethering his horse. Skylar stood up quickly, and he whirled toward the sound.

"Where are you going?" she asked as she moved to him.

Sun Hawk found it hard to believe his eyes. He had not expected she would discover him gone so soon, and he had never imagined she would come after him. "You are safe now, and if Gray Fox's promises are good, I will take my punishment and return to my family."

Skylar shook her head. "That is not the Apache way. A husband takes his wife's family and lives with them."

Sun Hawk's heart was beating so hard that it was difficult for him to think. "But your home is with your white family."

"My home is with you," she said forcefully, feeling a wave of anger rising inside her. "You had no right to try to leave without me. When you took me as your wife, you swore to love and care for me as I swore to love and care for you. Were your words a lie?"

"No," he said, moving to her. "But your heart has always been with them."

"My heart has been with you," she argued. "If you cannot see that, you are blind."

Sun Hawk shook his head. "You have lived in a world I do not understand. Now that you are free, you will never be happy in mine."

"I will never be happy without you." She looked at him defiantly. "Do you love me so little that it is so easy for you to let me go?"

"I love you enough to give you what I thought you wanted," he replied tenderly.

"You were wrong."

They looked at each other, letting hope and trust renew them. "I cannot live in your world," he said sadly after a long moment.

"Then I will live in yours, or we will find a place and make it our own. But we will do it together, because I cannot live without you."

The pain that had formed a cold wall around Sun Hawk's heart began to fade, and the wall crumbled. She was right. He had been foolish not to trust her. He pulled her roughly into his arms and clung to her. "You are my beloved," he said, his voice hoarse with emotion.

"You are mine," Skylar whispered. "And it will always be so."

They held each other close until Skylar finally stepped away from him and took his hand in hers. "Will you come and meet my other family?" she asked. "Or do we leave here alone?"

He hesitated a moment, then nodded. "I will learn to love those who love you."

She smiled up at him tenderly. "You will not be sorry."

AS SHE LEANED against the top rail of the corral, Libby looked up at the graceful hacienda, taking in the lacy balconies, graceful arches, and lovingly tended gardens. Rancho Verde was a beautiful place, but what was most important to Libby was that Meade was happy here with Rayna. He was finally living the life of a gentleman rancher, and if his days weren't always as placid as he'd once anticipated, at least they were never boring.

Though Case had made the trip to Rancho Verde nearly a year ago with Rayna, Meade, Skylar, and Sun Hawk, this was Libby's first visit. She had been here less than a day, but already she loved the Templetons, and it had eased her mind to see for herself that Meade was really as happy as his letters had indicated. It made being separated from him much easier to bear, and she knew that before long, a network of railroads would connect his part of the world with hers. Their visits wouldn't be so infrequent, and that would make them both even happier.

"There you are," Meade said as he approached her. He'd been giving her a tour of the stables, relishing the opportunity to show off Rancho Verde, and enjoying even more the chance to visit with her alone for the first time since she'd arrived. Then Gil had stopped him with a question, and when he turned around, Libby had been gone. "I thought I'd lost you. What are you looking at?" he asked, letting his gaze follow hers up to the house. "Has Rayna been drying her petticoats on the railing again?"

Libby chuckled. "No, I was just thinking how lucky you are."

"That is something of an understatement," he said, draping his arm across her shoulders. It felt good having her close to him again. "I do miss you, though, dear sister."

"I don't see how you could," she said with a teasing smile. "Between your medical practice in Malaventura and helping Raymond and Rayna operate the ranch, I would think you keep quite busy."

"Rayna and her father run the ranch. I just ride over it now and then, looking lordly."

"Something you do very well, I'm sure," she said drolly as she turned toward the corral and rested her forearms on the top rail. Case was in the center of the ring with Sun Hawk, who was working at gentling a rather rambunctious mustang. "How's your brother-in-law doing, really?" she asked him.

Meade glanced at the two men. "Which one?"

Libby poked him in the ribs. "Don't play dense. I mean Sun Hawk, of course. I know he had doubts about living on the ranch. Every time I get a letter from you, I expect you to tell me he's decided he'd rather live on the reservation."

"Oh, I think he got a little more than he bargained for when he agreed to try living here, but he's adapting nicely. You heard for yourself earlier how well his English is coming along, and he and Skylar are able to visit his family fairly often. I actually think he likes it here."

Like everyone else, Meade had been delighted when General Crook had used his considerable influence to get the Mescaleros transferred back to their own reservation. The citizens of New Mexico weren't too happy about having the Apache tribe back, and some of Rancho Verde's neighbors were still complaining because Consayka's people had been permitted to come back to Verde where they belonged, but to Meade's way of thinking, everything had worked out for the best.

Since Skylar was an Americanized citizen, more or less,

Crook had been able to persuade the head of the Indian Bureau to allow Sun Hawk to live on Rancho Verde with the other Mescaleros. Meade was happy about that because it had made his wife happy.

"How do Rayna and Sun Hawk get along?" Libby asked him.

Meade chuckled. "They manage. Rayna hates it that he refuses to live in the house and prefers to camp among the Mescaleros, but she tolerates it because she doesn't have any choice. You mark my words, though, before the year is out, she'll have her brother-in-law sleeping in a bed."

"Oh, Meade," Libby said with a sigh as she turned back toward the house. "Life is a never-ending series of changes, isn't it?"

"It is at Rancho Verde," he commented dryly.

"What will you—"

The sound of a woman's shrill cry cut her off, and Meade's tanned face turned pale as a sheet. "Rayna!" he yelled as he began running toward the house. Libby hurried after him, and they heard another shriek and the sound of Lucas's and Jenny's high-pitched voices as they darted through the walled garden and into the arcade.

"Rayna, what's wrong?" Meade called out urgently as he burst into the courtyard, and then stumbled to a halt. Rayna was standing in the courtyard blindfolded, her arms flailing wildly as she tried to find the giggling niece and nephew who were dancing around her just beyond her reach. His beautiful seven-months-pregnant wife was playing blindman's buff!

"Where are they, Meade? Am I hot or cold?" she begged him to tell her as she spun around, lunged at Jenny, and came up with an armful of air.

"What the devil do you think you're doing?" he asked, charging across the courtyard. He yanked the blindfold off her face and threw it to the ground.

Rayna sighed with exasperation and looked at Jenny and Lucas. "Obviously your Uncle Meade's education has been seriously lacking if he doesn't know a game of blindman's buff when he sees one. Shall we show him how it's played?" She stooped to retrieve the blindfold, but it required Meade's hand on her elbow to help her back up again. She smiled at him sweetly and offered him the strip of cloth. "Would you like to be the blind man for a while?"

Meade bit down on his tongue and reined in his temper before he finally answered, "No, thank you. Three children in the house are more than enough." He looked at Jenny and Lucas. "Why don't you two run out to the corral? I think your father and Sun Hawk are about ready to ride El Niño."

"Yes, sir," Lucas said gravely. Then he and Jenny were off and running.

Meade turned back to his wife. "Rayna, don't you have even a single lick of sense? You could have fallen and hurt yourself or the baby."

"Don't be silly," she scolded. "I had a little peephole in the blindfold that allowed me to see everything."

"Oh, wonderful. My wife is not only reckless, she's an unscrupulous cheat."

Rayna batted her eyelashes at him and grinned. "Of course. How do you think I keep beating you so badly at poker? No one's luck is *that* bad, darling."

Meade sighed heavily as he pulled her into his arms. Her swollen belly made it a little more of a stretch each day, but he couldn't complain. "Good Lord, what am I going to do with you?"

She laced her arms around his neck and looked up at him coquettishly. "The same thing you've always done. When you get the urge to strangle me, kiss me instead."

He cocked one eyebrow at her. "I suppose you realize that means we're going to have a very large family?" he asked, and then his lips closed over hers, silencing her laughter.

If you enjoyed this book, take advantage of this special offer. Subscribe now and get a

FREE
Historical Romance

No Obligation (a $4.50 value)

Each month the editors of True Value select the four *very best* novels from America's leading publishers of romantic fiction. Preview them in your home *Free* for 10 days. With the first four books you receive, we'll send you a FREE book as our introductory gift. No Obligation!

If for any reason you decide not to keep them, just return them and owe nothing. If you like them as much as we think you will, you'll pay just $4.00 each and save at *least* $.50 each off the cover price. (Your savings are *guaranteed* to be at least $2.00 each month.) There is NO postage and handling – or other hidden charges. There are no minimum number of books to buy and you may cancel at any time.

Send in the Coupon Below

To get your FREE historical romance fill out the coupon below and mail it today. As soon as we receive it we'll send you your FREE Book along with your first month's selections.
